Praise for *Out of the Shadows*

Carlson's rich novel takes readers on a journey of discovery from a young woman's quest to survive tragedy to the healing discovery of sufferings beyond our own world. This is one of those novels that impacts readers for years to come.

    —Cindy Martinusen Coloma, best-selling author of *The Salt Garden* and *Orchid House*

Kimberly Carlson's *Out of the Shadows* is a moving, lush, exotic novel that evokes the best psychological investigations of John Fowles, the moody atmosphere of Poe. The devastating atrocities of our dark century hang over every page of this brooding book as Jamie seeks to heal from a personal loss as bruising to her body as it is to her spirit. Readers will feel an intimate connection to the residents of the mysterious Fallow Springs mansion, and, at times, as trapped there by pain as the heroine. This is a surprising tale of the families we must make for ourselves in a brutal world that often rips mother from child.

    —Tony D'Souza, award-winning author of *Whiteman*, *The Konkans*, and *Mule*

Kimberly Carlson's novel is remarkable for its keen observation and compassion. It is about nothing less than what it is to be human.

    —Sandra Scofield, author of *Occasions of Sin* and *The Scene Book*

Carlson's captivating novel proves to be more about the journey than the destination.

    — *Kirkus Review*

Carlson's debut novel sparkles with vivid characters and evocative settings, the author equally at home with both the familiar and the exotic. She adroitly serves up mystery and suspense while delivering a heartfelt and thought-provoking message at the same time. A fresh story with substance and style, *Out of the Shadows* provides the reader with both red meat and delectable dessert. An excellent read.

— Celeste White, author of *The Last Good Fairy*

Kimberly Carlson beautifully captures the journey from one's internal struggle to survive to being part of changing the way the world responds to mass atrocities and humanitarian disasters. Too often our personal lives are barriers to our participation in our local and global communities. *Out of the Shadows* inspires us all and reassures us that we can heal through our work with others.

— Katie-Jay Scott, Community Organizer for Stop Genocide Now

Out of the Shadows is a memorable read — an inspired work from the heart of an activist!

— Paul Freedman, writer and director of *Sand and Sorrow* and *Rwanda: Do Scars Ever Fade?*

Dear Kimberly,

Below is an extract from my memoir, *Tears of the Desert*. I sung this to my son when he was a baby. When I read your novel, I felt it reflected the same feelings. Your novel is a dream, a kiss, a hug, a home, a story. You show that there is a life for every Darfuri woman. Thanks for writing it.

Come here my love,
I have a song for you.
Come here my love,
I have a dream for you. . .

Come here my love,
I have a kiss for you.
Come here my love. . .

Come here my love,
I have a smile for you. . .

Come here my love,
I have a home for you. . .

Come here my love,
I have a hug for you. . .

Come here my love,
I have a life for you. . .

Come here my love,
I have a story for you. . .

Halima Bashir, author of *Tears of the Desert*.

To my mother, Marcella Ann,
for life, love, and bravery.

Out of the Shadows

Chapter One

I tipped the wine glass and watched the deep red stream fall. The baby book was on the carpet next to me, open to the page where it offered a space for a mother to write her newborn's eye color, length, pounds and ounces. The wine bled into the clean page. I poured more, soaking the wet pages. Before I emptied the glass completely, I realized this act of drama was not soothing, just stupid.

I scooted away from the book and rested my back against Lily's couch. From the coffee table, I picked up my own baby book, the one where Mom had carefully filled each page, writing in the margins when the lines given weren't enough. I flipped to the page where my mother wrote that I, Jamie Virginia, weighed six pounds, two ounces, was 20 inches long and had dark blue eyes. In different-colored ink it said, "changed to brown at five months."

I heard keys and the front door click open. Quickly I slid both pink books under the couch, picked up my wine glass and bottle off the floor, and sat on the couch.

"Charles Shaw," Lily observed. "Is it a good one?"

I realized I held the bottle like a wino.

Brianna, her five-year-old daughter, flew onto my lap. "Whoo," I said and set the glass and bottle on the table. I pulled her into my arms, and for a moment life felt right. I squeezed her and took in her cedar smell, the smell of the bark from her preschool's playground. But the wine ... I hadn't taken notice if it was a good one or not.

"It's okay, I guess," I said.

Lily dropped three pieces of mail onto the seat next to me, nothing I could possibly want. "Did you get out today?" she asked, without looking at me.

I thought of lying, telling her that I went and dropped off job applications or even that I went and saw a movie. I could tell her that I went for a run, but then I noticed as she opened a letter that she wasn't wanting me to lie. She knew that I hadn't even gone down to the mailbox and picked up her — and now my — mail.

"Tomorrow," I said, "I'll look for work."

"You said you could get your job back at the bank." She was no longer reading her mail, but me.

I thought about the last forty-three dollars and thirty-eight cents in my wallet. "Let me go to the store and get food. I'll make tacos."

Lily left the room, saying, "I've got plans and Brianna's going to my mom's."

As Lily showered, I read to Brianna. She curled into me. I wrapped a blanket around her. To comfort herself, she sucked her thumb, and I didn't say a word, though I knew Lily was trying to break her of the habit. She worried about Brianna's teeth, the kids teasing her at school. I read eight books, every one that sat on the coffee table. She was almost asleep, her breathing deep and relaxed, but then her mother came out looking well made up in her fresh, dark eyeliner and straightened black hair.

"Time to go."

Brianna slid off the couch and lay on the carpet. "I'm tired, Mom."

As Lily checked her cell phone for text messages, I got up and whispered in her ear, "She could stay here." I felt invigorated by the suggestion, of having a purpose.

"She's staying the night. And don't you think it would be good if you got out?"

Lily was tired of me, through with me sleeping on her couch. Maybe she was feeling taken advantage of, used. It had only been for the last six months, not so long.

"Let me carry her down." I slipped on the flip flops I'd left by the door.

"She can walk."

"Oh, Mom," Brianna moaned.

"You need to learn to walk on your own some time."

Brianna grimaced. "I can walk, silly Mom."

I knew this comment was for me, not Brianna. Lily could parent harshly but she wasn't insensitive. I watched them from the window. Halfway down the stairs, Lily picked Brianna up and carried her to the car.

I thought about what I could do. Call another friend. My brother. Go get a bite to eat. Sit back down and finish the bottle. Nothing appealed to me, and I hated this more than not having any place to go. I felt empty, listless. The fact that sitting and staring at the wall was what I desired pushed me to pick up my keys off the kitchen counter and place my purse over my shoulder. I swallowed back tears of despair.

I drove out of the parking lot. At the first stoplight, I checked my gas. The tank was a bit over half full. I pulled onto the highway and headed west, out of Grass Valley toward the big city of Sacramento.

With no air conditioning, I rolled my windows down and drove recklessly, over the speed limit, in and out of traffic. The adrenaline rush of danger fueled my emptiness and set fire to the anger that was easily found lately. As I left Sac and its suburbs, the anger subsided and driving felt cathartic. If only gas weren't so expensive, this would be what I could do every day. I wasn't sure where I was going. I was no longer on the I-5 but took the I-80; maybe I'd stop in at Davis and eat at a fun college hangout, pretend I was one the students, studying, trying to get ahead, living off my daddy's work or a college loan. Knowing this didn't happen, I felt bitterness seep in.

I drove through Davis.

The dry grass on the hills was crisp, almost ready to ignite after the long summer. Farms were scattered in between towns. The farmers in central California must work like mad to keep their strawberries, corn, and olive trees alive, I thought. A large green tractor was stopped in the middle of a newly tilled field. Its shadow fell on the dry dirt, offering shade to all the bugs and gophers that chose a respite.

Maybe I could make it to the ocean before it got dark. It would be cooler. I had heard people say it was healing to walk in the sand and listen to the waves; most of these people were new age hippies, something I wasn't, yet the thought of sitting in the warm sand appealed to me. But already the sunlight was softening, and I began to think I was crazy for traveling to nowhere with little gas and little money in an unreliable car. I got off somewhere and began driving side roads. I was somewhere in Sonoma. In the dim light I could see grape vines and thought I could smell grapes and wine.

In a small town, I found a coffeehouse. This was the end point, I knew. I would get a cup of coffee and head back. My hands were shaky from driving. I had a little less than third of a tank of gas left, maybe enough to get home.

The coffeehouse had only one customer. He sat by the window reading a book. He didn't look up when I entered. And I thought how marvelous to be so engrossed that the bells that hung on the door didn't distract him.

"What's brewing?" asked the barista. She wore long brown braids. I liked the look, trendy, earthy, even a bit Danish.

"Excuse me?" I asked, confused.

"What can I make for you?"

And for a moment I felt like a cheapskate when I said, "Oh, just a medium drip."

"You got it. To go, or would you like a real cup?"

"To go, please. Cardboard is real enough for me," I attempted to tease back, but my comment felt dimwitted. She handed me the coffee, then rang it up. She glanced over my head when the doorbells chimed.

"Hi, Akasha." To me, she said, "You're not from here? Wine-ing?" I turned to glance at the newcomer. The woman strolled up behind me. Again, I wasn't sure what the barista was saying. I must have appeared puzzled because she then said, "Were you wine tasting?"

"No, never have."

"You must be new in town. Have you recently moved?"

"No. Wish. I wished I'd moved. You hiring?" Her nametag said Camilla.

"Not today anyway."

I set my purse on the counter to retrieve my wallet. I couldn't find it. It wasn't there. I thought it must have fell out in the car. I dug deeper to see if maybe I had a couple of bills at the bottom or enough change.

"I finished reading *West of the Night*," Camilla said to the person behind me. "It was beautiful. Thanks for recommending it."

"'He was a good lion,'" the woman said. "'He had done what he could about being a tame lion.'" I turned to look at the woman — I assumed she was reciting from the novel. "'Who thinks it just to be judged by a single error?'"

At the bottom of my purse, I found a quarter and two nickels.

"Yes. I remember that part. I loved it when the father says, 'A domesticated lion is an unnatural lion — and whatever is unnatural is untrustworthy.' Makes me think of humans, too, and what's natural behavior for us and what is unnatural."

Though I thought their conversation interesting bordering on weird, I worried about my wallet and having no money. "I can't find my wallet. Help her, please." I motioned toward the woman.

"No problem," Camilla said.

"It must be in my car. I'll be right back."

"Makes me want to go to Kenya," I heard Camilla say as I scampered out holding my purse and the coffee. For a brief second, I remembered a girl I knew who was from Kenya. Nostalgia fell on me — I hadn't heard or even thought about her in years. In the car, I searched for my wallet on the floor, under the passenger's seat, and then I remembered I had taken it out to count my money. I must have left it on Lily's lamp table. Shit, shit. I looked for fallen change. On the floor of my car, I found fifty cents. A folded ring dollar bill in the center console. Heading back inside, I felt revitalized by my success at what I first feared to be an embarrassing moment. The lady named Akasha was walking out. I kept the door open for her; I looked up and smiled. For a moment, I felt almost shy for no other reason other than she was stunning. Her hair was pinned up, showcasing her cheekbones and full lips. She stopped, holding a cup with a tea bag string hanging down, and said, "This door is one of those heavy ones. Thank you." She let me hold the door open but didn't continue through. I thought she was going to say something else, but didn't, and finally walked out. I hurried to the counter and handed Camilla my money.

"No need, Akasha paid."

"Who?"

"The woman who just left."

"I have the money. I really do." I grabbed my coffee and hurried out. I hadn't sunk this low that strangers were paying my way. I looked down the street and then up. She was stepping into a black car. I ran, dripping coffee down my hand and wrist.

Before she closed the car's door, I said, "Excuse me. I really did have the money. See." I held out my hand like a child's, holding precious quarters and a ring dollar. She looked at it as if it were dirty, as if the money I held was wrong. I thought she might not take it. But then she folded her fingers around the cash.

"Thanks, I really had the money. It was in my car. I wasn't trying to rip the place off."

"I didn't think you were. You're no thief. Maybe a bit down on your luck, but you're not a thief."

"No. I'm not." I took a deep breath then stepped away so she could close her door. I looked to make sure no cars were coming. She peered at me again, and I felt warm.

I thought again she might say something else, but when she didn't, I turned and said, "Bye." I walked back to the sidewalk and licked the drips off my arm. I took a sip of my creamless coffee, hoping it would still be hot and, when it was less than warm, I thought I might cry. I hated tepid coffee.

"Hey."

I turned back toward the voice. Akasha walked toward me.

"I heard you say you were looking for a job."

"Yes."

"I am actually hiring — an assistant to do research, if you're interested."

I nodded my head yes, although I wasn't sure what I was interested in, other than work and a paycheck. On the trunk of her BMW she wrote her office number and told me to call the next day to set up an interview.

"I really need to get going," she said, making her way to the driver's side. "If you get the job, it comes with room and board."

I folded the paper and stuck it in my pocket. I went back in the coffeehouse to get a couple of napkins and cream, and to see if I could get my coffee warmed.

"Let me get you a new one," Camilla offered.

"What does she do, that lady? She said she was hiring."

"I don't know." She dumped my coffee out. "But you should be thrilled. She lives in a mansion. I guess you're in for a trip."

"I haven't been hired."

"No, but I have a good feeling." As she pumped my coffee, she smiled over her shoulder, a fleur-de-lis tattoo on the back of her neck twisting with the movement.

Driving home, I placed my cruise control one mile an hour below the speed limit to conserve gas. I had no wallet, owned no cell phone, and now it was pitch dark. I kept my windows rolled down, wishing the wind could grab hold of my broken heart and carry it wherever wind goes, out to sea, over a mountain, down a cave. But just like the ceremonious pouring of wine hadn't helped any, I knew the wind wouldn't either. I wasn't sure what would help. But waking in the morning and calling Akasha, giving life another go, seemed like a start.

Chapter Two

I set up an interview with Akasha, although I never spoke to her directly. I was told she was out of town, that she would see me in a week, and that I should send my résumé, a letter of application, and any college transcripts I might have. Writing the résumé and letter would be easy, but I had no worthwhile college transcripts. I hoped that the fact that she met me in a coffeehouse meant she had no expectations of a college degree. I spent the rest of the day updating my résumé and writing the letter of application. It was short, only two paragraphs, since I had no clue what I was applying for. When I finished, I stuck the envelope in the mail. I spent the next six days cleaning Lily's tub, helping her with laundry, and scrubbing and picking paint splotches off her kitchen floor that doubled as her art studio. Six days with no money. Six days trying not to think, not to feel.

On the seventh day, I drove with a destination.

Listening to a Brandi Carlile CD, I began to look ahead, thinking something awaited me, something new and exciting that could fill me. These thoughts of adventure, purpose, excitement were the kind that used to sustain me, but now they felt scary, so midway through, I turned off the music, rolled down my window, bit the inside of my cheek, and hummed, keeping my mind busy and feelings numbed.

Once off the highway, I watched the shadows that fell on the road. Hills like the curve of women's hips seen lying under the sun, vines dripping with plump grapes, and road signs all lay lined and distorted. I welcomed the warm breeze as I drove, looking for the sign into Fallow Springs Estate. The scrap of paper upon which I had scribbled the directions flapped in my left hand. I glanced at it to see if I'd gone too far. The wind blew the corners down, shadowing the mileage I was to travel. I glanced in the rearview mirror, making sure no vehicles were behind me, and then slowed. A life-sized statue of a lion sat looking stern-faced on the west side of the entrance. Right next to it, canopying the drive and barely visible beneath a flowering vine that embraced it, was the sign I had been looking for. I turned in.

The driveway was long, as long as the entire street I'd grown up on. Dense forest grew on both sides. I had passed miles of neat rows of grapevines on my drive. Small wineries were open for tasting, yet, so far, I hadn't seen one grape on Fallow Springs, though it sat in Sonoma Valley, the heart of California's wine country.

When the mansion came into view, I stopped my car. Its grandness struck me as something out of a Jane

Austen movie, or Scorsese's *The Age of Innocence*, or maybe even the Hearst Castle in *"Citizen Kane"* — I didn't know my architecture. I did know I felt small and that adrenaline vibrated through my veins.

I got out of my car, walked up the stone steps, and knocked on the front door. A woman wearing a tight bun and black tailored dress answered.

"I parked in front," I said, pointing to my car that looked out of place in the circular drive. "I didn't see any marked places." The woman didn't look at my car.

"Are there marked places at your home?" I wanted to ask if she'd ever lived in an apartment building but thought better of it. "Generally, people introduce themselves when they appear at someone's residence," she added.

"Jamie Shire. I'm here for the interview with Akasha Duval."

The woman stepped aside, and I walked in. She hadn't told me her name. She closed the large door using both hands, then slid a thick board into a slot to bolt the door. It reminded me of the kind of lock used on the outside of barns, designed to keep in animals. A stained glass window was in the center. From outside it looked like black glass, but from the inside, I saw that it portrayed a boat filled with swans floating on a dark blue lake.

She took me into what I assumed was Akasha's office, told me to wait, then left. The room was long, the ceiling high. The only light came from a window at the far end of the room. I approached two identical chairs in front of a desk. My heels sank into the thick rug, making me feel unstable and foolish in the shoes. I sat. My hands rested on the seat's cushion. The silk was smooth and thick, colored in whites. I thought of "Round Here," by the Counting Crows: "Where no one notices the contrast of white on white." On her desk a single folder with a pen on top looked exposed on the polished wooden space. The large window framed the desk. I had a feeling that the desk's owner spent more time looking out the window than working at the immaculate workplace. Thick, purple velvet curtains hung on the left side of the window. I liked the unequal feel of placing the drapes only on one side and not neatly divided. The curtain rod stopped at the window. I decided the drape's purpose was to add beauty, like that of embossed wallpaper. Then Akasha stepped out from the curtain.

Startled, I stood. I felt caught in a private thought, but the truth was I hadn't expected her to enter the room from what I assumed was a wall. Remembering the purpose of my visit, I smoothed the wrinkles from my skirt. She was at least a foot taller than I, wearing what looked to be a pearl satin nightgown. Around the neckline were long white feathers draping over her breasts. When the feathers fluttered, I could see dark areolas. She sat behind the desk. I began to perspire, not knowing what to think about being in front of this woman who wore a nightgown in front of an almost complete stranger, who would wear a nightgown to an interview.

I touched the back of my hair. It was short, too short to be pulled into a band. She stared at me. I couldn't maintain the eye contact, though I tried, knowing that body language held just as much information as words. She asked me to sit back down. I did.

Her hair was long and unadorned, the color brown, but it was also gold, as if the sun had raked each strand. She opened the folder that sat in front of her, picked up my résumé, and began reading. On the back was a faint strawberry jelly smudge. Brianna had accidentally set her toast on it. I had decided the stain wasn't worth worrying about, that no one would notice. But she turned the résumé over, tried to rub out the stain in vain as I had done, and began reading my letter of application.

She possessed the kind of beauty given to some women without compromise. Delicate lines etched the skin around her green eyes, and I was sure I'd be able to see them more distinctly when she smiled, but she hadn't smiled. She hadn't done any of the things other employers would have done. She hadn't shaken my hand. She hadn't asked how my drive down was. She hadn't dressed.

"You're nervous. Why?"

My eyes widened. I was nervous. I hadn't even been sure I wanted this job. In fact, I wasn't even sure what kind of job I was applying for. But I needed a job. I needed out of Grass Valley. I needed to get away from all that defined me. I unfolded my legs and looked down at the floor, wishing for a folder filled with letters of recommendations, college transcripts, anything to make me feel worthy of something better.

"You're thinking." She leaned back in her chair and lifted one leg onto the desk. Her shoe was off. "Take your time."

The bottom of her foot was soft, pink flesh. She pointed her toes like a ballerina. The red polish must have been from last Christmas; the nails were grown out, the polish chipped. I thought of telling her, as an explanation, as a point of interest, that I could see the contrast of white on white, but instead I blurted, "I'm good with numbers."

"You mean you can add and subtract? Aren't those skills taught in the second grade?" She swung her leg off and sat on the edge of her chair.

"Takes more than adding and subtracting to work as a teller." I felt I was defending myself. The fact was I hated being a bank teller. The fact was, all it took was someone who could add and subtract and be sweet to customers. For some reason, wearing my own clothes and not a uniform from Blockbuster or Outback Steakhouse gave me the sense that I had moved up in the world.

She stood to look out the window. It faced east. The sun was setting, shadows darkening the tree outside the window. Shadows distorted her face. Good directors used shadows to create powerful feelings, feelings of mystery, infidelity, crime, intrigue, but also passion, and love. I felt I was watching a movie, but didn't know what to feel. She stared out the window and I at her for longer than any contemporary director would allow, telling me this was no film.

"Okay," I said. "The truth is I'm 27 and never graduated from college. My best paying job was at Outback because of the tips. Didn't work for me because I got into the party crowd. And I hated the stress of needing to get table 10 more bread, table 12 another pint of Fosters, and of course sending 13's steak back because it was overcooked. I actually liked working at Blockbuster."

She leaned closer to the glass to peer at a flock of geese aloft; their talk quieted mine. She continued to stare at the sky until we could hear them no longer.

"A change would be nice," I said, and then slumped back in my chair, knowing the interview was over but waiting to be excused.

A mosquito flew by Akasha's face and landed on the window. She smashed it with her index finger, and then wiped her finger down the glass.

Neither she nor I spoke a word for several minutes. My mind began to spin. Was I having a nightmare? Maybe I, too, was wearing my pajamas, and not a skirt and blouse. I looked down just to make sure. The room had little light in it. There was a purple and green lamp on a table next to me. I turned on the switch. The peacock-colored glass shone, the glass more like amethysts and emeralds. This lamp wasn't bought at JC Penney's, but at Tiffany & Co. This place wasn't for me. I belonged among the knockoffs, with a job that paid barely over minimum wage. Nothing in my life had ever panned out, nothing. I wouldn't expect things to change now. Akasha came and sat in the chair next to me.

"What are your passions?"

"Passions," I repeated, taken back by the question. I thought for a moment, then quickly said, "I have none."

"Bullshit." The feathers around her collar fanned her neck.

I squinted as if I were trying to understand some difficult mathematical equation. I had a passion once, feeling my baby kicking inside me. If I had other passions before her, I couldn't tell Akasha, myself, or anyone else what they were. Even if someone showed me an old journal in my handwriting spelling out passions, I would have laughed and said there must be some mistake.

I became lightheaded and nauseated, feeling as sick as I had felt during my tenth week. At first, I thought I must have caught the flu, then worried that I had eaten some bad meat. But all I had eaten was a bagel, a Snickers bar, a few chips and a vanilla latté. I reached for a trashcan, but there wasn't one, so I leaned over and threw up on the carpet what little I had in my stomach. Wiping my mouth on the back of my hand, the horror of throwing up in a strange woman's office, on her expensive rug, during an interview, washed over me. And yet she hadn't moved. Didn't try to comfort me. She wasn't patting me on the back saying, "It's okay. Let me get you a tissue."

Stomach acid burned my throat. The smell was pungent. I could make out the artificial strawberry smell. "I'll clean it up. Where can I get some towels?" I stood.

"So we won't talk about our pasts," she said.

On the other side of her, hanging in a glass frame, I could barely make out a sketch of Van Gogh's *Bedroom in Arles*. There was a letter next to the sketch. Akasha followed my eyes, then stood to look at the sketch. Everything in the picture, for the first time, seemed to make sense; everything looked symmetrical. I no longer thought the pictures were going to fall on the bed's sleeper. The bed wasn't pushing the back wall away.

"You can start on Monday or Tuesday," she said, her eyes on the sketch. She turned and walked out the double doors. "Beah," she called, as she disappeared from sight. Less than a minute later, the woman who had answered the door walked in with a bucket and towels.

"I'll take those," I said.

I didn't want her to have to clean up my vomit. The smell was rancid, and it now permeated the room. Throwing up was something a person was supposed to do in private with the door closed, hoping no one could hear the primitive guttural sounds. It wasn't for others to clean up.

"You can leave."

"After I clean this up." I took the bucket from Beah, then got down on my hands and knees. She stood over me.

"You're the first to throw up." I looked up, not understanding her comment. "In her presence, some fall in love. Some feel fear. Then some become babbling idiots. But you are the first to have gotten sick."

"She didn't make me sick." Again, I thought of the reasons I must have thrown up — food poisoning, a sudden case of vertigo.

"I can see that." She leaned against the desk and watched me as I soaked up as much liquid as I could. "Are you moving in?"

"Yes, I guess I am."

"You'll be fun to have around, young and full of life. We'll see how you fit." I saw that her smile was sincere. When I was finished, I asked where I could dispose of the rags. "I have it from here." She took the bucket and walked out of the room. "You can let yourself out," she said.

On my way out, I stopped to look more closely at the sketch. I guessed it was an original. The letter was written in a foreign language. I could make out his brother's name, Theo, but that was it. I couldn't remember if Van Gogh was French or had just moved to France. Several years ago, I took an art class at the college. It was one of the few classes I finished. I found Theo's support of and faith in his brother powerful.

On the glass, I traced my finger over the bed where Van Gogh had lain. He had been filled with so much passion, with love, with a desire to create. I hated the fact that he had sold only one painting in his life. Now, people traveled from all over the world to see his work. If only he could have had a glimpse of the effect he'd leave on the world, of his worth, maybe his depression would have been less painful, maybe he wouldn't have been filled with despair. Maybe he would have lived to create fifty more paintings and all of them would have sold.

It wasn't that I felt despair. I had a hard time feeling anything. I guessed I should be excited that I got this job, a chance to start anew, but what I really wanted was to crawl into that bed and pull the covers up over my head. But, of course, that would be impossible.

I slid the large wooden bolt aside to let myself out. It was easier than I thought. The wood fit perfectly in the metal groove. The door clicked when I shut it. Somehow, I felt that if I told Akasha about my desire for the impossible, she would listen and at least consider it possible.

Before heading back to Grass Valley, I stopped at the coffeehouse where I'd met Akasha. Unlike the previous time, the place was full. I was glad to see Camilla. Although she was busy, she did take the time to welcome me and asked if I got the job with Akasha. I told her I did. But I became I bit unnerved when the lady behind me said, "Oh, the lady who won't help our local teenagers but will harbor an Afghan terrorist!" Camilla looked at her.

"I think maybe you're just upset that your cause isn't hers, Ginger." Camilla put both hands on my shoulders. They smelled of caramel. "Don't listen to what others say."

On my drive home, I thought about what the well-dressed woman behind me had said, wondered where her anger came from, wondered why Camilla stood up for Akasha. Exhaustion was seeping in and the thought of doing something different now felt daunting. I really didn't have the energy to try. I had expected her to describe what kind of research I'd be doing. I hadn't asked. As soon as I had seen the mansion, the grandeur of it all, I didn't think I'd get the job. And then throwing up … I shivered with embarrassment. Yet she said for me to come back. But who was I to try to be something different, something I wasn't? Maybe that was why I got sick. Something didn't feel right. I decided I should listen to my unease.

When I got back to Lily's, I showered, took out my blankets and lay on her couch, my bed. Lily and Brianna weren't home and there was no note. I watched TV until past midnight. Then, during a commercial, I picked up the phone and dialed Akasha's office number, wanting to leave a message at an hour I figured no one would be in the room. I didn't want to have to tell her directly that I decided that the job wasn't for me. I didn't want to have to explain that I wouldn't feel comfortable living in the mansion with people I didn't know, doing something I didn't know how to do. Sitting in the comforting warmth of my blanket, I now knew that living in my familiar small town was for me. I'd miss the mountains. I'd miss Lily and Brianna. I'd miss the checkout lady at Safeway. I wished I could say I'd miss my dad or my brother.

Beah answered the phone after the second ring. "I'm sorry," I said, "I thought I'd get the machine." I turned the TV to mute.

"You didn't." She sounded as if she hadn't been sleeping. I wondered what she was doing up, answering the office phone.

"No. I guess I didn't." I stuttered. "This is her office number?"

"There's only one number. Would you like to call back and leave a message, or would you like to tell me why you called?" There was sarcasm in her voice.

"Please, tell Akasha that I can't take the job."

Unable to fall asleep, I turned the volume back up and waited for Lily. Maybe we'd have a beer before bed like we used to. She had been a good friend, my only friend really. I had been staying with her ever since I couldn't pay my apartment's rent, ever since Lonnie at the bank said I needed to take some time off because lately my numbers were off. But now that I was thinking more clearly, I would take my old job back. It really wasn't so bad. The hours. Weekends off. Free banking. My co-workers were nice. I missed them. I'd get my own place again. Or maybe Lily, Brianna, and I could move into a three-bedroom. I could help Lily with Brianna. Lily was a good mother. She was. But she worked a lot, and she liked to date. She liked to have a man in her life. If I lived with them full-time, I could help take up the slack, help with Brianna, pick her up at daycare so she wouldn't have to stay for nine hours a day. We would sit down and outline a schedule.

Eventually the workers at Starbucks, my old boss, my old friends, and their mothers would stop looking at me as the girl to pity. Some other local or tabloid-worthy tragedy would happen, and I'd be forgotten.

Lily opened the front door with her sleeping child in her arms.

"Hey," I said, and went to pull down Brianna's blankets.

Back in the living room, Lily said, "So, did you?"

"Yes and no. I decided I didn't want it."

"I thought you wanted out of Dodge. Yesterday you were saying how you hated this place." She left to get a bottle of water.

I knew then that Lily was tired of me. Her meter had run out. "Want a drink?" She handed me her bottle and I took a sip. "Keep it," she said. "I'm going to bed."

The next morning, I dressed in the same skirt and blouse I had for the interview with Akasha and went to see my old boss at the bank. Lonnie gave me three days a week, said that's all he had, but that he was glad to see me back on my feet. I wanted to tell him I never really was off my feet. "My cousin had a miscarriage," he told me. We were in the break room standing by the coffee pot. This was the place all conversations with Lonnie took place. It wasn't that he was never at his desk, or that he was a slacker, any time one of his employees asked to talk with him, he'd say, "Let's go get a cup of coffee."

"I'm sorry to hear that," I said, but what I wanted to say was, "Screw you." I wanted to ask if she had felt her baby kick. "I'll see you on Thursday. Thanks, Lonnie."

"It's good to have you back. Your customers were asking about you."

He was trying to be nice and supportive and all that crap, but none of it helped. Instead of heading right back to Lily's to tell her that as soon as some money came in, I'd be out, I went to the Internet Café. I was happy I hadn't taken the job at Fallow Springs, but I couldn't get Akasha Duval out of my mind. Sitting in front of the computer, I Googled her name. I wasn't sure what I was looking for, but nothing came up. This surprised me. I made sure I spelled her name correctly. A woman with that much wealth had to be on the Web somewhere. I tried just Duval. A bunch popped up. Duval County in Florida. Robert Duval. The Godfather. Maybe somehow Akasha was related to the mob, I mused. But no Akasha Duval anywhere, nothing to feed my interest. Then, on a whim, I typed 'Jamie Shire' in the search box, and when I saw the newspaper articles pop up, I quickly turned off the computer, paid, and left. I didn't want to read what others had to say about me.

I worked Thursday and Friday. On both days, my till's numbers were perfect. I heard, "Glad to see you back," at least ten times. Instead of making me feel all warm inside, these comments pissed me off — it wasn't like I'd taken a trip to Puerto Vallarta.

On Saturday, I took Brianna to the park. More than the slide or the swings, she loved us sitting on the large quilt having a tea party with her little tea set. I told her we could have done this at home, but she told me it wasn't the same indoors, that all great tea parties happened outside. "I believe you are right," I told her.

"I know I am," she said. I smiled and kissed both her cheeks, loving her confidence.

Back at Lily's, I went to talk with the complex manager to see if there were any one-bedroom apartments available. She told me there was one and that, because she knew me, I wouldn't have to pay the last month's rent, just the first. "I would like to help you," she told me.

"I should have enough money in a couple of weeks."

"Would you like a cookie?" she asked, as I was on my way out. There was no plate of cookies in her hand, nor did her house smell as if she had just baked.

"No, but thanks."

As I was walking back to Lily's apartment, a little girl who was playing hopscotch in the parking lot caught my eye. She sang, "One, two, I love you, three, four, shut the door, five, six, pick up sticks, seven, eight, stand up straight, nine, ten, big fat hen." I began to say it over and over in my head, "I love you, shut the door, pick up sticks, stand up straight, big fat..." I sat on the curb. The little girl's long hair hung in her face. She hopped back and forth, back and forth. She was good; only twice did she touch the chalked lines.

Without warning, sadness fell on me. My eyes stung. Maybe I should have accepted the apartment manager's offer of a cookie. Friendship would be nice. Maybe the manager wasn't trying to befriend me but needed a friend. I felt self-centered.

The little girl looked content with the repetitive fun. She continued with, "One, two, I love you." It came to me then that she had the nursery rhyme wrong. It was, "One, two, buckle my shoe, three, four, shut the door, five, six, pick up sticks, seven, eight, lay them straight...." Why had she changed it, I wondered. Maybe she was just repeating what she had heard. I hoped that she had changed it — I hoped she was creating her world, not allowing it to be created for her. I thought about asking her why "I love you," why "big fat hen." The girl's mother called her in for dinner. She left her chalk behind. I continued to sit. The last few days had been good. They had been. I said this to myself again and again. I was comfortable with my job. I was comfortable with my decision to stay.

I walked over and stood in front of the seven large squares. I hopped once. Twice. I laced my hands behind me like I used to. When was the last time I'd hopped? A third time. I felt foolish, yet the movement felt good. In the middle section, I threw my arms out along with my legs, hopped two more times, and then turned around using my arms to propel me. I hoped no one was watching. I hopped back. I used to number my hopscotch squares. The little girl's squares were empty. Why had I numbered mine? I must have seen it that way at school or from the older neighborhood girls. I hopped again. I felt less foolish. Then a third time. I no longer cared if people were watching. By the fourth time I was smiling, almost laughing. Maybe this was it. Comfort was about making yourself do something that at first felt foolish or uncomfortable. My life did feel comfortable, but not fulfilling. I wasn't getting anywhere, only surviving. I wanted more than to just survive. I would have to push myself to try something different. Something different had been offered to me. I ran back to the apartment.

Calling Akasha, I decided I was going to be okay with feeling uncomfortable.

"I made a big mistake. I want the job. I can still be there by Monday." I was breathing deep quick breaths. "Well, maybe Tuesday would be better."

"She wants you here Monday," Beah said. "She told me to tell you Monday." Hanging up the phone, I wondered how Akasha knew I'd call.

Chapter Three

When I pulled up to Fallow Springs, I saw Beah standing at the top of the stairs. The front door was open behind her. Before I started up the steps, I stopped and asked her if she was waiting for someone. I had never said what time I'd be arriving. She didn't answer. Maybe she hadn't heard me. I had my suitcase and duffle bag in my hands.

"Is that all you brought?" Beah asked. She walked down the front porch stairs, quickly, though unsteadily. She took the duffle bag out of my hand.

"Yes, thanks." I looked up at the house I would be living in, tilting my head all the way back. The mansion had to have at least three floors. Halfway up was a patio. There were large and small windows, all curved at the top. The columns were decorated with engravings. From the second floor shelf, gargoyles peered down at me. "I didn't know people actually lived in homes with gargoyles."

"They keep evil spirits out," Beah said, already up the stairs. I shuddered as I followed her.

"They look rather evil."

Several large pots filled with flowers hung from the porch awning. In my nervousness, I had failed to notice them when I came for my interview. "Beautiful flowers," I said, gesturing toward the pots.

"No pink," Beah said. "Akasha doesn't care for pink."

I thought her comment odd since I hadn't said anything about the color of the flowers. Looking at the pots again, I thought that although there were no pink flowers, there were white pansies with pink on the inside of each petal. Nothing was absolute. I was going to say something about this but didn't. Beah might think I was being a smartass. Lily was the one who said everything that came into her head. I already missed her and Brianna. Yet I knew I didn't want to go back to Grass Valley. Something had changed in me, something that felt faintly familiar as I stood on the massive porch. Beah was now standing inside the house, holding the door open.

"Come. You're letting in flies." I looked for flies and didn't see or hear a single one. "I'll show you to your room and you can unpack and get settled." When I entered, she closed the door. Again my eye caught the stained-glass window, and I wondered if anyone ever tires of beautiful art. "That is, if you're staying. Well, you're here now and she'd said she'll see you at one." I heard the clicking of a clock. Our breath filled the silence between each tick. Beah didn't speak or move. I thought maybe she was waiting for me to assure her that I was staying.

"Okay, one it is," I said.

A wide marble staircase lay just past the entryway. It cascaded down the three stories. The first couple of steps were worn, indented. I wondered about how old those steps were. There were several doors on the top floor. One door stood out with a large iron knocker. Beah saw what I was guessing. "Her room is up there."

"What about the other rooms?" I hadn't taken any of this in when I was here for the interview.

"Just rooms waiting to be used. If rooms can wait, that is." I thought perhaps not, yet I understood the feeling of emptiness and needing something to fill up the vast space inside.

The chandelier above the staircase reminded me of one I'd seen in *Doctor Zhivago*: large and small tear-dropped crystals hung in massive quantities. The movie took place during a time before communism had made opulence the crime of the powerful.

We headed down a hall past Akasha's office. I peeked inside and saw that the rug I had thrown up on had been replaced with a new, more brightly colored one. I felt shame, but I thought if a friend had gotten sick at my place, and I had to throw away my $12.99 rug, I wouldn't have given it a second thought. Maybe it was relative.

Beah's laced, two-inch heels clicked on the hardwood. A piano sat in the middle of a large open room where the walls were all wood. Before I could ask if Akasha played, Beah spoke. She told me that I was replacing someone who had left almost a year ago and that I'd be living in her quarters. The word "quarters" struck me as odd. If she only knew what that word meant to me: a drinking game with the sole purpose of getting everyone drunk.

We walked through a corridor to another set of stairs, spiral, wooden and brilliantly polished. Walking up the steps, Beah told me that Akasha and I were both upstairs, though not on the same floor. She and Ana, the cook, were downstairs. Zahir, the gardener, lived in a small cottage next to his greenhouse.

As we passed by two more closed doors, Beah offered no information as to what or who lay behind them, and I didn't ask, thinking there'd be time for that later. Maybe Akasha would give me a tour. I touched the doors as we walked past. At the end of the hall, Beah stopped. She was still out of breath from climbing the stairs. She opened the door with a key and handed it to me. I took it and stuck it in my jean pocket.

"We respect each other's privacy here," she said.

"What happened to the woman I'm replacing?"

"She married and is back living in her home town."

I shuddered, not wanting to return to my hometown, not wanting to go backwards. Beah must have sensed my discomfort because she then said, "What's the best for one person isn't what's best for the next."

I stepped into the room and became lightheaded. Was it from not eating? The few steps I had climbed? The newness of all this? It certainly wasn't from a foul smell in the room. Jasmine and lemon clung in the breeze from the open window. I couldn't recall the last time I had smelled jasmine. A good feeling fell on me.

"The lemon is for your weak stomach," Beah smiled. A potted lemon tree grew next to the opened window. Several lemons hung on the limbs.

"I really don't have a weak stomach," I said. Beah pointed out the bathroom, the small kitchenette. She showed me how to use the thermostat.

Standing next to a Masonic fireplace with a large stone mantel, she said, "Let Zahir know when you need wood." Then she closed my door, leaving me "to get settled."

I looked around the room without moving. The bed was veiled in chiffon. The desk, new and elegant, although it didn't have the opulence of Akasha's. I knew little about furniture; maybe it was Mission, or Asian. I stood in front of the fireplace, remembering my love of the smell of smoke, the sound of wood crackling. I slipped off my shoes and went to the window. The wooden planks felt cool under my bare feet. A jasmine vine crawled up a trellis from below. The window faced east. I would have morning sun. For a moment, I looked forward to the soft light, to something new and better, a time when possibilities gave birth. Yet I wasn't ready to be happy, just busy somewhere else, out of Grass Valley, away from people who knew.

A man I guessed to be Zahir was on his knees feeding a duckling out of his palm. All I could see was his bent back and his black hair lined with silver. Several other ducks and one swan floated in the pond next to him. The mother of the stray duckling quacked noisily.

I opened my suitcase to unpack. As I pulled out a few of the outfits I had worn at the bank, I wondered what I would be wearing to work. I preferred jeans. Akasha hadn't told me what she wanted me to wear. Remembering our first meeting, I thought maybe my pajamas would be good enough.

The drawer to the wooden dresser opened easily. A Henkel Harris pamphlet was in the top drawer that smelled of sawdust and varnish. There were no dust balls, or tiny scrapes of lint, or gum wrappers. I thought about the fact I was replacing someone who'd left not long ago and wondered what had happened to the dresser she had used. I had never had a new dresser before, and, although it really didn't belong to me, I liked placing my bras, pajamas, and jeans in it. As I closed the drawer that held my underwear, I was surprised at how neatly I had folded each pair. Normally they all ended up in one big heap. It felt good having something nice.

By now, it was a little after ten; I sat in the chair by the window. Gazing at the brick fireplace, I thought a fire in the evenings might be nice. The book, *The Red Tent*, was on the table by the chair. I picked it up and read the back cover. It was about ancient women's traditions. This sounded intriguing to me, but I fell asleep while reading the first page and dreamed of nursing a baby. In my dream, I felt joy, but then woke with a shudder. Oddly, my breasts were tender even though I'd just gotten off my period. When I was pregnant I never dreamed about babies or pregnancy or motherhood, and now that was all I dreamed about, making me curse sleep. I slipped on my shoes and headed down the stairs to meet with Akasha, not bothering to lock the door as Beah had suggested. I was ready to work. I hoped it was hard, all-encompassing work, that when the day was done I would be exhausted and would fall into a seamless, dreamless sleep.

With pen and tablet in hand, I went and sat in the chair I had occupied when I interviewed for the job. Akasha wasn't at her desk. I studied the velvet curtains, thinking she'd enter again from there as she had six days ago.

"I'm over here." I turned. She rested on a couch. One of her legs was pulled up behind her. She wore a long caramel-colored dress. It was fitted at the top; small buttons ran from her waist to her throat.

"I didn't see you."

"Move your chair. The light from the window was hurting my eyes."

I picked up the chair to sit closer. She closed the book she had been reading and set it on an issue of *People* magazine.

"*The Count of Monte Cristo*, a classic," I said.

"You've read it?" She placed her hand on top of the book.

"No." I felt myself grow warm. I imagined a woman like Akasha had read all the classics and now was rereading them, unlike me. I never read. "I saw the movies. The French version and Hollywood's." Instead of asking me which one I liked best, she got right to business.

"Where do you think help is needed the most?" This question felt vague. Maybe she thought I knew more about this position than I did, which was nothing, but I also thought she wanted a concrete answer.

"Help as in —?"

"Medical care, food, housing, education."

I hesitated. I didn't want to tell her I'd never thought too much about it. That I'd never been a news junkie. The news was depressing. Never had a beginning, middle and end. I took a stab. "New Orleans. The people who were affected by Hurricane Katrina." She squirmed on the couch. She wasn't happy with my answer.

"Hmm, I guess."

"Afghanistan," I countered, thinking of the Taliban and terrorism.

"Maybe I shouldn't have used the word 'most.'" She stood, pulled a yellow daisy out of a vase, smelled it, and then began pulling the petals off as young girls do, as I have done. "Do you think revenge is ever justified?"

I felt she was talking about me again, changing the subject, prying into my private life as she had during my interview, a life I didn't want to talk about. But how would she know? She didn't know about my baby, about Santos, the man I'd like to see hung up by his heels. Then I remembered the book she was reading.

"Maybe revenge is too strong of a word. Retribution," she corrected herself.

"Maybe not justified. But understood."

"What I want you to do is," she said, pausing as she placed the plucked stem back into the vase, "research, acquaint yourself with all the needy spots, needy people. I have money to spend. I want to spend it. But I hate hearing about people suffering — that's your job." She picked up *The Count* as if she were going to leave. I felt myself panic — that couldn't be all she was going to say.

"For instance ..." I waited for her to continue. She didn't. She stood studying Van Gogh's sketch, just as she had during my interview. She truly enjoyed it and didn't simply take it for granted, like a necklace or dress that someone like her could afford, but never wore. I wanted to ask her about the letter that followed Van Gogh's sketch, what it said, but I also needed to know what I was supposed to be doing. "You want me to research organizations like the Red Cross to see where— "

"The Red Cross. Or something else." Her mind was no longer on our conversation. "But frankly, I don't need any more information on the benefits of condoms. I already give to World AIDS and Planned Parenthood."

At least I had two more examples.

"Beah has a laptop for you, unless you prefer a stationary computer." She turned toward me.

"A laptop will be fine." I hadn't written one thing down. Glancing at the tablet, I felt bewildered, without the least idea of what she was asking me to do.

"I just don't want to think about it all," she reiterated.

I guessed I would just start Googling, reading. I hoped she'd give me more direction, maybe in a couple of days when I had more to say.

"Do you feel at rest when you look at this painting? Not this sketch, but the finished painting?" she asked.

I came and stood next to her. I recalled my first look at the actual painting and the feeling I'd had, that the walls were caving in. "No," I said and suggested, "You should put a copy of the painting next to the sketch."

"That's what he wanted. That's what he tells his brother in this letter." I guessed she didn't like my suggestion.

"You read French? Of course, you do." Again, my perception of the very rich: well-read, fluent in French.

"Beah does — and Dutch. This letter is written in Dutch. He tells Theo that the painting of his bedroom is to evoke rest. Vincent then writes the color of each object and says that all the shadows in the room are suppressed." I needed to see the painting again. I had missed his point. I'd call Lily later, Van Gogh being one of her favorite painters, maybe in line after Tamara de Lempicka and Frida Kahlo. "Goodbye, Jamie." She had her hand on the curtain.

"Akasha?"

"Yes."

She didn't want any more questions. She didn't want to have to elaborate on the work she was paying me to do. She was done talking about revenge and Van Gogh's room that was meant to evoke rest.

"I'll go find Beah to get the computer," I said.

She nodded her head, but her eyes were cast down. I felt I had missed something.

"Don't hurry. I'm not sitting around waiting for you to get back to me."

Chapter Four

*F*or the next couple of days, I worked in my room. I read websites and took notes. I felt like a college student studying, learning, but with no real direction, no clear assignment. I focused on learning about humanitarian organizations and what I now knew as NGOs, non-government organizations. On each NGO website, there was a link to the places that it served. There were so many places — countries I hadn't even known existed. People suffering all over the globe.

I thought about the stacks of *National Geographic* magazines that Aunt Gazella had in her living room on the coffee table. She wasn't an aunt by blood, had been a neighbor. I was drawn to her and she loved me. I'd sit in her lap, and she'd read me stories and later, when I was too big, I'd lay my head in her lap. "Close your eyes,

mademoiselle," she would tell me, "and let the magic play."
She always called me "mademoiselle," though she wasn't
French. She did those kinds of things, like serving me tea
when I was only eleven and baking fresh bread, when
everyone else I knew served store-bought bread.
Sometimes we'd flip through a *Geographic* together, but I
was more interested in the stories, in showing her my
homework from school that Dad never seemed interested
in seeing. She was the one who would hang my pictures in
her kitchen, place my 100% spelling test on her
refrigerator.

My desire to work hard hours and fall into a
dreamless sleep was gone. Sometimes in my dreams, I'd see
long lines of women waiting to fill up water jugs. Or
children playing soccer with legs as thin as American
children's arms. A man from Uganda said that what was
going on in his country was beyond the fiction seen in
movies. I thought about that for a while. Hollywood wasn't
a place to sugar coat violence.

Before I had gotten pregnant, I had taken a film
class at Sacramento State. I hadn't been registered for it. I
met the professor, Dr. Irving, at the Sacramento Film
Festival and he invited me to sit in. I did.

"There has to be a logical reason for the climax.
Read Shakespeare," he'd say, which I never did and
doubted any of the students did either. But his point was
clear and the man from Uganda's point now made sense.
There was no logical reason, no buildup as to how a person
could take the eyes out of a young boy, leaving him
screaming in agony.

On my third day, I looked for Akasha. I wanted to
know more of what she wanted from me. When I found
Beah in the kitchen, she told me Akasha had left for a few
days. Beah had told me when I'd arrived that I was

welcome to come down to the kitchen any time for food and that dinner would be ready after 6:30 in the evening. There was always a hot plate waiting for me but there was never anyone sitting eating at the kitchen table or in the dining room when I showed up at 6:30. I'd eat sitting all alone, wash my plate, and leave.

Beah was now sitting at the long wood table. She had a roll and coffee in front of her. The smell of warm yeast and cinnamon filled the space. The back door was open and the early morning fog was just beginning to burn off. A woman stood at the counter, braiding thick strands of dough, her hands and arms patterned with age spots. Her light gray hair was pinned back in a loose bun. She wore a yellow cotton dress with large side pockets that opened though no hands were inside of them. I knew it had to be Ana although I had not yet met her. I thought she'd turn and introduce herself to me or that Beah would introduce us. When neither of these things happened, I said hello. A ray of sun came in the opened door and shone on the side of her face. She smiled and continued to braid. When she came to the end, she dotted butter on the thick dough.

"The chicken dish you made last night was amazing." Ana smiled again and muttered her thanks. Not getting the information I needed, and wondering how I should ask it, I picked up a magazine that sat on the table and glanced at the cover.

"Do you need something else?" Beah asked.

"Yes. I'm not exactly sure what I'm suppose to be doing." With her hands folded around her cup, Beah continued to look up at me, as if she were reading me, not knowing how much information she could share. I didn't feel any warmth in her stare but maybe understanding. I wondered if she'd ask me to sit down. "What do you do here?" I asked, wanting to keep the conversation going. Beah looked at her roll and broke off a tiny piece and placed it in her mouth.

"What do I do? Well, you know I answer doors. You know I give out computers." It seemed this question had offended her and I couldn't tell why. "I keep this house looking and running ..." She broke off. "Just continue doing what you're doing. She'll be home in a couple of days, maybe sooner. Maybe she will tell you more, maybe not. But don't worry. Try to look at your stay here as a rest."

"A rest?"

"Yes." Seeming to sense my confusion and frustration, she added, "Have a seat and a pastry. Tell me a little about yourself." I froze. I didn't want to explore my past. "Or just sit and listen," she said. "I was telling Ana about getting pulled over yesterday for rolling through a stop sign. It was the first time that an officer let me out of a ticket. I was amazed. When I told him I wasn't driving my BMW, that I was an employee at Fallow Springs and it belonged to my employer, he said, 'Be careful, ma'am,' and turned back to his car. How about you, Jamie? Ever been pulled over?"

Although I appreciated Beah reaching out, I left the kitchen longing for Lily, our friendship, the feeling of familiarity, her passion for people and art. She was tired of me sleeping on the couch, tired of me not moving forward, but I couldn't blame her. I was tired of me, too. On the way up to my room, I stopped and called her. I hoped the long distance personal call would be okay. Maybe I'd get a new cell when I got paid.

At the sound of her message and the beep, I told her, "Thanks for being there."

❊ ❊ ❊

Akasha didn't come back in a couple of days. Beah advised me to be patient, but I felt I had hit a brick wall with the work I was supposed to be doing. There were many places, many organizations Akasha could give to. Why couldn't she just pick one and write a check? I wanted to admire her desire to be more thorough than that, but it didn't make a lot of sense.

When not reading or researching, I welcomed the long hours of quiet. Sometimes I feared I was becoming too much of a recluse. I felt as if sadness draped over my shoulders, and I wrapped myself in it, trying to forget the past. I lost track of time. An hour would go by that felt like a few minutes.

In the cool mornings, I'd build small fires in the fireplace in my room. One day, I watched the logs burn to ash without ever getting off my knees. I was trying not to think about my past, but at times, vivid snippets would fill my mind. I would try to recapture what happened before the memory. I'd think of things I could have said or done to change the final picture. As if willing something made it come to be; as if the desire to change our pasts were enough.

When I was a little girl, I went to camp. Mom let me use her camera, our only camera, a camera we couldn't afford to replace. When I got home, it was nowhere to be found. I looked through every little section of my suitcase, every inch of my sleeping bag, in every sweater pocket, and still no camera. I prayed. Still no camera. I went outside and sat under our apricot tree and envisioned myself sitting on the dusty cabin's floor placing the camera in the side pocket of my suitcase. Then I went back inside ready to find Mom's camera, but still it wasn't there, and I felt a crushing weight, knowing I had disappointed my mom, and for believing that God didn't care about the little things, and if He didn't care about the little things, where would that leave me with the big things?

Still, twenty years later, I tried this crazy visualization technique that I thought should work. But of course it didn't. It was better not to think about the past and move on.

My loneliest times were in the evenings. It seemed that Beah, Ana, and Zahir disappeared. I didn't miss living in Grass Valley. I had wanted out of my hometown since I was a girl. I remembered all the places Aunt Gazella had been — Munich, Salzburg, Ciguatera — even the names were enchanting. "You'll go to these places, too," she had told me. But I hadn't. It felt good to at least be out of my hometown.

One night, I tried Lily again.

"Sorry, I know I said I'd call." She sounded winded. "But he's just the shit." Then she laughed, and I was glad to at least hear that, even though I was beginning to feel rejected. Brianna was at Lily's mother's again, which made me sad. Any time Lily fell for a man, Brianna suffered. Any time Lily had a new interest in anything for that matter, Brianna suffered. When President Bush had launched Shock and Awe on Iraq, she had gone and got a peace sign tattooed on her shoulder and had spent her paycheck on a ticket to Washington, DC to demonstrate against the war. She even slept with an Iranian while in DC to prove that she had nothing against Iraqis. I told her that Iraq and Iran were two different countries. "I made my point," she said.

"To whom?"

"To that guy, to myself, to Bush."

"Okay."

"And don't be so pompous. I know Iran and Iraq are different countries, but not all Americans know this. So, you see the irony?"

She painted an anti-war series. Some of the paintings were pretty good, especially the one of the Iraqi child holding his dead father's head in his lap. But, now, if you asked her what was going on in Iraq, she'd shrug, and say, "No fucking clue."

She embraced me with that same passion the day I told her I was pregnant. She was the one who drove me to Target to buy baby clothes.

Sadly, until today, I hadn't known any of the repercussions of the U.S. invasion on Iraq. I just read about soldiers who came home, many injured, most with posttraumatic stress disorder, and once back in the States, unable to reassimilate into society. Many, unable to find a decent job, were forced to return back into the service or to take a civilian job stationed in Iraq. And then there were the Iraqi civilians who had nothing to do with terrorism, nothing to do with Saddam Hussein, the building — or not — of nuclear bombs. And yet, close to one hundred thousand Iraqi civilians had been killed since the United States invaded their country.

It seemed no one was winning.

On the farthest side of the garden, under a maple tree, I could get good Internet access. In the late afternoon, the shade was good, so I could read the computer screen. I leaned back on the trunk. The spot overlooked the pond, with bright flowers floating on top — some were fuchsia, some purple, others white. It was the first time I noticed how stunning white flowers were, like a pure blanket of fresh snow that never melted. I watched the ducks and the swans float around the lily pads. A Japanese-style bridge arched over the water. I found myself simply sitting and gazing at the ducks, almost feeling at rest. This place did evoke rest, even peace, and although Beah advised me to take it easy, Akasha never did. Feeling guilty for not being productive, I decided to go back to my room, thinking I'd get more read being less distracted; maybe I'd eat and then at least that task would be accomplished for the day.

On my way back to the house, I found Zahir digging in a flowerbed. I stopped him and told him that his garden reminded me of a Monet painting. He looked at me solemnly and said nothing. Maybe he didn't know what I was referring to. "Your garden, the bridge — it's all so picturesque." He may have tried to smile, but as if those muscles hadn't been used in a while, his expression took on a frown. He continued to dig up bulbs, their purple flowers falling limp, petals blown off. "What are those called?" I asked.

"Autumn crocus. Naked ladies."

I wasn't sure but I thought he might have blushed at giving me the flower's common name. And before he was finished, he picked up his bucket of bulbs and headed toward the greenhouse.

"I need to check on something."

Had I offended him by talking to him first or was it simply because we were alone? Beah had confirmed he was from Afghanistan. Middle Easterners were supposedly sexist. How could he be sexist and work for Akasha? She was strong, opinionated, and independent. I'd like to talk with him, maybe even have a meal with him. I'd never known anyone from the Middle East, but clearly he had no interest in getting to know me.

Changing my mind about trying to get some work done and now determined to have dinner with a friendly face, I headed out of the garden. Several bulbs had fallen out of Zahir's bucket. I picked them up and set them in a pile next to the shed.

My keys were still on the floorboard where I'd left them when I first arrived. But my car wouldn't turn over. I hadn't gotten a new battery since the last time my car didn't start. I had called Dad that day, like I always did when I had car trouble. It was the day I left the courthouse for the last time, the day Santos was sentenced. After he was escorted out of the courtroom, I watched the judge close a folder on his desk. Knowing it was over for him, I got up and left, as if it were all over for me.

"Your battery is old," my dad said. He stopped looking directly at me. He opened my driver's side door and reached down to open the trunk.

"Don't open that." I moved toward him, needing to take his hand off the lever. He looked up at me.

"Where are the jumpers I gave you?"

"Not sure." He popped the trunk. I rushed to the back of the car and shut the trunk. "Don't open that, I said! Can't you use your jumpers?"

"What in the hell do you have back there?" I wasn't ready to get rid of the onesies, the gowns, the stuffed animals, and the car seat, and I knew he wouldn't understand that I didn't want to lift the bags with the carefully folded clothes and set them on the pavement where men spit.

"Can't we use yours?" I felt hot tears on my cheeks. I wiped them quickly hoping he didn't see them.

He slouched to his truck, shaking his head. When he came back, carrying his jumper cables, he muttered, "You never were very strong." I wanted to hit him. I hated him in that instant. But, instead, I sat on the curb and cried. I didn't care if he thought I was strong. I didn't want to be strong, not yet, not for him.

"Why do you hate me so much?" I asked when the battery had charged and the car turned over. He rubbed his hands on a stained red cloth. He looked like he didn't understand what language I was speaking. "Is it because I remind you of her? The woman who never loved you?" I wanted to hurt him. I wanted him to know how it felt to hurt. I wanted him to feel just a fraction of my pain. I wanted to be able to congeal my pain and give it to him. The pain had to be solid and measurable for him to get it, like steel or a bolt size.

"Jamie, you don't know what you're talking about. You're such an ungrateful brat." He climbed into his cab the way shorter men do, using the steering wheel to pull themselves up. He hadn't even asked me about Santos' sentencing.

"Ungrateful and weak!" I screamed, trying to give the words back to him. He closed his door and was pulling away. I sat in my car, behind my steering wheel, but I was shaking too badly to drive.

"You sonofabitch."

Later that night, sitting on Lily's couch in the dark while she and Brianna slept, I questioned if hating a parent was the same thing as hating myself. He was cruel. I couldn't figure out why he hadn't asked me about the judge's ruling and how I was doing. He was self-centered and ignorant. I felt flames of hatred again burning my heart and mind. I envisioned myself turning to steel-grey ash and, with a slightest breeze, I'd be blown away in fragments, never to be made whole again. I didn't want to hate myself. I wouldn't hate myself. It was then that I knew that, in order to survive my life, in order to thrive just a bit, I'd have to detach myself from him.

I couldn't call him now, not this time, to fix my car, and I was glad to be so far away, that he was out of my reach. I was out of his reach. I slammed the car door and walked away from the mansion. I was going to town.

Chapter Five

*F*allow Springs was eight miles from town. It took me 10 minutes just to get down the driveway to the road. I stopped, rethinking my decision. My jeans dragged, catching under the heel of my leather flip flops as I walked. I needed to hear people talking about boyfriends, kids, or work. I needed to smell junk food. Maybe I'd get a hamburger and a Pepsi. I stuck my thumb out, although there weren't any cars coming, and kept walking. It had been about four years since I had hitched a ride. A friend and I had thumbed it to a pub in Sacramento; we hadn't wanted to have to count our beers.

A half-hour later, a beat-up old Honda stopped several feet ahead of me. I ran to the car and peered in the passenger side window.

"Just to town," I told the lady. She looked to be in her fifties. The window was rolled down, and her short red hair took the messy hairdo to the extreme. Her lipstick was a poppy color, applied thickly. I had seen this kind of woman while working at Blockbuster. They generally rented classics or contemporary G movies. Women who placed bright lipstick on an otherwise makeup-less face had to be safe. They always returned their movies on time and generally called me "sweetie" or "honey."

"Hop in, missy." As she pulled back onto the highway, she told me that I shouldn't be hitching rides in this day and age and she shouldn't be picking up people either. Then, she laughed.

The sun lit the top of her head, but cast her body in shadow. Although her dashboard was cracked, I smelled Armor All. Around her rearview mirror hung a faded red garter belt that had Knott's Berry Farm written across it. I asked when she got it; if she'd been to Knott's lately.

"Never been there. I've always wanted to go. I bought the garter at a garage sale. Wore it a few years ago when I was dating a younger man. I've always wanted one." I didn't know if she were referring to the garter or the younger man.

She was watching me and not the road. An oversized farm truck was headed our way. I held tightly to each side of my seat.

"Uh, there's a truck in our lane," I said.

"He'll move over." With her eyes back on the road, she went on, "With his teeth, that was the fantasy. See?" she said, looking at the truck. "All's well …" The truck had moved over. A box with clothes hanging out of it was lying in the opposite lane. "I wanted him to use his big sharp canines to pull the garter from my thigh, down my leg and off."

She glanced over at me and smiled an awkward smile. "Do I have lipstick on my teeth? I hate talking to someone only to discover later I had lipstick smeared on my front teeth." I shook my head.

"You seem like such an innocent girl, but I know looks are deceiving." At the moment, I didn't care if she thought I was innocent or not. A black sports car whizzed by in the oncoming lane. Again, I grabbed and held tightly to the seat. I really wished I had waited until her car passed before I threw my thumb out. Her driving was scaring me, and I didn't want to hear about her sexual fantasy. "You are such a nervous passenger."

"It's just that two-lane highways can be very dangerous," I said.

"Sure. Yes, they can be." She stopped talking and gazed out her side window. I was relieved that she had stopped talking, but then, picking up where she'd left off, she said, "As I remember it, he laid me on the bed and slowly, with his beautiful white teeth, grabbed hold of this very garter." She took one hand off the steering wheel and pulled on the garter. The rotting elastic gave a weary snap. "Slid it all the way off my leg. I could hardly believe it. Was everything I could have ever hoped it could be. I felt young, alive, and horny as hell."

This is just great, I said to myself.

"'My turn,' he said."

I wished I hadn't asked about the Knott's Berry Farm garter belt. I was beginning to wish I had stayed back at Fallow Springs, or walked the eight miles. I just wasn't in the mood to hear about some fifty-year-old's sex life. But that's the thing when you're hitchhiking — you're at the mercy of the person driving. The driver can ask you anything, tell you anything, but you have to keep your mouth shut. I thought about the opening scene in Ford's

The Grapes of Wrath. I was glad when Tom told the driver off, that, yeah, he'd been in prison for killing a man. Changed the power roles. I thought about trying that approach, but Tom was being sincere. I'd be acting. I was a terrible actor.

I wished I could rid my mind of her story. I thought about Lily. She would have loved this story. The thought of having a beer with Lily and telling her about this crazy woman sounded like fun. I'd be lucky to get her on the phone. I hoped her anger toward me would subside, now that I was out of her apartment.

"Are you a runaway?" the woman asked. It was my turn to laugh.

"No. I'm 27 years old. I came from Fallow Springs."

"Fallow Springs … don't think I've ever heard of it. A winery?" I thought this funny since she would have just driven by it.

"No. No, it's not. It's a mansion, a home."

"I worked at a winery once." She looked pensive and fell silent. Just as we reached the edge of town, she pulled over. "Town," she announced. Both of her hands were on the steering wheel. She was finally looking at the road.

I stood at the side of the road and watched as she drove through town on the main road. I wondered why she hadn't asked me where I wanted off. We hadn't even made it to one building. Just one more rejection, I thought, bitterly. I had needed a change in my life, but I was beginning to wonder what I had gotten myself into. My old life seemed normal. Maybe that was what I really wanted. A job with clear expectations. Safeway on the corner of 5th and Oak. My brother, Joel, pestering me about needing to be in church.

I walked the last bit of road into town, and when I got there, I was hot and smelly. Despite the sudden desire to be back in Grass Valley, I thirsted for the peach and lemon iced tea that Ana would make and leave on the kitchen hutch, next to a jar of cookies. I settled for an Italian soda at the coffeehouse I had gone to before.

Camilla wasn't working. Some other person that barely even smiled handed me my drink. Just now, I realized I had been hoping she and I could be friends. Sitting at the window table, I picked up a local magazine. I thumbed through it, looking at all the winery advertisements. Four women sat at the table next to mine. They had planners and pen and paper spread out before them and drank tall coffees. From what I could gather they were working on fundraising for a new football field, planning a dinner, dance and auction. Their conversation wasn't too interesting, but, then, neither was the magazine. My ears perked up when one lady said, "Maybe we could get Ms. Duval to donate something for the auction."

"Yeah, right. Try it, Diana." The others laughed. "Plus what would it be, a night's stay in her mysterious home?"

"Spooky," the heaviest lady said.

"Maybe I will give her a call. She can only say no."

I wondered why the anger toward a woman they apparently didn't know.

"I don't understand why she doesn't get involved in anything. Have you ever seen her anywhere?"

"I've seen her in here."

"That's not what I meant."

Camilla came to my table, holding a red apron. "How's it going?" I was glad for the distraction.

"Camilla! Oh, hi. Would you like to sit down?"

"Almost on the clock. You were deep in thought."

"Not really." Then I whispered, "I was listening to them," my thumb pointing toward the table of women. "They're talking about Akasha."

"Yes, people around here like to do that. Frankly, I think people don't like women who know their worth. And Akasha knows she has nothing to prove." I wondered if Camilla were right.

"Do you know yours? Your worth?"

"Hmm, good question. Sometimes. Maybe. Today, sure." She moved her hips like a belly dancer.

"Camilla," a voice called. She went to work, and I tried to rest my legs without listening to the women's conversation next to me. I thought about what my worth might be, but it was too depressing. Ten dollars. A million, I teased myself, but I knew this wasn't what Camilla was talking about. A woman who I guessed to be about seven months pregnant entered the coffeehouse. She breathed with difficulty. Her feet were red and swollen, and she wore no rings. She was radiant, though. As she was standing in line, she folded her hands on her large belly. From my seat, I stared. She caught me examining, watching her, but instead of smiling, I turned away and touched my own stomach. It felt so empty, just a roll of skin from a child I never held. I turned my gaze out the large windows smeared with fingerprints and saw that the sun was setting. Quickly, I sucked down my syrupy drink. I wanted to simply leave, but decided I should say goodbye to Camilla. As I walked toward the barista bar, she caught my gaze. I stopped. "See ya."

Camilla held up one hand. "Just a second." She went to the rear of the store and came back with a piece of paper. "Take a look at this. It's a rally in Frisco. We could drive together. It'd be fun." She wrote down her phone number.

I glanced at the paper, then folded it and stuck it my pocket. "Thanks, I'll let you know."

The sun traveled over the hills, and I strode toward oncoming traffic. Once out of town, quail scurried about. I watched them walk, their small feet moving as fast as they could go from beneath the blackberry vines to an open field and then back again.

The heat released fragrances: first, the smells of a deserted apple orchard, then road kill. I placed my palm over my mouth and nose. After walking over an hour, knowing I had about another hour left, my legs began to ache. It had been too long since I had exercised. I had given up running while I was pregnant. To compound my aching legs, I now had a blister. I sighed. I'd been one smart cookie deciding to head to town. Remembering what my counselor said about using words of affirmation, I said, "Jamie, you are smart. You are good," but I was being a smartass. Remembering what Camilla said about Akasha knowing her worth, I said, "Jamie you are worthy of …" but then it was my turn to fall silent. I couldn't think what I was worthy of. I tried the breathing thing, deep breaths. But then I came upon another road kill, so I held my breath.

I envied the pregnant lady at the coffeehouse. Was her baby kicking when she placed her hand on her belly? Did her baby have the hiccups every evening? I was tired of having all this time to think, and when I wasn't thinking about me and my screwed up life, I got to think about real suffering, people who were dying from malnutrition. Families without homes. Children who weren't given vaccinations and were dying of diseases forgotten about in America. With a hand on either side of my skull, I squeezed and screamed. I stopped walking and screamed as loud as I could. When I stopped to catch my breath, I worried about someone hearing me for a second, but then I screamed again. I wanted it all out of my system. All the hurt and frustration. All the anger. Then, as spontaneously as the screams came, they stopped. I felt out of breath, but I started on my way again.

Maybe I should go back to counseling, I thought. I had stopped going when I was tired of talking about the tragedy — that was the word marriage and family therapist Susan Stephanopoulos had used, "tragedy," — tired of talking about why I decided to marry Santos, tired of crying, and tired of thinking about Santos and the trial. The months had crept by as our justice system prolonged my pain. The law said it was illegal for a man to harm a woman, killing her baby in utero — involuntary manslaughter. Santos and I had made eye contact the first day of court. I was the one who turned away when it should have been him. I hated him all the more for having the ability to look me in the eye. He wore a faded orange jumpsuit. I wondered what other criminals had worn it before him. Were they embezzlers? Druggies, or rapists? Child molesters? Killers?

During the rest of the court proceedings, I never looked at him once. I was told that he always had his tear-filled eyes on me, with his mother tearing Kleenex tissues to shreds behind him. I'd dream of Santos and his eyes full of tears and then awaken, cold and drenched in sweat.

I went through each day, each court day, each cancelled court day, waiting for his final sentence, seeing him and his repentant face that I couldn't look at. The day before Santos was to be sentenced, I was walking down the courthouse steps with Lily and my brother. Amongst all the pain and chaos, it felt good having two people by my side. But then Joel said, "You'll have to forgive him someday or God won't forgive you for your sins."

I stopped in my tracks, stunned. I turned toward Lily. And, then, I looked at Joel. I wanted to say that I didn't care, or "Fuck you!" I didn't have the guts to say what I really wanted, and that was, "That really hurt."

"Are you kidding me?" Lily said to Joel in amazement. "Get lost!" She took my hand and we paused to let Joel walk slowly down the steps by himself.

My life felt like a *Twilight Zone* episode, a life lived in fuzzy black and white, where I was constantly confused. After the trial, I told my therapist, "I need a break. I just need to get on with my life." She didn't say she thought it a good idea that I quit counseling, but I noticed that she didn't take out her appointment book when my time was up.

There were no cars, no other walkers on the road. There was a small winery that had its "Closed" sign up and maybe there were people inside washing wine glasses. Maybe they heard me scream, but if they did, they remained focused on their tasks. As I continued on my walk, I watched the sky turn red, then orange. I had heard from a friend that colorful sunsets wouldn't exist if it weren't for smog and pollution. This information had made me sad at the time, wanting to believe that the beauty was another one of God's wonders, not man's folly. But I never checked to see if her assertion were correct.

Remembering what my therapist had said about needing to be more positive and learning to count my blessings, I said aloud, "I am blessed because I get to watch this sunset."

I figured I was about halfway back to the mansion but couldn't be sure. The days were getting shorter, and I didn't want to be walking in the dark. A large bright moon was already settling itself in the sky. The sound of a car grew louder behind me. I moved farther away from the road and turned to see. The BMW was one of Akasha's — she had two exactly alike — and when it stopped, I figured it had to be her. Wiping my tear-stained face, I went to the passenger window. "Hi. You're back," I said.

"Probably not a great idea walking on a side road in the dark. Get in." She pressed the button to unlock the door. I climbed in.

"It's not dark just yet." I felt glad for the ride, but I wanted to be alone. Funny how fast emotions change. I had set out on this little adventure needing company, and now I just wanted to be left alone to pull myself back together.

"Next time you need a car, take one of mine. The keys are always on the dashboard."

"I think my car battery is dead." I was getting goose bumps from her air conditioning as it dried my sweat. Trying to be inconspicuous, I looked around her car, wanting to know more about her. There was no Coke in the holder, no gum wrappers; there wasn't even any music playing. In the back, sliding against one another were several books that looked like textbooks and a notebook. It was getting too dark to make out the books' titles. She reached over and turned off the air. "Thanks," I said. I thought she must have seen my chill bumps. "I need to talk to you about what I've been reading, what you want me to do next."

"Not now," she said. "I have a lot on my mind." I was glad. Though I felt I had little direction, all I wanted was a bath and a movie. The moon shone more fully, softening the darkening sky. "You walked all the way to town?"

I told her about the lady I hitched a ride from, how she kept a sexual relic hanging on her rearview mirror to remind her of her younger man. She laughed and I did, too. "There was something really sad about the lady," I said.

"I hope I'm not sad when I'm old."

I hadn't thought about it before, but there was something sad about Akasha. It was the first time she exposed anything about herself. She parked, and then gathered her things from the back seat.

"Do you need help with anything?" I asked.

She said no. I thought she might retrieve a suitcase from the trunk, but she didn't. As we walked to the mansion, she gazed up at the sky. "What a beautiful moon. It has a purple cast to it."

Wanting to see what she thought beautiful, I glanced at the moon. "Maybe me and you and Camilla from the coffeehouse can get together sometime. She's been kind."

"I think she's moving soon." She didn't accept my invitation and I felt jilted and hurt. Inside, she went up her stairs without even a goodnight. She wore white linen pants and a sleeveless fitted top that exposed her willowy arms. Like a bird in flight, they floated above her head. When she reached the top of the stairs, she took the large clip out of her hair. Her hair fell over her bare shoulders. I combed my short hair with my fingers, feeling envious of her hair, but more envious of her ability to move through her life with confidence. It didn't appear that she played by anyone else's rules.

Sleeping restlessly, I woke with the moon's beams shining on my face. I thought about closing the curtains and trying to go back to sleep, but instead I put on my flip flops and quietly walked down the steps and out the side door to the garden.

The air had finally cooled.

I slid my shoes off and carried them. I liked the feel of the rugged stone path. A breeze played with the leaves in the maple trees. Smells of jasmine and roses composed a melody of fragrance. I closed my eyes to breathe in the smells; it was almost too sweet. I walked past Zahir's place as I headed to the pond. His light was on. Through his front window, I saw him kneeling, his forehead touching the floor. I turned away and wondered to what God he was praying to.

Soon I came upon a large Buddha sitting under a canopy of tree limbs. Moss sprouted on its head and cheeks. I smiled at what my brother and father would think.

"There is only one God, one religion," my brother would sermonize. Dad would attempt to say something funny about the Buddha's stomach. "I won't have what he had," I imagined him sputtering. Yet, the paintings and marble sculptures of Christ's concave belly weren't any more inspiring.

Sitting on the bridge over the pond, I saw what I had come for: the moon's reflection shining on the water. One night during our last summer together, my mother had told me that watching the moon on water was a time to reevaluate what was real in my life. I was ten. It was a night I used to try to forget. Now I didn't want to forget any moment I'd had with her. At Crater Lake's edge, Mom had reclined back onto her elbows.

"Look up at the sky." Sitting on my knees, I tilted my head back. She sat back up, brushed the hair out of my eyes, and added, "See the moon?" I nodded. It was a cloudless night. The moon, though maybe not full, was large and bright. I was sure she was going to ask me to find the Big and Little Dippers, or Orion, or Pegasus, like she had done before. "Now look at the lake," she said. "What do you see?" Still trying to locate the Little Dipper, but wanting to play a new game, I looked.

"Water."

"And ..."

Was she asking me to find a fish? Or a boat? Maybe name the leaf that was floating by?

"See the moon? It's also on the water. It's now fluid; it now knows how to dance. Look at yourself in the water. What do you see?"

"I see my reflection dancing with the water." I had caught on to this new game.

"What is more real?" She unclasped my barrette and began to comb my hair with her fingers. I told her the real me.

"What is the real you?" In reply, I placed my hand on my chest as if I were going to say the pledge of allegiance.

"What makes you think so?"

"Mom, why are you being so funny? This is me." I could feel little rocks poking into my knees.

"But when you see yourself in the water, you see yourself dance," she said, "dancing on the water in the moonlight." She took both my hands and lifted me up. And we danced around in circles. I watched our reflection on the surface of the water. She laughed, and I tried to.

When we sat back down, she said, "Don't forget to dance on the water with the moonlight. Don't forget to create beauty. Don't forget that I am always with you even if you can't feel me, even if you think I am gone." She then turned her head away from me, but she was too late because I had already seen the tears in her eyes.

The next day she told me she had cancer. At ten, I didn't know what that meant. I learned that cancer meant hospitals. Cancer meant watching my mom throw up, finding clumps of her hair in the bathtub drain, smelling rancid, rotting flesh that had been fed too many chemicals. Cancer meant slowly watching the person who loved me the most die with tubes up her nose while surrounded by beeps and more beeps from equipment I was told never to touch. Cancer also meant people telling me *it* would be okay, and my knowing that *it* was dead and I'd have to create a new *it* in my life. And the only person who could show me how to have another *it* was gone. That was cancer: a dead mother.

I bent over the bridge now to see my reflection, but it was blurry from tears dropping, one after another. There was no beauty in my life and I guessed I was the one responsible for that. It wasn't that I'd forgotten about beauty; it was that I didn't know how to create it, or didn't feel worthy enough. Maybe that was the it, the knowledge of what I was.

And, although Mom had said she'd always be with me, I hadn't believe her. How could something be if I didn't feel it?

When the tears finally stopped, I looked again in the water and saw not my reflection but that of a man. I gasped and pushed myself up. My head hit the railing. I turned, lying on my back, and saw Zahir.

"Zahir. You scared me." I pulled down my nightgown.

"Sorry." He offered me his hand. I took it. I was surprised at how soft it was. He worked with his hands.

"I didn't mean to disturb you. I know it's late," I said. I wiped a stray tear. The moon shone behind him, casting his face in shadows.

"You're okay?"

"Yes." I appreciated his concern.

"I could get someone, if—"

"Really, thanks. I'm okay." He turned and headed back slowly toward his home. I looked again at the water, wanting to recapture the moon's dance, my need to dance, my need to feel what was real, but a cloud now covered the moon.

Chapter Six

*T*he next morning, although I was still hurting from Akasha's rejection, I knew I had a job to do, so I dressed and went to look for her. Right before the spiral staircase, I saw a door ajar, one I'd never seen open before. Caught by curiosity, I peeked inside. Akasha stood by the window. In the center of the room sat a small white-canopied bed. Unlike mine, it was low to the floor. Above it hung a bright pink crystal chandelier. The room smelt stale from disuse, more like a room in a museum than a bedroom.

"What do you think of this room?" she said. I hoped she didn't want me to move. I liked my room.

"The chandelier is beautiful." I moved closer to the bed and to her.

"Does it feel like a child's room? A little girl's room?" She glanced at the pink chandelier.

I thought about the crib Santos and I had bought at a garage sale. I had placed it in my bedroom next to the changing table a woman from work had given me. Although I had planned to get a two-bedroom eventually, I'd liked the thought of having my baby close.

"I guess. Where would the mother be? I would want my baby's room next to mine."

"Yes. I suppose you're right." She walked out of the room. I followed. "You want to talk to me?"

I wondered if Akasha were pregnant. But then dismissed the thought since she didn't say anything more about a space for a little girl. Downstairs, she went into the room with the piano, looked around, as someone would do who was evaluating a home they might buy.

"Do you play?" she asked me and twiddled her fingers, one hand on top of the other, as if she were strengthening her fingers, an exercise she'd learned from a teacher.

"No. I wish I did."

"I'm not sure I can help you. That is what you are going to ask, isn't it?"

I had two thoughts at that moment. If she couldn't help me, the woman who hired me, then who could? And I had never seen Akasha act so unsure, almost nervous.

"I asked you this before. What are your passions? If I told you mine, you'd learn what motivates me, why I behave the way I do, why I choose one line of work versus another. But, of course, passions change. Or maybe we just redirect them as we get older. Think about it. I can't talk anymore right now. Maybe later. No, let's meet in two days at three o'clock. Stop second-guessing yourself."

She left the room quickly, and I wondered if she had an appointment or something. I wished I knew more about her. What she did with her time … how she made her money ... who her friends were... Maybe I should have asked what her passions were.

My passions weren't helping the homeless, getting clean water to a war-torn village, making condoms available to everyone all over the globe, or even saving the whales, yet this was what Akasha was paying me to do: to care. I felt at a loss. I worried that this job, my life here, was in jeopardy. And I wasn't second-guessing myself; I really didn't know what she wanted from me.

I spent the next couple of days and nights investigating humanitarian websites: Amnesty International, UNICEF, American Jewish World Services, Care, Mercy Core, Oxfam, and Human Rights Watch. The needs were so high all over the globe. Everyone asked for money. I made a list of issues to talk about with Akasha during our meeting. Then she could choose what organizations she felt compelled to give to.

1. Colombia — 3.5 million displaced people due to the fighting between guerrillas, government officials, drug traffickers, and right-wing paramilitaries.

2. Thailand — child prostitution, stemming mainly from poverty.

3. South Congo — boys being kidnapped and forced into military camps and eventually war.

4. Female castration —Sudan had the largest practicing population.

5. AIDS orphans — estimated in excess of 20 million.

6. USA — child abuse, inner city children at risk, poverty.

At our scheduled time, I smiled when I saw Akasha dressed and sitting behind her desk. There'd be no surprise entries from her today. Giving her copies of the articles I'd sourced, I sat and presented the information. She never looked at the printed sheets. But she listened, as I listed off statistics and told her stories of boys from the Congo being given marijuana and forced to shoot and kill, parents selling off their twelve-year-old daughters in Thailand for prostitution and how many American men visited these child prostitutes. One story didn't move her any more than another. She listened as a therapist would: interested and empathetic, but not shocked.

When I had said all that I had prepared to say, physically and emotionally tired, I waited for her to reply. I thought she might say, "Good work, now you're on the right track." Instead there was silence, and then continued silence. She stared at me, as if I might have more to say, but I didn't.

"That's all I prepared," I said. She turned her chair to look out the window. Zahir was in the distance pulling weeds. Akasha and I watched him. I didn't have anything else to add. My job was to give her the facts, do the research. For a brief moment, I wondered if maybe my job was done. What would I do if this job were already over? Go back to Grass Valley? The bank? No one would ever give me a paying job like this one. Sure, I could always find volunteer work, but I had to support myself. And then a thought popped into my head, one I hadn't entertained for a while. I could move to Hollywood and work in the film industry. I had made it this far. A six-hour drive and I would hit Hollywood.

"Zahir blames himself." She turned her chair back around and faced me. "There's so much suffering in this world." Her eyes were red, but there were no tears.

"Blames himself for what?" I felt hurt that she had no response to what I had just said. I felt all the work I did was in vain. But I also wanted to hear about Zahir.

"I'm always asking myself what is my responsibility and what is not." She pulled her hair back and tied it into a knot.

What was Zahir beating himself up for? I could have gone out of my way to be kinder to him. It was easy to concentrate on my own pain, as if I were the only one with heartache, the only one with problems, when in fact I now knew from all the research that people all over the world suffered. Everyone had a story.

"What now?" Akasha said. "I feel like I just watched *Nightline*, all the horror with no sane solutions, no hope." Her voice was kind, without being condescending. "Jamie, I am paying you to do the thinking, the work. Don't you get it?"

I had just given the best report of my life, and yet, it still wasn't good enough. "No, I don't get it."

"I don't want to think about these places, these people. I want you to."

I sat at the edge of the chair, feeling frustrated, ready to leave her office. I looked over at the wall where Van Gogh's picture hung. Some minimalist painting seemed more appropriate. A canvas full of nothing but red paint, and the viewer was supposed to "get it." But I didn't. "I'll try harder."

She picked up the paper clip I had used to clip my research together, then bent it back and forth until it broke. Walking across the room, she threw the pieces in the trashcan. She was wearing a long silk skirt, the only woman I knew who wore long skirts. The elegance was stunning, and I wondered why more women didn't dress like her. She walked back to her desk and picked up the handouts I gave her, then quickly laid them down. Sitting, she opened a desk drawer and took out a bottle of generic aspirin and swallowed three pills with no water.

"Tea, anybody?" Beah walked in holding a tray with a teapot, teacups and cookies. She placed the tray on a side table, not waiting for an answer, and poured two cups. She handed Akasha a cup. "Jamie, cream or sugar?"

I asked for both, as I'd always found plain tea bitter. Beah poured cream and a teaspoon of sugar into the small cup and stirred.

"Lovely day, isn't it?" Beah asked.

I liked the sound of the spoon hitting the thin china cup. Wearing her standard tailored dress, stirring tea, Beah reminded me of a British caricature in a *Saturday Night Live* skit. Even though I knew she wasn't addressing me, seeing that Akasha didn't answer, I said, "I haven't been outside, but it looks nice." I wished I hadn't taken the tea or the oatmeal raisin cookie but that I had left the room instead. My hurt feelings were bordering on anger. Akasha wasn't going to say anything else to me about my work and now she was being rude to Beah.

"Thank you, Jamie. Akasha, what do you think? " Beah said.

Akasha, holding her tea, faced toward the window again. "I'm leaving. Please pack my bags."

I looked up, thinking finally I'd get some information about where Akasha goes and why.

"Scheduled or not scheduled?" Beah asked.

"Does it matter?" she asked angrily and turned and looked at Beah. I was glad that voice wasn't directed at me, but then she did turn to me and started to say something but changed her mind. She peered down at her tea and drank the whole cup in one gulp. And here I thought the proper way to drink tea was to sip it. As I took a coffee-sized swallow of my tea, she said, "Do you and your father get along? What about you and your brother?"

"Sometimes my brother and I do," I said, but I could tell she wasn't too interested in my answer. She left behind the purple velvet curtains. Cookie crumbs had gathered on my lap. I brushed them off, trying to remember if I had ever mentioned to Akasha that I had a brother, if I had ever told her anything about my family. I was sure I hadn't.

Eying the now empty cookie plate, Beah said, "There are more in the kitchen." She took the tray. I followed, not because I wanted more cookies, but because I wanted to talk to her about my meeting with Akasha. She told me that Ana was the best baker she knew. Beah was sniffling. Though she was several steps ahead of me, I saw her take her hanky and wipe the drips from her nose. I wanted to ask her what was wrong. Beah didn't strike me as a woman who cried often. Maybe she was hurt by Akasha's curtness, too. I picked up my pace and placed my arm around her waist. Touch sometimes said more than words, so I kept my arm where I had placed it.

Ana was pulling a sheet of cookies out of the oven as we walked into the kitchen. Her hair was up, braided and tied on top of her head as usual; she wore a soft blue housedress. Setting a small plate of cookies on the table, she touched my shoulder with her warm palm before heading back to the sink.

Beah made coffee and sat down. "I get so damned tired of tea. I'm glad she's leaving." But I could tell this wasn't how she felt. Akasha was the glue that kept the house running.

Ana sat next to her and placed her hand on Beah's. How sweet it was that these two had each other's friendship. I'd often catch them talking and laughing. I ate another cookie.

"These are very good, Ana, thank you." She smiled. I then told them about a time I had made cookies with my mom. I was six years old when Mom had taught me the ingredients for oatmeal raisin cookies. She had said, "One teaspoon of baking powder to make them rise, cinnamon for zest." But, unlike the times we baked before, this time she cried. I tried making her stop by asking questions.

"What's the sugar for, Mommy?" I was silenced when I saw two large tears fall in the batter as she stirred. Sitting on my knees on a chair next to the cutting board, I fell silent. If Mommy was sad, how were I to be happy? I began to cry, too, like her, and since my head wasn't over the bowl, my tears dripped off my chin onto my neck. She looked at me and, with her floured index finger, wiped two tears from my cheeks and placed them into the batter.

"We won't need salt today," she said. Then she smiled. "Give me a hug. I always feel so much better after I feel your arms around me." And with that hug, Mom was back to her strong self. And yet I'd catch her crying at unusual times for the rest of her life. Later, I decided that my mother had been sad. Maybe she had felt trapped being married to my father, or maybe she had dreams that were left unfulfilled — but with all that, I never sensed that either Joel or I were her burdens. Her tears wouldn't have been about the news of her cancer; that didn't come until years later.

It was the first time I had shared that story about my mom with anyone. It was the first time I had talked about Mom in a long time. It made her feel more alive, as if I had been keeping her memory locked in a cellar, fermenting but never enjoyed. Now, when I thought about her in the sunlight, with freshly cut flowers and the smell of rosemary coming through an open window, I could almost feel her next to me.

When I got up to leave, Beah said, "Take your time. I may not know Akasha all that well, but I do believe she is not in any hurry. Why don't you just rest? We are living to heal in this house."

"That wasn't my agreement with Akasha," I said. "This wasn't a charity case." I felt hurt.

"No. But all jobs come with perks not stated in the contract."

"Yeah, if only I had a contract," I said, walking out of the kitchen. As I made my way to my room, I thought she must be referring to my story, the death of my mother. But then maybe she sensed I held a newer heartache, one that still haunted me.

When Akasha left, everybody retreated, staying in their rooms. Ana cooked less. The house was still kept mysteriously clean, but I rarely saw Beah cleaning even when Akasha was around. I began to wonder if mice and birds mopped floors and waxed the staircase in the middle of the night. Zahir also made himself scarce. Though I didn't spend any time with Akasha, I wasn't looking forward to her being gone.

Even though Beah advised me to rest, I felt on edge; I wanted something to do to keep my mind busy and feelings at bay. I sat down at my desk to begin researching. As I turned on the computer, I found myself missing my job at the bank, the simplicity of it. I knew exactly what I was to do, plus, my manager never asked me personal questions other than the standard, "How are you?" Never expecting or wanting a real answer. It would never occur to him to ask me about my passions, or perhaps he would be afraid of what my answer might be. I had been passionate about my baby. It was a feeling that arose with no warning and was more intense than anything I had ever felt before, more than my first love, more than my love for my mother. The need to nourish her and protect her felt archaic, something that had been handed down to me in some genetic code from generation to generation of women.

I then reflected about my passion before getting pregnant. It was a silent passion. Everyone knew that I loved movies, but my love was more than watching movies. The part that I didn't tell people was that I really wanted to work in the industry. I read books about the cinematic arts. Watching the director's cut was sometimes more intriguing to me than the actual movie. I went to film festivals when I could. When the film professor at Sacramento State told me I could sit in, I did.

The Safari browser wouldn't open, so I read some articles I had previously printed. One was on solar ovens, something of which I knew nothing about, but according to the article, they were easy to use and inexpensive, making them great for people living in small villages or even refugee camps. Another talked about the opium trade in Afghanistan, of how traditional crops were being replaced by opium and that Afghanistan was now the world's leading producer of opium. On a whim, to balance out world affairs with local issues, I read the *Sonoma Valley Sun* newspaper. Then, I painted my toenails, hoping Italian Pink would brighten my mood. Instead, I brooded.

How was I, through Akasha, supposed to end the desire for opium, or keep fathers from selling their daughters into prostitution? What could I do to help the millions of African orphans, whose parents had both died of AIDS? Plus, didn't she already say she had heard enough about condoms? I read in the *Sonoma Valley Sun* that parents and city officials wanted to build a teen center close to the local high school, the one I had driven by on my way to Fallow Springs, that money was needed. Yet she had said she didn't want to "just write a check." Why not help good kids in our neighborhood, I wondered.

Again, I doubled-clicked on the Safari icon. I watched the address bar, waiting for my Yahoo page to open. It didn't. I tried Explorer. I turned the computer off and back on again and, while it rebooted, I made some coffee. Next to the coffee pot was the folded piece of paper that Camilla had given me. I unfolded it. There was going to be a rally at the San Francisco Golden Gate Park. "Stand Up for Women in War," the flyer said. In smaller print it said there would be speakers from Iraq, Afghanistan, the Democratic Republic of the Congo, and Sudan. I set the paper back down. Although I thought it might be interesting and educational, and related to my work, I wasn't the rally-attending type.

Safari still wouldn't open, so I went downstairs to find Beah. On the kitchen table there was a note, not addressed to anyone, saying she had gone to town. I called AT&T just to see if someone might know what happened to the Internet service. The customer services agent said someone was working on it, but service might not be up for another few hours. I thought about dinner. There was no food prepared on the stove or the table. I really wasn't hungry anyway.

Back in my room, a white and red envelope on the dresser caught my eye. It held the DVD that I had ordered and Beah delivered. I decided, instead of pacing the room and waiting for service, I'd watch the movie. Then I could send it back, giving me a little sense of accomplishment, as if I had finished something. I climbed onto my bed, set my computer on a pillow in front of me, and pulled my knees to my chest, wanting something diverting.

The movie was a Don Cheadle film, *Hotel Rwanda*. I loved him in *Crash* and the fun, sleek *Ocean's* movie. I knew little about *Hotel Rwanda*, but because Cheadle was in it, I assumed it would be good. I read the DVD's sleeve cover: "Tutsi extremists lead genocide in Rwanda." This should be uplifting, I thought, wryly. I remembered watching *Schindler's List* in a history class. I couldn't get the images from the concentration camp, of the gas rooms, of children hiding in shit holes, of the emaciated Jews out of my mind. I had no idea that humans could be so evil. Three days after my teacher showed that movie, he moved on to the war in Vietnam. I wasn't ready. I wanted to know more about why the Nazis thought there was "a Jewish problem." Was it a religious issue? And what did the other Germans think? The Germans who were moms and dads who went to work at grocery stores … did they think there was a Jewish problem? I wanted to know about the Jews today and how they assimilated their past. I asked my teacher these questions but he didn't know. He said he'd look for some books for me to read, that he'd get back to me, but he never did. So I watched movies looking for answers.

Hotel Rwanda showed men's and women's throats sliced with machetes. Children killed, their innocence drained and soaked into the soil. "We will cut down all the tall trees," Rwanda radios pronounced in the movie. The Tutsis were tall trees, not humans, to these extremists.

Paul Ruseabagina, the hotel manager played by Don Cheadle, was at first confident that help would come and save the Tutsis. Though he was Hutu, his wife was Tutsi. "How could they not intervene when they witness such atrocities?" he asked a reporter. He was convinced that, after the West, America in particular, saw the footage of Tutsis being slaughtered, they would send help. Joaquin Phoenix, playing the cynical reporter, shook his head: "They'll say, 'Oh my God that's horrible,' and then go on eating their dinners." I wondered if this were true. Did we? Did the world learn anything from hearing about concentration camps and gas chambers?

In one scene, Hutu rebel men kept Tutsi women naked in cages. They called them Tutsi whores, as if they deserved being raped. I guessed that people had to dehumanize in order to rape and slaughter. Something had to separate "them" from "us." Otherwise how could any of this have taken place? There had to be a good guy and a bad guy. Or, maybe, because these men were acting unnaturally, they became untrustworthy, like from that book Camilla had talked about.

The movie showed UN troops transporting Tutsis with exit visas. The Hutu killers stopped the trucks and jumped into the back with machetes, ready to slice throats. Mothers threw their children on the truck floors and lay on top of them. Instinct and fear melded fiercely with their only desire, their only reason for living — to protect their young.

I thought of Santos. I hoped he was suffering in prison.

But where was I when this genocide was taking place? I had the excuse of youth, didn't I? The excuse of being a motherless child, wrapped up in my own pain. This happened over ten years ago and no one can go back in history and act. It was easy to say I'd have treated the Jews differently.

I watched the movie extras, wondering how much of this actually happened and how much was Hollywood's need for sensationalism, movie tension. I wanted more information. I thought information would give a clue, a reason, why one tribe would want to exterminate another. But, with more information, I only became more upset. With more information, reasons why people would slaughter other people became more absurd. What made a person Tutsi and what made a person Hutu wasn't that easy to decipher: width of nose; dark black versus light black; tall men versus short men. It would be easy to confuse the two.

Over eight hundred thousand Tutsis were killed in one hundred days. Almost all of the murders happened with knives and machetes, where the killer saw the fear in the eyes of his victim and felt life inside himself. I wondered what could make a person hate with such fervor. Maybe it was brainwashing or fear for their own lives and families.

Dad never talked about politics, other than to say he hated this person or that one. My teachers at school never mentioned it. Maybe my government or English teacher did try to tell us apathetic kids about people being slaughtered. I didn't remember learning about Africa in any grade, except in geography class, and even then all we had to do was label the continent AFRICA. I thought about Nick Nolte's line, as UN Colonel Oliver in *Hotel Rwanda*: "You're not even a nigger. You're black, an African."

After the movie was over, I had no problem getting online. I began to research the Rwandan genocide. Ten years was long enough to say that genocide couldn't or wouldn't happen today. I assured myself that there was no way; after all, everyone had had enough time to reflect on the Holocaust and ask how. I was glad when I read that President Bush said, "Not on my watch." This assured me, gave me a sense of hope and safety and even pride in being American.

Yet what came up in my search wasn't only the Rwandan genocide, but also a genocide in the Darfur province of Sudan, Africa, happening now. When I saw the word "Sudan," I jumped off the bed and reread the flyer that Camilla had given me. I slipped on my shoes and trotted down stairs to call her.

I wasn't sure what I was getting myself into, but maybe Akasha would even consider it work. Camilla and I made plans to drive down to the city together in three days, early Saturday morning.

"I'll bring you a sign to hold," she promised.

"A sign? What kind of sign? Like a peace sign?" I had to laugh; this seemed so out of my comfort zone.

"Perfect! Peace for All Women."

Chapter Seven

Camilla and I drove down in her blue Bug to San Francisco. We talked nonstop, and this getting-to-know-you conversation lifted my spirits. I found myself laughing and drumming my thumb to the beat of her music. She told me she had a degree in engineering from Cal Poly and that she had joined the Peace Corps. She would be leaving for Panama in two weeks. I felt sad. I'd just found her and now I'd be losing her. Also, it was becoming clearer to me what a college education could do for someone. But then I thought about the awesome job I had with no education and the weirdest interview anyone could ever experience.

"I wanted out of the Americas," Camilla said. "I really did. I don't even speak Spanish — zip, *cero, ninguno Español.*"

I told her about living at Fallow Springs, the richness of it all and how foreign it felt, how strange it was that I still didn't know Akasha, or anyone really for that matter.

"Beah and I talk the most. She seems the most socialized." I laughed when I thought about it. The rest of us seemed to pitter-patter here and there, doing this and that, like mice in Cinderella's story.

When we crossed the bridge into San Francisco, Camilla became visibly excited. Her energy was contagious.

"This is going to be great. You'll see." She smiled so widely that I could see her gums gleam. She rolled down the car windows and turned off the music. "Okay, I need to concentrate now. I'm not exactly sure how to get there." She leaned closer to the wheel. The smells of the sea, car exhaust, and city life filled the car. I took the map from her lap and became her co-pilot.

At the rally, we went to different booths to pick up information. I took a bumper sticker from Amnesty, a pencil from Mercy Core. Camilla knew people so I was left to my own devices much of the time. This was fine. I could take it all in when I didn't feel the need to talk or listen. I had thought there would be mostly young, hippie-looking people, but there were people of all kinds and ages: older men in wool sweaters, children toddling on the grass, women wearing tight pencil skirts and heels. People held signs, wore t-shirts with logos. Some said, "Genocide No More: Save Darfur."

The sky was an exceptional shade of blue. It looked to have purple bubbles floating among the clouds so white and fluffy. I had imagined the day to be grey, overcast, a bit chilly. It didn't seem to be the kind of day to talk about the rape and torture of women here in the USA or anywhere. I knew I was being silly. The weather was simply the weather.

I sat on the grass with the sign that Camilla gave me propped in front of me. I felt like an imposter. I really didn't understand the politics behind the rally. If someone asked, I'd just stick my sign in their face and say, "See? I want peace."

Quietness tumbled over the crowd. The coordinator of the rally, an older lady, came to the stage and introduced herself. Her mother was a Holocaust survivor but had lost all her family. The woman removed her sunglasses, although it was exceptionally sunny, and began to speak.

"As a child, I watched my mom move through the world passionless about everything except me. I knew as young as five that I wouldn't keep quiet when wrong was being done.

"I've heard activist and actor Mia Farrow say that her family mantra is, 'With knowledge comes responsibility.' Today we are going to share with you stories. Then, my hope is that you will take a bit of responsibility. It us up to the people who have a voice to help women around the globe, as well as on our own streets, to stay safe."

People around me clapped. The little boy next to me looked intently through a patch of clover for a four-leaf clover. He asked his mother to help him, but she shushed him. I willed him to find one so I could see him smile.

"I am honored to bring to you a Kenyan who works for the World Food Program. She was stationed in Darfur, Sudan. Inaya Atudo experienced firsthand war at the power of the Janjaweed, a Sudanese-funded militia."

"Who?" I said, leaping to my feet. "What did she say her last name was?" The lady next to me shook her head. "Inaya who?" I repeated. Inaya, possibly a common

African name. I made my way through the crowd to the front of the stage. The woman was tall with black hair, brown eyes, large white teeth and a crooked smile. Could be any Kenyan. Her forehead was rounded, her neck long and elegant, almost like a ballerina's. She wore gold sandals and a vibrant blue and yellow dress. I forgot what she called the native dress, what all Kenyan women called them. I could see this woman's perfect right ankle and her mangled left, where a snake had bitten her as a child. She was lucky to be alive, she had been told, but forever would limp.

I wanted to run up on the stage, call out her name, and say, "Do you remember me? You were our exchange student. We slept together as sisters for nine months." You were the only one who asked how I was doing after my mom died. I remember the paper you wrote the letter on. It was brown and stained; your penmanship was perfect, always perfect, while mine sucked. You said your mom used to make you practice for hours, copying poetry. I thought your mother must have been cruel, too strict.

"But look at my penmanship," you had said to me. People can read my writing, understand what I am thinking. You," she had teased, "Well, you had better learn to type."

I made myself listen to her story, this story that she was telling in San Francisco, California. So far from Africa. I wasn't surprised she was back in the States, speaking to a crowd this large. She was a voyager; she was strong and capable, smart, and from a good Kenyan family. Even as a child, I knew life would be hers, in the palm of her hand, as they say.

I had felt I was average in her presence, colorless, forgettable. But she had never made me feel this way. She would hold me tight before we fell asleep, and she would tell me stories of Africa. Of watching the differences of how geese fly. "Did you know geese fly differently when going to water than when they are leaving it?" Of Kenyan poets. She'd recite, "Daughter, take this amulet; tie it with cord and caring." And of dancing by fire. Her mother would send her during the school holidays to live with her cousins, who lived in a village far from Nairobi, "to learn the ways of your people," she had been told. Sometimes Inaya and I would dance in my room until we'd fall down, sweaty and exhausted, or until my dad would bang on the door, telling me to turn the noise down, that he was watching television.

Listen, Jamie, I told myself, as I gazed at her. I took a couple of steps back from the stage.

Inaya still smiled, but something was gone. Her smile used to make me laugh. It was so big, real, evoking goodness; I'd laugh and then she would. Listen, I said to myself. On stage, she cleared her throat and then smiled, a bit unsure. Maybe it wasn't Inaya. I looked at the wounded ankle. A breeze picked up the fabric of her shawl; she wrapped her scarf back around her neck.

"They took me and Dafina." I couldn't remember who the announcer said the "they" were. "I was thrown into a hut. I wasn't sure what they did with my friend." Her voice lowered. "She came to Darfur because I had asked her to come with me." She shook her head as if a fly landed on her nose. "The first man called me a black whore slave, good for two things, work and rape. I counted the men at first. The first day, one...two...three...four...until twenty. The second day, number twenty-five came in. I said to him, 'You are black. You are African.'

"'I am Arab. Sudan is for Arabs.'

"He used his bayonet. 'You are no good black woman.'

80

"I stopped counting. Only saw colors surround me, purple, red, black, the colors of my mother and her birth of me. I wished I had never been born. I desired to be back in my mother's womb and hear the rhythms of her heart, the food she swallowed, the songs she sang, the laughter she released.

"When the Janjaweed moved on, they left me under a tree. It was there I saw Dafina again. Why didn't they leave us in the sun where I would have surely died? Did they want others to see their evilness? Sometimes I think one cared enough, but probably not. Care and kindness can be wiped clean from the spirit of an unnatural man.

"If, though, if we were in Kenya, a lion would find us and eat us; this sounded welcoming, something that made sense. But, in Darfur, the lions don't even roam.

"Dafina died. She never spoke a word. I held her hand and prayed and thanked God that she had peace. I prayed for peace, too, but instead, UN workers found me and took me. Someone gave me water, and later food, and later, I thanked them not for peace, but for life, because with life I can do something, help other girls and women. Still, I have little peace — I still pray for peace."

As Inaya left the stage, the crowd broke out in applause. I wondered what they clapped for. Did she entertain? Inspire? Was it because of her courage? I followed her steps. Two women came to be with her as she exited the stage. Words were exchanged. One lady took Inaya's hand. There were no tears. I wondered how many times she had had to share this story to make the tears stop. The announcer called another guest to the stage. The woman holding Inaya's hand mounted the steps.

Dragging my peace sign, I made my way to her side. She watched the woman on the stage. I wiped my tear-drenched face then whispered, "Inaya."

"Yes?" She took in my gaze and her eyes flickered. She grabbed my hands, and held me with her eyes, and then we embraced, just like on the day she left my home. Our love and friendship returned like a dried riverbed left to drought finally rained upon.

"Sister. You found me. Oh, life is good today." And we kissed. I tried to tell her it was only by chance that I came, but she assured me it wasn't. "I knew we would meet again as women and here we are. Fate it was." We still held each other with our eyes. I thought maybe she was right. Maybe this day was meant to happen, in just this way.

After the rally, she made herself available to talk. People lined up to say hello or give her a hug or tell a story that sparked when she had relayed hers. I stayed by her side. Many times she reached for my hand and held it as she wished people well, accepted information, gave information. Some man from the *San Francisco Chronicle* snapped her picture; she held me close. Told him, "This is my sister."

"Your sister?"

"Yes. Jamie Shire. Write that down."

"She's white," he said, disbelieving.

"Yes. She is white."

Camilla waited patiently. She came by a few times to check in and then went and visited with friends. I knew she was ready to head back.

"You fly out at what time?" I asked Inaya, as I saw Camilla approaching again.

"Not until 10 a.m. First, I am going to Chicago and then back home."

"Are you speaking at another rally?"

"No. A playwright has asked to meet me, Lynn Nattage. Do you know of her? She is writing a play about war through the lives of women. I am happy to help her. Stay here with me, Jamie." She slipped her arm around mine.

"Jamie, you about ready?" Camilla looked at me expectantly.

"I want to stay."

"I would," said Camilla. "It's just that I work in the morning. It's my last shift. I don't want to miss it."

"Sure. I understand," I said, wondering how I would get back.

"Maybe there is a bus," Inaya said.

I thought about the check from Akasha I had deposited a few days ago. Then with confidence, I smiled. "Yeah, something. I'll take a cab if I have to."

"I like your style," Camilla grinned, as I hugged her goodbye. Inaya left to thank the woman who had organized the rally. When she returned, we strolled around the park. She told me more of her story and of the work she was doing now.

"It is difficult to come to America. American visas have become more challenging to get. Tickets are expensive. I need to, though, because here in America, there is power. The people here have power to help change things. In Darfur, the people have no power. The government is taking their homes, their means of life, and their dignity. So I will keep speaking. Here and wherever people want me to."

I told her about my job and living with Akasha.

"When I think about the situation logically, it makes no sense. A beautiful woman hires me to research and pays me crazy well. I get to live not in a house, but a mansion. I haven't even been in all the rooms."

"Maybe you shouldn't think of it logically. Take this chapter as a gift. I don't know why she is doing it. Maybe she does not know why. Seems like a gift. Like today is a gift."

We walked and talked until I thought I might pass out from hunger. Then we took a cab to an Ethiopian restaurant. She loved the *doro wot*, a spicy chicken dish that sent my throat screaming. I settled in to eating a simple lentil dish and salad. She talked of her days at the University of Nairobi and how she fell in love with one of the young teachers. "He married another woman. Crazy man," she said, as she watched the waitress set food down at another table. "My life would have turned out differently had he wanted me." I reached for her hand and held it. I told her about a man I had loved.

"I never felt good enough for him. He eventually left me. Or maybe it was simply love I didn't feel worthy of — either way, gone, gone, gone."

"Now this wasn't how it was supposed to work out for us. We were queens, rulers of the world, back when we were young." She held up her glass as if toasting.

"Men want princesses," I said, never really having articulated this before. She laughed, a short shallow laughter, yet it still sounded reassuring. I simply smiled.

"Oh, it feels good to laugh. Sadly, I think you are right. Paupers and kings both want princesses — only wise men want queens, and there are so few of those here on this earth."

Back at her room, I showered, and then she did. She gave me her pajamas to wear, a red cotton capri set, smelling of her, a subtle sent of jasmine and sandalwood. She came out of the bathroom wearing a t-shirt that had an American

Eagle logo on it, exposing her long, muscular, ebony legs. On her right thigh, several two-inch scars puffed out, red and swollen. I thought about saying something, but wasn't sure what. That looks awful? Painful? Seen a doctor? Instead I said, "I never got to ask my mother why she took in an exchange student."

"And a black one from Africa. I am sure there are many questions you wish you could ask your mother. The mystery of me is just one."

"I know she wanted to travel. Maybe that was it, maybe partly."

"I remember she loved to read." I had forgotten this about my mother. I sat on the edge of the bed and watched Inaya as she brushed her hair. "She always had a book in her hand, purse or on the table next to her," Inaya recalled. "She told me reading was her teacher. I think about her whenever I pick up a book. I am sorry I could not be with you after she passed. You should have come and lived with me."

"I should have. My dad and I never got along. I mean, I shouldn't say 'never.' There were..." I hesitated. "I guess, some good times."

"You two are different. I was always just a little scared of him. I was not sure he wanted me in his home."

I wasn't surprised. My dad had a prejudiced streak and the fact that a black girl lived under his roof probably wasn't his idea of what home was all about. But I was sad that Inaya had felt it.

"We used to dance," I reminisced. "Do you remember? You'd place a pile of dirty clothes on the floor and tell me it was a fire and you showed me how to dance, how to move my hips." I suddenly remembered nights I'd spend in bars dancing until closing. I never thought about Inaya during those drunken nights, even though people had marveled that I really knew how to groove. I wished I did. Somehow, maybe her image next to me would have made my life a bit lighter. Her life, I guessed, would have taken the same path.

"Sometimes we'd fight. You didn't like me borrowing your stuff and I wanted to look American."

"Sorry about that."

Inaya went into the bathroom and turned on the faucet. I followed her into the bathroom and sat on the cold lid of the toilet.

"I should have asked," she said, before she stuck her toothbrush in her mouth. She spit and then rinsed off her toothbrush.

"You always let me use what you had. I wore your bangles almost everyday."

"I didn't have much."

I swept my tongue across my teeth, wishing I had a toothbrush. Knowing I didn't have a toothbrush, Lily would have handed me hers after she brushed. We had shared toothbrushes on many of overnight trips, or the times one of us crashed at the other's house.

"Do you mind if I use your toothbrush?" I stood up to reach for the toothpaste. Inaya froze, a thin white hotel towel glued to her mouth. I flushed, worried that I had crossed an etiquette line. I was smart enough to know that Lily and I were special this way, the way my elementary school girlfriend and I had shared chewed gum.

"No," she finally said, not looking at me. "You cannot. Please. Call for one to be brought up. I will call for you."

"I'll just use my finger. I'll be fine." I squeezed some paste onto my index finger. She was still standing behind me. I wished I hadn't asked. The energy felt thick, almost like the question stifled her very movement. "This is perfect. Thanks for the toothpaste." I smothered my front teeth in paste, pretending I still cared about the grime that I had felt on them a few seconds earlier.

"I have AIDS," Inaya whispered. "Maybe I should have told you earlier, before inviting you in." I held on to the porcelain sink to steady myself. I turned on the water. Of course, all those men, those beasts who raped and killed. Why hadn't it occurred to me? She placed her hand on my shoulder before walking out. I needed to say something, but I had no fucking clue what to say. I spat the rest of the minty crap out. I splashed cold water on my face and used her towel to rub my face dry.

She sat in the middle of the bed, legs crossed, one on top of the other. I crawled onto the bed and took her in my arms. She smelled of soap and her earthy perfume.

"Remember talking about our dreams? You were still so much younger than I was. Your dreams were about stories where good triumphed. Do you still dream about that?" she said, sliding her legs under the covers.

"No. I think about revenge. Ways to hurt those who have hurt me."

She nodded. "Good. Me, too. Who do you have vengeful thoughts about? Are you broken-hearted again? Does your brother still tease you about your lack of sense of humor?" she teased affectionately.

"I have a sense of humor, " I said and then I told her, "I was pregnant." I pulled the covers over my body and lay on my side facing her, propping my head with my elbow.

"Oh. Tell me, was it with the man you loved?"

"No. Let's not talk about me. I want to know more about how you're doing. You look healthy." I felt it selfish to discuss my life and my pains. She, this amazing woman, had lived through such hell and now the story would continue for her, no erasing it, no amount of counseling or prayer was going to change the end of her story.

"Did he touch like this—?" She tickled my ribs. I squirmed away, screaming out in ecstasy. "Or was he more gentle, like the touch of a cat's tail when it slithers through your legs?"

"I didn't love him. His touch repulsed me, mostly. But, I loved my baby."

"Then tell me about what happened to the baby you loved."

I let my head rest on the pillow. She reached over and flipped off the lights. I closed my eyes.

I had been watching a *Seinfeld* rerun, I told her, when Santos had unlocked my door and walked in. My feet were swollen, and I had them elevated on the coffee table, like the doctor had told me to do. At times, when I became bored with the show, having seen the episode two other times, I read sections of *What to Expect While You Are Expecting*. At that moment, I wished I hadn't given him a key. Then I reminded myself that we were going to be married a month after the baby was born and he'd live here full-time. I would have to get used to it.

Santos stood in front of the television. I could smell alcohol. He looked pissed off as well as drunk. He thought I had robbed his life from him. He didn't love me, just like I didn't love him. We were together for one reason only, our baby. I would never feel the love for Santos that I had felt for Sean, the man I had loved.

My dinner plate, scraped clean, was on the coffee table. He was staring at it. I thought maybe he was mad that I'd eaten without him, so I began to explain.

"You were late and I have to eat at least two hours before bed or I get awful acid reflux." He didn't say anything. But he lifted the crucifix that hung around his neck like I had seen old ladies do and kissed it. "Did you have to work late?" I sat up straighter, though pulling myself up was getting progressively harder to do.

"No." He glared down at me. His eyes looked evil, or sad; I couldn't tell which. The whites were bloodshot. I turned my eyes to the television, hoping he'd get the clue to move, to leave me alone. Kramer was looking in Seinfeld's fridge, not finding anything. He pushed the door shut.

"My father said I was a disgrace."

"Mine thinks I am, too." I smiled, hoping he'd smile, hoping we could have a common ground.

"You did get pregnant out of wedlock. Any father worth a damn would think you are trash." I gaped at him.

"How dare you!" I retorted. "Me? What about you? I didn't get pregnant by myself." I looked away from him and turned the television's volume up with the remote. My anger gave me strength, yet physically I felt weak. I was thirty-six weeks pregnant and could barely get off the couch. Faking physical agility, I quickly bent down and picked up my plate and took it to the kitchen sink.

"If you were Catholic, you wouldn't have screwed me." He followed me into the kitchen. I thought about the day that we "screwed." I had passively — not willingly — opened my legs for him. Not for sex but for the future I wanted so desperately, a future filled with love, acceptance, and adventure. I became lightheaded at the memory. The baby kicked. I placed my hand on my stomach, wanting to protect her from this fight, this world she'd soon be living in.

"Maria called my parents' house today."

"Your sister? Has she got her papers yet?" I was grateful for the change of topic.

"Maria is not my sister. Marie is my sister. Maria is the woman I was supposed to marry. She is in Miami now." I think he thought this statement would hurt me. He said it with sarcasm that was bathed in pride.

"So, marry her," I said.

He hit the table with both fists. The salt and pepper shakers fell and shattered on the floor. My utility bills fluttered down on top of the pieces of red ceramic. I edged away from Santos. I wanted to get out of the kitchen, out of the apartment. But he blocked me with his massive body.

"I cannot. Do you not understand? You ruined my life, you and that bastard girl baby." I heard *Seinfeld*'s laugh track. And then the show's theme song. "How do I even know she is mine?" he spat.

I needed out of the kitchen. It suddenly became clear that I had to leave him. Being a family wasn't worth a minute of this anger, this abuse. My baby, yes, my baby girl didn't need a father like him in her life. She would have a mother, a mother who would devote her life to her. I would be there, provide for her. Take her to ballet lessons or soccer practice. I'd attend back-to-school nights at her school, teacher conferences. I'd hold her all night when she was sick. I would live and wouldn't die of cancer. I'd be there for her prom night, graduation night, and the night her first boyfriend broke up with her. The day she started her period. I'd even get an education and a real job so she'd have someone to look up to. I would be strong and loving. I thought all this as Santos went on about Maria and how much he loved her.

"We grew up together," he moaned.

I willed myself to move past him. I walked toward the small door that led out of the kitchen. My right shoulder touched his ribs. He pushed me back. I tried again and he told me I wasn't going anywhere. He wasn't through with me. He said I hadn't answered his question.

"How do I know you are not trying to trap me? That the baby does not belong to some idiot American?"

"Don't you think when she's born it will be obvious?" I said. The sound from the TV was irritating. I wished I had turned it off.

"My papá said I was always a disappointment. Marrying Maria was going to be my way of showing him that I was not. She comes from a good family."

"Good family?" Immigrants from Cuba? What could he mean? I almost said, but I have gringa blood. Something that he had said was impressive to his mother.

He pulled out his pocketknife and opened it slowly. I watched the knife and not him. He laughed. I felt totally drunk at that moment, as if I couldn't concentrate. But also I felt in that moment that no other moment in the past or the future mattered, or would ever matter. I was sure he was going to use that knife on me. Would he slit my throat? Or just maim me? He laughed and then threw it across the room. It embedded in the wall above the coffeemaker.

"Did you think I was going to stab you?"

I didn't answer him. Instead I expelled a breath that had been caught inside my lungs. This was my chance to get by him and leave. I'd have to get the front door lock changed. Maybe even move. His shoulders fell and his jaw flopped open as I stood next to him not saying anything. I took a step.

"You're right. She doesn't belong to you. She isn't yours." I said those words partly out of defiance, partly to get rid of him forever. He pushed me back against the wall. My head hit a picture I had just hung, pomegranates, one whole and one cut in half. I had bought it for fifty cents at a garage sale, the same garage sale where we'd bought Clara's crib. The picture fell onto the floor and the frame broke. I watched it, trying to concentrate on something besides Santos's weight against me. Glass shattered. His eyes that had seemed disturbed and filled with hate were now empty.

I gasped raggedly, unable to get enough air. I knew I was crying because I felt tears on my cheeks, dripping from my chin. He stepped away from me. I thought that was the worst of it. When Dad and Joel wanted to know why I wouldn't marry Santos, I'd tell them exactly what happened. They'd have to understand, and if not, I'd have to rid them from my life as well. Clara turned in my belly, and I felt life. I had a reason to live. I smiled. His large hand formed a fist. I closed my eyes and willed that fist to hit my face, to knock out a few teeth, to even give me a concussion that would send me to the hospital.

"Please, God. Please," I said to myself. While praying, I felt the blow. But not on my face. He hit my baby. She moved. At every doctor's appointment the nurse asked, "Do you feel fetal movement?" I always said, "Yes."

I fell to the floor, vomiting. I curled into fetal position, then began inching my way out of the kitchen toward the front door. I heard myself sobbing. I couldn't feel pain. I felt heavy. But I had to get out of the apartment, away from him. Santos was yelling in the kitchen, first in Spanish and then in English. On the television, I saw a woman dancing and then a Kotex with wings appeared on the screen. My body was getting heavier. I stopped to rest, but only for a moment. I began crawling toward the door again. When I could no longer see the TV, I heard a Jack in the Box commercial. I felt thankful I couldn't see that white, creepy, expressionless head. The theme song to *Friends*. I'm almost there, I said to myself.

When I got to the front door I tried to stand, but couldn't. I had put on four pounds in the past week. Instead, I reached and turned the knob, opening the door. When I smelled the rubber from the welcome mat, I saw lights from an ambulance and cop cars. I let myself fall limp, knowing they were here to help me. My neighbors must have heard all the shouting and called 911. I rested my head on the inside of my arm. Tears dripped down. They felt so warm against my cold cheeks. I wanted to sleep but knew I shouldn't. A woman bent down. Her warm, minty breath flowed past my ear.

"Help my baby," I wept. "Please. I love her." She told me she would. I thanked her.

"She's not moving. She always kicks at night."

"We're here to help." More people surrounded me. They all talked at once. I tried to concentrate, to hear what they were saying. "One, two, three." I felt myself lifted onto a gurney. They took me downstairs and pushed me into the ambulance.

Chapter Eight

*O*n my cab ride back to Fallow Springs, I looked out the window at hotels offering free Wi-Fi, vehicles of all kinds with people looking anxious, bored, apathetic — so many talking with no one else in the car, ear pieces growing out of their skulls — billboards advertising products that claimed to make us all desirable ("We all know sex sells and the whole world is buying," Creed sings to us), and finally, trees and wineries. I so wanted to spend more time with Inaya. Although she had only lived with us for nine months, those nine months had been so rich and full, and my life in that brief period had seemed so open to all possibilities. I could be whatever I desired. And the prospect of something ever happening to my mother hadn't entered my thoughts. I guess it's what some people might call a time of innocence.

How does one lose contact with someone so special? Was it simply distance? Time? After my mom passed, I never returned one letter and Inaya eventually stopped writing. Last night, Inaya recalled times back in Africa when she would see from the corner of her eye a person's shadow and she'd think, here comes Jamie. Of course it wasn't me, but I loved how she brought me with her to her home so far away.

No one greeted me as I slipped in the side door and made my way to my room. I wanted to lock myself up. I needed the solitude. As soon as I closed my door and flung myself on the bed, I broke down. I hadn't seen it coming. I had woken, eaten breakfast with Inaya, watched her mount the steps to the airport shuttle, all with little emotion. But now, I felt so raw to all of Inaya's hurt, the fact that she would eventually die from what those bastards did to her. Her strength also felt painful, as I knew I would never possess it. I didn't have it. What I had gone through was minor compared to her suffering and yet my pain was still real, still toxic. I still hated Santos virulently. I was glad I had told her. Sharing it helped me to feel less of a prisoner.

I fell asleep. I was naked, on display in front of dozens of men. Laughter permeated the room. Darts and bullets, penises and knives flew at me. I heard a voice I thought might be God's say, "The target, you need to aim at the target." I woke sweating, unable to lift my head from the pillow.

Sometime during the night, Akasha and Beah lifted my head and made me sip water. At one point, I heard Beah — with Ana? — discussing my temperature. "Maybe we should call a doctor," Beah said. "Jamie, take this. Your fever needs to come down."

When I next awoke, it was late morning. I slid out of bed. The cool wood floors felt smooth, solid and real. I wore my yellow PJs, only vaguely wondering who had put them on me. As I made my way to the window to look outside, the door creaked open. Beah entered.

"You're up," she said. "Good. How are you feeling?" I mentally examined my body.

"I feel fine. Was I sick?"

"Yes. Had a fever. Slept for two days." She came and touched my forehead. "Not a speck of one now. Not even clammy. You should probably rest." She laughed. "I've told you that before. If you would have taken my advice the first time, this might not have happened."

I smiled. "Beah, thanks. I know you took care of me."

"It's what I do. I help where I can. Go take a warm bath, and I'll bring up some food."

I'd lost two entire days. In the bath, I wondered when I had ever been so sick. I thought I must have caught something down in the city, but the larger part of me wondered if the fever had to do with the psychological trauma of hearing Inaya's story and reliving mine.

The next day, I felt strong and clearheaded, ready to work. I got online and researched The World Service Program, where Inaya had worked. I researched Darfur. And what I found was no less a reality than what Inaya had talked about. In the last three years, 2003 until now, there were more than two hundred thousand people in refugee camps, nearly two million international displaced persons in Darfur, and four hundred thousand men, women and children murdered.

I read about men called "Janjaweed," or evil men on horseback, who were destroying homes and villages, raping and killing. These were the men who had taken Inaya and her friend, Dafina. In a mixture of disgust and horror, I read of how the Sudanese government were funding the Janjaweed. Military helicopter, "gunships," would fly over the villages, shooting men, women, boys and girls. Old Russian transport planes, Antonovs, would drop bombs, sometimes car chasses, old appliances, or 55 gallon drums of petrol, anything that could kill someone or annihilate something on the ground. And then the Janjaweed, the evil men on horseback would ride in and kill men and boys, rape girls and women, and steal the livestock and destroy the water wells.

I read some long, convoluted historical background on Darfur. By comparison, America's was short and concise. Most of the Janjaweed were Arabs, like the Sudanese leaders were Arabs; the people in Darfur were black. All were Muslims. The Janjaweed were nomads; the people in Darfur, farmers. The Janjaweed had guns, made in China. There were many humanitarian groups asking for money, wanting to save Darfur.

The information threatened to overwhelm me, yet adrenaline pumped through my veins. It was a weird feeling: a sense of urgency, passion, and purpose; sadness, horror, and loss. I sat back down and began reading personal Darfuri stories told to aid workers.

Many of the stories began the same way, with bombs being dropped. Then the Janjaweed rode in. One woman's eleven-year-old son was shot as he stood between her and the invaders of their hut. I thought of the agony that mother must have experienced watching her young son fall in front of her. Three men beat and raped her. She was six months pregnant. The next day she miscarried. I imagined the mother holding her two dead children, bloodied and emptied of life, while blood still pumped through her veins, feeding her empty womb, giving oxygen to crazed thoughts.

African and American mothers were more similar than different, regardless of race, religion, country of origin, or even what century they happened to be born into. I was sure of this — women would always be bonded through motherhood, more than man's universal need for food, water and sleep. I walked over to the window, stood looking out at nothing in particular. A fire took hold in my belly. I was done hurting, thinking of only my pain, my loss. By comparison, my life was good. I was emotionally and physically able to give to others. I could help Inaya speak to the world. Suddenly, I felt like the right person for the job Akasha hired me to do.

I ran out of my room and down the stairs to Akasha's office. It was empty. I heard a noise coming from across the house and followed it to the library. A pile of books lay on the floor.

Beah was coming down the wheeled ladder holding a book bound in red leather. I hurried over and stood next to the ladder to hold it steady. Although I wasn't a reader, I loved how this room had a ladder that led to another floor of bookshelves. Books lined every wall, except the one with a large picture window that looked out onto an elegant, sprawling magnolia tree. Beah shooed me away.

"I do this all the time." She began to climb down faster. "Do you like the classics? Or contemporary? Oh, probably contemporary. Who's your favorite author?"

"Beah, I'm looking for Akasha."

"Haven't seen her. Important?" She stopped and scrutinized me. "You must be feeling better," she observed. "You have color in your cheeks."

"People are being killed. Children slaughtered." I felt an urgency I hadn't felt in a long time. She gave me a quizzical look. Was she waiting for an answer to her question? "I don't have a favorite author," I said.

"Sad, but people have always been dying unjustly." She pushed the wheeled ladder aside. "I'm glad to see you. I've been meaning to come up to your room. Your father called earlier. Before you were up. I wanted you to rest, thought you needed to. I hope that was the right call."

"My dad?" I stuttered. "Are you sure? What did he say?" It seemed unbelievable. How on earth had he found me? How did he get Akasha's number?

"Yes, I'm sure. He said, 'I'm Jamie's dad.'"

"How'd he get this number?"

"You didn't give it to him?"

"No. He didn't ask for it and he knew I no longer had a cell." I turned and bumped into a small end table. A vase on top wobbled. I caught it before it crashed to the floor. It had to be Lily, I thought, but how did he get Lily's number. From Joel? Weird. Dad wasn't one to give me much of his energy.

"*Jane Eyre.* Would you like to read it?" Beah held the book out to me.

"I don't read." My thoughts flashed to Inaya's memory of my mother — always with a book in her hand.

"If I see Akasha, I'll tell her you're looking for her. Glad to see you looking well."

I headed back to my room. I'd talk with Akasha later. I wondered why Dad had called. Maybe Joel had been in an accident or something. Maybe I should call Dad back. Maybe he was just calling to chat. I gave a derisive laugh. He and I didn't have a chatting kind of relationship. Thinking about our relationship, I felt my desire to help the people of Darfur fizzle like a dying firework. Doubt crept in. I questioned my ability to help mothers and children in a land so far away, where men think nothing of killing. I questioned again why Akasha had hired me. Who was I? I had no education. I had no skills. I was the daughter of a mechanic. I was kidding myself.

Back in my room, I showered, thinking it might make me feel better, distract my mind from old insecurities; yet as I turned off the water, I didn't feel any better, just cleaner. With one towel knotted on my head and another wrapped around my body, I stepped out of the shower and spied a spider on the floor. I screamed and grabbed the nearest shoe. I threw it as hard as I could, but the spider had already disappeared under the rug that lay in the middle of the room.

When I was a child, my dad would kill any spider I asked him to. Even if it was in the middle of the night, he'd wake and slap the spider with a shoe and take it to the toilet. He never teased me about this fear or refused to rescue me. It was during these moments that I loved him best. One night about a year after Mom died, I saw a black spider crawl into my covers just as I was about to go to sleep. I called Dad to get it out. He threw back all my covers, but couldn't find it. Then he took the comforter, blanket and sheet, and shook each one out. Neither of us ever found the spider. Dad and I carefully remade the bed, making sure the spider was gone, but I was still scared to climb in. He then said that I could sleep with him if I needed to. And, although his bed no longer smelled like Mom, I felt safe.

I gnawed my thumbnail. Maybe I had been too hard on him. If I had been different, would things have been different between us? I could have been less bitter about the things he enjoyed, football, old cars.

Now, as I lifted the corner of the rug, I saw the spider dart further under it. With my back to the bedpost, I pushed backward, sliding the bed part way off the rug. I pulled the rug off the floor as far as I could, which wasn't easy, and when I saw the spider, I stomped, forgetting in my fury that I wasn't wearing any shoes. I screamed again, feeling the gooey warm bloodsucker on my foot, and shuddering, ran back into the shower to wash off the remains.

Dried and dressed, I started to put my room back together. As I lifted the heavy wool rug, I heard Beah calling my name. It felt much heavier than when I'd moved it the first time. She called again. I hadn't time to move the bed when she knocked. I opened the door but only a few inches. Her eyebrows rose.

"Are you hiding someone in there?" she laughed.

I opened the door a few more inches. "No. No one." I leaned against the jamb. I didn't want her to see my room in such disarray, with the rug skewed, the bed tilted and unmade, and my towels and underwear on the floor.

"I didn't tell you why your dad called. You asked but I never answered."

"Oh, yeah." My breaths were shallow and short from the scare and the physical exertion. I breathed in deeply, hoping she wouldn't notice.

"To say, 'Happy Birthday.' So, today is your birthday?" I paused and thought. I hadn't thought about dates, months, or holidays as being significant for a long time. "It's September," I said, "September 21st. Yes, it is."

"Well, Happy Birthday." Beah turned and walked back down the spiral staircase, humming the birthday tune.

I closed the door. With my back to it, I slid to the floor. I felt sad and confused. I took the towel that lay on the floor and hid my face. I didn't know why I was crying.

Was it for my baby that I never got to hold? For the woman in Darfur who lost first her son, and then her unborn baby? Inaya? Because I'd stepped on the stupid, ugly, disgusting spider? Or for the love I needed so badly from my dad? And did the reason I was crying fucking matter?

Birthdays weren't forgotten in my family, despite all the coldness and lack of intimacy, despite the fact that Dad rarely wanted anything to do with me. My dad, brother and I always had dinner and cake, and we'd buy each other gifts. I was grateful that Dad, Joel, and I at least cared enough to have a meal to celebrate each other.

I climbed into bed and fell asleep. When I woke early that evening, I picked up the phone and called Dad to thank him. He wasn't home. On the machine, I thanked him for calling and told him that I was doing well.

My room was a mess: towels, sweats, a dead spider smeared on the floor. Drawers opened. Bed and rug still out of place. But I didn't want to clean. It was my birthday. I pulled out a dress I'd bought online after I'd deposited my paycheck. It was a silk dress with long sleeves that wrapped around and tied. I had fallen in love with it when I saw it online. And now I could afford such things as a new dress. I would take myself to dinner. I would call Camilla. I hadn't talked to her since my return and now she would be leaving any day. Beah was the only person I lived with who I felt comfortable asking. If she wanted to come, great. If not, I'd be fine with that, too. Maybe she could recommend a place.

It was dark by the time I got ready. The days were getting shorter. In the foyer, I dialed Camilla's cell — no answer. I went into the kitchen to look for Beah, but she wasn't there. I knocked on her bedroom door. No answer.

The house seemed eerily quiet, even more quiet than normal.

"Beah?" There was no answer. I called out for Ana, and when there was no answer, I got even braver and yelled for Akasha. I was both a bit spooked by the fact that no one answered me and a bit upset. No one had told me they were all going out. We all lived in the same house, but not one of us ever really communicated. Or maybe they all did, and I was left out. What did I expect?

It dawned on me that, if no one was home, all the cars might be gone. I became panicked, needing all the more to get out. I should have taken care of my car. On Monday, I vowed to myself, I'd take my car in.

The cars were parked in front of the garage. The moon was full and shone brightly on Akasha's black BMWs. I stopped, more confused by the quiet, knowing everyone was home. I shuddered at some unknown feeling, but shrugged it off to chills. I touched the closest BMW as I walked past. It was cold. I opened the door. I looked on the dashboard where I'd been promised the keys would be left, and then on the floor, under the mat, in the tray between the seats — no keys. I got out and slammed the door and then looked inside the other one. "Damn," I cursed.

I opened a door to the garage, thinking inside there might be a key holder nailed at eye level, like in my dad's garage. Even though Akasha had said they'd be inside the car, maybe Zahir or Beah typically placed them elsewhere. As I felt around the wall with my right hand, a hand grabbed my left which was gripping the doorknob. I gasped, startled. I heard Akasha's voice pierce the darkness.

"Found you! I've been looking all over. Beah said you were looking for me."

Chapter Nine

*T*his was the first time Akasha had ever touched me. Her hand was thin and warm. "I heard you were looking for me," she said. I was, I wanted to say, but I'm not anymore. I didn't want to talk about the unfixable problems around the world. Genocide. Or Inaya who was raped by so many men she stopped counting, stabbed with a bayonet. I wanted to have a nice dinner, a glass of wine, tasty food, laughs. That was all — didn't I deserve this? I wished I had made plans.

"Come with me."

We walked up the front steps and back inside the house. She pushed the lock back into its slot. We passed her office and headed toward the library. I felt frustrated and angry, wanting to tell her that work hours were over, that I liked keeping bankers' hours, but I knew that she didn't and I wasn't expected to, either.

Akasha wore a vintage gown. I thought of Greta Garbo and wondered where she would be going dressed so elegantly. She opened the door to the library. Shouts rang out.

"Surprise!"

Beah, Ana, and Zahir were all there. "Happy Birthday," Akasha added. Beah gave me a hug and kissed my head. Ana stood next to me with her hands cupped around her beer glass. It sounded like she said, "Happy special day." It came to me then that maybe she came from another country, that maybe she couldn't speak English well. Zahir nodded from across the room.

"What would you like to drink?" asked Beah. I stood, speechless in amazement. I willed my head to stop spinning, to believe that this moment had actually just happened. What about all the suffering in the world?

"Snap out of it," Beah teased. "Beer? Wine? Or something a bit harder?" She snapped her fingers with astute confidence.

"Beer, please," but when I saw how everyone else was dressed, I changed my mind. "No, wine." Beah wore a blue tailored dress. The back dragged a bit on the floor. I had to wonder where she had bought it, and for what purpose. Ana wore an ivory wool dress; lace trimmed the collar and cuffs. Zahir looked different. Younger. He looked like a man who wouldn't know the difference between an azalea and a geranium. If I didn't know better, I would have thought, wearing that periwinkle-blue starched shirt and a silver tie, he was on his way to a jazz concert with a woman who owned pearls.

It took me several minutes to take in everything. For, although we were in the library and I had been in here a few times before, the furniture was arranged differently. The velvet couch, the leather chairs and the settee were on the opposite wall. And a movie screen stood facing the fire that burned in a stone fireplace. I stared at the silver screen. A blank screen always set my heart to beating. How on earth had she known?

"*All the King's Men*, and *It's a Wonderful Life*," Akasha said. Her hair was loosely curled and pinned up. Her eyes looked teary and passionate, like the old stars from the forties. I couldn't seem to move.

"How did you know?" I stammered.

"You worked at a video store for over five years — you sent me your résumé, remember? I just figured." She was right. But she couldn't have known that one of my all-time favorite movies was *It's a Wonderful Life*. I used to watch it every year on my birthday; for me it was more of a birthday movie than a Christmas movie. After all, it was a movie about what would have happened if a man had never been born.

Beah came and took my hand and sat me on the couch with a glass of wine. "How did you know to dress?" Before I could explain that I'd intended to take myself out to dinner, she added, "Isn't Ana's suit beautiful? It's over forty years old, her wedding suit."

"It is beautiful."

"Which one first?" Akasha asked. I felt like I was on stimulation overload. I took a sip of my wine and decided.

"*All the King's Men*. You know, it's recently been remade. Should be out — soon, I think."

"'Humpty Dumpty sat on a wall …,'" Beah began.

"This is the remake," Akasha said. She filled her wine glass.

No, I thought, no way. She couldn't possibly have known that Sean Penn was one of my favorite actors, that I was always in line before anyone else when he had a new movie out. I had never told her this.

"But *All the King's Men* isn't even in theaters yet."

"Not yet," she agreed. She must know someone in Hollywood.

Beah said, "You're thinking too much. Just enjoy." Akasha turned on the movie projector.

I sat between Akasha and Beah. Ana stretched out on the settee. Looking at her, I thought, if I were an artist, I'd paint her. She reclined so gracefully, wearing her well-kept wedding suit, her grey braids tied on her head. Zahir sat in the leather chair. Never once did I get a feeling that anyone was bored or would prefer to be doing something else. Not only were they all here for me, but they were enjoying themselves.

After the first film, we stood to eat. Ana had laid a beautiful table of food that I was becoming accustomed to quickly: strong cheeses, hummus, crab cakes, and salmon pâté.

"Jamie, what did you think? Thumbs up or down?" Beah asked. "It followed the book, I guess. It's been a good thirty years since I read it."

"Sean Penn is, well, fantastic. I know he's popular and sometimes it's uncool to like the popular actors, but it would be like saying Monet wasn't great just because everyone has one of his lily pads somewhere in their house, on a book marker, napkin — you name it. But that doesn't take away from how great he was, right?" Everyone was listening as I continued.

"When Penn plays a role, he becomes the man. I don't know the book. I saw the original movie years ago. I prefer this version. I think the screenwriter was trying to tell too much in the first film, maybe trying to stay too true to the novel." I was thinking out loud, but they were all still listening and I was getting energy from talking. "And though Jude Law's performance and his looks are similar to the first guy who played Jack Burden, I like how Law was more unmotivated. His presence spoke of underachieving without the script needing to go there. And the cinematography... I felt old money and aristocracy at Burden's childhood home. We saw but also felt New Orleans's opulence and depression. And the shot where Jude Law walked in the street by himself, bereft." I smiled. "Yep. Thumbs up."

Zahir stood and took a lone carrot from a platter. I waited for him to dip it. He didn't. "The screenwriter stayed too true to the novel," he mused. "Wouldn't that be his job?"

"Yes and no. In all art, I think artists are after some sort of truth. The truth of what it means to feel fulfilled, to be happy, to suffer and experience pain. But, untruths may have to be told in order to get the truth out. For instance, Anne — Kate Winslet — felt deeply rejected by Jack. Maybe that rejection wasn't a sexual rejection in the book, but the way it was written and filmed here, I sure felt her pain. His weakness. So — the truth was told."

"Hence, that sums up Willy Stark," Beah said. "He played crooked to get good things done. And was that right? Was that something the public could accept? Could America handle it now? We want our politicians to be nice people and take care of the dirty work without dirtying their hands." She held her hand out, her fingers positioned as if there was a cigarette in them. "I'm not sure if it can be done," she said. "What do you think, Ana?"

I looked for smoke rising and thought she must have surely smoked in her day. Then I turned toward Ana, suddenly interested as to why Beah had asked her. Maybe Beah was worried Ana was feeling left out, maybe because they were closer in age. Ana picked up one of the half full trays. "Pray for our leaders," I thought I heard her say, and then she whispered something in Akasha's ear before she headed out with the tray.

"What did she say?" Beah asked.

"And keep the faith in the people," Akasha said, looking into her almost empty glass of wine. "You know, from the movie. Doesn't Stark say something like that?"

"My favorite," Zahir said, "was 'there are a couple of moments that determine your life, maybe one.' Doesn't seem quite fair, but it seems to play out that way." He set his mug down and then said, "Excuse me," and left the room. There was unease. I wasn't sure why. This was why I sometimes avoided discussing movies with people. When a movie really had something to say, the discussion could cause disheveled feelings.

"My favorite," Beah leaned forward, "was 'Time,'" — she attempted to mimic Sean Penn — "'brings all things to light. I trust it so.'"

"Oh, bullshit!" Akasha said.

As if on queue, Ana returned with Zahir and a beautiful coconut birthday cake, aglow. Leaning down to blow out the candles, I longed to wish for what I could never have, Clara, my baby. I quickly reframed my wish. I wished to see Inaya again. Akasha filled champagne glasses. As cheers were given, I smiled at the attention and the sincerity of it all. The tension I had sensed moments ago was all gone. We sat down to watch *It's a Wonderful Life*.

My favorite and least favorite scene was when George Bailey gives away his honeymoon money to help the people of Bedford Falls. He passionately hands over his cash, his ticket to his dreams. It hurt to watch him do this. He deserved to travel, to get good use out of the suitcase that had been sitting too long under his bed. Yet his actions saved The Bailey Savings and Loan. As this scene played, I closed my eyes and took a deep breath. I was glad for this new life that I chose. For a moment I became proud of myself for packing my suitcase and driving out of Grass Valley. I tucked my feet underneath me and I thought how priceless this evening was.

Beah and I were sniffling at the end of the film. I was glad no one got up during the credits. I liked to watch them. It was the time I slowly transitioned from the world of make believe back to my life.

When the lights came on, the night ended. Beah and Ana said they'd clean things up in the morning. It would all be spotless before I woke, I knew. That was how things worked. We all walked Zahir to the front porch. Maybe it was simply my fear, but it seemed we were all going back to our former ways, distant, elusive. Zahir said goodnight. He walked toward his bungalow with his hands in his pockets and his head bent back, as he looked toward the heavens. I looked up also to see what he was looking at; it was the Big Dipper — large and obvious, but still remarkable. I called out, "Wait!" He stopped and turned back toward the porch.

"Thank you, guys. Thanks, Akasha. The food and the movies were perfect." I wanted to also say something about friendship and about caring for one another but I lost my nerve. I hadn't known them for all that long and friendships took awhile to grow.

"I loved your baklava, Ana," Akasha said. Ana turned and smiled, enjoying the compliment. Ana didn't walk back in the front door with us; she went around and I imagined her going through the kitchen door.

"She told me that it is an old Jewish recipe," Beah said.

"Is she Jewish?" I asked, but as was the fashion, I received no answer. Inside, Akasha walked up her stairs toward her room.

"Thanks again," I said. She did reply, but I didn't hear what she said, either because she said it too quietly, or because I was too preoccupied noticing for the first time that she was walking with a limp.

The next morning, on the worn kitchen table there were freshly cut white roses. As I bent to smell them, I realized there was still dew on the petals. I touched the length of one of the larger flawless petals. Dew gathered and dripped down my finger.

I heard Ana behind me gasp and yell, "No!" She stood in front of the stove, holding a spatula, wearing the same clothes as she had on the night before. "Don't touch." As she approached, I quickly moved out of her way. She picked up the vase of roses.

"Sorry."

Beah could always be found in the kitchen in the morning, drinking coffee and eating breakfast. I wanted to sit with her and feel like I had last night, but she wasn't there, only Ana. This was our first time alone, and it wasn't going well.

"Where's Beah?" I had offended her and I wasn't exactly sure how. It couldn't have been from simply touching her rose.

Ana pulled the rose that I had touched from the vase and threw it out the back door. Setting the spatula down, she turned the stove off and left the kitchen without a word. I picked up the rose off the lawn, rinsed it off, and placed it in a glass of water. On a sticky note, I wrote, "Sorry." Waiting another several minutes for Beah, I poured some coffee. When she didn't show, I took my coffee out the kitchen door toward the garden.

There was a light mist in the air, and the clouds were beginning to break. I cupped my hands around my coffee to warm them and sat on a wooden bench. This wasn't my usual favorite place, for no other reason than I felt more exposed, preferring the feeling of safety I felt from having bushes and flowers on all sides. The bench was against a vine trellis and on both sides water sprinkled down over rocks. There were a few lily pads, but no other flowers bloomed. With my feet pulled up to my chest, I drank my coffee before it got cold and thought about the events moments ago. Why the odd behavior with the roses? And why did Ana still have her clothes on from last night? Maybe she wanted to get another wear out of the suit before sending it to the cleaners? That was a crazy thought. It was her wedding suit, not something she should wear to cook in. I hoped that she hadn't been up all night. Maybe Beah was sick. Maybe Ana had received a phone call and some relative had had a heart attack or was in the hospital. Tragedies happened all the time to all people. I remembered when Dad had called to tell me that Aunt Gazella had a stroke. I hadn't been to visit her in over six months. I was twenty-two and getting on with my own life. She never regained consciousness.

So, yes, tragedies happened to everyone, but horrors only happened to some. Images of dead bodies from the movie *Hotel Rwanda* popped in my head. The women in cages, moving and moaning as if they were sick zoo animals, begged me for attention. Like the women in Darfur. Like my Inaya. What she went through stabbed me as too horrific. It felt too evil.

I spied Akasha and Zahir off in the distance, walking over the stone path. The way he was gesturing to the foliage, I imagined that they were discussing the garden. I wanted to go to them and be a part of their conversation, tell them about my friend, Inaya, and the awful things that had happened to her, and that after all these years we'd met again. But I didn't, believing if they wanted me to be with them they'd call me over or walk my way. I stayed and watched.

I felt myself inexorably begin to withdraw. Depression crept in through a door I thought I'd closed. When would my emotions level out? Be consistent? Why was I always the spectator and never the doer? I loved the hero. Everyone loved the hero. And this was why the crowd had broken out in applause for Inaya. She was a hero. She's the kind of woman screenwriters seek out. But me? No one ever said, I loved the teller's performance in the latest Western, or bankheist film: "You know, the woman who looks scared and hands over the money."

Even before my baby died, there were times when I fought depression, "fought" being the right word. It started with just pure sadness after my mom passed away. And then, in my teens, that sadness fermented into depression. Always a good student in the past, during my senior year of high school I couldn't get myself to focus on the latest research project, on my tests. Every time I sat down, my mind would wander. I'd read a paragraph three times and still not be able to say what it was about. I wanted to do well in school and get A's like I used to, but the belief that I could was gone. Aunt Gazella helped by reading assignments out loud to me, but this didn't write my papers, didn't help on tests. I began skipping school to go to the movies. Gazella urged me to go to the movies after class. I stopped telling her how poorly I was doing, and when she told me she was moving to London for six months, I stopped telling her anything. And, although she came back nine months later, our relationship was never the same.

Teachers and my brother told me that I watched too many movies, that they'd be the ruin of my brain, but if they only knew — it was movies that kept my brain going, kept passion alive.

In the darkened theater, I'd feel my inertia disappear. I'd no longer want to go to bed. I'd watch a movie like *Fargo* and feel the chill of the horror, see how one man's greed could lead him to such desperation. How others could kill as if life were a play and all the other people were props available for slaughtering. Watching, I was not so fascinated with the actors as I was with the directors and writers, the Cohen brothers. How did they make a seven months pregnant cop the hero of this murder mystery? I loved them for doing so. I loved how the movie entertained, and how it made me think.

I wanted to be a director, work in Hollywood. I never voiced this dream, even as a child when dreams were for all to have and think possible. Then, finding out how many directors actually made it, I became discouraged. Of course when I reached twenty, the dream became impossible. I had no education. No contacts. Couldn't make it living in Hollywood. Plus, someone had to be the moviegoer. It would be as if everyone who read books wanted to be a writer. Or if everyone who bought a Coldplay CD wanted to be a musician.

Yet I never stopped loving movies. I never stopped thinking about directing or storyboarding scenes. For five years, I volunteered at the Nevada City Film Festival and attended the Sacramento International Film Festival, where I met Professor Irving. And once, while I was drunk, I told him that I had eight folders full of ideas. "Just come and sit in. You'll teach the students something," he told me.

Even though I held sacred my brochures to the festivals and my plastic folders where I placed my worked out movie scene ideas, I still didn't believe it could ever happen for me. But once, I think, I had a belief that I could be whatever I set myself to. Mom had told me that, when she'd drop me off at preschool, I sometimes wouldn't even take the time to say goodbye to her. She'd have to chase me down to get a kiss. I couldn't wait to get my hands on the tambourine. I'd gather my friends and give them each an instrument and tell them what to do with it and we'd perform for whomever would watch. Where did that energy go? Where did that person go? I blamed everything on my mother's death. How many times I wished it had been my father who'd died instead of my mother. I'd feel guilty for thinking this, but my life would have been richer. I'd have someone who would inspire me, love me. But the gods don't let us choose our destinies.

"Right, Athena," I said to the generic, Greek-looking statue in front of me. Akasha and Zahir stopped walking, and both looked at me. I grew embarrassed from staring. At the least I should go over and say good morning and thank them again. Zahir turned and left. Akasha met me on the bridge.

"Hi," I said. "Last night meant a lot to me. It was the best— "

"I don't do well with too much flattery," Akasha said. I felt like I just caught a surprise ball right at my belly.

"Okay." I had to look up at her to make eye contact.

"What were you thinking about over there? You seemed deep in thought." She turned to face the water. I followed, leaning on the railing.

"Well, I was thinking about last night. I liked us all being together." I guessed I was being true to my secret dream, not wanting to tell her all I was thinking. Wishing to take the focus off me, I asked, "And wondering why Ana still had her clothes on from last night."

"Was that all?" I began to sweat even though the sun still hadn't made its way through the clouds. There was a moment of quiet. I liked this about Akasha, that she didn't need to fill every second with talking. I wanted to share my thoughts, my dreams and pain with her. I wanted her to tell me I was okay, that I was capable.

"I was thinking about the fact that I'm a spectator, that I lack self-confidence. Don't you think everything comes down to self-esteem? The job we choose ..." I trailed off, hoping she'd answer, and give me some insight. She didn't. She looked at me, not staring but waiting for me to continue. "The friends we hang around, the men we believe we are worthy of." Then I worried that she might think I wasn't thankful for this job. I quickly said, "Taking this job was hard for me, but I knew I wanted something different, something better."

"I think we are all born with such raw abilities. If yours weren't shown to you and sculpted, then it becomes your job to dive in and become what you want. We all have our struggles, Jamie." She said "we," as a person who had also struggled. I wondered what her struggles were.

"And, about Ana — she wears her clothes until they need laundering."

116

Chapter Ten

I only had one email in my inbox. It was from the Save Darfur Coalition, asking people to write to President Bush. I had signed up to receive emails from them as well as Mercy Corps and Amnesty International. I was hoping for a long, funny email from Lily replying to the one I'd sent her, but she seldom turned on her computer, claiming she was a Luddite, a word she'd heard from a no-name rock band, literally called "no name." Lower case, she had stressed. But she was full of shit. She loved her iPod, her television, her blender, her scale that talked back to her, and I won't even begin to mention all of Brianna's Leap Frog toys and every other electronic toy she owned. I emailed her again with a simple, "Are you there? Did I tell you she has an original sketch by Van Gogh?"

I had never thought about writing the President. I guessed I thought writing him would be like writing to Santa Claus in the North Pole. Who would read it? Who would care? But intelligent people wrote to him. Someone had to be reading the letters and getting some kind of response. I opened Microsoft Word. "Dear President George W. Bush ...," I began, then stopped. All I could think to say was, "I care. Please help. Children are being killed." It all sounded naive.

I went downstairs to ask Beah if she had ever written a letter to the President. She was in the library again, towering overhead on the wheeled ladder, holding on with only one hand.

"Beah, what are you doing up there?" She made me nervous; I was afraid she might fall.

"Jamie, I am alphabetizing the books." The library was immaculate. The books were lined in neat rows. I was surprised they were out of order.

"How'd they get out of order?"

"Years of use."

This seemed crazy to me. How many people used this library? But, I decided, alphabetizing a library used by two or three people felt more doable than writing to President Bush.

"I'm an expert," I told her. "I used to work at Blockbuster, and one of my jobs was to keep the videos in alphabetical order and then, at the bank, I was always filing some form or another." She said, "Fine, do it." I tried to help her down but, again, she wouldn't let me. "How old do you think I am?" Beah demanded.

"I'm not sure." But then I added, with honesty, "The ladder moves easily. I just wanted to help."

"This is where I left off." She handed me *To the Lighthouse*, by Virginia Woolf.

"Woolf, you must be almost finished."

"That book was in the A's."

As she walked out, I thought, good, I will have something to keep myself busy. But alphabetizing books only takes so much brain energy. I still had time to think about the children in Darfur. Children who had lost parents, sisters, brothers. Children who were hungry or injured. Children who were told to believe in God's love. Parents could rationalize God's workings as His will, or man's free will, or even that God won't fight Evil, not now, not in this lifetime. But children felt love, not out of faith but from full stomachs, pains that were cared for, safe homes, and strong, loving arms. No. No amount of alphabetizing could distract me completely from those facts.

At five-thirty, when I decided to quit, I knew I had accomplished something. Reading websites all day was filling my mind with horrors, but I really wasn't getting anything done. I hoped Akasha would be happy when she heard that her library was almost back in order.

Feeling tired but also restless, I went for a run. I hadn't run since I'd become too pregnant to do so. And when I asked myself why I hadn't started again, I came up empty. Maybe because it took too much energy. I would be starting at the beginning again and starting at the beginning of one more thing felt daunting.

I hadn't even made it to the main road and I was huffing and puffing, telling myself, just make it to the next tree and then you can go back. My shin muscles were stiff; breathing hurt. I stopped in the shadow of my designated tree, not quite making it to the tree itself, turned around, and instead of running back, I walked, not reaching that runner's high that I'd once found so addictive. Darkness was coming quickly. I made a mental note that I needed to run earlier. Maybe in the mornings. The shadows from the trees darkened the drive. I walked faster and then began to run again, wanting to beat the darkness, and then I remembered that animals and people chased prey that ran. I walked. The ocean mist, though miles away, was settling in. I could smell it.

I heard a noise in the blackberry vines and jumped. When I was a kid, I believed that every noise that came from within blackberry vines was a rattlesnake. Although I learned that snakes tend to move without sound while birds were the noisy ones, I still jumped any time I heard any rustling sound in vines.

As the woods grew darker, I concentrated on the lights coming from the mansion. I heard another sound, like the rustling in the blackberry vines, but coming from deeper in the trees. I looked into the woods, but couldn't see anything, my eyes still adjusting to the darkness. I heard the noise again. I'd never been afraid of the dark, of the unknown, but ever since the loss of my baby, fear loomed. I walked to my car faster at night. When I'd get home and Lily wasn't there, I'd look in closets, under the beds, check the windows.

I saw white. Whatever I was looking at in the forest was white, and it was moving. I heard voices, and then no voices. Certain that they were voices and not a wild animal or rabid dog, I kept listening. "Trust your instinct," the voice said.

Then I heard laughter. Akasha laughed. I was sure of it. I took a couple steps off the road into the soft, uncertain ground. She began moving again. Her white clothing shimmered in the mist. The last of the sunbeams and the moonlight both were lightening up this clearing. She grunted as she moved. Was she dancing? I walked closer, staying in the shadows of the large pine tree. I saw she held a sword. Her movements were fluid and strong. Her sword appeared to be an extension of her arm. She turned toward me in one sweeping movement and thrust the sword. I took in air and held it in my tired lungs. Was she pointing the sword at me? Could she see me? I leaned against the tree trunk.

The other voice said, "Again."

I heard and saw her breath in the mist. She turned and began what I assumed was her fencing training. With little noise, I eased back onto the road and walked back to the mansion.

Back in my room, sitting in the chair by the window, I ate a Cliff Bar and yogurt. The image of the sword tattooed on Sean Penn's back in *Mystic River* came to mind. In one of the last scenes of the movie, when Laura Linney seduces her husband, the father of her children, to remain strong and engaged in their lives, Penn's sword pierces us with his heartbreak. I watched that movie several times in the theater, amazed at Eastwood, at Penn, amazed at how much I could cry, until *21 Grahams* was released.

I had received another movie in the mail. Beah was the person who got the mail and distributed it.

"What are all these red envelopes?" she had asked. I received three a week. My dad used to say I was just lazy when I'd watch movie after movie. Like all comments coming from Dad, I'd refute them to his face, but then I'd take the hurtful words and let them seep into my heart like water into dry ground. What I should have said was, "What about all the hours you spend watching football, basketball, hockey?" That's what I'd say now.

Sitting on the bed, I stuck *Citizen Kane* into the computer. I had seen *Citizen Kane* more than fifty times.

The first time I sat down to watch it, I was sure it would change my life: after all, it had been said by many critics that it was the best movie ever made. But, sadly, when the film ended, I felt disappointed. I wasn't even sure I understood what it was about. So I watched it again and again. I watched it so many times, I knew the lines and, of course, the plot progression by heart. I had heard Orson Welles say that "Rosebud," the word Kane mutters on his deathbed, was his least favorite part of *Kane*, though this was the most quoted line. After watching the movie about twenty times, I agreed. The magic in the movie was the cinematography. In the opening scene, the camera zeroes in on the "No Trespassing" sign that hangs on the chain-linked fence and sets the stage for Kane's own imprisonment, his isolation. Maybe our own isolation. And though it would be easy for viewers to say they have nothing in common with Kane because of his millions and opulence, I believed we did. We felt Kane's loneliness as our own.

Now that the movie was a strong, familiar presence, I often watched it while I was doing other things, not in a flippant way, but as one plays their favorite music to help them feel better.

My room was still a disaster. I began to pick things up, starting with the easiest, my dirty clothes. I left the rug and the bed for last. Trying to move the rug back to its original place was difficult. Working on my hands and knees, I laid all four corners on the ground. There was a wrinkle right in the middle, not to mention that it wasn't straight. I needed to move the bed farther off the rug to fix the problem. With my back against the bedpost, I pushed.

The bed inched along. With half of it now off the carpet, I could straighten the rug. Thinking it would be easier to move, I began rolling the carpet. I stopped when it revealed a door in the floor. The handle was grooved inside the wood, keeping it from poking up. I lifted it to see if it opened. It did easily. A stairway headed down, and because it was dark, I couldn't tell how far. The air that came into the room smelled of dirt and a child's hand after it had been holding a fistful of pennies. Closing the door, I told myself I should just replace the rug over the door and forget about it, like one does a breaker box in a closet. Or ask Beah or Akasha about it. There had to be a simple, uninteresting explanation. But I did neither of these things. I opened the trap door again and suddenly heard a noise outside my door. I froze, listening carefully. Nothing, no one, just nerves.

I wanted to find out more about Akasha, about this mansion ... where she made her money, where she went when she was away ... and this staircase might offer some kind of clue, I decided. At the same time, I thought, maybe she didn't want me to know more about her.

I liked my job, liked living here, and I was beginning to feel comfortable with Beah, Ana, and Zahir. Even though we didn't share much time together, their presence now felt familiar. I wanted nothing to ruin my situation. Maybe I'd find out something I wished I didn't know, like she was involved with the mafia, or drug trafficking, or even that she was part of the sex trade, and my job was to ease her conscience.

I looked down the darkened hole. Then I got up and lit the candle that was on the dresser. I was like some character out of a bad movie. If this were a good movie, an Oscar-quality movie, the heroine would know what to do and she'd do it with a sense of purpose, or at least confidence, like with Kane. This seemed like a horror movie, and even when the heroine of a horror movie has a sense of purpose while looking down the mysterious black hole, no horror movie had ever made it to the Oscars.

I'd take this a step at a time and at any moment, I could retreat. The passageway was narrow and there were stairs heading down. I couldn't see the end. The walls were lined with wooden planks, not simply earth, and this was a huge relief — if this were earth, it would feel like some kind of grave. I then remembered I was on the second floor.

Before I headed down the stairs, remembering what Lucy said in *The Lion, the Witch and the Wardrobe* about never going into a wardrobe and closing the door, I placed my laptop and a book on top of the opened door. I didn't want any mysterious wind to close me into this darkened place.

I stepped onto the first stair, holding the candle in my left hand while my right braced the wall. I didn't even know how old these steps were, or if they could hold my weight. I placed half my weight on one. It felt secure. When I was on the second step, my hand felt something on the wall. My first thought was: shit, another spider! But it wasn't moving. I held the weak flame up to it. A light switch. A flipping light switch, I chided myself. Maybe I had been watching too many movies. After turning on the light, I blew out the candle. With the light on, I could see as far as the bottom, where the passageway turned.

When I was five stairs down, I did something I shouldn't have. I looked behind me, up the steep staircase. What if I got trapped down here, or if I really did see something illegal going on? For a brief moment I thought about heading back up the stairs, but instead I quickly walked down the next twenty or so feet. I was sure I had gone below the first story of the house. This fact was not comforting, but I kept going.

Turning left, I came to a large wooden door. And although this discouraged me and made my heart pump more rapidly, I couldn't help but notice how beautiful the door was. It was curved at the top, making me think of some old Catholic cathedral. I tried to open it. The knob turned and clicked, but it was stuck. I pressed my hip against it and pushed it open. The room that it led to was dimly lit. Bottles lined the walls. I looked around, not knowing anything about wine. The bottles were surprisingly clean, almost sparkling. In the center of the room was a round table. I knocked my knee on one of the chairs and yelped out in pain. They were just as heavy as the door. I sat down to look at my wound. No blood, but I was sure I'd bruise.

There was another door at the other end of the cellar but it was locked and there were no windows. I thought it odd that my room, out of all the rooms in the house, led to a wine cellar. This place seemed to fill me with more questions than information. I went back up the well-lit stairs, feeling I had discovered nothing.

I fixed the carpet and the bed, and fell asleep watching the rest of *Citizen Kane*. I woke at three in the morning, feeling cold and disturbed. I had been dreaming.

In my dream, an invitation came in the mail. It was formal, like a wedding invitation. "You are cordially invited to walk through the wooden door," it said. And I did. Nothing was like the way I was used to seeing things. Trees grew from the tips of their leaves up, their roots swaying in the wind. A man sat on a bench nursing a baby, the baby content, wrapped in a fleece blanket. Couples with grey hair kissed passionately by a water fountain that squirted snowflakes. Children wearing police badges ice-skated on mud puddles. Though I had walked through the door, I hadn't moved once I got inside this other land. I watched people, but no one noticed me. There was nothing unusual about me just standing and watching. Or maybe they couldn't see me? My feet began to grow sprouts that rooted themselves in the soil, which wasn't soil at all but small Greco clay pots. I picked one up. On its sides, a woman held a bow and arrow, aiming it at a centaur. It was the most realistic image I gazed upon.

My mind couldn't grasp and make sense of this new world. As I began to reject it, the images became less vivid, the laughter from the children muffled. A wind picked up and blew snowflakes from the fountain in my face. I woke with my blankets kicked off on to the floor.

The next morning, Akasha came to my room.

"Hi," I said. She had never been to see me. "Did you sleep well?" I thought about telling her about my dream, but she didn't give me time to talk.

"I came to invite you to a wine tasting party. Today at four. It's in the cellar. Go through the kitchen pantry door." I flushed, sure she had caught me, caught me going where I hadn't been invited. "I'll be leaving in the morning," she tossed over her shoulder. I wanted to ask to where but I knew I had already crossed a line and I didn't want to push her any further.

At the tasting, I couldn't relax. I couldn't drink much or enjoy the wine because I focused on the fact she was having this wine tasting event to embarrass me, to show me that she was no fool. That she made the rules around this place. There were no outside guests, just Beah, Ana, and Zahir.

The beautiful door I walked through the night before now had a heavy chair in front of it. I took it as another sign that I had crossed a line. Zahir sat in his chair with beautiful posture. I set my half-full glass of wine on a tray, sure it was the most expensive wine I had ever had, yet wanting to leave this so-called wine tasting event. I said goodbye and then glanced and waved at Zahir. He looked me in the eye for the first time. But then Akasha looked at me.

"I'm not paying you to do busy work," she said, and turned away.

What in the hell did she want me to do? She gave me little instruction. I was angry with Beah for telling her that I was alphabetizing and dusting. I was hurt that the work I had done wasn't appreciated. But mostly I became fearful that she'd think I wasn't capable of the job she hired me to do and that I'd lose this position; that I'd be made to leave and go back to my hometown.

Chapter Eleven

*A*gain I read into the night. I woke to the book *Darfur Diaries: Stories of Survival* hitting me in the face. I was pretty sure I had read more in these past weeks than I had in years. Akasha and I would meet when she returned. I'd learn as much as possible and research which organizations I thought Akasha should give to.

In many of the Darfuri stories, people from different villages would give the same account. The only difference was the level of cruelty the Janjaweed performed. Gunships would come first, bringing shots from the sky. Antonovs would drop bombs. Fires would ignite and homes would burn. And, then, the Janjaweed rode in. They would rape, kill, and then pollute wells and pillage. Many people escaped, finding their way through the desert to a camp for internally displaced persons, or IDPs as they called them. Many would escape the country and go to refugee camp. I watched a short video showing a young woman wearing a canary-colored scarf around her head telling her story to an aid worker. Tears fell and, as she used her scarf to hide them, she told how the Janjaweed killed her mother, father and brother. Alone, she walked two days to a refugee camp in Chad. On another video, a man, a schoolteacher by profession, told how the Janjaweed made him watch as they shot his son. He, too, walked days to find safety in a refugee camp. And, now, he was building a mud-bricked school for the children in the camp. I couldn't help but wonder how a person could walk in desert heat and sand storms to a refugee camp after he saw his son being shot. I didn't question his devotion or love; I questioned why the body had such a need for survival. I imagined this was some crazy, no longer useful gift from God.

I read about a man who watched his wife get raped and then taken, his son killed. He said that because the killer had mercy his life was spared. Mercy. I thought I knew what that word meant, but it didn't make sense. I looked it up again.

Not knowing how to process all this information, my stomach cramped. I needed to have some plan, some intelligent thoughts solidified before Akasha came home. If I didn't, she might find someone else who could, and there had to be hundreds, maybe thousands of women more qualified than I. She said she didn't want to hear the stories but the solutions. How was I to be a part of the solution? Maybe Beah would have some clear answer for me.

I wondered if the letter I'd finally penned to the President had made it. And who had actually read it? Some young political hopeful? My heart ached to be with Inaya again. How would she advise me? I wrote her a letter asking just that question: How can I help end the genocide in Darfur?

After I addressed the envelope, I decided to escape and head to the movies. Though I loved watching movies in bed, nothing would take the place of being in a theater. The large screen, the darkness, the velvety curtains that many theaters still had, the smell of popcorn, and my shoes sticking to the floor all worked for me — an escape, I supposed. It was the place I dreamed, the place where the impossible was possible, a place I became inspired. Hollywood had her many faults, but I forgave her for all of them after seeing *Casablanca* or *The Shawshank Redemption*.

The evening air was misty. I walked on what I'd come to call the religious path to Zahir's. A large child-sized Buddha sat on a rock facing eastward. There was another small one sitting in the pond with water spurting out its belly. Past a crepe myrtle tree, there was the Mother Mary holding her son. Her expression was both happy and sad. Faded purple petals from the tree had fallen on the baby, making him look blood-stained — I brushed them off, figuring his death was imminent enough. By the pond, several Greek statues stood — I wasn't sure what the statues were of, but they reminded me of the movie *Clash of the Titans*, which was still one of my all-time favorites.

A light was on in Zahir's place. I knocked. He came to the door wearing some kind of nightdress, like Ebenezer Scrooge in *A Christmas Carol*, the version with Patrick Stewart being my favorite. Except for the night of my party, I had always seen Zahir in jeans and a t-shirt or sweatshirt. More questions about him and his life came to me. How long had he been in the U.S? I figured he had to be a Muslim, being from Afghanistan, but was he Shiite or Sunni? While doing my research, I was beginning to understand that there was a big difference, or at least some people thought so.

For a brief second, I lost my words. He said hello and I felt embarrassed, like I had caught him wearing something I wasn't meant to see, like his skivvies. I wanted to look inside his house, out of curiosity, but his eyes held me. They were black, not brown. I had always thought that all black eyes were actually brown, like all lake water was really green, not blue. He cast his eyes downward when he said, "Hello." His quietness no longer felt like a put off, or arrogance, but it was because he suffered.

"Do you know if the keys are in the car?" I asked, not really meaning to, wanting to ask him to join me, but suddenly too nervous.

"I think they are. I can go check, if you'd like."

The garage was closer to the house than to Zahir's cottage. He must have thought I was being foolish for going to his place and asking him. Yet I was amazed at how he didn't make me feel like a fool for asking. I thought about the many times my brother had called me stupid for asking what he'd call stupid questions, like, why do I need to get my oil changed? Or, why do Americans call football football when the rest of the world calls soccer football? Or what does the grace of God feel like?

I liked Zahir all the more.

"That's okay. I can." I turned to leave. "Sorry for bothering you." He didn't answer. And when I turned back to see if he was still there, I saw he had already shut the door.

When I was almost to the garage, Zahir came up behind me, wearing jeans and a plain blue t-shirt, hands deep in his pockets. He opened the car door, bent down and picked up the keys from the floor.

"I was the last one to drive that car. Just wanted to make sure." I took the keys.

"What I really wanted to ask is if you'd like to go and see a movie."

He folded his hands together as if in prayer. Did he think Hollywood was filled with a bunch of heathens? And those who watched what came out of Hollywood as sinners or simply shallow?

"Thank you, but I can't."

I was ready to excuse him for staying true to his convictions.

"I dated a man once, and I mean once, who wouldn't watch movies. And my brother will only watch PG-13 movies that don't have any sex scenes or witchcraft. Of course, he wouldn't watch *Harry Potter*. I'm sure he'd love them, but he will watch *The Lord of the Rings* trilogy, although there's witchcraft in them." I shook my head at my brother's logic. My babbling wasn't easing my discomfort. Zahir had watched two films just the other night.

"I'm sorry, I'm not judging you or anyone else for enjoying themselves. And I don't give a damn about religious dogma." His expletive surprised me. "I can't go for other reasons." He took a couple of steps back and before he turned, he said, "Have fun."

"Thanks, I will," I said, glad I had invited him.

As I sat in the theater before the movie started, feeling both excited and calm as I always did right before the lights went out, I knew that my problems would be forgotten for two hours while watching someone else's story, and afterward, I'd feel more capable of dealing with my own. Yet I also couldn't help but wonder why Zahir couldn't have come.

When I returned, Beah was in the library reading.

"I've been wanting to talk to you," I said. I sat on the floor at her feet. "I feel confused. What does Akasha want from me?" Beah placed her hand under my arm to get me to stand, and we moved to the settee.

"I don't know," she sighed. "I do know she admires people who trust their intuition. People who leap forward with what they want even if they fail. Maybe you're playing it too safe."

I, too, admired people who went after what they wanted, without arrogance but with confidence. "I suppose I am, but I feel blinded. I don't see what I am supposed to leap toward. If she'd give clear instructions ...."

"She's not that kind of woman." In a relaxed fashion, she twisted to her side, bent her arm and leaned against the back of the settee. She rubbed her cheek gently with her index finger.

"What kind of a woman is she?" I pressed. "Tell me about her. Who is she? How does she make her money? Has she ever been married?" I turned toward her, tucking a leg underneath me.

"Remember what I told you on your first day. No gossip." I looked at Beah, thinking by now she'd give me a smirky grin, as if to say, yeah, right. But her expression was serious. She believed what she was saying, or else she wanted me to believe what she was saying.

"How does she know so much about me? You should be able to tell me that."

"You'll have to ask her. Maybe somebody told her." She sat back up, no longer relaxed.

"Told her? Who?" I felt myself grow anxious.

"I don't know. Maybe someone wrote a letter."

❊ ❊ ❊

The next day, I couldn't get the thought of someone writing a letter out of my mind. My intuition said to keep busy. Do something you'll feel good about. I dusted and alphabetized books, even though Akasha said she wasn't paying me to do busy work. Cleaning was never just busy work. I doubted that Beah considered it a waste of time. Plus, this was after I read for over four hours. My thoughts went back to the letter. It was easy to think about, I mused, as I held *The Scarlet Letter* in my hand. Maybe someone did write her a letter. But who? I then remembered that Beah picked up the mail and distributed it. I suspected my dad. Maybe he was feeling guilty about how he treated me when he came to jump-start my car, or about not being more supportive of me during the trial. But even if Dad had written Akasha, she knew things he didn't, like my passion for Sean Penn movies.

I couldn't stand the questions anymore. I wanted to know who and what was said about me. I set the book on a shelf, then left to look for Beah. She wasn't in the kitchen, or her room, or Akasha's office. It was raining, so I didn't think she'd be outside. I stood in the foyer and called out, "Beah!" Someone knocked on the front door. I slid the latch back and opened the door. It was Beah.

"You called?" She held a folded newspaper. I saw that it was *The New York Times*.

"What are you — "

"I couldn't open the door." Beah pointed to the nineteenth century lock. "Only opens from the inside. I was reading. I love the smell of rain."

I closed the door. "When did my dad write to Akasha? Did you read the letter? What did it say?"

"I don't know anything about a letter, sunshine."

Sunshine? She had never called me that before. She took her coat off and set it on a chair by the door. "Yesterday, you said you did."

"I said maybe. I feel damp. I believe I need a soak in the tub." She walked toward her room.

"But you get the mail," I said to the back of her head, knowing that was all the information I was going to get from her.

It had to be Dad. He always butted into my life after the fact. His words in the past had been to "pick up your broken pieces." I really didn't trust him to be looking out for my good. Ironically though, I was more upset with Akasha for reading it. She should have told me about the letter. He probably gave her all his so-called informed opinions of me, like he did to my principal in high school when I started ditching school, like he did to my correctional officer when, at sixteen, I was picked up for shoplifting, like he did to my lawyer. He said things like: she doesn't choose friends wisely; she's usually in the wrong place at the right time; she doesn't use her brain. How could a father dislike a child so? If he couldn't be a positive person in my life, I would think he'd at least let me be. But it was almost like he didn't want me to be happy. He didn't want good things to come my way. Yet, as I slumped down in the chair that held Beah's coat and stared at the marble stairway, I felt pretty sure that Akasha did.

Chapter Twelve

*T*he rain had stopped, and I heard Beah humming far off in the distance. I was still sitting in the chair wondering what to do next. I was pretty sure Beah was the only person to deliver the mail and she did so on a tray like in some Jane Austen movie. I had watched her sort the mail as I waited impatiently for the new movie I had ordered. Junk mail went directly into the trash. Utility bills went into Beah's stack. And the occasional letter was placed on the silver tray.

Instantly, I made my decision, knowing Akasha was out of town. I walked up the steps straight to her bedroom door. I turned the door handle, expecting it to be locked. After all, this was the most sacred of sacred places, and no one would dare enter without permission. The door opened, and I walked in, closing it with my back, and looked around. The French doors to her balcony were open. The smell of rain lingered in the room. Akasha or Beah must have forgotten to close the doors. Silk curtains fluttered in the breeze. The light blue water in the pool flanked by stone seals spurting water and the large red bridge looked picturesque from the third floor. A statue of the Virgin Mary stood in the center of the balcony, overtaken by vines. Why hadn't she chosen Venus, Aphrodite, or Athena? But what did I know of her and her life?

I didn't know where to start looking for my dad's letter.

Akasha's bed was unmade and pillows were thrown onto the floor, but other than that, everything looked immaculate. I stood still just inside the door. I felt paralyzed. The wrong of intruding where I wasn't invited had already been committed, so what was keeping me from stepping forward and opening her bedside tables, her small desk by the window? For one thing, I feared getting caught. But I also I feared not finding what I came for, and also feared finding the letter and reading it, seeing what my own flesh and blood had to say about me.

I took a breath and tiptoed forward. The floor creaked. I stopped momentarily and then headed toward a desk. I lifted the chair out from the desk. The legs banged against the desk. "Shh," I said to the chair, to me. I expected to have to open several drawers to find the letter, if I found it at all. She didn't appear to me the kind of person to keep anything that wasn't of value. She wasn't the kind of woman to have a box full of sentimental treasures. A rose from her first love. A baby food jar lined with melted snow from the day she believed that love had come to her. A ticket stub from a Dave Matthews concert.

No, she wasn't that kind of woman. That was me and we weren't anything alike.

The top drawer slid open easily. All that was inside were pens, paper clips, and a single envelope addressed to Akasha Duval, with a return address of Mr. Joel Shire. My brother, not my dad. I couldn't tell if I was more hurt or relieved. We weren't close. I never felt I was good enough for him, always judged by some absurd conservative religiosity he believed in. The pain came from believing that siblings should stick together, be supportive. But this new, ideal, brother and sister relationship wouldn't start today, so I was relieved that at least the letter wasn't from my only surviving parent.

I picked up the letter, but before I opened and read it, greed for more information overcame me. I wondered if there might be more letters sent by my brother or my father. I opened another drawer and shuffled through blank greeting cards and birthday cards addressed to Akasha. I read one, looking for some clue to the mystery: "I miss you, happy birthday." It was written in flowy cursive writing, but there was no name just a "Love ya." I picked up an unsealed, unaddressed envelope heavy with pictures. An infant wearing a red and green Christmas dress; a toddler playing in the sand, same toddler sitting in a swing, smiling with pure joy; a preschooler showing off her hands with blue finger paint all over them.

A toilet flushed, not outside in the hall or downstairs, but just a few feet away. My heart pounded against my breast, struggling to get out. Quickly, I shoved the photos back in the envelope and stuck it back into the drawer. The breeze had stopped, and a blue jay chirped angrily. Without closing the desk drawers, I moved toward the door, not taking my eyes off the open bathroom door. I heard another noise, almost like footsteps, but not quite. I hoped to see a plumber walking out with a waist belt full of tools. It wouldn't be Beah. She was still downstairs. Ana? Zahir?

No. Neither of them. Akasha appeared, hopping on one leg to the door where she leaned against the doorframe.

Joel's letter, Mr. Joel Shire's letter, fell to the floor. I stuttered and bent to pick up the letter, keeping my eyes on her. I studied her blank face, the white t-shirt, yellow underwear, perfect thighs, the stump. Her right leg was gone; where the knee would have been was a stump.

"I'm sorry, I'm so sorry." I ran out, leaving the letter, slamming her door.

Once in my room, I shook my hands as if ridding them of poison. I paced, not able to keep still. Hot tears fell. I wouldn't dry them. I deserved the tears, the pain. To calm my nerves, I took a beer from my motel-sized fridge and drank it down in one gulp.

After another beer, I slipped *Citizen Kane* into my computer to distract me; I fast-forwarded it to the end when he lived in Xanadu. I began taking my clothes out of the Henkel fucking Harris dresser and sticking them in my Targét duffle bag and my childhood suitcase. Akasha pounded on my door. I knew it was she, could tell from the anger in her knock. I told her to come in. She opened the door and hopped across the floor, still wearing only a t-shirt. But she wasn't the one being humiliated, the one hopping; I was. She may have been physically deformed, but I was emotionally deformed, unable to finish a job she asked me to do, unable to follow the simplest of social rules, unable to pull my life together, unable to make anything of myself.

"Here." The one word came out sharp. Her cheeks were flushed; several strands of hair stuck to small beads of sweat on her forehead. She tossed my brother's letter at me. It floated weakly onto the bed.

I didn't say anything, even after she stood in the doorway for what felt like a full minute but was probably more like two seconds. Finally, she left, closing the door gently behind her. Why hadn't I apologized? I could have gone after her. I mean, how hard would it be to catch up with someone hopping on one leg? But I didn't go because I felt guilty and afraid. I was in the wrong. There was no other way around it. I could've let my anger toward my family, my anger toward myself bury this fact, but I didn't.

I closed my computer, and quickly unfolded the letter. She gave it to me, and I was going to read it.

Dear Miss Akasha Duval:

I felt a flash of irritation at my brother and his way of thinking, by the simple fact that he called Akasha "Miss" and not "Ms." He could be so sexist. He had said the only women who used Ms. were career women who were afraid to settle into married and family life.

Thanks for contacting me.

Contacting me? Why would she contact him? If she wanted to know something about me, why didn't she just ask me?

I'm glad she is doing good. You ask what she loves. That's easy, and I'm sure you'll soon know for yourself. She loves movies, all kinds. Now, I don't know her favorites. I've never asked her, and we don't go to the movies together. She likes foreign movies and chick flicks, but I know she'll watch anything. As a girl, she watched The Wizard of Oz *over and over again.*

My sister and I aren't close. Before our mother died, we were. We used to sleep together. She hated sleeping alone. And we used to play together. She'd make these elaborate worlds, and we each had to play a good guy and a bad guy. Once we were playing Jaws *with small plastic figurines. I only wanted to be the great white, but she threw a little boy at me and said play both roles and see if you can still eat him and, if you can, then he deserves to die. And while the great white was thinking about this, her little skiff made it to shore. Makes me laugh to think about it. It's good to think and write about those times.*

We both suffered when our mother passed away. Mom was awesome. She was so kind and loving. Our dad has a hard time expressing his emotions. So the hugs and bedtime stories stopped. He relates more to me than to her. We have sports and cars in common. He can't relate to her at all. Some might think I'd enjoy getting more of his attention, but I haven't. It makes me feel sad. I've never said this before but it makes me not like him as well. And it's not easy having those feelings about your father.

My sister hasn't found her place in life. I don't think she knows how smart she is. She could have gone to college and made something of herself. I know she wanted to. I always looked up to her. School came so much easier for her than me.

I pray she gets back in church. Maybe you can recommend one to her ...

Sincerely, Joel Shire

I used the sleeve of my sweatshirt to wipe my face. Joel never told me that he'd also felt that dad seldom gave me much of his time and love. He was more sensitive than I had given him credit for. And it was true that he and I did used to play and sleep together. Mom used to tease us, saying she was going to sell Joel's bed if he didn't start using it. It hurt to know that he knew me better than I had thought, and more than I knew him. Why had I chosen such isolation from him all these years? But I knew why. After Mom died, he'd ask Dad to take him to church, and by the time he was a teenager, his niceness was always punctuated with his comments of "I'll pray for you," or "Church is what you need." Judgment with a soft pat on the back and a calm tone of voice. The church invited all people to worship, but once inside the doors, asked for transformation or required people to pretend to be or feel something they didn't. There were a few times I went to church with Joel. Once, I even went up to the altar and the preacher's wife prayed over me. After the call to prayer was finished, she'd kept asking if I felt anything, if I felt changed. I didn't. I had wanted to. But to get her off my back I said yes. The church said, "We accept everyone." But how could it accept and condemn at the same time? I didn't feel accepted when, another time, the pastor said he could deliver me from my need to watch sin. I looked at Joel. He said, "I told him that you were addicted to movies." I turned and left and hadn't been back.

Reading my brother's words unnerved me. I got out another beer; a Hefeweizen was all I had left. I opened it, wishing for a slice of lemon. Then I set my beer down and went to look for Akasha.

I found Akasha with Beah, sitting at the kitchen table. When I entered, they both looked up at me, and it was obvious Akasha had said something to Beah. Akasha's brow was tense. She waited for me to speak, offer some kind of explanation, apology. A wave of heat and the smell of yeast rolled over my skin; I turned to see Ana opening the oven. She moved gracefully, reaching her gloved hand into the oven and pulling out a baking sheet.

"I had no business being in your room. Please forgive me." Akasha's face softened. She looked into my eyes. She was accepting my apology. "It's just that I needed to know what my dad had to say about me." As I continued, her expression became rigid again. "Now I know it was Joel. But I thought maybe my dad had said some awful things about me that weren't true." I talked more, trying to get her to understand. "But I should have known that my dad would never write. "

"Apologies should never be followed by a 'but,'" Beah said. She looked stern, even parental. Akasha turned to her, and her gaze fell back to her cup of coffee.

Beah was right, but I felt I needed to explain myself. I wanted to talk about my dysfunctional family, about the letter. What was she hoping to accomplish by writing to Joel? Actually, what right did she have? Wasn't this also a form of betrayal? Because I worked for her, did she think she could pry into my life? She must have done it for my birthday, but still, she could have just asked me. It dawned on me that Joel hadn't mentioned anything about *It's a Wonderful Life* or Sean Penn. My head reeled with confusion, yet I needed to take responsibility for what I did wrong.

"I'll try again." I wiped my clammy hands on my legs to rid them of their sweat. "Akasha, I'm sorry for sneaking into your room. No excuses. I'm sorry I hurt you and betrayed your trust in me." I looked down at her healthy leg. "And mostly, I'm sorry about your leg. I had no idea."

"That's one thing you shouldn't be sorry about." She speared her teabag with her fork. Soggy leaves fell out and clung to the tines. She licked them off. There was silence. The conversation was over. I left the kitchen, not knowing what to say, how to fix what went wrong.

While I was throwing stuff onto the back seat of my car, Beah slipped out the front door and came to me. I thought maybe she was bringing me my last check. I hoped she was coming to say goodbye. What I wanted was a hug, but I was afraid if she did hug me I'd fall to pieces.

"She wants you to take one of the BMWs." For a split second, this offer upset me, as if I were being manipulated.

"I'm leaving, Beah. For good. She couldn't possibly want me to stay."

"She likes you."

I didn't feel manipulated by these words. I just felt sorry once again that I failed her. I opened the door to my car and sat behind the wheel. If I didn't act fast, I'd lose my momentum.

"I sucked at whatever job I was supposed to be doing," I said. I had snuck into her room and had pilfered through her belongings. I caught her half-naked. Shit, I caught her without her leg. If she wanted me to know she had a fake leg, wouldn't she have told me? Bad. Bad. Bad. I was so wrong. I ruined my chance to change. "It's time for me to go, Beah. Go back to the life I was living in good old fucking Grass Valley." As much as I bit the inside of my cheek to keep from crying, the more I lost control. I took both my hands and swiped at my face, my tears, my nose.

"Take the car."

"What for, Beah? I am not coming back." For a moment, I was stopped by the tears in her eyes. But then, determined, I turned the ignition. Click, click, click. I tried again. Same thing. Damn. I can't even leave with dignity, I raged. Last week, I charged the stupid battery. Zahir helped, just to see if it still worked. What's wrong with my car? I wanted to leave and make it on my own, like I did before meeting Akasha and would continue to do, but the truth of the matter was, there was a lot wrong with my car.

"Take a few days off. What you're doing is stressful."

I got out of the car. "You mean my job? I work about twenty hours a week. How stressful can that be? Have you ever waited tables? Now that's stress. I need to leave." I thought of the mothers in Darfur who had lost their babies. The women who had been raped. I thought about Inaya. "It's not like I can help, anyway." Beah took my suitcase and duffel bag out of the backseat and walked toward Akasha's car. She popped the trunk and set them in.

"Go."

"What if I don't give the car back? How can she trust me?"

"That's a silly question."

"Which one, Beah? Which question is silly?" Tears flowed down my face again. I pictured my face with ruts from the constant flow, like on hillsides after winter, water always taking the same path. She wiped my tears away.

"Drive safely."

"No promises," I sniffled.

As I drove away from the mansion. I resolved to get Akasha's car back to her somehow. I replayed in my brain how I had walked uninvited into Akasha's room. When she saw me, I could see how angry she was, but more so, she was disappointed. It was just plain stupid. I was just plain stupid. This was my real chance to make my life better, and I blew it.

Zahir was on his hands and knees in a flowerbed at the edge of the drive. He had been in that same position, digging that same hole, planting small purple flowers yesterday. I wondered why he'd dug them back up; they were beautiful. It seemed everything he touched flourished. Part of me wanted to drive by him without even acknowledging him. I felt self-conscious about what I did and he'd soon know. I just lifted my hand up. He nodded.

Ana walked by, carrying a basket full of flowers. Although she waved, she didn't meet my eyes. I guessed she was disappointed in me, too.

I drove west, thinking maybe I'd go to the ocean and take a long walk on the beach. Like, when I came this way before, the thought sounded appealing. A few miles later, I knew the thought was an illusion. I wouldn't be sitting in the sand all tranquil and thanking God for the beauty surrounding me. No. I was angry. Yes, angry with myself for being so stupid. But also angry at Akasha for not being forthright with me, not telling me she wrote to my brother. My birthday must have been the reason she wrote to him. It was such a great evening. My eyes narrowed. Wait a minute. I hadn't even told her I had a brother. Why would she go prying? And why couldn't she be more honest about the job I was supposed to be doing? Was this all some kind of psychological game? And, then there was the familiar anger I kept handy toward my dad and brother. How I wished I could just throw it away. Maybe I should go and talk with Joel, make peace as they say. Find out what Akasha said to him in her letter. I pulled over. Driving was stupid in my condition. I felt irrational — drunk with anger. I tried to picture a time when my life didn't feel so complicated, and then it came to me where I needed to go. Who deserved my anger, who deserved retribution. Just like in *The Count of Monte Cristo*. It was Santos. I hated him more than anyone. He was the one who took what didn't belong to him. All this other stuff was petty. I wanted him to look me in the eye. I'd let him know that he wasn't going to get my forgiveness. Forgiveness was a luxury, one he didn't deserve. He had stolen what was most precious to me.

I turned the car around and headed toward Folsom Prison.

Chapter Thirteen

*E*verything I knew about prisons I had gleaned from years of watching movies: *The Shawshank Redemption*, *The Green Mile*, *Escape from Alcatraz*. Yet none of these movies gave visiting hours. I drove slowly past an empty parking lot up toward the entrance of the prison. A large gate loomed, sealing the high, thick walls. A tower held light and a guard.

Although it was drizzling, I didn't turn on my windshield wipers. I began to shiver. My anger had simmered during the long drive. I wanted to see Santos while I was angry. I wanted him to feel the punch of my words, words that said how I hated him, had never loved him. I wanted him to feel the heat from my eyes. The gray entrance gate, the gray electric wire that stretched on top of the wall, the gray sky filled me with the loss of Clara, the loss of a life filled with smiles and a tiny fist wrapped tightly around one of my fingers. Thinking about my loss refueled my anger. As soon as I saw his pitiful face, my words would wound.

I drove to a hotel a few miles down the road, even though I was only forty-five minutes from Lily's. I didn't want her to see me in a worse state than when I'd moved to Fallow Springs. I wanted to be alone with my anger. At the hotel, I would call the prison and ask when visiting hours were. I would see him. It occurred to me then that Santos didn't have to see me.

There were many times he had tried to see me, talk with me when he discovered I was pregnant, and I had avoided him. I hadn't wanted him in my life. He had pursued me, wanted to be a father to his child. "A good father — that's the most important job," he had said. I had believed him. And I wanted a good father for my baby. I'd wanted help. Plus, I hadn't wanted to be a single mom. I wanted to make my dad proud. Most of all, I wanted what was best for my baby. So I'd agreed to marry him. I had convinced myself that I would learn to love him, and we would be a family.

I should have read some of the early signs. The day of the ultrasound when we'd find out the sex of the baby, Santos had paced around the waiting room glancing at the cheap, way too feminine art. I had thought he was scared, like I was, that we'd see only one heart chamber, or a clubfoot. "If it's a girl, I want to name her Clara, after my mom," I said.

"It is not a girl."

"How do you know? Santos, have a seat. You're making me nervous."

"In a minute."

He never sat down. Twenty minutes later, I was called in.

As Dr. Franco moved the ultrasound knob over my belly, he said, "The heart looks good. See all four chambers? Here is the spine." I choked up. The baby was kicking, moving, looking just like a little tiny baby. But instead of allowing myself to cry, I looked back at Dr. Franco.

"Can you tell the sex?" I could hear Santos take a deep breath. He wasn't holding my hand like he had at the previous visits. His hands were thrust into his pockets.

"Here is the femur." He moved the ultrasound, pressing firmly over the warm gel. "Here is the genitalia and, unless the little thing is hiding … looks like a girl." I reached for Santos's hand, grabbed his wrist. He moved away.

"Are you sure?" Santos asked.

"Can never be one hundred percent sure." Dr. Franco said. Santos was rocking back and forth. The chain that hung out of his jeans pocket kept hitting the edge of the bed. He seemed oblivious to the ching-ching-ching. The baby moved, giving us a better view.

"Pretty sure it's a girl. Nothing better than being a father and having a daughter to spoil." He was a smart man. He watched Santos and then at me and smiled. "Your baby looks great."

Santos didn't open my car door like he had before the ultrasound. On our way back to the apartment, he slammed his fist on the steering wheel. "I thought it was going to be boy."

"Don't be so old-fashioned." Secretly, I was glad the baby was a girl. I thought about Mom and our relationship.

"I'm the fifth generation of firstborn sons. It's expected." We were at a red light. Before it turned green, he pressed his foot down on the accelerator, almost hitting a car coming through the intersection. I placed one hand on the dashboard, the other over the baby, thinking I could protect her.

"You're scaring me." He didn't stop at the next red light at all, driving as fast as his old Nissan would go. I held on to my seat, pleading with him to slow down. When I saw that wasn't working, I started to bargain, "If you slow down, I'll make you barbequed prime rib. I'll give you a foot massage." That didn't work either. Then I got mad. I yelled at him to slow down. This made him drive even faster, until he pulled into the driveway by my apartment.

"I need some time," he said calmly.

"I guess you do."

After a prison guard searched my purse the next day I went through a metal detector, and then sat on a cold aluminum chair. There I waited for Santos. I placed my hands on my lap, not on the table that would separate us. I hadn't seen him since he was convicted and sentenced. I had never wanted to see him again, ever. But I now needed him to know how much he hurt me, that what he did was irreparable, no matter how many years he spent in prison.

Looking around the room, I saw men who had raped, battered, killed. I was also in a room with fatherless children who would never know a normal life, who had to learn the art of survival, who had learned to fight on the schoolyard to prove their worth, and to feel alive, even if it was by punching a kid in the face. I saw the angry wives who wanted to love the man who committed the crime. They must love them — why else would they be here? They also needed to feel love, but their man was locked up. I saw the mothers who thought the system was unjust. My son is innocent. It's the system's fault. Yet the mothers' faces held the weight of guilt — they didn't really blame the system.

A little girl with a pink velour dress sat in the chair next to me. She couldn't have been more than two. She played with the little kitties that were embroidered on her tights. "Meow, do you want a toy, maybe some string to play with?" she said. She traced a squiggly line up her leg. I wanted to tell that little girl that she could change her life, that she didn't need to continue down this same path. I looked up to keep the tears from falling, not wanting my life to be ruled by one man and one experience.

When I saw Santos walking through the door, fear tightened my chest and anger blazed in my skull. The fear paralyzed me, and anger made me feel like attacking. These two polarized emotions grew stronger as I watched Santos being escorted in. Seeing him with handcuffs helped me to feel safer but they did nothing for my anger.

"I'm glad you finally came to see me." I was relieved he didn't smile, but looked solemn, hurt almost.

I didn't respond. I thought about the word "finally." Did he expect me sooner? His hands were on the table. Other men's hands embraced their loved ones' hands across tables. He couldn't possibly expect this from me. He sat with his back straight, only his head bent in remorse.

A couple of unwanted tears fell down my face. I felt I was observing myself, not really in my own body. My tears weren't a sign of weakness, submission, or remorse, but I think that was how Santos read them. Why else would he have the audacity to take his index finger and wipe a tear from the table? With his thumb and index finger he rubbed my tear into his skin. His eyes dropped and all I could see were his long lashes, his beautiful long eyelashes.

"How come you haven't written back?"

Written back? He must have been writing to me, but to where? Did Akasha hide this from me, too? He must have seen how confused I felt.

"Haven't you received any of my letters?"

"No," I said. My thoughts quickly turned an unexpected corner. He couldn't be writing me letters. Writing letters was so personal, almost too personal anymore. How could Santos even think about writing to me? I had no intention of talking about why I hadn't been writing him; that wasn't what this visit was about.

"I've been sending them to your brother's address. It was the only one I had. The jerk must not be giving them to you. I've written over thirty."

I'd have to spend time later thinking about what in the name of God my brother had been doing with the letters, but at the moment I focused on Santos and the fact that he'd written me thirty letters and that he thought that I was sitting in front of him because of them. Had he been asking for forgiveness? Explaining his brutality to me? I leaned in.

"Don't call my brother names. Got it?" He nodded. "What in God's world do you have to say to me in one letter? Let alone thirty fucking letters."

"Well, I ..." He was choosing his words slowly, carefully.

"Yes?" There were other things going on around me — tears, chairs moving back and forth from underneath tables, conversations about lawyers, drugs — but I stayed focused on what he was going to say.

"Of course, I was apologizing. That night, I lost control. And if I am good, which I have been," he sat up even straighter, "I can get out in four years, maybe."

It was like I was watching a movie where I knew what was coming next. I knew what the villain was going to do, but still I was riveted. I sat at the edge of my chair, my heart pounding in my chest.

"An angel has come to me. God has told me that the only way to right what I have done is to take you back and have another child with you. You have to believe me. I have been reading the word of God."

I was no longer an observer. I was fully in my body. I stood up, and I punched him right in the nose. I wanted to hurt him, wished I had something like a crowbar. "Never," I said, almost in a whisper, as a guard restrained me, "will you touch me ever again." Santos looked surprised. He touched his nose to see if he was bleeding. The armed guard wrapped his arms around me and dragged me out. I yelled, "Only by making you pay can I ask the baby to forgive me." People clapped. The guard was squeezing the breath from my lungs. I kicked. "Read the letters," Santos shouted after me. Another guard had him stand, restraining his arms and cuffed hands. Blood dripped down his face. I was thrown out of the room and told to never return.

I returned to Akasha's car, shivering. The wind blew, beating me with rain. I had left my coat behind, giving me yet another reason to hate Santos. The keys dropped three times from my numb fingers before I managed to press the button to unlock the door.

I drove to Lily's, but she wasn't home, and I no longer had a key to her place. I thought about going to see her at work, knowing I needed something to help me gain clarity, somebody to tell me I was okay and that my life wasn't going to be a series of Santos. But I didn't want to go to the Chili's Restaurant where she worked and sit at the bar and have a cold one. I needed something deeper, more meaningful.

I drove to the cemetery where Mom was buried. Desperate to get to Mom's grave, I parked in a handicapped parking place, though there wasn't another car in the lot. I ran and threw myself on her grave, like I had thrown myself onto her legs as a toddler. I had known she'd catch me, pick me up, hold me, and make me feel safe and loved. The grass was wet, the dirt turning to mud — the ground smelled of death. There was nothing romantic, nothing beautiful or reassuring about death.

"Mom, help me. I needed you, need you." No answer. Sitting up on my knees, wet and shivering, feeling so alone, so lonely, I no longer sobbed. I felt a touch on my shoulder.

My brother peered down at me, from beneath a large black umbrella that he angled over me. I scooted away from his shelter.

"Jamie!" He was surprised to see me. "What are you doing?"

What did it look like I was doing? Mourning. Paying my respects. I turned back to Mom's grave. I was annoyed that he showed up; this was my private moment. Her gravestone dripped with water. I leaned toward the headstone. With both hands, I brushed off the rain as if I were trying to get it to stop crying. It had been a sunny day in August when we buried her, yet I remembered being so cold that I couldn't stop shaking. I wore a black and red dress that my aunt, my dad's sister, had bought. It looked like a Christmas dress. I heard her tell Dad that she had a hard time finding an all-black dress for a ten-year-old, but there had to be a catalogue for death clothes, like the ones for gravestones, gravestone engravings and caskets that the funeral home had given to my father. The sound of dirt thrown on the casket had paralyzed me. As the earth dropped with a thud, I envisioned myself in the casket, hearing that thud ... the thought of being buried dead or alive felt terrifying. Then I felt awful for thinking about myself and not my mother. My mom used to tell me that I was perfectly beautiful, a wonder, a gift from God. I felt that this gift — her gift — was useless unless it had a receiver and my receiver was dead. I was now like Mom's costume jewelry. What should we do with this? We can't just give it to the Goodwill. Dad never called me his gift, his angel. I was his daughter, his responsibility.

Joel didn't try to share his umbrella with me again. I liked him for this. I was trying to hold the sobs in — I didn't want Joel to know I couldn't stop crying.

"Crying is good," he preached.

"Fuck you." My response was harsh, but I was tired of his judgments of me, his I-know-what's-best-for-you comments.

"She's my mom, and I love her, too." I turned around. His eyes were red. Joel and I should be on the same side. We had something we could share. Why did we always fight?

"I know," I said, almost in a whisper. "I'm sorry." He knelt down, tossing the umbrella aside, and hugged me. I held on tightly to him while our strong facades broke. He felt strong — I was glad he didn't walk away from me. As we made our way back to the parking lot, I let him hold the umbrella over me, though I was already sopping wet.

"You come here often?" I asked.

"Every other Saturday. What are you doing here?"

"I needed a hug." I laughed, realizing that I got what I came for. We walked on in silence. I glanced back at Joel. "I came to see Santos." Joel's head whipped around and his gaze met mine. "Wasn't exactly sure why at first, but then I punched him. And it felt so good."

"Are you serious?" His face shone with excitement and disbelief. I smiled.

"Did you read them, the letters Santos sent?" Joel flushed red.

"Not at first. But as more came, I thought maybe there was something that you should know."

"Is there?"

"Just that he's sorry." I braced myself for the forgiveness speech, but he didn't say anything else.

"I don't read them anymore. They all say the same thing. Do you want them?"

"No. Burn them. Really. Burn them," I repeated, to let him know I was serious. Some things don't need to be remembered fifty years later.

"Where you going?" he asked.

My shoes were soppy and caked with mud. Akasha's pristine car had probably never carried someone so wet and filthy, maybe not even someone so emotionally wounded. But I thought I knew her well enough to know that she wouldn't care if mud fell all over her floor or if her leather seats got wet, not if I were ultimately okay. "I'm going home," I said. He looked surprised.

"To Dad's?"

"No. To Akasha's." I opened the trunk and pulled out some dry clothes. "Maybe we should talk some time."

"I'd like that."

I changed clothes in the back seat. Joel kept watch, although there weren't any other cars in the lot. We hugged again, and he waited for me to drive away, then followed me in his car to the highway, where we went our separate ways. As I pulled onto the freeway, I realized that

I didn't even ask him about the letter he wrote to Akasha. Maybe it really didn't matter anymore.

Chapter Fourteen

*H*eading down the long driveway to the mansion, I decided I needed a break from myself. I was tired of feeling on emotional overload. I wanted to rest my mind, to rest my body. I wanted to laugh. I thought about movies that could help. I remembered Beah telling me to rest.

The other BMW wasn't parked in front of the garage. I sighed, wanting to tell Akasha how sorry I was again, to tell her that I was back for as long as she'd take me, that this was where I belonged. And even if we didn't all sit down to dinner together, I wanted to confide in Beah, to experience Akasha's intensity and sensitivity, to enjoy Zahir's quiet sweetness and concern, and to see Ana's smile, even though she seldom uttered a word to me.

Ana was the one who sat in the swing on the veranda near the front door. Her braids were not pinned to her head like they usually were but instead hung down over her breasts. She was drinking peppermint tea. She always smelled of it.

Approaching the steps with my duffle bag and suitcase, I said a simple hello and kept walking toward the door, ready for a warm shower, a good movie, and an end to my tears.

Ana patted the spot next to her, but still she hadn't said a word. I didn't want to join her. I was tired. She held a book, *The Collected Poems of John Keats*. For a brief moment, I felt Aunt Gazella's presence and warmth. I sat.

We rocked back and forth. After several minutes I began to feel frustrated, for she hadn't even said hello. Why should I talk when she didn't? But then, why did she invite me to sit? I rocked for a couple more long minutes. Finally, I stopped the swing, placing both my feet firmly on the ground, ready to stand. "It's been a long day. I need a shower."

Ana laid her hand on my thigh. Holding the book in front of me, she pointed to a poem. I read out loud.

Why Did I Laugh Tonight? No Voice Will Tell

Why did I laugh tonight? No voice will tell:
No God, no Demon of severe response,
Deigns to reply from Heaven or from Hell.
Then to my human heart I turn at once.
Heart! Thou and I are here, sad and alone;
I say, why did I laugh? O mortal pain!
O Darkness! Darkness! ever must I moan,
To question Heaven and Hell and Heart in vain.
Why did I laugh? I know this Being's lease,
My fancy to its utmost blisses spreads;
Yet would I on this very midnight cease,

And the world's gaudy ensigns see in shreds;
Verse, Fame, and Beauty are intense indeed,
But Death intenser — Death is Life's high meed.

"It's beautiful," I said, closing the book. "I'm not sure exactly what it means. Something about having no voice? No words for what he wants to say?" I wondered if she related to this poem, but I had heard her talking with Beah. She'd stop when I'd come into the room. She couldn't be saying the poem is about her. "It's also about how painful our suffering is and yet we laugh."

Ana smiled. Her eyes were light blue, very clear for an older woman, although I wasn't sure of her age. I loved the fact that she always smelled of peppermint and yeast and garlic and rosemary. She took my hand. I turned to look at her. I thought she was going to tell me something. Instead, she opened her mouth and stuck out her tongue. Her tongue had been severed. The end was white and pink and squared, not rounded or pointed. I pulled away. I didn't want her to feel I was freaked out by it, but I was.

"I don't like to talk," she said, sounding as if she had a wad of cotton in her mouth. I don't like the way I sound. People react and treat me as if I were stupid."

"I'm so sorry," I said. "I didn't know." I wanted to ask how and why. I was ashamed again at my self-centeredness, how I had assumed our strained relationship was because of me.

"Go shower," she said.

I wanted to stay and comfort her, but I also wanted to get away. I got up and walked to the door. And then I did something that surprised me. I walked back and gave her a hug. Starting for the door again, I stopped with my hand on the handle. I felt worse than empty inside. All the pain and loss from losing my mother to the loss of Clara to hating Santos made me feel polluted. I wanted to feel normal.

People said there was no such thing as normal, but I believed there was. Normal to me was represented by those who were innately more balanced, those without extreme, extreme anything — intelligence, athleticism, sensitivity. Not everyone hurts and suffers like others do: not every person has the capacity to feel as fully as others. I guessed John Keats did. Maybe poets do. Sensitivity is like intelligence. Some people are just smarter. Leonardo da Vinci was a painter and a sculptor, but also a scientist, an engineer, an inventor. Mozart, who heard entire symphonies in his head, wasn't normal. Those who can catch the ball that others think is out of reach, or those who can ride down a half-pipe with speed and grace are not normal. I wished my feelings to simmer down, my tears to dry. I sat back down.

"Ana, I'm sorry for touching your rose. I know how it is to care about things that other people think are stupid. My mother had told me not to touch flowers. She said the oil in my fingers damaged the tender petals. But I would whenever she wasn't watching. I couldn't resist. Petals are so soft, and smooth, almost like the palm of a baby."

Ana nodded. "My mama told me not to stick my fingers in the cream." She spoke slowly and deliberately, almost like she was trying to learn a language and needed to search for each right word.

"Did you?" The clouds broke, opening the sky to colors of blue, purple, and pink.

"Of course." Ana smiled and the lines around her eyes softened.

"My mother always told me to look both ways when crossing the street. And I still do."

"Children know when to obey." She turned serious again. "My mama told me to never tell anyone we were hiding Avrum and Eidel. And I never told."

"You just now told me," I teased. But I also wondered who Avrum and Eidel were. She laughed.

"Now doesn't matter. That time is gone. Now is the time to get the bread out of the oven." She got up and walked inside without having to look at her watch, without hearing a timer chime. I followed her inside, went to my room, and took a long bath. When I came back down looking for Akasha, or Beah, there were two loaves of braided bread on the kitchen island. Ana was chopping chives into small tubes.

"Can I make you some tea?" I asked. I used to leave the kitchen when I saw that it was just Ana. I no longer felt the need to quietly walk away. Now, I knew why she hadn't talked and it had nothing to do with me. She turned the burner on under the kettle while I got out two cups and the assortment of teas. Picking up the cutting board, she scraped the chives into the pot.

"If life were easy, we wouldn't learn how to cling to people."

"No offense," I replied, "but I've never had anyone to cling to." I thought of Mom, then Aunt Gazella. "Not for very long anyway." True, Lily had been there for me, especially during the trial. But I hadn't heard from her in two months.

"My mama and papa were good people. They taught me to trust and cling to those we love, the values we believe in. The only thing that helps a person get through war is time with no war. That is how hope is installed. These people who come from lands where war is continuous ..." She stopped and poured hot water into our cups and, after placing the kettle back on the stove, sat down. On the table were two tablets. She picked up one and with the palm of her hand dusted the top, although there wasn't any dust that I could see. She slid the journal toward me. "Read it if you would like."

I cracked the cover open. My heart beat with nervousness at the thought of reading Ana's private thoughts.

Before the war, my life was filled with light and tenderness. Light coming through the slit in my curtain to tell of a new day. Light shining through Papa's corn stalks. The light glinting off my mother's hair. Light shining through the stained glass window at church, brightening Mother Mary's face as she held her son. Tender laughter throughout our day. Tender kisses and hugs.

When the war came to our town, bringing the Germans, everything became dark and harsh. The lightness and tenderness of my childhood gone. Even their language sounded discordant. Mama began to kiss me and hold me as if I would vanish in the middle of the night. The rain that spring turned to hail on several occasions, pelting me and my sister, Sarah, in the face as we walked to school.

I stopped reading the journal. I felt self-conscious, as if the act was too personal. Ana twisted the string of her tea bag around her spoon then pressed the bag against the cup.

Zahir came into the kitchen with a bundle of firewood. This kitchen with its large open fireplace, speaking of days long gone when women cooked over real flames, comforted me. There had been times that I'd seen Ana cooking in it, even though she also had two ovens. Zahir's hands were full of wood. For a moment, I felt lazy and spoiled. Ana, Beah and Zahir all had more exhausting work than I did. They were always busy, and often I had too much time on my hands. He nodded hello as he sat to unload the wood.

After he stacked the wood, Zahir stoked the fire on bended knees, carefully rearranging the burning wood, placing a fresh log on top. His face looked younger, the lines no longer deep. As he got up to leave, Ana jumped up, grabbed one of the braided breads, and handed it to Zahir.

"Good person," she said as he left.

"How old is he?" I asked softly, although he was already gone. "I can never tell." I guessed she took this as a rhetorical question because she didn't answer.

"Only if you want— " she patted the open book, then turned to wash a couple of dishes.

I don't remember the day the Germans occupied Nostldorf, or the day some Jews closed shops and began to migrate, or the day the others were made to wear the Star of David. It all happened like a tree sprouting its leaves, slowly, continuously, and, other than chopping that tree down, nothing could stop the leaves from taking over.

I disliked America when I first came. Nothing was familiar. American life was easy and me and my family weren't Americans; our history was more painful. My family migrated in 1945 after the Allies saved Belgium. Papa said that our land betrayed our values, and that he no longer wanted to live in a country that bordered Germany. After the war, I didn't know what to look forward to. I used to dream of the war ending and, when it did, Mama still held tightly to me and my sister and cried as if her Sarah and Ana could still disappear during the night. She nursed baby Delly until people began to talk. Papa had to tell her, "No more," that the child was big enough to eat with the rest of us.

We had lived on a farm in a small town in the Flemish region of Belgium with my Papa, Mama, and my sister, Sarah. We were close enough to town to make weekly visits to the store, to attend Mass, and to know what was going on when the Germans occupied.

During the war, my parents took into our home two Jews, Avrum and Eidel. One day, our priest had come to speak with Papa and Mama. It was too cold to go outside, so Sarah and I went upstairs. He asked my parents to hide this young couple until he could get them new visas. With weighted hearts and minds, my parents said yes. When Sarah and I were called downstairs to be told, Mama smiled but had tears in her eyes. I wanted to be excited about having guests, but I felt the tension and fear in the room. So instead of asking what they were like, I asked, "Will they be staying in mine and Sarah's room?" Papa said, "Probably not." At first we thought Avrum and Eidel's stay would be just for a few weeks, but the weeks turned into months and the months turned into almost two years.

I heard Mama warning Eidel and Avrum against getting Eidel pregnant. Mama would say there would come a day when they could try for a child as often as they liked, but this wasn't the time. To the Germans, a Jewish baby was simply a Jew.

Eidel used to brush my hair and braid it, never hurrying. Once I had told her that I hated my hair. It was too thick and had no natural curl like hers had. I wanted hair just like hers. "If you're going to waste your wishes on something so absurd as hair, then you shouldn't be allowed to have them," Eidel told me. She was right. I knew this even then.

"Do you wish you weren't a Jew?" I asked.

She stopped braiding. Then I became scared, thinking I had offended her and began to apologize. "No," she said. "But I wish my child weren't." That was the day I discovered Eidel was pregnant.

Avrum and Eidel slept hidden in the attic on top of Sarah's and my room because Germans were known to come into people's homes at all times of the night. There were times I heard Eidel crying. She didn't know where any of her family had been taken. They had lived in Brussels and a neighbor had said the Gestapo came and took her papa, mama, and brother. Avrum would sing to her those nights, and, I imagined, hold her tight. Soon she was with child, and soon after that so was my mama. I always wondered if Mama got pregnant on purpose, thinking that somehow it would end up helping Eidel, which it did.

Almost nine months later, Mama, Papa, Avrum and Eidel left to go to a midwife's house. Sarah and I knew we'd never see Avrum and Eidel again. At least not until the war was over. I cried and cried, aching from missing them after they left, yet there was also a part of me that welcomed feeling safe again. I thought maybe Mama wouldn't need to pray so long for me at bedtime.

One night while our parents were still at the midwife's, Sarah and I ate supper, then Sarah brushed my hair by the fire. When the knocks sounded, Sarah dropped the brush.

"Papa's back," I said.

"Let me do the talking," Sarah said.

Then I knew it wasn't Papa. I stayed in the chair and watched Sarah open the door. Three Germans, wearing Gestapo uniforms, hats pinned with a skull, towered over her. Mama had pointed them out to us, telling us to keep away from them, that they didn't know right from wrong. Mama used that saying even before the Germans occupied, saying it was her job to teach Sarah and me the path of the righteous. I wondered what the mamas were like of those men. I imagined all the ugly men to be orphaned.

In that harsh language that hurt my ears, one of the men spoke. His face was red and his hair very blonde, like the color of bones left in the sun. I heard and understood "die Juden."

These were the men that Mama had warned me against, telling me never to speak to them, or even look at them. And here they were walking into our home without being invited.

Sarah was forced to step back. I'd always thought Sarah was so much bigger than me, growing into a woman, but next to these men Sarah looked like a child. Her cheeks turned bright red. "I don't speak German," she said in Flemish. One of my classmates had told me that it was going to be the new language of our country, of the world. I had told him that I didn't care. I'd never learn it.

"No German. I speak Flemish," another man spat out. He had a double chin, and a round face. And he spit when he spoke. I was glad Sarah was the oldest.

"Where are your parents?" that man asked.

Sarah told them that our papa had to take Mama to the midwife's. He translated to the red-faced man. The red-faced man pushed past Sarah into our home and the other men followed. The one who spoke Flemish and the tall skinny man looked in the rooms of our house. It didn't take long for the tall skinny man to find the attic. The door was hidden by a large tapestry. Mama cherished the tapestry. It was the one luxury she took with her when we moved to America.

The red-faced man said something and pointed toward the front door. The man who spoke Flemish left. I was glued to the chair and couldn't speak.

The skinny man came down from the attic, and, with a long piece of steel that had a hook at the end, began pulling up the floorboards. Sarah cried. The man in charge spoke German again saying something about "die Juden." Sarah kept shaking her head; her words stuck like mine.

The man who had left came back; words we couldn't understand were spoken.

Sarah was asked where the midwife's house was. She said it was a full day's journey, to the west.

"What kind of women travels a full day when she's ready to give birth?"

I thought about saying Mary, Christ's mother. But didn't say anything. I must have smiled, or maybe a sound escaped my lips for the skinny man stopped destroying our home for a moment and came and tickled my chin as if I were a goat. He asked me something. I knew it was a question because he waited for an answer. I was glad I didn't speak German.

Sarah explained how our mama had difficult births and this was the only woman who could help her deliver. He seemed to understand this. I thought maybe he was smarter than he acted. He spoke to the man in charge.

I now thought that they'd leave soon. There was a moment of quiet. The man who was pulling up boards had succeeded in discovering we had no one hidden under the house. He set the tool on the table. Sarah's tears stopped. I smelled the bread Sarah baked earlier and thought it funny that I hadn't realized how good it smelled while it baked or while we ate it.

The man in charge reached inside his jacket, took a flask out, drank, and then gave the flask to the man who spoke Flemish. The man in charge said, "Ich riechen Juden."

He took the flask back before the other man took a drink. He looked at Sarah again. He spoke loudly, spitting in her face. The round-faced man translated, "He smells Jews."

The one in charge grabbed the back of Sarah's hair and pulled her head back. I screamed and she screamed.

The skinny man said something and they all laughed. Sarah was pushed toward that man. He coughed. He pushed her back to the one who spoke our language, said something and laughed again. The Flemish-speaking man picked up Sarah like she was a pile of soiled laundry and took her into our parents' bedroom.

Sarah screamed and cried at the same time. I tried to run and help her, but the man in charge grabbed me and pulled me back down. He took a chair and sat in front of me. I hated that man. I hated the man who was in the room with Sarah. It was the first time I felt hate and how it burned the heart, yet gave me such energy. I kicked the man and darted again toward Sarah. The two men laughed. The skinny man threw me back in the chair and then said, "Boo" before he stepped away.

They continued to pass the flask, talking and laughing while Sarah and I cried from opposite ends of the house. When I heard Sarah begin to scream in pain, I yelled out her name. "Sarah!" I couldn't stop. Their laughter mixed with our screams sounded like coyotes making a game out of killing. I thought this must be hell. I thought that my sister and I must have died.

The man in charge slapped me. I stopped screaming, though I couldn't stop the sobs and tears. Sarah had stopped screaming, too, but I could still hear her crying. The man who spoke our language came out of our parents' room, zipping up his pants.

Then the skinny ugly man went in. It was then that I knew that the man who spoke our language had taken Sarah's virginity. I worried if our mama would ever stop crying when she found out.

When Sarah began screaming again, I begged the man in front of me to help her. I was slapped again.

"Where are the Jews?" I was asked. I stopped crying, looked at the man who spoke Flemish and called him evil, a worker of the devil.

The man cackled, "Or God," he said.

The man in charge took out a pocketknife. And asked about "die Juden" again.

I believed he was going to kill me, but death didn't seem to scare me. I was scared for Sarah and what was being done to her, scared too for what these men would do to Avrum and Eidel, and Mama and Papa.

"Tell me!" He grabbed my arm, squeezing it and bruising it, maybe even trying to fracture it.

The man who spoke our language said something to the man in charge. I heard the word, "kind." The man in charge got angry. His face turned red and he pointed the knife at the other man, yet he let go of my arm.

He asked me again about "die Juden." I closed my mouth. My chest heaved. I was shivering, like they had left the door open, but the man in front of me was sweating. Perspiration flowed down his cheeks like tears flowed down mine.

Again he said something as if I could understand. His face was so close to my face that I could smell his breath and see the white hair on his chin.

I looked at the man who spoke our language. The fire burned at my back, but still I shivered with cold. I pretended not to understand his question and shrugged my shoulders. But I knew he was asking where Eidel and Avrum were. Squeezing my eyes shut, praying that they were safe, I shook my head no.

The man who was in charge stuck his fingers in my mouth and pulled out my tongue. I gagged. He flipped out his pocketknife then sliced off my tongue. I screamed out, but couldn't take a breath. Blood poured out from between the fingers I'd clapped over my mouth, down my chin, onto my dress. The pain was awful. I thought I was dying. I watched the man throw my flesh into the fire and then clean his knife slowly on Mama's towel. He spoke, his voice even, though I didn't try to understand.

The man who spoke Flemish gave me his handkerchief. "Hold it," he said and pressed it onto my tongue.

I did what he told me to do. The white cloth smelled of cigarettes and spicy cologne.

I ran into our parents' bedroom. This time no one stopped me. Sarah was lying on the bed sideways, head dangling off the edge. The man was still on top of her thrusting his hips. Sarah no longer screamed or cried. She stared at the ceiling. I pulled at the man's arms, trying to get him off of her. He hit me across the face. I let go of the handkerchief and blood spilled out of my mouth. I went back to my sister and cradled her head in my arms.

Chapter Fifteen

*T*aking my eyes off the page, I saw Ana anew, although she was just standing with her hand on the open refrigerator door peering in, a common enough pose for her, so I guessed something must have changed inside of me. I couldn't see what she was after. When she closed the door with her hip, she held two armfuls of vegetables. She laid them on the large cutting board in the middle of the room and organized them in a row: carrots, potatoes, celery, radishes, zucchinis, tomatoes, and an onion. Tears dripped down her cheeks. I guessed she was reliving the words I had been reading. She picked up the onion and began to dice it.

I turned the page of her journal seeking to discover what happened to Sarah. What happened to Avrum and

Eidel? What happened to the babies? The page was blank, along with the next one. I closed the book.

"May I help?" I washed my hands in the sink, thinking that was all she would share now.

"No," she smiled. "This is what I enjoy. Please, go rest."

"Your story. How awful. I'm sorry." Again, like when Inaya released her story, I found language inadequate, like how a floating stick would be if it were stranded at sea.

"Yes, the story is painful. Go rest, Jamie."

Ana wanted time to herself. I knew this feeling.

When I got to my room, I was exhausted. So much had happened in the last twenty-four hours, I could have slept for two days. Akasha sat in the chair next to the open window. A light breeze blew in, lifting the top strands of her hair. The moon shone directly above her, though it wasn't completely dark yet.

"I saw you pull up. I hope it's okay that I let myself into your room." I flushed, although she didn't appear to have made the inference intentionally. "Thought you might want to talk to me." In her lap rested the same book I had attempted to read on my first day, *The Red Tent*. It looked like she had made it through several chapters.

I had left the bedroom door open. "I left. And it wasn't my room anymore." I looked at Akasha and bit my lip. "I want to finish the job I started." I had so much more to say to this woman, but I was too tired. "Akasha..." I leaned back against the large dresser.

"You've been with Ana — kind of makes you grateful, doesn't it?" Akasha closed the book and set it back on the table.

"Kind of does."

"I'm glad you're home," she said, standing. I looked to see if her eyes spoke the same message as her words. I smiled.

"Me, too. Thanks for letting me come back."

"Maybe tomorrow we can talk. I'm sure you need some rest, so rest."

I looked at the book she had set back on the table. "That book isn't mine. If you want to read it."

"I have."

"I must look really tired." She didn't respond, so I added, "Ana just told me to rest as well."

When I went to sleep that night, a movie played out in my head, set in Belgium on a little farm outside of Nostldorf.

The next morning, I wrote letters to two senators. I called the White House, asking the President to support the United Nations and the African Union. And I vowed to call every day until something happened. Late that afternoon, in my meeting with Akasha, I recommended Akasha send money to the United Nations High Commissioner for Refugees, Doctors without Borders, the World Food Program, and the Save Darfur Coalition to help the people of Darfur.

Akasha asked me to create community awareness. I squirmed in my chair when she said this. I hated the idea. And once again I was at a loss. Did she want me to speak to people? Pass out flyers? Go door to door like the Jehovah's Witnesses? I did better behind the scenes. I liked researching, writing letters, and calling President Bush, but I must admit all that didn't take long.

"Around this community?"

"What other community do you live in?" She sat back in her office chair. The only time she ever seemed to be in her office was when she met with me. I thought this odd. "Yes, this community. Didn't you say that this genocide was going to be stopped through grassroots?"

"I did." This was what she wanted from me; but I had no clue what to do.

"Do you have anything else you'd like to say?"

I looked down at my notes, happy she wanted to hear more about what I had learned. I hadn't given her the Sudanese government's reason for attacking. "The Sudanese government says that it's fighting rebel groups, that this isn't about killing off the black farmers. There is the SLA and JEM. SLA stands for Sudan's Liberation Movement and — "

"You've done good work. You know what you're talking about. I believe you. I just thought there was something else."

She wet her perfect lips in such a way as to remind me of a scene in the movie *The Girl with the Pearl Earring*, based on the life and work of Johannes Vermeer. Vermeer's Muse, his love during those moments of creation, was a beautiful servant girl. The Muse living and breathing for him alone.

"Jamie?" Akasha's eyebrows rose. "Are you still with me?"

"I am." I looked down at my hands. My nails had grown out, needing to be trimmed. She knew I had more on my mind. I hadn't really given her any kind of explanation for my abrupt departure. "I saw my brother. I was at my mother's grave and he showed up. We don't get a long that great but ... I need to focus on what we share. He loved her, too."

I told her how painful it was that our dad had always sided with him and that I felt my brother judged me for how I spent my time, who I hung out with, and that church wasn't a part of my life; yet he was the one who would call when we hadn't seen each other for awhile, and he was the one who'd initiate our hugs. It was the first time I didn't feel like Akasha was in a hurry to leave, to get away from me. She leaned forward, rubbing her middle finger in an absent-minded gesture that seemed comfortable and at ease.

"Sounds like your brother loves you. But maybe he's having a hard time loving himself." This comment surprised me.

"Why do you say that?"

"It's been my experience that people who are overly zealous, overly involved in any religion, are trying to calm the demons in their own head."

"Yeah. Maybe. I'm not sure he'd see it that way."

"No. I wouldn't think he would."

There was a quiet that told me we were finished. I stood.

"Ana, Beah, and I are eating dinner tonight, together in the kitchen," I said. "I asked Ana if we could do dinners together. We're starting tonight. Would you like to join us?"

"Thank you, but I like to work while I eat. In my room. Maybe some other time." Akasha passed me and headed toward the marble staircase.

"Work at what?" I blurted.

"Make sure you invite Zahir." She started up the steps to her room.

"I will." I hadn't, figuring he wouldn't come, and I hated to be rejected. Yet Akasha had rejected my invitation and I was okay.

When I reached the kitchen, Ana was placing food on the table.

"I'll be right back." I jogged on the stone path, over a small bridge, and knocked on his door. When he answered, I was still trying to catch my breath.

"Is everything okay?" Zahir asked. A large curl hung on his forehead. He brushed it over.

"Yes." I caught my breath. "Please come and eat with us."

He looked over his shoulder at a pot on his stove where steam rose. I smelled onions. He wore no shoes, and his shirt was unbuttoned, revealing his chest, light brown and muscular. I remembered seeing him for the first time bending over, back hunched, graying hair shining in the sun. He had moved so slowly, an attribute of the old. I tried not to stare at his chest, willing myself to look at his face.

"I see you have something on the stove. Maybe some other time." I turned to leave.

"Why?" he slid his hands into his jean pockets.

"Why what?"

"Why do you want me to have dinner with you?"

"Not just me. With me and Beah and Ana."

"Why?"

I didn't have an answer. Neither Ana nor Beah had asked why, not even Akasha. Then I felt insecure. What I was asking for was friendship, family, intimacy. Could a person ask for those things?

"Ana is a great cook and she—" I didn't finish because I wasn't sure exactly what to say. I was retracting, not wanting to tell him what I really wanted was friendship.

"I have food on the stove."

"I like it here," I confessed. "I feel like I belong." I wasn't sure how much I wanted to say. "I just thought, maybe it would be nice if we hung out a bit." He began to button up his shirt.

"Give me a minute." He turned off his stove, slipped on his sandals.

"We'd better run," I said, smiling.

"Run?"

"The food is on the table. I don't want to be disrespectful."

"Okay. Let's run." Together we jogged back over the stone path.

When we sat down to dinner, I told them what Akasha had asked of me and how uncomfortable I felt. How I didn't even know where to start, and what did I know, really? I had just learned about the genocide and the people of Darfur from listening to one victim and then reading stuff off the internet. That didn't make me an expert, and I was sure people wouldn't really care, anyway.

As Ana slowly buttered her bread, listening, I thought about how she and her family had sacrificed so much, and how here I was complaining about putting myself in an uncomfortable situation for a few hours, days, or weeks.

"I thought about going to the local high school and asking the principal if I could talk with the students."

"Good idea," Ana said. "Don't be afraid. You don't have to change the world. If you get one student to write a letter and several students to talk to their parents about Darfur, what a success." I was already used to hearing Ana's wonderful voice, with all the slurs and round sounds.

"Yeah, I guess you're right."

That night I told them about my childhood friend, Inaya, and how we had found each other and the horror that had come to her. I talked about how the Janjaweed killed and raped people right in front of family members and then set fire to their homes, forcing them to leave without any food or possessions.

"They usually end up in international displaced persons camps or refugee camps. There are over two hundred thousand refugees."

"Jamie," Zahir interjected, "there are refugees everywhere. In Pakistan there are over three million Afghan refugees."

I didn't know what to say. Here I was talking about a place and people so far away, people I'd certainly never meet, and Zahir might have family who were actually living and experiencing the same terrors as those in Darfur. I thought about praising Ana about the soup, but the timing would be wrong. Zahir methodically buttered a piece of bread as if lost in thought.

"Maybe when Jamie is finished with her work on Darfur, she can start to educate people about the problems in Afghanistan," Beah said. The thought threw me, reminded me that this kind of work would never be finished. Even if I no longer worked for Akasha, the needs would still be there.

"Chances are you won't get one person to care. Fighting the war on terror began in Afghanistan. The news says America won that war. Clean deal," Zahir said quietly, yet with bitterness, as he sipped his soup.

It was the first time I heard Zahir mention his homeland. The tension was painful. I felt to blame since I was the one who brought up Darfur and my assignment to educate the community. This must be the source of his pain, that his people, maybe even a father or a sister, were suffering, and there was nothing he could do.

"Not everyone feels that way, Zahir," Beah said. "Sometimes people don't know what to do, to think. The media feeds us with snippets of emotionalism." I admired her wisdom.

"I know. I'm sorry." He finished his soup and bread. No one else said much. It was obvious the subject was painful and personal for him. He stood and washed his bowl, set it to dry. "Ana, thank you. The soup was wonderful."

"You're welcome." She kept her eyes on him. In fact, we all did as he walked out the back door. I ran after him. I needed to say something, apologize, or something.

"Zahir, wait up."

"Jamie, please." He stopped and turned. "I do better on my own. Before you came, I ate alone, I worked without being interrupted. No one invited me to wine tasting parties."

"And you liked it better that way?" He opened his mouth to speak, but didn't say anything. He was frustrated and hurt. "Tell me you're okay," I added. "And if not, what I can do to help. I'm sorry about what is going on in Afghanistan."

"It's not your fault. I'm not even sure whose fault it is. Our history is complex." He looked up at the starry sky. His features softened a little.

"I like us having dinner," I said, looking at him as he gazed at the stars, "and talking. I know this sounds sentimental and cheesy, but you guys are my family right now."

"Don't take it personally. I just need some time alone. I have become used to it." He headed down the path toward his cottage. I watched him, wondering if there was something else I could say. A star shot down from the sky and for a moment I thought about making a wish.

"Did you see that?"

"Yes." As I turned to head back inside, Zahir called, "Jamie, can you tell Ana that I'll be eating dinner tomorrow night."

I smiled and stuck my hands in my pocket to warm them. "I will tell her. I will."

Ana and Beah were still at the table when I walked back in.

"Nice of you to check on him," Beah said.

"War leaves its victims so empty and scarred," Ana said. I filled my glass with water at the tap and sat back down. Ana and Zahir had more in common than I initially could have guessed.

"He's going to have dinner with us again tomorrow. Maybe we can talk about the weather," I joked.

"Let's not," Beah said. "I've spent my whole life talking about the weather."

I took another piece of bread, not because I was hungry, but I wasn't ready to get up.

"Ana, I've been wondering. Since we're not going to talk about the weather," I said hesitantly, "could you tell me what happened to Avrum and Eidel? Was your sister okay after those men …?" I stopped. Ana turned. I worried that I shouldn't have brought her past up. She took from the counter another notebook and handed it to me.

"Take it to your room. Beah and I will visit."

I made a small fire and sat in the chair and began to read.

After the evil men left, Sarah and I moved from our parents' bed to our own, where the sheets still smelled innocent. There we held each other. My arms wrapped around her waist, one of her arms around mine, the other holding a warm rag on my tongue to stop the bleeding. My sister must have woken before the sun, for when I stumbled out of bed, Doc Gilbert was there, ready to look at my maimed tongue. The man I had always thought of as grumpy and mean had tears in the corners of his eyes when he told me it was a clean cut and that it probably wouldn't get infected. The bleeding had stopped and that was the best we could hope for. He then took his glasses off and rubbed his eyes. "And you, Sarah. Do you need anything from me?"

Sarah squared her shoulders and told him no, that they hadn't hurt her. I thought about protesting. But I knew she had her reasons for keeping silent about her pain. She walked with a limp for several days but did appear fine when Papa and Mama and baby Delly eventually came home.

After the doctor left, we cleaned Papa and Mama's sheets. We did our best to hammer the floorboards back down. Even though it was cold and raining, we opened windows and the front door to air out the house. I often wondered if Sarah would have ever wanted our parents to know about the men if it weren't for my tongue.

Mama walked in the door first. Papa tended to the horses. She held the baby so tightly to her breast I thought she might be suffocating it. The pain that floated in the room as Mama shut the door was so thick, I swore I could see it: little particles of soot, never landing, held up by our breaths. Without one of us saying a word, we all stood there and cried. At the time, I didn't know why Mama cried. I wondered if someone had already said something to her. Maybe Doctor Gilbert had found them on the road.

"Here is your sister, Delly," Mama said. She held her out, uncovered the baby's face so we could see. Sarah didn't move, so I did. Awkwardly, I took the infant and sat down.

"Mama?" Sarah was looking at her, concerned. Mama fell into her rocking chair and rocked, though I was the one with the baby. "Are you fine, Mama?" Mama looked up and brushed her tears away.

"How were things while we were gone?" Mama asked. "You both look pale and frightened." Sarah fell to her knees and placed her head on Mama's lap.

"They came, Mama. The bad men came." Mama stroked Sarah's hair. "They came looking for Avrum and Eidel. I was glad you had already left." Mama held Sarah's face between her hands, so she could look at her straight on.

"Did they hurt you or Ana?" I nodded my head and I was glad to see Sarah did, too.

"Mama, they took Ana's tongue."

Mama leaped to her feet. She lifted my chin and told me to stick out my tongue. I had never seen such worry and hatred in my mama's eyes. I was afraid.

"Now!" she ordered.

"Doctor Gilbert said she will heal."

I opened my mouth, while being careful not to disturb the baby. Mama clapped her hand over her mouth, and then she ran outside and vomited. Papa didn't come in that night. He stayed out chopping down a beautiful maple tree and had the whole tree ready for firewood in the morning.

My Mama and Papa never went back to Belgium. Sarah, Delly, and I did though, seventeen years later. Mama was ill and begged us to go and look for Avrum and Eidel's child.

"Just make sure he is safe and happy," she said.

I wanted to go back to our farm, but Sarah didn't want to. We later heard it was gone, burned in a fire.

"Good," Sarah said when she heard.

"But we had good times there, too, Sarah. Don't forget the good," I reminded her.

Delly was the whole family's blessing. Her lightheartedness and her sense of humor kept us all from madness. She had never known the heartache we all knew. She had never met Avrum or Eidel, although, as a child, she used to name her dolls Eidel. After all, she was named after Eidel. We didn't care that it was a Hebrew name. Mama said it was her child, and that Catholics could name their child a Hebrew name if they wished.

We went to the Bayen's farm where Avrum and Eidel had to leave their baby. Our parents had never contacted them, not because they didn't want to, but because the Bayens had said they never wanted to hear from any of them again. They had adopted the baby as their own and wanted the child to believe they were his parents. Mama and Papa had respected their wishes all those years. But now Sarah, Delly and I respected Mama's wish to find Eidel's son.

Pulling up to Dylan and Florine Bayen's farm, we could see a fence that surrounded the pasture. It hadn't been painted in years; part of it leaned over, and boards were missing. The pigpen was kept up, and several pigs slept in dry dirt. Summer was in full bloom, and as I stepped out of the car, a familiar feeling fell on my heart. Memories came to me I could barely make out; in my mind's eye they looked like rain on photographs. Sorrow fell on me. I had to remind myself that I had had a good childhood.

Delly, only seventeen and still full of wonder, said, "It's beautiful here. Do you think they would mind if I took pictures of their orchard? And those hills over there?" She wanted to be a photographer. She had told me she wanted to capture the beauty of the world.

"You should ask," Sarah said.

A man walked out of the barn. His cheeks were sunk inside his face. We greeted him. Sarah apologized for inconveniencing him, told him we were from Nostldorf and had migrated to America after the war. As she was talking, his wife came out, and when she discovered we were Belgian, visiting from America, she invited us into her home. Her husband trudged back to his work.

Our mama had said the family that adopted Avrum and Eidel's child was well off. At one time they might have been, but nothing was kept up. It wasn't that anything was dirty or unclean, just unkept. Steps and walls hadn't been painted. Windows hadn't been washed. Furniture with rips and stuffing sticking out hadn't been replaced. But the saddest thing was that there were no current photographs. This gave me an eerie feeling. There were old wedding *photographs: one of the Bayens and maybe one of each of their parents. There was one photo of their farm years ago, maybe when Mama had seen it. Although the photograph was in black and white, everything sparkled brightly: trees filled with fruit, a freshly painted swing, smiles, and in the arms of Florine Bayen, a child. Was he a year old? Eighteen months? His grin was broad, his eyes large and wide set. I tried to see if he resembled Avrum or Eidel. I couldn't tell. My memories of them blurred unless I concentrated. I closed my eyes to bring them both back to life.*

Mrs. Bayen asked us to sit. Sarah took her time getting to the reason we were at their home all the way from America. She was like that. She could talk and not say anything.

"Who did you say your parents were?" Mrs. Bayen finally asked.

"I didn't say."

"Arnaud and Delphine," I said quickly before my tongue could be a hindrance.

Mrs. Bayen's eyes fell on me. Sarah glared. Sarah took over talking again. Delly then told the story. "We're looking for a child, a man. He would be my age, seventeen. You adopted him, took him right after he was born. He's Jewish."

"Jewish. No. He wasn't Jewish. We made sure of that. He was Catholic, like us, baptized Catholic," Mrs. Bayen said, sitting more toward the edge of her worn chair.

"Maybe he became Catholic, but he was Eidel and Avrum's child. They were killed at Auschwitz a few months after she gave birth. They lived with us for almost two years. Mama is ill and she requested we make sure he is doing well, that he doesn't need anything. May we see him? May we meet him?" Sarah asked. "I know Papa and Mama …" Sarah's voice trailed off when she saw tears rolling down the woman's cheeks.

"Are you the other baby?" She gazed at Delly. "The one that was born the next day?"

"Yes," Delly said.

"You are the Jew. I told the priest I wanted no Jew baby. Your mother took the Jew as her own. And I took ... and we took Simon."

Delly stood and turned toward Sarah and me. We both shook our heads.

"No. Delly is my mama's child," I said.

Delly's usual cheerful expression faltered. She waited for Sarah or me to tell her that the lady was lying. Yet hearing this story was shocking to us, too.

"Your mama's child is dead. Simon died of pneumonia when he was two years old."

Delly ran out of the house, and Sarah and I ran after her. She was younger and leaner and faster, and we would have never caught her if she hadn't tripped over a fallen tree branch. I didn't know what to say and Sarah must not have, either. We all sat in each other's arms and cried. My heart broke for Delly. But I felt Mama's pain, too. Though she loved Delly as her own, every day she must have ached to hold her son, the son she never raised or even spoke of. I never loved anyone that day as much as I loved my mama.

When we got back home, Delly stopped going to school and stayed by Mama's side, reading to her, brushing her hair, painting her fingernails. Delly smiled, but not often and always with tears in her eyes, as she held our mama's hand.

"Simon is a beautiful young man," Sarah told our mama. "He has all the good a Belgian man could have. His wide set eyes miraculously look just like yours, Mama. He's a miracle."

On the day our mama died, she asked us to tell her about Simon again. And as she was fading off towards death, she said, "I think I see him. Thank you, my children."

Chapter Sixteen

While eating Ana's cooking and sitting by Zahir's large crackling fires, Zahir, Beah, Ana and I became friends. Ana's new openness invited us all to talk and laugh and share. When I had returned her journal, she took me in her arms and held me for a long time. I held her, too, but her arms were outside of mine. I thought it odd that she was the one holding me until she said, "It feels so good to still love."

During our dinners, I shared with reserve, as I believe Beah and Zahir did. They knew my mother had died. They knew my relationships with my brother and father were strained. They didn't know that I had been engaged to be married; they didn't know that I had loved my baby and that I had lost her. I knew Zahir was from Afghanistan, that he moved to the United States when he was nine, that he didn't go to movies or anywhere for that matter, that he loved bread that had "air" in it, that he didn't like lukewarm food, that he wore shoes purely to be respectful to others. "Even when it's cold?" I asked one drizzly evening.

"Yes."

"What about when it snows?" I asked.

"It doesn't snow here."

"What if it did?"

"He says he prefers no shoes, Jamie. Why don't you leave it at that?" Beah said.

"She's asking me to be exact. She knows that no one could prefer to be barefoot all the time and in all circumstances. She's also wanting to be right," he smiled, as he buttered another piece of Ana's homemade bread.

"That's not true," I countered. "I don't need to be right." But the truth was I liked teasing Zahir. I liked that it was okay that I could be "right" around him. This was a new feeling for me, a feeling I had a hard time naming. My first year of high school I aced an algebra test. The teacher had me stand and bow. I felt mortified, not proud. That same day I also received an A plus on an English essay. The next night, my dad had had conferences with my teachers. He came home and teased me, calling me smarty pants. From then on, out of unease and a desire to blend in, I donned the coat of ambiguity, of ignorance. I wore that coat not proudly but with the belief that this was what my father, my teachers, my employees, and even my friends wanted from me. Except with Aunt Gazella. She told me that I was smarter than I led people to believe.

Ana, Zahir, Beah and I talked about our days. I kept them updated on the government policies concerning Darfur. I told them about being turned down to speak at the local high school because I had no credentials — that was the word the principal used. I told them that I could hardly blame him. I had only recently discovered that there even was a place called Darfur.

"Go to Sudan. Visit the camps," Zahir suggested.

"Okay," I said, dismissively. "And then I'll run for Senate." I thought everyone would laugh — no one did.

Ana told us of her visit to see Delly's daughter, Delphine, named after their mother. Ana lived and worked at Fallow Springs to be near Delphine and her son. They lived three miles away. Ana would often walk. "Sarah never married. She's been gone since '78. Delly died five years ago. Cancer got her. I feel blessed to be able to live so close to Delphine and Connor." I loved Ana's resilience, her ability to feel blessed in the light of such tragedy and heartache.

Occasionally, Akasha joined us for dinner. When she did, we ate in the dining room instead of the kitchen. As far as I know, nothing was said about this; it was just where Ana told me to set the table. I enjoyed the formality, the china, the tall upright chairs, the Raphael copy of *The School of Athens*, and the tall candles in the center of the table, although conversations seemed stilted. Beah, who was always asking questions about Ana's recipes, or Zahir's work in the garden, or the cute Fed-Ex man, sat quietly. Akasha asked about Ana and her niece and grandnephew. She knew their name, ages, and many of their likes and dislikes. No one asked me about my work in front of Akasha, and for this I was grateful. I didn't want her to know how I struggled with the new assignment of community awareness.

It was weird to me that I had initially thought of Zahir as an old man. Beah had told me he was thirty-two, only five years older than I was. It took several weeks for this fact to penetrate. The night I saw him with his shirt unbuttoned, it was plain that he was in great shape. Although not often, sometimes he was jovial, almost lighthearted, like a younger man. The more I got to know him, the more his actual age became apparent. I told Ana and Beah this one day when we went to the grocery store together. They both laughed. We were in the produce section, helping Ana with her list. I now welcomed this average outing almost as much as I used to dread it.

"Maybe he was feigning age because he was interested in Ana," Beah said.

"The thought of romance hasn't passed my mind in thirty years." Ana tore a plastic bag off the roll and began to assess mushrooms.

"Romance isn't usually felt in the mind," Beah said, waving a zucchini.

"Maybe you should have propositioned him then," Ana countered.

"Hello," I said. "Neither one of you is too old for friendship."

"Friendship?" Beah turned and pointed the zucchini at me. "I'm capable of more than friendship, thank you very much." I tried to continue, but Beah was on a roll.

"His hair has gray. He is constantly bending with his hands in the dirt. He has the soul of an old wise man — we know," Beah said, placing a bag of zucchinis in the basket. "But, I'm sure there is youthful blood still running through his veins." She slid her arm around my waist.

"What else do we need?" I asked Ana, looking to change the subject. She was still picking out mushrooms, inspecting each one. I would have just grabbed a handful. I looked at my bag of red potatoes and hoped they were to her satisfaction.

✿ ✿ ✿

Zahir and I had nothing readily in common. He was born and raised in Afghanistan, a Muslim, educated, patient. He didn't own a television or a computer. He spoke proper English and never cussed, even though, I argued, there were appropriate times to use profanity.

"Like when?"

"Yeah, like when?" Beah demanded. We were cleaning the dishes after dinner one evening.

"You're one to talk Beah. I've heard you cuss," I retorted.

Ana laughed, and Zahir asked again when it was appropriate. My hands were submerged in dishwater. Ana preferred hand-washed dishes to using a dishwasher. I had already scrubbed all the plates, glasses and most of the silverware. I searched for more spoons, swishing my hand along the bottom of the sink in the lukewarm water. My finger found the blade of a knife. I felt it slice fast and deep.

"Damn it!" I pulled my hand out of the water. Blood pooled on my fingertip. "Damn."

"Once is enough. You made your point," Beah said, as she left to get the first aid kit.

"I wasn't trying to make a point." Zahir and Ana laughed. "I'm okay, really. Thanks for asking," I said, sucking the blood from my finger. Zahir walked over and took hold of my hand.

"Is it deep?" he asked, looking at the cut. "Not bad. But I'm sure it hurts." It was the first time he had ever touched me.

Zahir rarely mentioned his family, as if their lives didn't parallel his. I talked about my brother and dad as if their lives defined mine. He was a good listener. And he was funny and his laugh was infectious. And because we basically lived together, sort of as a family, our relationship deepened. I could be myself, and what a relief that was. But he was still reserved with me, with all of us.

One Sunday afternoon, rain settled in, making the daylight gloomy. I had been trying to write a letter to Joel, wanting to tell him that it had been good to see him and that I was grateful he kept Santos's letters from me. I didn't know that finding the words would be so difficult, so painful. I wrote, *Thanks for the hug. I really needed it.* All the times during the trial or when I was pregnant when I needed a hug, all Joel could give me were words taken from the Bible. And then there was Santos. He really thought we could get back together. He really thought that I could kiss him again and let him lie next to me. When, I wondered, would he become a distant memory, just a small ache in my stomach as my therapist told me he would? When? I set my pen down.

I hadn't told all this to anybody. Despite their invitation to share.

I looked at the movie schedule I had printed yesterday, glanced at my watch, and then slipped on my shoes and coat. I ran over to Zahir's. I would ask him again. He had enjoyed the movies at my birthday party. Maybe I could convince him to see another. I hoped he wasn't working in the greenhouse. On many rainy days that was where he'd spend his time, planting this, hammering that. But the greenhouse light wasn't on. I knocked on his door. He didn't have an overhang. As I waited, I got wet. Although I'd never been invited inside his place before, at the moment I would have welcomed a dry spot. He opened the door. I expected him to say something like, "Come in out of the rain." If we were in a movie that's what he would have said. But we weren't in a movie.

"Jamie," he greeted me. "Is there another spider in the house?" After that first spider incident in my bedroom, I had taken to running over to Zahir's anytime I stumbled upon a spider, stumbled being the right word. Zahir would kindly come over, catch the spider in a jar, and take it outside.

"No, no spider," I said, feeling embarrassed. What must he think of my petty fear? "I came by to see if you wanted to go to the movies."

"No."

"Sean Penn is in it."

"It's the middle of the day." This statement struck me as odd. I had never thought that movies were supposed to be seen only at night. Yet he was no longer simply saying no.

"It's raining." I looked up. My coat dripped.

"Oh, yes. Come in."

I stepped into his home and slipped my hood off. Water fell onto his tiled floor.

"Sorry." He wore khakis and a Stanford sweatshirt, and, per usual, no shoes. His home was warm, but I felt chilled. For a moment, I didn't know what else to say, but then, glancing at his sweatshirt, I asked, "So you went to Stanford?"

"Let me get you a towel." He walked to the bathroom and on his way answered my question. "Yes." He fetched me a towel and laid one on the floor. He hadn't invited me in to sit down or offered me something to drink.

"I've taken a few classes. Withdrew from most of them." I thought about telling him about the film class I sat in, but I knew being a guest in a class wasn't the same as being in college. I hated that I felt stupid not having a degree. But the truth was I respected people who had college educations. I wondered if Akasha went to Stanford? Harvard? Yale? Maybe Cambridge?

Looking past Zahir into a sitting room, I remembered the night I saw him bending in prayer. Cushions and a bamboo mat lay on the floor. Candles and a fire were burning. On an end table next to the front door was a pile of books and a magazine: *The War*, *Aircraft Down*, and *A Short History of Iraq*. The books seemed appropriate, but the magazine struck me as odd. *Maxim*. It didn't fit with my image of him like the books. I reminded myself that all of us spilled out in different directions.

"Did you want to go to school?" Zahir asked. I thought about my job at Cinemark, at Outback, at Blockbuster, at Trinity National Bank.

"Yeah."

"You're still young, Jamie."

"I know I'm still young, Zahir." I thought about telling him how in this country, "the land of promise," there were still the haves and the have-nots. There were still those who were born to go to school and make something of their lives and those who are bred just to struggle and get by. "In high school, I stopped caring about schoolwork. I think my teachers and dad just hoped I wouldn't get knocked up or on drugs."

"What did you want?"

"I wasn't sure exactly. I was a teen in angst." I pulled my coat tighter for comfort though I no longer felt chilled. "At the end of my senior year, a school counselor came into my English class one day and instructed us average kids to pick a vocation. 'What's a vocation?' one kid asked. And then this jerk of a so-called counselor spent fifty minutes explaining what a vocation was and the different ones we could choose." I began to sweat. The anger quickly came back as if this had happened yesterday. "I still remember some. Let's see ... carpentry, concrete, plumbing, carpet cleaning, car towing, blah, blah, blah — but none of that appealed to me. He asked what interested us. The kids in front of me said motorcross bikes, bike repair, business, and mechanics. I said, 'I like movies.' Then he laughed, saying, 'Being a movie star is a pipe dream. I'm here to ground you.'"

"That pissed me off. So I told him, 'I didn't say I want to be an actor. You asked what we were interested in.' He said, 'I like movies, too. Nothing like a John Wayne movie.'

"Then this girl to the side of me raised her hand and said, 'Mr. Anderson?' and he spreads his feet apart and pulls his shoulders back and says, 'Don't call me uncle. I ain't your uncle.' Trying to imitate John Wayne, I guess. The girl with the question looked totally confused and scared, and he went on, 'No need to call me sir, neither, or grandpa, or Methuselah. I can whip you to a frazzle.' Boys behind me laughed. Mr. Anderson's eyes were still on the girl, so she asked, 'Well, what do you want me to call you?' This must have been what he was hoping for, because his eyes got all sparkly and he goes, 'Name is Coach Anderson.' Then he dropped the John Wayne persona and told us, 'Once a coach always a coach!' For the rest of the period we had to sit there and listen to him talk about his football coaching experiences."

"Did the girl ever get her questioned answered?" Zahir asked.

"She never got to even ask her question."

"Okay, I'll go." He smiled. "I'll even wear shoes."

"Is that an Afghani thing?"

"What?" He opened the closet nearest the door.

"Not wearing shoes."

"It is not. It's a personal thing."

After the movie, we drove home by the Fallbrook Winery. I asked Zahir if he wanted to stop and taste and then wondered if it were against the Koran to drink. Yet I had seen him with wine before. Without answering, he pulled in. I had never been to a winery before. The idea was romantic to me, like sipping coffee in Paris.

As he parked the car, we continued our conversation about working for Akasha and how much we liked being around Ana and Beah. He hadn't mentioned anything about the movie, which made me feel a bit uncomfortable.

"Don't you think it's funny that we don't know anything about Akasha or Beah? It wasn't until recently that Ana told me how she lost her tongue." I stopped short. I didn't want to expose Ana's tragic past if she hadn't already told him. I didn't feel it was for me to tell. What he said next surprised me.

"Yes, I know. Beah told me."

"She did? Beah is always contradicting herself," I said, walking into the tasting room. "The day I moved in, she said that people in the house respected each other's privacy. She even gave me a key to my room, insisting that people locked their doors. But no one locks anything. Keys are left in cars. Secret tunnels to wine cellars are left unbolted." We walked slowly to the entrance, the sound of gravel crushing under our feet.

"My privacy has been respected. Until you came, days would go by and I wouldn't see or speak to anyone." This statement hurt. But I knew he didn't mean for it to.

"And that's what you wanted?"

"That is what I wanted. What I needed."

I loved his honesty and his ability to communicate who he was.

"And you can still tell me no if I become too annoying." I pulled at his sweatshirt and smiled. I told him that ever since Ana told me her story, I'd been dreaming about Belgium and World War II, although I knew little about it.

We stood at the counter inside the winery. Several other people were already tasting. Zahir picked up a sheet of paper, glanced at the selections, then placed two twenties down. He had done this before, which I was glad about. I was afraid of looking foolish. For some reason, people who knew a lot about wine seemed a bit snobby. I thought about the movie *Sideways* and Miles's line, "I am not drinking any fucking Merlot!"

When we received our first tastes, Zahir told me, "A small village in the Netherlands, called Nieuwlande, unanimously decided that each of the 117 homes would shelter at least one Jew during the war, insuring that no one would tell the Gestapo. A town in France called Le Chambon-sur-Lignon sheltered five thousand Jews, more Jews than any other town in Europe. I have always had an admiration of the French ever since I heard that story. When the Nazi patrols came, the Jews ran and hid in the woods. After the Nazis had left, the villagers would sing. That was the clue that it was safe, the Jews could come out from hiding."

I asked him where he'd heard this story. He said, "School, books … I'm not sure. But the image of all these farmers, clerks, moms, children all singing while the ones they harbored came out from hiding has always stuck with me. Humanity at its finest."

We tasted a Pinot Grigio, then a Chardonnay. The description said light, crisp, buttery, and fruity. And, you know, I did taste the buttery flavor.

While we were waiting to be poured a Zinfandel, Zahir told me that Jewish mothers would give their children to be raised in Christian homes or in monasteries.

"It must have been difficult for Jews to trust any Christians at that time," I said.

He sat silently for a moment then said, "If one looks at history and how many people died at the sword of God's word, it's obvious that today is no different. God wants America in Iraq, Allah wants Westerners punished. The Bosnian Serbs killed Bosnian Muslims. Eight thousand in less than two weeks. It would be easy to think it's religion that is to blame. But there are some beautiful things being done by religious people. I try to focus on those people. The people who see God as love in action."

The man behind the counter poured us some Zinfandel. Zahir told me about an Italian Catholic monk who saved Jews by forging documents. I had never seen Zahir so fired up. While he talked, he appeared less wounded.

"All I know about that war is what I learned from seeing *Saving Private Ryan* and *The Thin Red Line*," I confessed. "And it's only recently that I've learned anything about the Bosnia Genocide."

"I can give you some books to read if you're interested," he said. "Or I have some documentaries. *A Cry from the Grave* tells the story of the mass killings in Srebrenica, Bosnia. One of the most alarming statements I remember from that film was when the Dutch UN soldier says, 'I thought nothing would happen because the world was watching.'" Zahir swirled the wine in his glass and then finished it. "Did you see the series *Band of Brothers*? I'm sure you'd find it interesting and well done."

I wondered at this. The man who told me he didn't watch movies. Then, as if he read my mind he said, "I used to watch lots of movies, Jamie."

Zahir bought two bottles of Merlot. He held up a bottle. "One for Akasha," he explained. "Let's go to one more winery. There is a small one just down this road." He seemed to be having more fun wine tasting than he ever had at dinner, or at the movies. I guessed passion was what it had to do with. He liked wine and history.

"So Zahir loves World War II history?" I asked, to continue the conversation that fired him up.

"I loved all history."

"Loved. As in past tense. Seems to me you still love it." He made a sound but said no word. "Is that what you got your degree in?" I pressed.

"Yes. I thought that by learning about history — not just Afghan history or history of the Middle East, but as much about history as I could — I could somehow help people to not make the same mistakes. There is a saying to that effect, yes?"

"There is. 'History repeats itself.'"

Zahir became the quiet man I knew him to be again. I wished I had kept my cynicism to myself. He pulled into a winery that I had never seen before. The wooden sign was worn. The road leading up to the tasting room was dirt. Vines covered the brick building; smoke drifted from the chimney. There was just one other car in the lot when we pulled in, a small blue Toyota pickup truck, like the one Joel drove. I looked inside the cab as we walked past but when I saw the trash on the floor, the Wal-Mart oil change sticker, and the VOTE FOR PEROT button pinned to an old ballcap, I knew it wasn't Joel's car. I felt both disappointed and relieved.

"My brother has a truck like that one." I was beginning to think that I sometimes talked to keep from feeling or thinking. Talking could create a buzz inside my head that numbed. I thought of Lily and her incessant chattering. I missed her. Zahir looked over his shoulder at the pickup.

"Not his, I take it?"

As we walked inside, a couple was leaving. Zahir opened the door first for me and kept it open for them, saying hello. The man looked intently at Zahir and, as he stepped past Zahir, who was still holding the door, said, "I guess they let terrorists anywhere these days."

"What did he say?" My hands shook with anger. "Was he talking to you?" Zahir steered me toward the tasting counter. I wanted to run after the man and say something to him. All I could think of were cuss words. You fucking bastard; you ignorant jackass; he's my friend, you fucker. But none of these things sounded intelligent. If this were a movie, how would I script it? The hero would run and punch him in the face and he'd fall to the floor apologizing — I'd be a *Charlie's Angels* sort of woman. Or, I'd be articulate like Cate Blanchett and say something scathing, and the man would feel small and worthless. Instead, I stood in front of the wine counter and stared blankly at the scores of wine bottles that lined the back wall.

"Jamie?" Zahir held a glass out to me. "Wine tasting."

Zahir had already paid for the tasting. He leaned into the counter. I noticed his tan Sketchers for the first time; they looked new. I wanted to somehow make Zahir feel better, let him know that not all Americans thought that way.

"Jamie," he said again. "It's obvious that man's comment hurt you more than me."

"It's just that— " I touched his arm. He looked down at my hand. It was a disapproving look, the kind I'd seen in numerous movies, subtle without being mean. I pulled away. He didn't want to be touched or pitied for being an Afghan.

"I'm okay. I love my heritage, as sad and complex as it is. It is who I am."

I took a drink of the wine without thinking about the taste. "Not bad," he said, after tasting his.

"Not bad." My feelings were hurt — I didn't know whether by the jackass's comment or by Zahir's disapproving look. I took another taste of the wine. It was dry and bitter. "I don't like it," I said. I threw the last swallow in the ceramic basin.

The proprietor came over and gave us a taste of a Pinot Noir. I didn't say anything else. I wasn't sulking; I just didn't know what to say.

"This wine isn't my favorite, but people love it ever since that movie came out. Sales and the price have tripled," said the man behind the counter.

"I've always been more of a Zinfandel person," Zahir said.

"Cabernet for me," the man said, "What was the name of that movie? My mind isn't what it was. Or at least what I imagined it to be." He laughed.

Zahir smiled and placed his hand on my shoulder and squeezed. "This is your area. What was the movie?"

"*Sideways.*" My shoulder felt warm where he had touched it, and, happy to be talking about something I knew about; I thawed. "Won the best screenplay at the Golden Globes and the Academy Awards. It was great because the movie didn't rely on blockbuster names or special effects, just a wonderful script."

"Movie buff are you? A few weeks ago, Doris Day was in here. She still gets my heart throbbing. So many old men fall for the young ones. But my eyes find beauty in women my own age. Like you will always be beautiful. Beauty ages well." He held up his glass as if he was toasting me, but he didn't say cheers. I wanted to tell him I wasn't beautiful, that I was plain, that I had hips, that I was too short for my large feet, and that my breasts were too small. His compliment embarrassed me, yet I felt flattered. He told us that he'd lived and worked at the winery for forty years.

"You grew up here?"

"Grew up in Kentucky. Whiskey, moonshine country. Then I was in the Navy for four years. Back then, it was a great way to see the world. I had no action in the Fifties." He asked from where we were visiting.

"Just up the road. We both are employees at Fallow Springs," Zahir said.

"Fallow Springs. Now there's a place with history." He leaned in and placed his elbow on the bar and rubbed his scruffy chin. "Used to be Château la Louvière when a baron owned it. He planned to create a winery that would compete with the wineries in France. Was friends with Stanford, the lumber giant."

Zahir nodded his head in agreement. I wondered if it could be the same Stanford as Stanford University, maybe a relative.

"Then the place sat for ten years. I guess the bank owned it, just used by teenagers for late night ..., well, you know. Then, Takahashi bought it, and still no grapes would grow. Put tons of money into it, too."

"No grapes would grow anywhere on that property?" Zahir asked in surprise.

"Rumor is, not a one. Ms. Duval, your boss, had all the vines removed. She put in the garden and let the natural grass take over the hillside behind the mansion."

I was trying to recall if I ever saw a fruit-bearing tree at Fallow Springs. Zahir's gardens were so elaborate and beautiful, something bloomed at all times.

"What would happen?"

"I was told — this was years ago, by one of the growers who worked for Takahashi — that sometimes the vines would just wilt and die. Sometimes the plant would flourish but no fruit would grow."

"Has anyone tried to grow any other fruit on the place?" Zahir asked.

"Not that I know of. After the Takahashis gave up on the land, they lost lots of money. I heard they moved back to Japan. A young couple bought it and turned it into a hotel. Beautiful place. I went to the open house. This was about thirty years ago. Guests said it was haunted. I never heard of any ghost sightings, but people would hear things and leave saying that they felt a strong energy. Before, it was just known for its barren land."

The story was becoming more and more enchanting. I wondered if he knew more about Akasha, too.

"I'm the gardener. Everything flourishes. Except she's requested no grapevines or fruit trees. I've always questioned this. The soil is rich, fertile."

"Amazing place." He shook his head the way people do when they are processing information — known, new, forgotten. He stuck a corkscrew into a bottle and slowly twisted. After the corked popped, he placed three glasses on the counter and poured wine into each. He turned the open sign to closed, then pulled up a chair. "Not in a hurry, are you?" He swirled the wine in his glass and then stuck his large nose into the wide opening and inhaled. "Here, one on the house. It's our '94 Cab Reserve. One of my favorites." He slid a glass toward me and then Zahir.

"Thank you," I said.

"What do you taste?" he asked, after we had our first sip.

"Leather. Tobacco," Zahir said.

The man laughed. He was more attuned to Zahir's sense of humor than I was.

"You two been working there long, at Fallow Springs?"

I said, "No," and Zahir said, "A while," at the same time.

"Long enough to know some of the secrets, I suppose. I hear that lady is very particular about who she lets work there or even step onto the place."

"Particular," I repeated. I had never made the cut into a "particular" crowd. Maybe he meant outcasts. "What kind of secrets?" I glanced at Zahir. Finally someone was going to tell me something about the mansion, about Akasha. Maybe she lost her leg on Fallow Springs? I considered telling him that I found a tunnel under my bed that led to the wine cellar, but every time I brought this up to people, they acted like it was a perfectly normal thing. Then again, I only brought it up with those who lived in the house.

Zahir grew quiet again. Did he know more about where we lived than I did? He never seemed inquisitive like I was. It was now dark, and the rain fell again, echoing in the stone room.

"Name's Demetrios Papadopoulos, by the way." The man threw another log on the fire.

"Zahir, and this is Jamie Shire."

"Ah, 'Shire,' like in Great Britain. Interesting last name."

I wasn't so certain it was interesting; neither was I so sure it had anything to do with Great Britain.

"Are both your parents Greek?" Zahir asked.

"Just Dad." Zahir and Demetrios then began to talk about his father's migration. Although it was interesting, I wanted to get back to the secrets of Fallow Springs. As Zahir asked more questions and Demetrios drank and elaborated more, I was beginning to wonder if Zahir was avoiding the topic on purpose. Instead of tuning them out and waiting for an opportunity to bring up Fallow Springs again, I tried to be polite and made a conscious effort to listen to Demetrios's history, confident we'd get back to the subject I wanted to discuss.

"My mother's history is far less interesting. She was born and raised in Anaheim back when Orange County was a beautiful place to live."

Zahir and Demetrios shared stories about the places they had been. Zahir mentioned Palestine, Iran, Turkey, France, and Germany. Demetrios had traveled to Italy, Germany, Hawaii, Chili, and Peru. Demetrios turned to me.

"And where have you been?" I thought about the world map that I had hung in my apartment, the red thumbtacks that I had forcefully pushed through the yellowed paper into the wall. And then I thought about the day I had to move in with Lily. I removed the tacks, leaving small holes in Paris, Arles, Rome, Tuscany, Venice, Salzburg, the Swiss Alps, the Island of Santorini in Greece, and then there were Thailand and Kenya, Machu Picchu. I had one yellow thumbtack, just one tack representing where I'd been.

"I've only been to Mexico," I said.

"Well, where would you like to go?"

"I want to go anywhere, but if I had to choose today— " I stopped, recalling my desire to climb the steps to the Parthenon, float through the canals in Venice, sip coffee at a café in Paris. "I'd go to Chad."

"Chad? Are you wanting to see elephants or Darfuri refugees?" I liked that he knew.

"Yes. The people of Darfur. I want to hear their stories. But an elephant would be nice, too."

"You must be a philanthropist."

"No, not really, but Akasha Duval is." I took this opportunity to ask what I wanted to know more about. "Tell me more about the secrets at Fallow Springs."

"Like I said, I haven't spent much time there," Demetrios said and drank the rest of his wine. "I do know that the house's original owner had a thing for medieval castles and hidden passageways. I'm told that not all of them have been found. I know that there is an underground lake a half-mile from the house. It's beautiful, and eerie."

Part of me felt fear. I began to second-guess my decision for working for Akasha and really liking it, feeling like part of something larger. The place was even more mysterious than I'd imagined. And yet I felt excitement, wanting to go see the lake. "An underground lake? Do you know how to get there?"

"Sure. But I won't go back. It's like going to the Parthenon; a place that used to be so alive with thought, art, beauty, and no longer is. Once is enough. It stays with you for a lifetime." He stopped himself and washed a wine glass. "That was an awful analogy. The truth is simple. I fell in love with a woman, and we used to go there. The visions in my head are painful enough. It would be too hard to see it again." He dried the glass, held it up to the light to make sure it was clean. "I loved her. You know what I mean?"

Zahir grunted something, almost inaudibly. I didn't understand what he'd muttered, but when I looked at him, it became obvious I wasn't supposed to hear. I swirled my wine and took a drink. Demetrios took Zahir's empty glass and cleaned it. Zahir and I took that as our cue that it was time to go. Zahir held out his hand. Demetrios wrapped both of his hands around it.

"Don't you want to know where it is?" he asked. "The lake?"

Before I could say yes, Zahir said, "I know where it is."

Chapter Seventeen

*T*hat night I dreamed of lakes — dried up lakes, forgotten lakes. I dreamed of deserts. I dreamed of Africa.

When I awoke, for a moment I thought I was in Africa. But then I rolled over and became fully alert. Why not ask Akasha if I could take a trip? It seemed so absurd, coming from someone who had only traveled to Mexico. I dressed, wondering what to do with my day. Write letters, ask Zahir to take me to the hidden lake, go to Africa? I wasn't leaving the thought alone. I emailed Inaya. I told her about the wine tasting, but then I asked what her thoughts were about me visiting the refugees of Darfur. I knew I wouldn't hear from her soon. I had emailed her a couple of times since we met in San Francisco; I had only heard back one time. Throwing out the question felt right.

She might say stay home where you are safe; she might say go.

After I pressed send, I paced my room. What do I think, Jamie Shire from Great Britain? I went to Akasha's office. She wasn't there, seldom was. I mounted the marble stairs then knocked on her bedroom door. I hadn't been to her bedroom since the day I'd sneaked in. It was only 8:00 a.m., but she was an early riser. There was no call of "I'm coming," although I heard something like footsteps head toward the door. I waited.

Akasha opened the door wearing a short nightgown. And although I tried not to look, I saw that she hadn't put on her prosthetic leg. Her stump was barely visible beneath the silk ivory gown.

"I'm sorry, I'll come back. Or can we meet later in your office?" I guessed she wouldn't want me to see her like this.

"Come in, Jamie."

She left the door open and started hopping back to where I assumed she had been sitting, on her verandah. She pointed her one foot, stretching the leg out. I thought of the legs of a horse, long and muscular. The sun shone through a potted Japanese maple. Leaf shadows appeared on her face, moving, giving life to this scene. Her good leg was stretched into the morning light. I sat down, totally submerged in shade. I felt underdressed in my jeans and Roxy t-shirt.

"Coffee?" There were two china pots on the table. Next to her sat a cup of tea. She poured a cup of coffee and held it out for me. Creamer sat next to the pot. I could smell the vanilla. I was the only one who used flavored creamer.

"Were you expecting me?" Once again I was struck by the oddity of her knowing things about me. She must have thought I was coming; why else would she have vanilla creamer?

"Why would you ask that?" She stirred her tea.

I poured creamer into my coffee — the black liquid swirled around the cream. Her stump was visible. The leg severed right about the knee.

"How did it happen?" I asked.

"Jamie, I know you didn't come here to talk about my leg."

"And I know you don't drink coffee. How did you know I was coming?"

"I didn't, not really."

"What if I did? What if I did come here to ask about your leg? What if I came to ask where you go when you leave for days at a time?"

"You wouldn't. You're sensitive to other's feelings. Asking those questions would make you feel uncomfortable. Just like I didn't come out and ask you where you went when you left last month."

Instantly, I was reminded of Santos. It was so easy to feel the pain of my loss, my empty arms. Instead of saying anything about my pain, revealing something intimate about myself, I said, "People ask where people are going all the time."

"That's because those people are going to their mother's for a visit, to a conference, to a Hawaiian all-inclusive vacation. That's not where I go and that's not where you went. And I'm not telling you anything you don't already know."

Before I could place too much thought into what she said, she did something I thought strange. She placed her hands on the back of her seat and stretched her right leg, the stump. I watched the muscles in her thigh extend and the movement run down as if the leg were still there and cramped or something.

"I heard this house is haunted," I said, knowing the statement was out of the blue. I explained the comment by telling her about the man Zahir and I met at the winery.

"Have you ever felt it haunted?" she asked. "Have you ever been scared?"

"No." What I felt was comfort, acceptance.

"I've heard the same thing but I love it here." She stared out on the hillside. For a moment she looked vulnerable. Maybe from revealing something she loved. But then she said, "What are you needing?" The sun rose above the maple; I felt the heat on my face, no longer in shadow.

"I think I need to go to Africa — Chad, to be exact. I want to see firsthand how the refugees are living. I need to educate myself. The principal at the local high school won't even let me talk to the students and, frankly, a part of me understands his position. I have no idea how much a trip like that would cost. I have no idea, at this point, how it would all work out. I mean, I'm not a doctor or a humanitarian aid worker. Zahir was the one who brought it up and— " I was starting to feel nervous, wondering if the idea was too crazy after all. "I don't even have a passport." I stopped. What I was asking for was scary, adventurous, and maybe even crazy. It could take months to plan.

"Money has a way of making those problems go away. I'll call Arnold." At first I wasn't sure whom she was referring to. Then I got it.

"Schwarzenegger. As in the *Terminator*."

She laughed.

"Why Chad and not Sudan?"

I explained to her that although most of the Darfuris were in IDP camps, camps for Internationally Displaced Persons in Sudan, that President Bashir had closed Sudan's borders. He was not letting people in. Americans who were going in were sneaking across Sudan's western border from The Republic of Chad, usually from a town called Tine. I had no plans to do that. There were several refugee camps in eastern Chad.

"What is the difference between an IDP camp and a refugee camp?" she asked.

"IDP camps are for people who are in their own country. So there are camps for Darfuris in Sudan, but it's becoming increasingly more difficult to get aid to these people. Refugee camps are for people outside of their country. There are Sudanese now living in Chad that I could visit."

"Yes, I want you to go. Bring information back on— " She took a sip of her tea. "Cold. I hate cold tea." She set her cup down.

I had to smile. I hated cool coffee. "On?" I said. "Information on …?"

"On whatever you see."

I spent the next few weeks planning my trip. Surprisingly, Beah was the person who helped the most. She knew how to get my passport, helped me with my traveling arrangements, and even found the name of the woman I'd need to contact once I reached Abeche in Chad. Her name was Heidi Zinsli. She worked for the UNHCR, the United Nations High Commissioner for Refugees. Beah was sure she'd be very helpful, and I was glad to hear this. Someone to help guide, who knew the ropes.

"Did you used to be a travel agent?" I asked her when she was helping me pick flights, looking over my shoulder as I worked on the computer. She laughed.

"No. Never even considered that profession."

Two weeks later, when Beah handed me my passport, I asked her if she'd worked for the State Department. She laughed again. "Well, I just wondered. I never knew anyone able to get a passport so fast. Never heard of it, except in the movies."

"No. Never worked for the government." She began to leave my room. "I wanted to dance at one point. Be a ballerina. But don't all girls?" I thought for a moment, and then shook my head.

"No. I didn't. But I did want to travel."

Chapter Eighteen

I made my way through the airport in N'Djamena, the capital of Chad, carrying my backpack and small suitcase, got a taxi, and went straight to my hotel. The man at La Meridien Chari check-in desk, used to business travelers, was nice and efficient. Before getting a bite to eat, checking out the hotel grounds, or asking where anything was, I went up to my room and locked the door.

I had wanted to travel my entire life. I had loved looking at Aunt Gazella's *National Geographic* magazines. As far back as I could remember, my fantasies had taken me to foreign places; the limits of my imagination expanded over lands, seas, and time. In my play, I'd explore the world fearlessly. And here I was in Africa, where, as a child, I had faced lions, played with black boys and girls, saved my mother from a cobra. And now I was sitting on a western-looking bed with my feet planted on orange tile, staring at a blank TV screen, wondering if I should turn it on or crawl into the sheets.

I had jet lag, but all the travel books advised getting on the new time zone first thing and it was only 4 o'clock in the afternoon. I showered.

"Where?" my father had asked when I called him a week ago to tell him I was going to Chad to visit refugee camps.

"Chad. Africa." Already, I had regretted the phone call. I hadn't talked to him but once since I'd left Grass Valley. But a part of me thought that since I was going so far away on what could be viewed as a dangerous trip, it was the responsible thing to do.

"What in the hell for? You haven't gone and joined anything have you?"

"Joined? Like what?"

"One of them organizations that don't pay. I heard you were making good money with that lady."

"No, Dad. Anyway, I won't be gone too long. Just wanted to say goodbye and that I love you. Tell Joel, too." I had intended to call Joel after Dad but now I'd decided this phone call was enough.

"You never told me why you're going." His tone changed. He must have known he was being too judgmental.

"Just a vacation. Call it that."

Inaya didn't answer my email until the day before I was to leave. This saddened me. I really thought I'd see her. After all, Sudan borders Kenya. I had called her home number and on the third attempt her mother answered. For a brief moment I thought it odd that I had never met her mother and that her mother was still alive — this was only because my mother was gone and in many ways Inaya did feel like my sister. Her mother said that Inaya was out of the country, working in Nepal. She then said to call if I needed anything while I was in Africa. I smiled at this; although Sudan bordered Kenya, I would still be about seventeen hundred miles away.

Inaya's email said she was proud of me, said to be careful and that she'd be in London in a couple of months. *Sister, let us meet up then*, she wrote. I smiled and wrote back, *I'll be thinking of you while in Chad. And yes, I will do my best to meet you in London.*

Ready to go out, I tied a bandana over my head like I had seen in many pictures of the aid workers who came to work in the camps. I wasn't sure if it was expected, or they did this out of respect, or just for comfort.

Once outside, I looked around a bit. The hotel was on one of the two paved roads in all of N'Djamena. Cars honked. Motorcycles whizzed by. Venders sold food. I was reminded of Mexico — my one trip out of the country with my then boyfriend. The aridness, the poverty, the lack of modern conveniences were like Mexico; I smelled exhaust, grilling meat. Dust floated up, meeting the sun. The similarities stopped there for me. Men wearing long white gowns hurried along the sides of the street. Women carried bundles on the tops of their heads. I smelled a spice I couldn't name. A camel trotted behind a boy.

I wore my "Fear No Art" t-shirt that had reminded Zahir of me when he'd seen it in a magazine. I wished he had come, too, or anyone else, Beah, Ana, or Akasha. This experience would have been much easier and fuller if Inaya were here, but I also liked imagining her in Nepal. Maybe her work there would bring her a sense of peace; whereas here there would be painful reminders.

Before heading east, closer to Sudan's borders and the refugee camps, I had to register with the local authorities, known as the *gendarmerie*, and meet with an advisor at the UNHCR. All that would have to wait until tomorrow. Then I hoped I'd be on a plane to Abeche, the fourth-largest city in Chad and out of which all the NGOs — non-governmental organizations — worked.

I stepped off a sort of curb, wanting to cross the street. A motorcycle came out of nowhere, startling me. I fell trying to get out of the way, then quickly scooted back away from the street. I heard a honk but didn't see the bike until it had already passed. I sat on the red dirt while several men from across the street stared. My eyes burned with tears that I refused to let fall. My side ached. I felt scared and humiliated.

No one offered me a hand. I had thought Africans would be different in this respect. I stood, dusted myself off, and walked across the street and said *bonjour* to the men who were still watching me. Not having anywhere to go and feeling defeated somehow, I went back to the hotel and ate a five-course French meal while looking out at the Chari River and watching fishermen in small boats.

The next morning, Dominique from the UNHCR gave me a press pass and said that there might be room for me on the World Food Program plane out of N'Djamena to Abeche. I would need to go to the airport and wait and see. Once there, I checked in with the pilot. He said that there probably was room but he had already okayed a doctor to join the party. He needed to see how much weight the doctor was going to bring. I couldn't place his accent. He could have been from England, South Africa, or Switzerland — accents were new to me.

"He'll be here soon. Always the last one to show up. I guess it goes with the M.D." I nodded, not really knowing if I thought it went with M.D. or not. He went to the front of the plane and checked the propeller. "How much equipment do you have?"

"Just what you see." My large backpack hung over my right shoulder.

"Good, good. Go ahead and take a seat. We'll make it work. I've flown overweight before." A plane overweight — was that something to be concerned about?

I stepped into the small six-seater plane and was greeted with hellos from four other passengers. I sat in the only empty row.

As soon as I got settled, the doctor climbed aboard. He took the place next to me. "Hey," he said. "Name's Doc."

"Jamie."

"Jim said you're press. Journalist?"

"No."

Before I could say anything more, he asked, "Are you famous? Must be famous. It's been so long since I've been up on who's hot in Hollywood. Are you the latest and greatest in Hollywood?"

I laughed. "Hardly. Although, I've been in the papers before." My words surprised me. It wasn't my way to make light of what had happened to me — I hoped he wouldn't ask.

"A woman with a past — my favorite kind."

Then the pilot's voice came through the speakers. "Welcome, ladies and gents. No peanuts, no cute, small bottles of al-co-hol. A bit overweight, but we should be okay."

"So have I," Doc added. "Maybe all of us white skins here in Chad have been in the papers."

"Maybe." He made me feel as if I belonged, that somehow I was like him.

Doc and I spoke some, though it was hard to talk over the sound of the engines. I asked him about Chadian hospitality. He said it got better once out of the capital. "It's kind of like comparing a New Yorker to someone from Tennessee."

When we landed, he told me that he and friends often met at the Sahel Café. "Ask anyone — they'll be able to help you find it. If you want to join us later, do." He grabbed his bag and, once outside the plane, began to gather up his boxes of medical supplies. A man was outside the plane waiting to help him.

I stepped down from the plane, needing fresh air. The recycled air from inside the plane felt thick. Sand and dust flew into my eyes and mouth. Fuel fumes saturated the arid air. As I stood deciding which way to go, sand kept hitting me in the face, even though the blades from the props had stopped turning. My cheeks were beginning to burn. There was no information desk, no customer service, no sign pointing me which way to go. The pilot noticed my hesitation.

"You okay, ma'am?"

"Thank you. I was just getting sand out of my eyes."

He laughed. "Good luck, ma'am."

Abeche, with a population over of 60,000 people, had no paved roads. I was told the town had swelled in size with all the NGOs using the city as their hub for reaching all the refugee camps. I finally found someone to drive me to the UNHCR where I could register and talk with Heidi Zinsli, the woman who was going to show me around Gaga Refugee Camp; I could have found a donkey more easily. Everywhere men and women rode on donkeys and used donkeys as truck beds. They were as ubiquitous as SUVs back home.

Heidi wasn't at the UNHCR compound. I was told I could wait or come back later. I asked about a hotel and the man recommended one not far from where I was dropped off.

"There may be something better," he said. "I just don't know. But I know there are worse."

A man wearing a nametag that said, "Idriss" checked me into a room. He had a wide, warm smile. Already I liked Abeche better than N'Djamena. I looked around the room and decided there was nothing to inspire me to stay — no television, no electricity. "We have water," Idriss had said, proudly, and water seemed like a good thing to have in the desert. The bed with its thin sheet and smokey-smelling blanket did tempt me, but instead of taking a nap, I put on some lip gloss and left.

When I came down the stairs, Idriss came out from behind his desk. He had been visiting with a man. He introduced him as his brother.

"She's from the U.S., California," he told his brother. That was when Idriss asked if I were a movie star.

"Oh, no," I said. I guessed it was the California stereotype. I asked him about the Sahel Café.

"The Sahel Café is not far, no. But my brother is a driver and has a new truck if you want a ride."

"I'd love a ride," I said. The roads were dusty and crowded. As I rode along with Idriss's brother in his new-to-him truck, I thought about the fact that I was oceans and countries away from home and I was getting around and doing fine. I felt just a tad bit heroic, like when I'd gotten my first job, my driver's license, the only A in my eighth grade English class.

At the café, four people sat drinking beer. I saw the back of Doc's head. As I approached the table, I instantly felt like an outsider. These people were dedicating and risking their lives. In my mind, they were on the same level as Martin Scorsese, Sean Penn, Nicole Kidman, and Russell Crowe. One man with a coarse, thick ponytail pulled up a chair for me even before Doc turned around and said hello. I guessed they were accustomed to welcoming new people.

"Join us," he said. I held out my hand and introduced myself.

"Jamie Shire," I said. If I had been asked to sit next to Russell Crowe, my body wouldn't have reacted any differently. My heart pounded.

"Saul."

Doc turned around. "You found us."

"Thanks for inviting me," I said. I took the seat and the beer that was offered me. I was sweating and dirt stuck to my arms. I felt it on my lips.

"Nice thing about working in Chad instead of Sudan," Saul said as he held up his bottle. "Beer." He asked whom I was working with.

"The woman I work for," I feebly began — I would stay with the facts, I decided — "she's wealthy beyond anything I can comprehend and she pays me to do philanthropic work. I'm here to, well, to see firsthand what's going on. I think I was given a press pass because I didn't fit into any other category. Sounds crazy, I know."

"Sounds like a good idea," said a woman who looked to be in her thirties. "I'm Sandrine." Her skin was beautiful and fair. I wondered how she managed not to get it sunburned and chapped from all the blowing sand.

"You work with Doc?" I asked.

"No. Doc and Thad work for Doctors without Borders. That's Thad." She pointed to a man seated next to Doc. He had a short, well-trimmed dark beard and wore a white shirt that resembled what the locals wore. "I work for the WFP, the World Food Program," Sandrine continued. "And Saul here is with the UNHCR. Thad is from South Africa, Doc and Saul the U.S., and I'm from Switzerland."

"Do you know Inaya Itudo? She works for the WFP."

"Sorry. I don't. It's a big organization."

"I know. It's just that she was here." I hoped Inaya's story wasn't already forgotten.

"In Abeche?" Sandrine looked puzzled.

"No, I don't think so." I thought of telling her Inaya's story, but decided maybe later. "I'm supposed to meet up with Heidi Zinsli from UNHCR. Do you know her?" I asked Saul.

"He knows her," Thad said. "In a carnal way." It was the first time Thad said anything.

"Why is it that you always use Catholic symbolism? It's disgraceful," Sandrine chided.

"Because my grandmother was a nun. I love Catholicism."

"Funny," she said, but didn't laugh. Doc and Saul both did and I couldn't help but smile. Several others whom I guessed to be aid workers walked toward us.

"And here she is," said Saul. "That's Heidi." He gestured with his head as she and her friends came in and sat at a table very close to ours. Hellos were exchanged by the two parties. Sandrine introduced me to Heidi. She was not overly friendly but said she'd meet me at the compound at 7:00 a.m. Then she sat down.

"Why are you here?" Doc asked, "if I may be so blunt."

I told them about Inaya, how she had lived with us, how she called me her sister, how she was taken and raped.

"Sorry to hear that," Doc said.

"I remember that story," Sandrine said.

A woman wearing a bright red and orange dress set food on the table. A fly instantly landed on some meat. Thad said something to her in French. I ordered rice and chicken and asked for another beer. "I'll try the Cameroon Castle this time," I said.

"You'll regret it," Doc warned. The server looked at me questioningly.

"Cameroon," I affirmed. "How did you all end up in Chad?" I asked, once she had left.

"We're all running away," Saul said. He tugged absentmindedly at his ponytail.

"That's not true," Heidi said from the other table. She had been watching our table since she sat down. "I'm not running. This is what I do, what I've always wanted to do." She was a lot smaller than I had pictured. Saul was almost twice her size, in girth and height. And she wore her hair short, almost manly.

"I thought you wanted to have a family some day. Can't do that here," Saul said.

"My dad was a surgeon," Doc said. I figured he wanted to take the conversation from Heidi and Saul. "I lived a cushy, sheltered life in D.C. Went straight to medical school, graduated when I was 27. I worked at the same hospital Dad worked at and hated it. Hated the politics, the prestige, and the expectations to be like Dad. I was tired of helping people who weren't helping themselves. So I joined *Médecins Sans Frontières*. Best decision of my life. This is where I fit." He took a long hit from his cigarette. "Plus, you can smoke in Africa without breaking any laws."

I had learned from my research that *Médecins Sans Frontières* was the same as Doctors without Borders. I was glad no one had to explain this to me.

Saul said that he didn't know any other life. His dad and mom were missionaries. He hated religion but loved people, so after college he joined the Peace Corps and then got a job with UNHCR.

"And what about you?" Saul said, looking at Thad.

Thad said the pay was good. The others laughed, nodding. Saul then asked about the woman I was working for: What was motivating her?

"I don't know," I said. "I know very little, really. She's beautiful, mysterious. Never been married. No kids. And did I say she's gorgeous?"

"Beautiful — same thing," Sandrine said. Sandrine was beautiful, too, but in the way that came from confidence.

"She hired you to spend money?" Thad asked.

"Yes, to help spend her money."

"To appease her guilt," Heidi suggested. She was now sitting closer to our table than her own. Heidi intimidated me with her curt ways, but I also felt sorry for her. It seemed that Heidi wanted Saul and I knew the feeling of wanting a man more than he wanted me. I thought of Sean, my boyfriend before Santos. I gave and gave; all he gave was disdain.

"Maybe she's a drug lord, or part of the Mafia, you think?" Thad asked.

"I don't think." I became defensive. "I know the situations sounds weird. All the people who work for her at the mansion are interesting, sort of misfits, like the toys in that movie, *Rudolph, the Red-Nosed Reindeer*. And I love them all."

"Never seen it," Thad said. Saul and Doc began to sing the tune.

"How did you come to work for this woman?" Heidi asked. Her question was innocent enough, but I thought she was more interested in how Akasha had become involved in my being here. I imagined that Akasha gave tens of thousands of dollars and that was why Heidi had to deal with me, another responsibility. Why did Akasha give? I wasn't exactly sure. Was it to appease her guilt? Her nightgowns cost more than my entire five-year wardrobe. I began to say I needed a change, the same thing I had told Akasha the day I went in for an interview.

"Maybe because I was running," I said truthfully — running from the pain of losing my baby, the judgment I experienced from my dad and brother, the continued loss of my mother, my mediocre life.

"From?" Doc asked. And then something weird happened. My whole life I had been relating my experiences to scenes in movies I had seen. But as I sat at this dusty table with these people in this unbelievable place, I began to see my life as my own movie, as if I were the director and not just the one who paid eight bucks to see the flick.

"I'm sorry," I said, after a lengthy pause. "It's only just occurring to me that maybe I have been running to something and not from something."

There was a moment of quiet and Doc lit another cigarette. Thad and Heidi took drinks from their beers. Saul and Sandrine kept their eyes on me. I took a deep breath.

"My mother died when I was ten. After she died, I felt so empty, and then insecure for the rest of my life, it seems. Two years ago, I was pregnant with a baby girl. Clara — that's what I named her. The man I was with, the man I was supposed to marry ..." I hesitated. Doc blew his smoke out and it enveloped all of us at the table, hanging like fog in central California. I brought my beer to my lips, chugging it until it was empty, the painful scene of what happened next crowding into my mind, its awfulness compressed into a few short seconds in my memory.

"Clara died," I finally said. "Santos, her father, punched me — punched her and killed her. And after that, I sat around hating him." I remembered what Ana had said about how hatred gave her energy, and how my hatred for Santos gave me the ability to sit in that courtroom day after day, how hatred fueled me and then, when he finally got sentenced, I felt empty again. I couldn't sustain the hatred even though I wanted to. I remembered walking around feeling transparent, weightless. There were moments I had to question if I were alive.

Sandrine said, "Hey, that's awful." Saul squeezed my shoulder. Everyone's eyes were on me.

"I met Akasha in a coffeehouse. I'm not sure what she saw in me or why she hired me. But I took the job. That job is what I'm doing here." I shook my head. "The whole thing is totally bizarre. Now, I live with Akasha, and Beah. She's the strong, loving housekeeper. And Ana, she's from Belgium. Her family harbored Jews during World War II. And Zahir, the Stanford graduate from Kabul, he's the gardener. And I love them. So that's it." I stood and opened my wallet. "How much?" Saul placed his hand up, as if to say, stop, I've got it. "I'm tired, " I said. "Goodnight."

"Take care," Sandrine said. Heidi nodded as I looked at her. Thad, who was by her, managed to get the beer label off his beer. Doc stood.

"Let me walk back with you."

We walked in silence. The streets smelled of dirt and donkeys. People were still out, but only a fraction compared to earlier. Some of the buildings had wooden porches that resembled facades in 1940s Westerns. On storefronts the writing was in both French and Arabic. I tried to make out words. I couldn't. The moon was bright but I could still see stars. Electricity was scarce in Abeche. I heard it was even scarce in N'Djamena, though Chad was oil-rich. As we came to the building before the hotel, I said, "Thanks for inviting me."

"A lot of refugee women have lost their babies," Doc said.

"So I've read. Babies that they were carrying on their backs. The bullets came from behind and hit the babies. And I know, Doc, I know that their suffering is worse than mine, which only makes mine that more putrid. If I were that mother, I'd want to die."

"Your pain is your pain, Jamie. You can't compare human worth and you can't compare suffering. I'm glad you're here, even if it's for a short time. New blood fuels us. Some of our hearts are drying up." He looked up at the sky. "I guess it's from being in this desert."

Chapter Nineteen

*T*he following morning, I drove with Heidi and another female aid worker to Camp Gaga, an hour-and-a-half's drive from Abeche. Our hired driver's name was Djudo, a Chadian who spoke little English. As we drove in the early morning light with the Land Cruiser rattling and coughing over piles and ditches of sand, no one talked. I welcomed the silence. I had read that this area of the Sahel used to have wildlife but most were gone. Giraffe, lion, cheetah, and oryx all gone. I looked for a long neck, a set of eyes anyway. Was it simply that they had all been hunted? Or were they smart and had left before food and water became too scarce?

The drive was bumpy. And although the Land Cruiser was enclosed, sand and dirt seeped through, coating me with a thin layer of grime. The aid workers had this long, hard drive every day, for weeks, months, and even years on end. I had always lived within fifteen minutes of any place I ever worked and I still usually walked in to work flustered and late.

The desert looked uninhabitable. It was easy to take for granted how beautiful Grass Valley was, sitting on the edge of the Sierra Nevada Mountains, and Fallow Springs, hidden in the wine country on rich soil bubbling with life.

There was the occasional umbrella thorn acacia, a light sketching of a tree compared to the brilliantly leaved green trees in *The Lion King*. Other than that, sand and wind. The wind in the desert constantly buried the dead and dug them back up. I didn't want to see any bones, bleached from sun. I didn't want to see any bodies fallen from dehydration and malnutrition. But I had read that many Darfuris were out here in unknown, unmarked graves.

My mother's sister, my aunt Erika, died in the desert. Mom used to tell Joel and me stories about how funny she was, about her dreams of being a model. She had wanted to keep Erika's spirit alive in us kids. I hadn't thought about Erika in years. She died while Mom was carrying me. She died alone in Yucca Valley when her Volkswagen Bug had gotten stuck. She tried to walk out, but collapsed a quarter-mile from a ranger station. Her body was found six months later by people dune buggying. I supposed she still had her hair, and some flesh — of course, the family never saw her body. She was identified through dental records.

When Mom talked about her death, a lesson was always implicit: if you get stranded in the desert, don't leave your vehicle. Don't forget you could drink the water in the window washer container. Try to burn your tires. Never go into the desert alone. My aunt had thought the desert was beautiful, and I suppose, in some ways, if I were to look at it differently, I could see the beauty, too. "Even if your goal is to pray and get closer with God," Mom would add. According to the family, Erika had gone to the desert for that reason. But how did they know? Because she had taken her Bible? Because she hadn't taken water or food? Of course, she had no cell phone. And she had been heartbroken. Was there a better time to try to hear God than when you were heartbroken? Erika had recently discovered that the man whom she was in love with and had been sleeping with was married. Also, she had recently gone to see a doctor who had laughed at her when she told him she wanted to be a model. "Your breasts are not the same size. How can you be a model?" he had said to her. Hurtful, yes. Unprofessional, yes. But true? Aren't all women's breasts slightly different sizes? If she were destined to be a model, couldn't that be remedied by padding? What about the fact that she was short? Pretty but not beautiful? With poor skin? With little self-esteem? These issues were never part of the story.

She died. Young. Ashamed. Heartbroken. Holding the Holy Bible. And thirsty.

My mother had missed her.

After an hour of driving, Heidi began to share information about the refugees in Gaga. Although she didn't address me directly, I knew she was talking to me. "Gaga is the newest of camps, though it's tripled in size within the last year. You'll get some fresh stories. Many children have been born in this camp. If God would strike the dicks of the men running the Sudanese government, the children wouldn't end up being raised here. The majority of the refugees are women and children. This is because Janjaweed either killed the men and boys, or they joined the rebel groups."

We came upon makeshift tents laced through the sand as far as my eyes could see. Some were UNHCR tents; others were simply made of bright fabric, maybe the remnants from women's clothing. Women wore bright beautiful reds, blues, yellows, and greens, while the men all wore white.

When the Land Cruiser rolled to a stop, Heidi parked and stepped out. I followed. "This is now the home for thirteen thousand people."

Children came running toward us. And for the first several seconds, small children were all I saw. We stood still while children surrounded us and touched our hands. I decided I'd do whatever I had to not to cry. The aid workers didn't have energy for my tears, and the refugees deserved something better than an American's tears.

Heidi hadn't said another word or taken another step. I guessed one never got used to the look of suffering, or of surviving in spite of all the suffering. I couldn't help but question what God saw from His vantage point. I wasn't in the habit of thinking about what God thought. I could only imagine that He must see what was happening here from a different perspective than I.

"This is Gaga," Heidi told me. We walked by a tent with "UNHCR" stenciled boldly on the top. "First, we find this." She reached down and picked up a handful of dirt, letting it fly away in the wind. "And then we set up these." She rapped the tent with her knuckles.

"Water, of course, is another big issue. When people are desperate, they'll drink anything, hoping that it will be okay. It usually isn't. Our doctor friends deal with a lifetime of diarrhea cases in one week in this place, and diarrhea kills here. It's not just an inconvenience." There were scraps of metal outside some of the tents. "Those are used for catching water. There are no gentle rains here —

it's either drought or floods. People drown every year during the rainy season. This land is almost uninhabitable."

A boy ran through the crowd of children to Heidi. He held a tattered piece of paper bearing a crayon drawing in his hand. He gave it to her and ran away. She stopped and looked at it. A small black stick figure was being held by a very large woman with golden hair.

"His name is Akaye. He's had a crush on me ever since I shared some chocolate-covered raisins with him. That was months ago." I liked this side of Heidi.

People watched us as we passed. I wanted to study each face and remember every one, remember every new sound, every color on every woman's dress. I wondered how many of these people in this camp Heidi knew, a camp larger than my hometown.

In the UNHCR tent, Heidi was greeted with hellos. She introduced me. I was glad that people didn't seem to be bothered by my presence. I secretly hoped that maybe they had taken me for one of them, someone who was there to help make a difference. I wondered whether, if my life had been different, if I had been introduced to this life years before, I would have chosen this.

An African man ducked through the door. Once inside, he stood tall, regal. "Another woman was raped last night," he said, "on the east side of the camp. I found her. She was just lying in the dirt; said she didn't want to come back." He had another accent I had never heard before.

When he noticed me, he introduced himself to me and I learned he was Rwandan. I so wanted to hear more about his life. Was he a Hutu? Or Tutsi? But why did I want to know this? Wasn't it illegal to ask that question now?

A reporter came in then, from the BBC. Heidi excused herself to talk with the reporter. I was learning that press was common here, and needed.

Jakob, a nurse, stopped in to run something by Heidi, but seeing that she was busy, talked with me instead.

"Would you like to come check out the Medical Clinic?"

"Go," Heidi said, when I looked at her. She was great at listening to two conversations at once. "Come back when you're ready."

"I think she likes me around," I joked to Jakob.

"Don't take it personally. She's like that with everyone. Saul just broke up with her. Have you met him?"

"I have."

"It's different here."

As we walked to the medical tent, we passed a woman who sat on her haunches, stirring a stew of some kind. The ancient scene contrasted with the modern conversation I was having with Jakob gave me a disoriented feeling.

"She may be sleeping with someone else next week and they'll all be eating dinner together. But the fact is, Heidi wants him back. They were a great couple. She laughed a lot more when she was with him."

Every time we'd pass someone, Jakob said, "*Salaam.*"

I'd smile.

"That's another thing, everyone knows everyone else's business. How long you here for?"

"Seven days."

"Long way for just a week. Maybe not long enough to get caught up in any of the drama. But who knows?" he teased. "People work fast."

"I had no idea," I said. "I mean, I had no idea what to expect. I don't want to get in anyone's way."

"There's always work to do. Always a hand to hold. Children to play soccer with." He kicked a ball that had rolled his way. "That's the thing I love about this work — gets me back to the basics of what we need in this life."

At the medical tent, five people lay on mats under a small tree outside.

"Good morning, I'll be back in a jiffy," Jakob said to the patients. To me he said, "Those are the sick who need monitoring but aren't sick enough to have a bed. We'll send them home by the end of the day." Then he laughed. It was hard for me to see the humor.

Neither guts and gore movies nor war movies have ever freaked me out. But when I walked into the medical tent, I immediately became nauseated. The smell was some kind of disinfectant, mixed with blood and rancid skin. I waited for Jakob as he talked to a man lying on a bed. I stood next to a bed with a woman sitting and gently rocking. I thought she must be the woman who was raped last night. I glanced over and smiled. She lowered her eyes and placed her scarf over her mouth. She looked to be sixteen, maybe younger. Jakob turned his attention back to me and spread his arms out.

"Welcome," he said. Then he gestured to the back of the tent. "Over there, that is the operating room. In front of it is Wing B and on this side, Wing A." Both Wing A and Wing B were rows of beds. "For very little money, we could add a new wing and you could name it anything you want. Give those people on the mats outside a bed."

His last comment made me feel weird. As if I were the one with the money, as though I could help but wasn't.

Jakob began with his good mornings to the patients inside the hospital tent. And then I saw him sit down next to the patient he said he'd been concerned about all night. It became clear that I'd be as needed and useful in this place as I made myself. No one held anyone's hands for very long.

Thad was across the room sewing up a young boy's leg. The boy sat trying to play with a small toy truck that had only three wheels. He winced every time the needle poked through his skin. Thad talked to the boy while suturing his wound. He was animated, telling him a story about his childhood dog. Maybe the concept of a dog as a best friend was lost on the boy, for the boy didn't respond in any way to the story, only the needle. It wasn't until Thad began to bark like a dog and say that he was done stitching did the boy smile. But his smile was worth waiting for, unadorned, unfettered, like a baby who doesn't know cruelty yet. Where it came from or how long he'd be able to muster up that smile, I couldn't say.

"Your dog is like my camel," the boy said.

Thad looked up and saw me and he smiled, a nice smile but different. He said, "Hello, Jamie," over the other noise. "Yes," he said to the boy.

After he washed his hands, he came over and asked me how I was faring. That was the word he used. I hadn't moved that far from the woman on the bed. She now talked in a soft voice to a woman wearing an African Union uniform. There was no place for me to go; yet I didn't want to encroach upon anyone's space. Thad went to the girl's bedside.

"She's bleeding," the AU soldier said.

"What is her name?"

"Nourasham."

"Tell her I'm sorry to keep her waiting," he said.

"She says she fell off a donkey. She says she speaks a bit of English."

Thad bent over her. "I need to examine you." She cast her eyes down. "Let's take her behind the O.R. curtain," he told the soldier. He and the African Union woman picked up the flimsy bed and moved it to the O.R., which was nothing more than a sheet separating space from the rest of the tent.

"Jamie, you can be my assistant." He didn't wait for a reply. The AU woman didn't give me any questioning looks. As I followed, Jakob looked over and said, "Like I said, always something that needs to be done." I moved, although I felt stunned, wondering how I could possibly help a doctor. Thad pulled on gloves and handed me a pair.

Nothing was laid out on a silver tray like it would be in the U.S.: speculum, KY jelly, and long cotton swab. Instead, Thad went and got the supplies he needed and set them on the bed. There were no stirrups.

He told Nourasham he needed her to open her legs. She opened her legs only inches. "Falls can be very painful and need to be examined," he said. She relaxed enough for him to be able to open her legs.

I felt her tension and fear and shame. She pulled her scarf over her eyes. She had blood caked on her thighs. Her pubic hair was dried in clumps from what looked and smelled like blood and semen. As if the wound had recently reopened and fresh blood had pooled on clumps of already dried blood.

"Jamie, get a wet rag."

I got one. He moved over and told me to clean her. The lips of her vagina were swollen. She had sores on the inside of her thighs as if she had gotten a rug burn. As I cleaned in between the lips, I tried to be as gentle as I could. I wanted to look her in the eyes to see if I were hurting her. But I didn't. I couldn't. She had gone somewhere else in her mind.

Thad asked me if I had ever seen what a healthy vagina looked like. I told him yes. "Good," he grunted. "A lot of women haven't." He pointed to a few white lines next to her vagina.

"She's been circumcised. I'll have to sew her back up." He said. "I need to examine you inside," Thad said to the woman. "It will hurt." She let her scarf fall from her eyes and nodded.

I watched Thad stick two fingers inside her vagina and saw his wrist move. My body reacted and I could feel the pressure of when I, too, had a doctor feeling for lumps. But I was sure he wasn't looking for ovarian cancer. I tried to imagine what this would be like with opened wounds. I saw a tear develop on each side of her eye, and I knew she was in great pain.

"We're out of local antiseptic, Jamie. You may need to help hold her while I sew her. Can't leave that sore open."

I felt myself wanting to protest, to say, are you kidding? You can't sew up a woman's vagina with no antiseptic! In that instant, I learned that different rules applied here. There would be no running down and purchasing the pain medication. There was no way she could simply reschedule her appointment. Instead, I held one side of her body still while the AU soldier held the other. But Nourasham wasn't protesting. Although her body flinched from time to time, she wasn't fighting the pain. I watched Thad moving his needle down and in and up. His movements were graceful, gentle. After he tied the last knot, he guided the girl's legs together, saying something to her in Arabic — she didn't respond in any way — and then he turned to the AU soldier.

"She'll be fine in a few days. She has no internal bleeding." He took his gloves off and threw them in a plastic can, then immediately washed his hands. He looked at me. "Are women ever fine after something like that? Now, let's hope she's not pregnant." He pointed to a table with a small shelf. "Jamie, there's our pharmacy. Give her the 500-milligram ibuprofen, enough for two a day for four days." He went and sat on a stool next to the man Jakob had been with earlier. I hadn't noticed before but now I saw that the man's leg had been amputated. Maybe from a gunshot wound. I thought of Akasha. It was because of her that I was here, in Africa, experiencing this surreal existence. I vowed I'd make myself useful.

I picked up several bottles looking for something that resembled ibuprofen. Many labels were in French. Pasted across a large bottle was a piece of masking tape that said IBUPROFEN. I opened the bottle and placed ten pills in a small envelope — giving her two extra just in case. Then I took another pill and a small Dixie cup and brought it to her. The women from the AU had left.

"*Salaam,*" I said.

With an open palm I held out the large white pill. Nourasham took it. "Have you ever swallowed a pill before?" I asked her. I opened my mouth and pantomimed placing the pill on the back of my tongue and then drinking the water. I helped her sit up and gave her some water. She swallowed the large pill. Giving her the rest of the pills, I explained what Thad had said. "Take two a day, one in the morning with food and one in the evening with food." I wasn't sure she understood.

I helped her off the portable bed. With her pale yellow scarf, she wrapped her head and left the medical tent. She had no visible wounds. She had both her legs. But it was easy to see that her dignity had been ripped away from her, as if it were a leg, a breast, or clumps of her hair.

❁ ❁ ❁

Later, at the Sahel Café, Thad told me that rape was especially painful for Sudanese women. "Darfuri women circumcise and infibulate girls, making sex painful, and I'm sure, rape excruciating."

"What is infibulation?"

"After cutting off the clitoris, they sew the lips of the labia, leaving only a small hole for urinating and menstrual bleeding. Maybe, when this is all over, that will change."

I thought about this. What caused a society to change an ancient custom? One that held no importance anymore? Weren't American men still being circumcised? Would that ever change?

After eating some chicken and rice, I wondered if this was really French cuisine or Chadian. Saul ordered another round, but I stood up and said, "Not for me." I couldn't keep my eyes open. I was even more tired than I had been the night before. The reality of the refugees' suffering was getting to me. I needed to lie down.

I said my goodnights and again Doc joined me until we came to my hotel. I thanked him. And asked him if his escorting me was necessary. Was Abeche so dangerous?

"No. I needed the fresh air. I like my cigarettes, but I don't appreciate others'."

As I fell asleep, I found myself praying, asking God to care for his African children. I tried to ask this without bitterness, but feeling as if He abandoned them.

The next day, I told Heidi that I wanted to find an interpreter. Heidi thought it was a great idea and said she knew someone who'd be perfect. "Listen to their stories and then share them with the world," she said. I smiled when she said this, for who was I to tell the world? That was George Clooney's job, Angelina Jolie's job. Mia Farrow's job.

I thought it would be great if a powerful Hollywood writer would write a screenplay. Maybe Paul Haggis. People would start to ask questions. What? Where? When? There would be tears. Did tears bring people to act?

My interpreter, Sashi, spoke Arabic, French, and English. She said she was from Khartoum, Sudan's capital. "I used to be proud to be from my nation's capital," she said. Her skin was black although she told me she was Arab. On our way into the camp, she told me that her grandfather had married an Arab. "It has been beneficial to be Arab for a long time, even in Khartoum: better jobs, better food, better place to live. Black is no good in Africa."

When she said this, my head jerked around. I stared at her, seeking some indication that she was kidding. I thought about what Zahir had said about pre-World War II. That many Germans had been very poor and hungry, and when Hitler promised employment, dignity, and food, many Germans easily became Nazis without looking at what it really meant to be a Nazi, what it really meant to hate.

"My brother is a Janjaweed," she told me as we walked out of the UNHCR tent into the dusty streets of the refugee camp. "At first I didn't know what that meant, but when I heard, I had to help fix all the evil he is doing. I pray Allah will help us soon. Until then, I will stay in this camp and help the people my brother is killing. He shames me."

Sashi's zest and ability to talk reminded me of Lily.

"I make it my job to meet people and see what I can do." She stopped and bent down. I thought she was going to pick up a handful of dirt as Heidi had done, but instead she fetched up a tiny piece of discarded paper and held it in her hand until she came upon a small cooking fire, where she placed the paper into flames.

That evening, before going down to dinner, I sat in my room and wrote everything I could remember about the day. I had never seen such suffering — wounds the size of lakes, wounds left unclean because the need for daily survival was so strong. I then began to storyboard a scene that had left me speechless.

I had sat next to a boy, Mohammed, who had been tied to a stick. When I first saw him, I gasped, wondering if he were being abused. Inside the barren tent, Mohammed sat with his knees pulled to his chest. He rested his thigh on a thick piece of wood that had been hammered into the ground, a tattered rope tied to his birdlike ankle. His eyes danced with fear — maybe with images that wouldn't go away no matter how many times he closed his lids.

"I try to sit and talk to him a little every day. He needs a friend," Sashi had said, "but today I'll leave you."

"Is he being punished?" We stood at the entrance of the tent. The blazing sun poured into the dim shelter.

"No. His mother is afraid for him. He runs off. She has five other children to care for. He was found covered in blood, blood that was not his own, the day after the Janjaweed attacked his village."

"And he hasn't talked since," I guessed. I walked into the tent, letting the flap close, wanting to close off the light, thinking it felt too bright for him.

"Not yet. He is from the Zaghawa tribe. He has fight in his blood."

I sat, pulling my knees to my chest like his. The ground was dusty and cold. But soon this desert heat would scald my skin, trying to reach my soul. I didn't know what to say to Mohammed. His chin rested on his knees, but he did look at me. I could see that his eyes held more than fear; they were eyes of a wounded child and eyes of prey.

I felt a small pinprick on my neck. I jumped, and fanned my shirt to make sure a spider or something hadn't crawled down my back. But he didn't lose his composure. I apologized.

"I'm sorry." I continued to look for the spider and for a moment I wondered if it had been a snake. Black mambas were fast. But were there mambas in Chad? I wished I knew. Reassuring myself that I was fine, I willed myself to sit back down and focus my attention on the boy. What could I tell him? Would the sound of a language he didn't understand help him to feel better or would it irritate him? I told him the story about David and Goliath, embellishing here and there, not really knowing the story all that well. I assured him that some day his Goliath would be slain, although I thought grimly as I told him this that I wasn't sure it would happen in time to save this boy.

It had been a long time since a Bible story felt comforting. Here I was thousands of miles away from home, in a Muslim country, and I was telling a Christian story and receiving comfort from it. In some way I hoped the story transcended language. I wanted to hug the boy. But that would be fulfilling my need and not necessarily his. It wasn't until Sashi returned that he had anything to say.

"He says he wants to touch your skin."

With open palms I held out both my hands. I was still bending down to be at his level. Using one fingertip, he touched the largest vein on my wrist and traced it inches up my arm. He said something and Sashi smiled.

"What did he say?" I asked.
"He said, 'The same.'"

Chapter Twenty

I thought about ways that I could communicate Mohammed's pain and his mother's need to keep him safe as I drew a small, stick-figure storyboard. But imagining his life on the silver screen felt impossible. I turned to a blank page in my journal and started writing.

The room was hot and, although I had just showered, my skin felt sweaty and dusty. I wrote more. I thought about the Darfuri loyalty to family, how they stayed with each other and helped each other, not with a sense of duty, but because that was simply what they did. Just like I breathed. All those years I stayed in Grass Valley afraid to venture off — was it because I needed intimacy? Sadly, the only person I felt intimate with was Lily, and her friendship was generally contingent on whether she had a man in her life. My relationships with

Beah, Ana, and Zahir were strong, although they hadn't been in my life for very long.

I heard banging outside my window. I stood and pulled back the curtain. Men were unloading chairs and a table; one stopped to smoke a cigarette. I breathed in deeply, but the smoke didn't make it up to the third floor. I wanted the men to look up. One was laughing. I wanted to wave to him. I loved their long white gowns. Were they called gowns? Dresses? I doubted it.

I sat back down on my bed and pulled the mosquito net closed even though it was still light out and I hadn't seen or heard any mosquitoes. I liked the net, the feeling of being enclosed in something. It was light and see-through, but it was there to create safety. I opened my bottle of anti-malarial pills and swallowed one.

I squirted lotion onto my leg, which was silly, for although I liked the moisture, sand stuck to my legs more readily with lotion. I rubbed the Japanese Cherry Blossom cream into my prickly leg, thankful that the hair was light. My calf still felt strong although I seldom ran these days. I examined an old scar. When I was fifteen, I had fallen off a kitchen chair onto a fork. It took years for the pain to go away. I gently rubbed the lotion into my other leg. When was the last time I had been touched? Held? Could I count my relationship with Santos? Did his touches and kisses count toward feeling loved, desired, needed? We did have sex after I agreed to marry him. He said he liked it a lot. It made him feel like a man. But for me, it was being pregnant that made me feel like a woman. My kisses were out of obligation. I'd close my eyes and kiss him like I'd pet the head of a neighbor's dog, without thought, without affection. It had been almost two years since I had had sex and then that was with him. Sex seemed tied to Santos, the man who was tied to my dead baby. And the funny thing was, as in sad-funny, I hadn't even thought about it, not for almost two years. Not even after watching movies where sex was used to stimulate the audience. Not even after listening to Lily go on and on about a great night of it. I hadn't touched myself. I hadn't bought a new bra or underwear. Nothing.

I unbuttoned my shorts, pulled them off. I slid my hand down my belly, to my pubic hair. What was the point? I wanted to forget. I wanted to forget about my sexual self. Sex was tied to pain. Sex was tied to getting pregnant.

My index finger made its way to the top of my clitoris. It was sensitive, yet dry. I told myself that I needed lubrication and wondered if my body was capable of making it, another thing I hadn't paid attention to.

I heard people talking outside my door. I froze. Then the noises moved down the stairs. I had heard that Africans were highly sexual. Was that simply another racial remark to explain away why so many Africans had AIDS? My skin was pale... it was absent of color. But looking more closely I saw the color beige, brown freckles, pink, purple shadows and blue veins — all this color telling me that I was alive. I was happy to feel a little wetness. I began to move my finger back up to wet my clitoris. But around my clitoris I felt pain. What about the woman being cut and then sewn? The pain she would feel from being raped. Her legs would be pushed apart, bruised. The perpetrator's inflamed penis thrusted in, tearing her vagina. Would she scream? Cry? Or would the shame silence her?

Images of the desert floated in my mind as I dried up. My stomach grumbled. I pulled my shorts back on and headed out for the Sahel Café.

I didn't know where to sit. The café was full. Part of me thought I should ask if I could sit at Heidi's table, but she wasn't the person I felt most comfortable with. Thad, Saul, and another woman whom I had never met sat at a table next to where Heidi sat. I was glad when Saul saw me and pulled out the chair next to him. I thought it interesting that Heidi and he were always close to one another but never at the same table.

He introduced me to Sharon, another doctor from Minnesota. She stuck her hand out. I lifted mine and then remembered that I hadn't washed it and rubbed it across my shirt.

"Sorry, sweaty." I burned with embarrassment.

"Sweaty?" Thad said, with a lift of an eyebrow. "We're all sweaty. Every single part of our bodies is always covered in sweat."

"And sand," Saul said.

"I'm always amazed at the places I find sand," Thad said.

Of course Thad couldn't know why I wiped my hand, although I knew what he was referring to.

"Leave her alone." Sharon poured half her beer into a glass for me. "His dry sense of humor is a cover-up."

I wondered if maybe Sharon and Thad used to have something going and it had turned cold.

My back was to Heidi. After I ordered, I turned to her and thanked her for introducing me to Sashi. "I haven't processed everything. I've met so many wonderful people." When I wrote about or tried to articulate my thoughts and feelings about the refugees, I felt like a fool, as if language was too elementary. Words like wonderful, heartfelt, heartbreaking, lovely, sad, and tragic seemed like vocabulary words from grade school. Maybe if I had a more sophisticated vocabulary I wouldn't think this way, or if I were an artist … or a cinematographer….

"I'm glad." Her face seemed devoid of the hard lines I was used to seeing. "Tomorrow you can choose what you want to do. Shit, do what you want every day. As you now see, my life isn't romantic. I do too much paper shit. Can you believe it? I'm in Africa to get away from a desk job, and here I spend so much time — " She didn't finish but drank down her beer. "The only difference, no high heels and no air conditioning. I guess in order to give up the heels I have to work in Satan's heat. Anyway, you're not what I would have thought."

What did she think? That I was a rich kid do-goody? And were those people so bad? "Thanks."

"Unlike that man there." She pointed at Saul, who shoveled two spoonfuls of rice into his mouth.

"This place makes me drink," Sharon said when I turned back around.

People's voices grew louder within the hour. The beer took away the feelings from the day. I sat back in the plastic chair. The smell of dirt, beer, sweat, and *nachif*, minced meat in sauce, penetrated the air. The night sky was black but glittered more brightly than I had ever seen a sky do. I wanted to stop this moment and frame it to be able to relive it later when I felt my life was mediocre. I ordered another beer, and then I told the waiter I wanted to buy a round for the whole table.

"No — for everyone," I said. "You, too. Or whatever anyone wants." What good was money if it wasn't spent? Akasha would approve.

"Are you going to stay with us? You seem to thrive. Not that I knew you before," Thad said.

"Thrive. I like that word." I said it louder, "Thrive." I leaned back in my chair, lifting the two front chair legs off the ground. "No, I'm not. I told Beah I'd come home.

But thanks, Thad. I don't remember if I've ever felt I was thriving before."

He smiled. I could have sworn he was flirting. I started to direct this scene, as if it were a script written by Christopher Hampton who wrote the screenplay for *The Quiet American*. Where was the next shot? The trauma, the suspense was already laid out. Would I focus on Thad's hand held loosely on his beer? Or Saul playing with his ponytail? Or on the flies that landed on the food, like I had seen geese land on a lake, elegantly, purposefully?

"Hey!" Thad, Saul and Sharon all yelled at the same time.

"Where are you, girl?" Sharon said, then thanked me for the beer.

"She's a daydreamer," Saul said. "Or drunk. Better be careful or someone will take advantage of a pretty girl like you."

I looked at Thad, wondering what Saul was saying. In that moment, Thad had me. I pushed the thought aside, wondering how capable I'd be of kissing, of caring, or even sex.

"Tell us some stories of the real world," Sharon said.

"If only I'd been living in the real world. For the past two years, my life has been … " I wasn't sure what word to place on my affair with Santos, my engagement, the death of my baby, the trial, and then moving in with Akasha and living in a mansion with Beah, Ana, and Zahir.

"Oh, come on. Nothing is more like hell than Darfur." Sharon took another drink. I thought of Inaya — and wondered if she'd compare her time in Darfur to hell.

Sharon probably was right. She hated that her assignment had led her to Chad. There was a time I had thought I was in hell. But against this backdrop, my life was good, even considering the loss of Clara.

The instant I knew that Clara had died, I felt more alive than ever before. Pain came, making every cell in my body alert to life. My whole body, my whole being woke to the suffering. And in that instant of suffering, of knowing that I was fully alive, all I wanted was death. In a flash, I felt her body in my arms, saw her smile, felt her suckle, and caressed her arms as she rested her fingers around my finger. Then the memory that would never be born died.

No one was in the hospital room when I first came to—no doctor, no nurse, not the woman who said she was there to help, not the father, not my father, not my best friend, not my brother. I placed my hand on my stomach. At first I was fooled; my body fooled me. My belly was still large. I pressed harder, pushing my baby so she'd wake and push me back with her femur, her foot. I then smiled, knowing that they must have taken her by cesarean. Dr. Franco — I liked him, trusted him. The nurse had told me that thirty-six weeks was considered full term. I was thirty-six weeks. Clara must be in the nursery. But then I worried that she was in ICU. I tried to stand, but couldn't. My stomach burned and my muscles failed me; my stomach was bandaged, the tape pulled my skin. I used my neck and back to pull my legs over the side. But now the cords held me back. Tears poured down my cheeks, and I screamed help. A nurse came in and said, "Sweetie, there is a call button."

"Where's my baby?"

"Let me get your doctor."

"Help me to the nursery, please." I tried to sound kind, thinking that would help. "I want her."

"Lie back down."

"Help me walk, please." Then I saw Lily and called for her. "Where is she?" I asked. She came to my bedside and brushed my hair back with her fingers the way I watched her do with her daughter when she was sad, heartbroken, or upset. Lily looked at the nurse. Then I knew.

I tried to get out of bed, but they held me down. Lily lay on top of me, keeping my body pinned to the bed. Sounds were coming out of my mouth that I had never heard before, but they were mine, all mine.

I pulled the IV out and stood. I felt a dagger in my lower gut. Physical pain was easy. My soul burned. I hated Santos. I hated God. Was it because I hated God that I burned? This was hell. I lived in a hell that God in his omnipotent laziness had sent me to.

I managed to get up from under Lily's body. I was now wild.

My father and brother walked into the room. At first they moved out of my way. I thought, good.

"We have to get her back in bed," Lily said. "She'll hurt herself." I laughed. Dad and Joel each grabbed an arm and dragged me back toward the bed.

"Don't touch me!" I screamed. They were strong. I felt stronger.

"Please, Jamie, lie down," my dad said. "Can't you give her something?" he asked the nurse. Both Dad and Joel had tears in their eyes. They hoisted me back onto the bed. Joel pinned me down while Lily again combed my hair with her fingers.

If somehow I could disconnect from my body, I wouldn't feel the pain. I floated out of my body. "You can't touch me," I said and disappeared, even to myself.

"Hey, Jamie." Sharon was waving her hand in front of my face. "Sorry — didn't mean to send you into la-la land."

"Oh, it's nothing. I'm just tired." I stood. The word "tired" seemed to be my evening mantra. I waved to everyone. On my way out, I handed the waiter a handful of CFAs, Central African dollars. "Does that cover it? And enough for your kids to have something really special." For a moment I felt like a big shot, but I also was aware of how the NGOs had made the price of food go up. Local Abechians were having a hard time keeping up.

"*Oui*, madame. *Salaam*."

When I was outside, Thad ran to catch up with me.

"Hey," he said.

"Hey."

He walked an arm's length or two away from me. I appreciated the space. "I liked having you in the clinic," he told me. "If you're interested in helping, stop by any time."

"Thanks. I was worried I was in the way. I will. I will come by."

In front of Hotel Aurora, I said, "Here we are, the Holiday Inn of Abeche. If only there were electricity … " Thad stood, waiting. Was he thinking I was going to ask him up?

"If there were electricity you'd …? I'm sorry, I thought you weren't finished."

And he was right. I was going to say if the hotel had electricity it would almost be like a Holiday Inn, and maybe I'd invite him for another drink from my mini bar. But, there was nothing to invite him up for, not even a movie or the news on a television set.

"Just a figure of speech," I said.

"Good night, Jamie," he said.

❖ ❖ ❖

I spent the first half of the next day with Thad in the medical clinic. I was given a ten-minute lesson on how to take vitals and, with my interpreter, that was what I did for four hours. I loved the work. Though I couldn't speak a lick of Arabic, some patients spoke a little English. I knew this from all the research I had done, but the fact still amazed me: African villagers speaking English.

As I was leaving the medical tent, Doc said, "Ride back to Abeche with us."

"Okay. I'll let Heidi know."

I spent the afternoon with Mohammed. I told him more stories, plots from movies that I liked and figured he'd enjoy, too, like *Star Wars*, and *The Lion, the Witch and the Wardrobe*. Good always conquered evil. I wished this would be true in Mohammed's life as well.

Thad drove on our way back. Jakob sat in front and I sat in the back with Doc. I hoped he wasn't hitting on me. But his friendliness turned out to be just that. He told me he was smitten with a woman who lived in The Netherlands. I was amazed how small the world appeared when talking with aid workers. When I was growing up, Sacramento was considered far away.

"We've heard your crap story. Now tell us something else, something good about you," Doc said.

We talked about movies for a while. Thad had met Angelina Jolie when she was in Chad as an UNHCR Ambassador. "He hasn't recovered since," Doc said.

"Fuck you," Thad tossed over his shoulder.

"Thad used to be the man around here. But some of the younger guys are moving on in."

For the rest of the drive, we listened to music while the three guys gave each other shit about stuff that had nothing to do with Darfur, genocide, refugee camps, or

252

medicine. At first I was taken aback by this banter, but I decided that this was how aid workers did what they did. They tried to leave their work in the camp. But I had a feeling that each one of them had heartaches that they carried, cases that haunted them.

I was dropped off at my hotel. Idriss, the hotel manager, was very friendly. Every time I came or left I'd spend a few minutes talking with him. He spoke Arabic, French, and as he said, a little English. He smiled easily. He had a gap from a missing tooth that he didn't seem bothered by or ashamed of.

The more I was here, the more Africa, Chad, the people, the land all intrigued me. I noticed new things all the time. And I began to write down information that had nothing to do with Camp Gaga. I thought about so many of the movies that I loved, *Out of Africa*, *Casablanca*. Movies in foreign places.

"Everything fine, madame? Can I get you anything?" Idriss asked as I walked in. I assured him that I had everything I needed and headed up to shower.

I looked forward to meeting people at the café. Every night there was someone new, someone who decided to stay back and work or write home, or have an intimate conversation with friends. But only being in Abeche for such a short time, I didn't want to miss anything. I was glad that I hadn't allowed the fear I'd felt in N'Djamena to take over.

Again, after a couple of hours of food, drinks, and laughter, Thad stood to walk me back. Most everyone else had cleared out. Every time I thought about Thad during the day, I pushed the thought away. But as he said his goodbyes and headed out my way, I knew there was no other person I'd rather be with in that moment. I closed my eyes tightly to squelch any other thought and allowed myself to be happy.

He kept his distance like he had before, though now I wished he wouldn't. An inch or two closer would have felt like maybe he enjoyed being with me. When we came to the hotel again, I thought about inviting him up, but I couldn't think what I'd be inviting him up for. Maybe Idriss could get us a couple of cold beers, or some cold water.

"I brought a candle," he said, as if reading my thoughts.

"And I have matches." I slowed my step to keep my heart from jumping out of my chest. But was I ready for this? And what was this? If it was sex, I decided I was ready. Sex wasn't something that I had consciously longed for or fantasized about. I hadn't thought about it in over two years, but apparently I hadn't needed to. Desire rushed into me as if I had been wishing for it all those lonely nights.

Thad followed me up the stairs. Idriss was sitting behind the front desk reading a book. He didn't look up. And I wondered briefly what the characters were doing or feeling, that he couldn't take his eyes off the page.

I unlocked my room door, holding it open for Thad. I could still smell the lingering scent of the lotion that I had used a few hours ago. I opened the window to let in the breeze. The moon was crescent — stars held more light in the night's sky. "Tell me about South Africa. Your family. Are you ever going to go home?"

Thad took the book of matches I held out to him, lit the candle, and set it on the nightstand.

"Johannesburg is a big city. People coming, going. People living and wanting more. Like anybody, I only knew what was in front of me: my home, Mom's car, my sisters, my friends. There was school and homework, football. Mom worked hard. Still does. I'll go home. Yeah. But when? I left when it was my time to register for the military — every South African male has to serve his time."

"I take it your dad is gone?"

"Yeah, he's gone. Alive but gone. Mom was the strong one. My older sister, Julie, is gone, as in dead gone."

Thad was no longer standing face to face with me but had stepped away. He watched the candle, and when a pool of wax floated around the wick, he stuck his index finger in the wax, and then his middle finger. "She wanted to marry a strong man, someone different from our father. He took control of her life and at first she liked that. Liked that he was always around, never wanted her to be with her girlfriends without him. She liked how firmly he'd take her by the arm. She said she felt safe with him. Safe. Until he saw her talking with their neighbor, a man, and later that night he firmly hit her over the head with a frying pan. He was dead sober, too." All Thad's fingers were now tipped in white wax. He rubbed them gently over his cheeks.

"Wanted to kill the bastard. Ever want to kill someone? Like, if you were given half the chance, you would have?"

"Yeah."

He sat on the bed. The energy in the room had changed. The lust that I could have reached out and touched and rubbed all over my body was now gone. I sat down next to him and took his hand and peeled off his wax fingertips. His hands were thick, and I wondered how he could have held such a small needle to sew up that boy's leg.

Neither of us said anything. The flame from the candle flickered and created long shadows on the wall. The shadows were alive. The tall colorless flames danced on the wall, growing short and then tall. Were they male? Female? Black? Arab? White? They're just shadows, I said to myself. How often did I pay attention to all that wasn't real? I watched the shadows because it was easier. They were larger. Not so painful to my eyes. The blue orange flame was hot and alive. Shadows didn't exist without life, without light and darkness.

As I sat next to this amazing man, I felt so empty. My heart ached from trying to fill the space in my chest. My mind spiraled down a long tunnel. When would it reach the bottom? I understood why Thad touched the wax. It was a deterrent from that moment. I wanted to touch something hot and soothing. I climbed onto the bed and sat behind him. I kissed the back of his neck. Reaching my hands under his shirt, I moved my fingers up his back. His warmth, his skin were real. I pulled his shirt over his head. And then he turned to me.

"I don't have a lot to give you," he said. And I thought I knew what he meant. He wasn't talking about commitment, marriage — those institutions were abstract, and silly here in Abeche, here in this moment. He meant of himself, at this moment. But in saying that I knew he was the kind of man who'd give all he had to give.

I thought about telling him that I hadn't been with a man since Santos, since the accident. But I wasn't sure what I'd want from him, what I'd need for him to do differently. I shivered though I was sweating. When his tongue entered my mouth, my belly growled from a primeval hunger. Our clothes came off and we held each other. Our kisses and caresses slowed. "I'm like a ship in a bottle," he whispered. "Women see the ship. They see travel, sails, a captain, and adventure. That's all they see. I'm just telling you the truth."

But I wasn't looking for the horizon. I wasn't waiting for someone to take me to a safe harbor. I simply wanted to see what was in front of me: him, the color of the water that splashed against the boat, sending a salty mist that covered my skin. I wanted to feel the surge of the ocean.

The talk on the drive to Camp Gaga the next morning was about two aid workers who had been killed outside of Guerada, a town five hours north from Abeche. Doc was pissed. He thought that the international community was "sitting on their fucking hands, while people all around were dying."

"You know, some people find this hard to believe," Thad ground the gears as he shifted, "but I can handle a small child dying of some disease because that's what happens. Kids die of disease. What I can't handle is people not giving a shit about the reasons these kids are dying. And now the people who are helping are being targeted."

"Tell us," Sharon said to me. "What is going on in America?"

Heat rose to my face. But I wasn't embarrassed; the question gave me energy. This was what Akasha was paying me to do. This was why I was here. But I knew most people didn't know a single thing about Darfur.

"Most people I know aren't aware of what is going on," I said. "Right now, people only have energy for so many foreign affairs, and the issue that's most talked about is Iraq, then Afghanistan. For many Southern Californians, the issue is with Mexican immigrants."

"Yeah, I thought so," Doc said. He turned and stared out the window.

"But I'm here," I said. "And that says a lot. If I can care, if I can be here caring and learning, then others can, too. I can't stress enough how unlikely a person I am to be in Chad. And there are so many grassroots organizations popping up. Stop Genocide Now tours with Camp Darfur. This man named Gabriel Stauring has been to the camps and he's created Camp Darfur. He sets up tents at colleges and high schools and people get to see pictures and hear stories about life in the camps. Paul Freedman's *Sand and Sorrow* documentary is out there. George Clooney narrated it. And John Prendergast, who wrote *Not on Our Watch* with Don Cheadle, is one of the co-founders of the Enough Project, an organization that focuses on mass atrocities in Africa. These movements are huge. I think people need to be taught to care and how to care, and that caring won't screw up their lives for the worse but actually make them more meaningful." I felt breathless when I was done talking.

"Woo hoo!" Sharon exclaimed, poking me in the arm with her finger. "You go, girl."

After we parked, Sharon went to talk to someone in the UNHCR tent while the rest of us headed toward the medical tent. Thad reached for my hand. My whole body tingled with embarrassment. I felt caught in the same web of love affairs the aid workers found themselves in. I wondered what Doc thought. Either he didn't care or didn't notice because he never said a word. Thad may have already said something to him. But why should I care? I did fall for Thad, maybe like a lot of other women, but that fact didn't erase my desire. As we reached the clinic, he squeezed my hand.

"Here we go."

I spent the morning taking temperatures, cleaning wounds, handing out medication, holding hands, cleaning beds. Never once did I look at my watch and wonder when the morning would end, like I used to do constantly at the bank, wondering how time could cease to move forward. This work was exhausting; it was meaningful.

After lunch, Sashi took me to meet a young woman who was caring for her sister and brother; both of their parents had been killed. She was only fifteen. I thought about the worries of most fifteen-year-olds back home. I held her two-year-old brother while she cooked. She said that she would like to finish school. She loved mathematics. But education was only available for the younger children.

"We hope to have a secondary school someday soon," Sashi said. The girl's name was Fata. She wore a jewel-blue headscarf. Her siblings' names were Abdul and Ache. Abdul and Ache. I would remember them.

The refugees were constantly working on making life better in the camp while also wanting to go back home. Without exception, everyone I met wanted to go back to her or his village. They couldn't understand why the government of Sudan would want to kill them, or why President Omar al Bashir had sent the Janjaweed, why he and his regime thought Sudan was an Arab country when blacks had lived on the soil for generations. They also wanted justice.

My last hour I spent with Mohammed. His mother said that he had a rough night, waking up screaming and crying for his dead brother. I simply sat near him humming songs that my mother used to sing to me. Before I left with Sashi, Mohammed asked if I had a mother and father. I told him my mother was gone. He asked if I had any brothers.

"Yes. He likes to work on the wheels of cars."

"Just one brother?"

"Yes."

"I am just one brother. And I like cars, too." I smiled. And before I walked out of the tent his lips twitched, maybe from trying to smile.

The front seat of the Land Cruiser was saved for me. People were tired. The stress of the day and the news from the morning had taken its toll. I welcomed being near Thad. I blocked thoughts of leaving in three nights. All I cared about was the now. All I wanted was for him to hold me, make love to me. All I wanted was to make love to him.

"I'm going to Guereda in the morning," he said, once we were underway. My heart sank. Wasn't that where the aid workers were killed? "There is plenty of help here, but docs have already pulled out of there. I want you to come with me. Maybe you can stay a few days more. It's a five-hour drive from here. We'll be working in Camp Kounoungou."

I looked over at him. And if life happened in snapshots like photos in an album, that was the moment I took over my life.

"Yeah, okay," I heard myself saying. "I'll go."

I told Idriss I'd be back in three or four days. I had to go to Camp Gaga at least one more time to say goodbye. I wouldn't just disappear, but would it matter if I did? Of course it would. When I told Heidi I was leaving, she didn't ask any questions. I thought this odd. She let me use her phone to call Beah, telling me, "You've given enough money to make a phone call."

Ana answered the phone, and with the bad connection and Ana's fear of talking on telephones, the call was short and to the point. "Tell Akasha I'll call when I'm in Paris." When I'm in Paris. The statement seemed crazy, like a line from a movie I had watched my whole life.

Chapter Twenty-One

*C*amp Kounoungou was older than Camp Gaga. A building had been constructed for a school. Three-and four-year-old children knew no other way of life. More families lived in mud brick homes than in makeshift tents. For over an hour, I watched children make bricks out of the dirt that they walked on, that they used to harvest on, that they grazed their donkeys and goats on.

The work with Thad and the stories I gathered were tiring. Needs were staggering. Yet smiles and hope filled so many faces. As did the pain. Salga, a woman I had tea with, told me that when a family member died back in her village, they'd get rid of all remembrances. All their clothes, shoes, and trinkets were sent to a neighboring village. I thought about all the unused baby items in the trunk of my car. What was I going to do with all that stuff?

Was my way wrong and theirs right? I had heard on a radio program back home that parents of U.S. Marines who had died in Iraq had transformed those boys' childhood rooms into shrines. Did this help with the loss? I didn't know, but I was pretty sure there was no right way to mourn the life of a child.

My new interpreter's name was Mohammed, such a common name among Darfuris. I was told it was the name given to first-born boys. Of course the name for me would always bring up images of a little boy with his leg tied to a stick, who believed that a white woman was the same as a black boy.

The refugees' stories all sounded so familiar. First they would tell of bombs being dropped from the sky, and then the evil men on horseback, the Janjaweed, would come into the village to kill, rape, and pillage. The few villagers who managed to escape from the attacks would then begin their trek to an IDP camp or a refugee camp. Sometimes this walk would take over fifty days. Sometimes death would come before they reached their destination. But inside each one of those stories that appeared similar was an individual living life.

"I was nursing my baby when the Janjaweed came into our hut," one woman told me. "My baby is dead now. The Janjaweed threw him into a fire. My other son ran away. I don't know where he's gone. Maybe to another camp. His name is Daoud. We are from the Masalit tribe." She then told me he had only three fingers on his right hand, that I would be sure to recognize him if I ever saw him. I promised I'd let her know if I ever did see him.

Whenever I had a free moment I wrote down every story, sketched every detail. I wanted to take these stories back home and share them. If people could feel the sameness, the oneness with them, as I had, they'd call their senators, too.

I'd have to leave Africa soon. An American shower and an American meal appealed to me. But it pained me to have these thoughts, knowing that the people in the camps had no option to go home to what comforted them.

And I had no desire to leave Thad.

There was love and then there was this. The love I had for Sean, my first and only love, no longer brought a pang. I was feeling glad he had left, had left me. And the other guys that had held my attention for a few moments or months vanished. Then there was Santos, the man I had agreed to marry but didn't love. People who hadn't known the love that I felt for Thad might caution me. But anyone who might question how I could have such strong feelings after knowing him for only days simply hadn't experienced this kind of love. Theirs was love, yes, love of a different kind, I'd guess. Thad was my Humphrey Bogart in *Casablanca*, my Ralph Fiennes in *The English Patient*. I was a woman with Thad, not a girl, a girlfriend, a friend, a fiancée; not someone to be evaluated for beauty, coolness, religious preference, education, or credit card debt as I had been in other relationships. I felt younger and older, sillier and wiser, sexual and intellectual with him.

Five new refugees came into camp. They had been sleeping outside the camp until they were registered. An eight-year-old and her father both came into the clinic. Thad asked the father where he had come from. He was told that they had been walking for three weeks. That there were eight of them.

"Did the other three pass on?" Thad asked. I held the gauze Thad was using to cover the man's gaping wound from a small piece of shrapnel, now infected. The smell sliced deep into my throat. I tried not breathing, but that only made me feel lightheaded. I placed a hand over my nose and mouth.

"One gone." He said the other two, a mother and a baby boy, had fallen behind. The baby had a small stomach wound. He hoped they'd make it. "I had to get my daughter here."

"I understand," Thad said. Thad asked a few more questions about how far the mother was from the camp. If she had any water.

"A little."

He finished bandaging the man and turned to wash his hands, then went and talked to the other doctor in the clinic. Finally, he came to me.

"Jamie," he said, "I'll be back."

He was leaving to look for the mother and her baby. In a land where death was as commonplace as texting back in the States, I wondered why he chose this mother and this baby to risk his life for. And wouldn't his search prove futile? I wanted to ask him these questions, but I knew two things: My questions wouldn't stop him, and when a person was about to do something that seemed futile to others, questions didn't help.

Instead, I said, "I'm coming, too." I grabbed my backpack, water, and camera and headed toward Thad's car. Ibrahim, our driver, was already behind the wheel.

Thad didn't say anything for the first forty minutes of our search. We were heading closer to Sudan's border; we were heading into more dangerous territory. No longer was it only the Janjaweed who were a threat, but also rebel groups, and Chadian bandits. The genocide in Darfur and the influx of refugees was negatively impacting Chad, a country whose government hadn't been all too stable to begin with.

I looked up at the sky. It was blue. A couple of lightly drawn clouds hung above us. When I looked at the desert, the vast emptiness that I saw, the horror, the pain that was occurring here, it stuck so differently in my mind than any field, mountain range, or lake back in California. But when I looked up, I could have easily have called the sky a California sky. The sun, the clouds, and at night, the moon and stars all looked the same. Maybe that was what Mohammed meant when he said "the same;" it was based on perspective. But differences could teach us to recognize different kinds of beauty. We could learn compassion, humility; we could become more insightful, thoughtful. Maybe we could learn that we humans were much the same. Even in Africa the sky was blue, filled with clouds and birds and constellations and a moon.

Ibrahim drove on sand. There were no roads. No signs that said, "Sudan, 50 kilometers." Or announced which gas station was at the next exit. He navigated assertively through what I called sand dunes and he called *wadis*. A cassette tape played low. The music sounded harsh to me. Nora Jones would have eased the tension more effectively. Sand dust flew up all around us. It was hard for me to see where we were heading, but Ibrahim seemed to know.

"Others are coming."

I tried to see where Ibrahim had spotted another vehicle. I looked straight ahead, to each side, and then turned and looked out back. Thad pulled his binoculars out of his backpack, gazed through them out the front window and said, "Yep. Two cruisers."

"Do you have any cash?" Ibrahim asked.

"A little. And nothing else. Jamie?"

"No. No money." I felt like a fool for having left my wallet back in the clinic. Of course money would come in handy.

No more was said. No "Should we turn around, drive the other way?" or "Let's try to outrun them." This was what Hollywood taught me. In an action movie, there always had to be at least one good car chase. We headed in the same direction. Within minutes the Land Cruisers were within a hundred yards of us. Two Cruisers with the tops taken off like the sawed off shotguns so popular with the gangs of Los Angeles. Men sat with weapons across their laps, across their shoulders. My heart began pounding. This is it, the end to my tale.

"Why didn't we turn around?" I asked.

"They'd have caught us and been angry for making them waste gas. Jamie, you give them everything. Except your passport. They won't want it. Take it out now," Thad said, never turning in my direction.

Ibrahim stopped the car. Thad got out at the same time as one of the men with a Kalashnikov slung across his shoulder. I opened the car door. Ibrahim was already out translating for Thad. The man was yelling at Thad, asking him what he was doing in SLA territory. Did he have permission? Did he think being white was going to protect him? Ibrahim kept calling Thad a *hawalya* doctor, who was there to protect the people, his people. He said that we weren't spies.

This kept getting more absurd. Us? Spies? What made him even consider such a possibility? Or was the term used simply to give reason to kill? I stayed by the open back door, unsure what to do.

A couple of other soldiers jumped down. One wore a Nike t-shirt with his faded, dirty military pants. I thought about getting back in the car but knew that would offer no real security. My legs shook as I stepped out next to Thad. He glanced at me. I couldn't read him; maybe there wasn't anything to read. He wouldn't have known if it were better for me to stay in the Cruiser or not. Two days ago, two aid workers were killed for a box of food and their vehicle. The man yelling at Thad wore dark wraparound sunglasses, the kind that men wore back at home. He was their leader, I guessed.

Thad stepped in front of me, covering half my body. His action was purposeful, but I wasn't sure what had happened to make him do it. Thad told Ibrahim to tell the man that we were looking for a woman and her child. They were in need of medical care. We were not spies.

The soldier wearing the sunglasses, the leader, laughed. The other said, "You expect us to believe you? There are women and children all over this land."

"Yes, but this mother is not far from the camp," Thad said.

The man in charge took out his cell phone. He dialed as I had seen people do thousands of times, placed the phone against his ear, pulled the phone back to look at the bars, and then placed it back to his ear. He talked. So much about being in Chad felt foreign to me, and much of the time it seemed like I was in another time in history, but here was a rebel leader in the Sahel surrounded by nothing but sand and death using a cell phone.

I imagined the phone call was determining our fates. He flipped the phone, stuck it back in his pocket. I looked at Ibrahim, wanting a sign of hope or desperation. My heart pounded; my blood ran scared. The man turned and said something to the rebel soldiers. Another one jumped out of the Cruiser. That one grabbed my arm and motioned for me to get everything out of the Cruiser. I did.

I gave him my backpack. Thad's medic bag. Our water. We didn't have a lot.

His eyes scared me. Were they empty? Filled with hate? Sadness? I couldn't read them, and it came to me that it was because he was only a boy, maybe thirteen. For some reason he reminded me of a boy I saw once who'd stuck his arm inside the blood pressure machine at a supermarket while waiting for his mother to pick up her prescription, but he couldn't get a blood pressure reading because his arm was too small and thin for the machine to grip. Like him, this boy was too underdeveloped to be able to know what to do with the absurdity of living in a land where his tribe and his family were being killed. His eyes reflected the confusion that comes with youth, that comes from still being primitively aware that life wasn't going the way it should. That life was supposed to reflect justice and love but didn't. That adults were supposed to care for him, feed him, educate him, wrestle and tickle him. But didn't.

I looked him in the eye, through my lightly tinted sunglasses. I smiled, as if to say hi, as if to say maybe soon this whole thing will come to an end. His eyes turned on me, flamed with rage. He flipped his Kalashnikov around and with the butt he punched me in the gut. I fell to the ground. Air escaped my lungs. Cheers came from the men in the vehicles.

Thad was held by the man with the sunglasses. "What the fuck is he doing?" he yelled. Ibrahim didn't translate.

The pain cut and burned. I breathed and much of the pain went away. I was afraid to move, worried the pain would come back or that I'd be given another blow. Was I bleeding internally? And if I was, would I die? Were we all going to die out here in this desert? Would my bones be found and reburied year after year?

The boy reached down and took my sunglasses off. And slipped them on. He stood next to me. And I felt like a dog he just reprimanded and wasn't going to feel sorry that he did.

I sat with my knees embedded in the sand. The sand burned my legs. The sun burned my back, and it was easy to see how death came easily in 120 degrees. Sweat ran down the side of my cheeks in large drips, and for a moment, I thought that I had started crying. I was small and weak in my position. Thad, Ibrahim, and I didn't stand a chance with these men and boys, angry males who were trained to kill. Men and boys who knew death was coming soon for them and this was their way to control the when and how. Men and boys whose hearts had been altered, their passion for love changed to revenge, their grace to power.

The leader said something to the boy. Then the leader turned to Thad and said, while Ibrahim translated, "We are going to leave you. My commander said you were okay." He then smiled. "And he said sorry. There are some *hawalyas* who don't support our efforts to bring peace and equality back to Sudan." He laughed. "Go look for your patients."

I lifted my eyes to the boy who had gutted me. He could now see that they were light brown, and scared. As if scripted and directed, I lifted my hand. He took it and helped me to stand. "*Salaam*," I said. "*Humdallah*." Thank you, God!

On his way back to the Cruiser, he said, "*Humdallah*," which was custom. He climbed back up next to the other rebels, men who were distinguished by their western t-shirts displaying capitalistic logos: Calvin Klein, The Lakers. Distinguished by wearing or not wearing a turban, a shal. Distinguished by having or not having sunglasses. They weren't distinguishable by their eye color or facial expression. Nor by their anger toward their country that didn't give them equal rights, or a president who took away dignity, home, safety and claimed rights no one should be privy to while killing their fathers and brothers, raping their mothers and sisters.

The commander and his sidekick got back in their Land Cruiser. Both vehicles took off in the direction they had come. There was no road. The tracks they had made were already blown over with sand.

"Let's go." Thad came to me and held me. I relaxed in arms that were strong. But he and I both knew they were not strong enough to protect himself or me from a gun. He nuzzled the crook of my neck. "I'm sorry for bringing you. Tell me you're okay."

Thad's body resonated differently from mine. He didn't shake. He would be still and then jump.

"I'm okay." I got in and out of habit placed my seat belt on. Thad stood by the back door a second longer. I thought he might sit next to me. But then he closed the door and sat in front where he had been before, leaning forward, looking for the mother and her son.

As we drove through the desert with no road, I thought about the opening scene in *Crash*. It played on stereotypes, almost confirming the stereotypes, giving them ground and validity. The rest of the movie unraveled our stereotypes, but in the opening, we questioned, do African-Americans always tip poorly? Were African-Americans to be feared by middle class white people? After this experience, I wondered if the next time I was in downtown Sacramento would I look the young black men in their eyes. Would I walk closer to Lily? Or even cross the street to avoid contact? And if I did, would I be such a bad person? Is fear really the basis for racism?

"The SLA commander said he saw them just over the next *wadi* next to a tree," Ibrahim said.

"Take your time," said Thad. Then he muttered, "She had water. She'll be okay."

I saw the tree rising in the distance, its sinuous branches becoming more defined as we drew closer. Red fabric waved in the wind. She must be trying to get our attention, I thought.

"There they are," I said. To save their lives was worth the run-in with the SLA. I would always hold onto that knowledge.

As we drove forward, I saw that movement was limited to the fabric of the mother's dress. I wanted to go back to that moment seconds ago when movement meant life. Maybe she's resting, I tried to convince myself. Sleeping. Nursing her baby. The red chiffon weaved in and out like the arms of a hula dancer, gracefully, meaningfully.

Even before the Cruiser rolled to a stop, Thad jumped out. "Jamie, stay in." As soon as he opened the door, the smell of rotting flesh hit me. Everything in my gut erupted. I couldn't get out of the vehicle fast enough, as I fell over my own feet and retched. The pain of vomiting felt good. For the briefest of moments I told myself to keep puking so I wouldn't have to face the moment of realization. To see what I'd have to see. But then I was empty. I stood and saw Ibrahim already digging a grave. Thad sat on his heels motionless, looking at the baby and his mother.

I stepped forward.

The baby was swaddled, no fabric moved exposing his face, or arms, or little feet. I thought about the mother's hands as they carefully, tightly, folded the sky blue cloth around her child, over her baby's face, knowing life was taken, gone. The mother lay on her stomach. Her head was in a hole dug by her own hands. Sand filled the hole, suffocating the breathe out of her. Her baby died and she killed herself. We all could see it. None of us said a word. The only sound came from Ibrahim as he dug the one grave with a branch from the acacia tree.

I reached and broke a branch, and began helping him dig. "It will need to be deep. The wind has a way of unburying those who shouldn't have died," Ibrahim said.

This mother's tie to her baby was so visual, so pungent, and so deeply spiritual. The wind vibrated the evil that was in this land. And I wondered how could man, all these good men, women, children, change the tunes of the wind? It was in the desert that Christ fought Satan. What tools did he use? Did he bury them somewhere? Somewhere the Darfuris, the people of the Zaghawa tribes, the Fur tribes, or the Masalit tribes could find them?

On the way back to camp, we all stayed locked inside our thoughts, pain, and confusion. I was shaking and cramping. I lay down on the back seat. "Don't fall asleep," were Thad's only words.

Back in our tent, I fell fast and deeply asleep. I awoke early in the night. Thad still wasn't back from "taking care of business." I stepped outside, and there he sat with his back against the tent, holding a bottle of whiskey. It was almost gone. I sat down, and he handed me the bottle. Used to my hard liquor being mixed with juice and sugar, I winced when I took a swallow.

Thad smelled of sweat and whiskey. He hadn't moved other than to hand me the bottle and take it back. "I'm going for a walk." He straightened up and stumbled to his right, then to his left, and then fell against the tent.

I helped him back onto his feet and held onto him, wanting to go with him, wanting him to ask me to go. There were other lights on in the compound. Laughter pierced the breezeless night.

"It wasn't your — " I began, wishing he'd just take me in his arms, or let me take him in mine. Wishing we could use our hands and tongues again to erase our pains like we had for the last five nights. But here was new, fresh pain.

"I don't want to hear anything about what was or is my fault. I don't want you to follow me or try to make me feel better, so I can in turn make you feel better."

"Why were you sitting outside where I was sleeping?"

He took a couple of steps away from me. "Where else was I supposed to go? The local café? There is nothing out here besides tents and sand."

"You're right. But— " I pointed at our tent, wanting to say you were here, by me, waiting for me.

"Don't make me into something I'm not, Jamie. I promise you'll only hurt yourself. I just want to finish this bottle." He pulled another swig. "And if you need one for yourself or some body to hold you, start asking around."

"Don't be cruel."

As he walked into the darkness, I felt the side of love that was more vivid, more lasting … the side that hurt like hell.

The next day, I drove into the camp with Ibrahim. I hoped Thad had found another ride. I worked in the medical tent and then played soccer with kids, although I had never played back home. The kids were patient with my lack of skills.

I worried about Thad all day. I was told he was just sleeping it off, that someone had seen him.

Later in our tent, I wrote and sketched everything I could remember about yesterday, pushing every thought about Thad out of my mind. It was a pain I could do nothing about. Tears streamed down my face as I recalled the mother's face poked deeply into sand, the smell of the rotting flesh, the baby wrapped so perfectly.

Thad walked in and saw me sitting Indian-style with my journal in hand. I looked up at him.

"Don't think these tears are for you," I said.

"I won't." He sat in front of me. The wind blew fiercely, pounding the tarps.

"Ibrahim is taking me back to Abeche tomorrow. I'm spending a couple days there and then heading home."

"I'm sorry. I'm sorry for my selfishness. I'm sorry for not letting you comfort me. I'm sorry for hurting you. And I wish I could say it wouldn't happen again, but I can't. And, yes, you should go. Not that I don't want to be with you, but I don't think I could be with you here. And I hate the fact that I wouldn't be able to protect you."

"It's not your job to protect me."

He slid down, his haunches resting on his calves.

"I've fallen for you, so don't you think it's only natural that I'd want to protect you?"

"Yeah, I think we all want to protect those we love, and that's the tragedy. We can't."

And now there were more than just Thad and me in the tent; there was his sister, my mother, my Clara. He sat closer.

"Let me see your sketches." Looking at the one with the mother's head in a self-dug hole, he said, "You know how difficult it would be to suffocate yourself? Usually the brain takes over and the body is pretty much forced to take a breath. She could have easily lifted her head. I wonder how long it took."

"Not long."

"Yeah. You're right." He finished looking through my storyboard ideas and closed the book. "Do something with these," he said.

"Okay, " I said, but he must not have sensed the sarcasm in my voice because he then said, "Fuck, I'm going to miss you."

Chapter Twenty-Two

*A*s I retraced my steps, my feet felt like boulders, my legs steel, my heart some unearthly material that took little space but weighed heavily. I thought of pictures of soldiers returning home, humping their packs, their broken hearts, their spirits that were forever changed. I knew that my experiences in Camp Gaga, Camp Kounoungou, with the SLA, with the mother and baby couldn't compare with the months — years — that a soldier spent at war, but I felt I could now empathize somewhat more with their cast-down eyes, their pained smiles.

I spent two more days with Sashi, and with Mohammed. I promised him I'd let the people in the United States know that he was here. He looked at me quizzically. So I explained to him that the U.S. was powerful, that maybe someday he could go home. He stood, then with his finger, he imitated a roller blade from a helicopter, saying "chu-chu-chu." When the helicopter made it to his chest, his finger became a bullet and his hands mimicked a blast. He sat back down next to his stick and wrapped his arms around his legs, then slowly rocked. Home for this boy didn't feel safe. It was in his home that his childhood had been ripped away from him.

Like I'd wanted to on that first day, I wanted to take him in my arms, and like that first day, I feared that it would be too invasive, too much touch for his wounded spirit and he'd only reject and fall deeper into his nightmare that came to life. But I decided to risk it.

I sat in front of him, then wrapped my arms around his slight frame. He didn't pull away. He didn't hug me, but we sat like that rocking as I sang, "Hush, little baby don't say a word, Mamma's going to buy you a mockingbird ..." until Sashi said it was time to go. Kissing Mohammed on his forehead, I left him in the same position I'd first seen him in.

After a flight out of Abeche, and then Chad, I saw my reflection in the departure monitor at the Charles de Gaulle Airport. My flight from Paris to Newark was three hours late. I pondered the extra time. I loved being in Paris although it was only its airport. If I had more time, I'd take a cab drive around the city, maybe glimpse the Eiffel Tower. I had more time, I told myself, really — another day gone wouldn't mean a thing. I ran to the ticket counter.

I asked the cab driver to take me to a hotel near the Eiffel Tower. He dropped me off at the Hotel du Champ de Mars. There I showered, using warm water and lavender soap, almost like an American shower despite the water pressure. I called Fallow Springs and told Beah I'd be a day late. "Strong move," she told me. I left to see up close the Eiffel Tower that to me represented travel, excitement, beauty, and love.

I worried that I'd feel lonely in Paris without a friend, without Thad. But the exhilaration of walking the steps of the tower, of being somewhere I had dreamed about, filled me with awe at the world, at what I was capable of. At the second level I took the elevator to the top. I took in the views, and then stood facing the Seine River until the sun set and I became chilled.

Back down in the Parc du Champ de Mars, I studied the travel book I'd bought at the gift shop, looking for a place to eat dinner. I held the book out, trying to orient the map to where I stood. A French man sporting a well-trimmed beard and wool ivory coat asked in English if I needed any help. I thanked him and asked him for directions to a nice place to eat within walking distance.

"I will show you." I followed him through the Parc, across a street to Chez Francis. "*Bon journée,*" he said. "Enjoy."

After I was seated, holding my wine, I reflected on the kindness of the Parisians and the common stereotype. Yet I sensed some exasperation in my waiter that I knew no French. I ate dinner while watching the lights flicker on the Eiffel Tower. Now I was missing Thad.

The next day I took the Mètro to the Louvre. I'd stay here, I decided, until it was time to head to the airport. At first, the Louvre, with all its rooms and corridors filled with masterpieces, was a bit overwhelming. I felt I was gliding from painting to painting, most by artists I hadn't even heard of. I stood in front of the *Mona Lisa* in wonder, not so much of the painting but of how she draws people from all times and cultures.

As I walked into another room, I was pulled toward a painting deep with shadows. Outside of the shadow lay Mary, Christ's mother. She lay stone cold dead, her arm flung out, not peacefully crossed. Her feet exposed. Her dress scarlet red, not virgin blue. No halo floated above her head. Her face, her body looked tired, worn. Her earthly job of mothering, nurturing, caring, keeping her babies safe failed — thus, life failed. Here lay the truth of her life, exposed for us viewers to see and take notice of. Around her, deep in shadows, men mourned. On the other side of her, Mary of Magdalena cried without being consoled. I found myself searching in Caravaggio's shadows for hidden meanings, yet always being drawn to the light.

In the museum's gift shop, I bought a book on Caravaggio. I read it on the plane until I fell asleep and it fell on the floor.

When I arrived home, Beah met me at the airport with open arms and I walked into them. She held me at arm's length for a few moments.

"Let me get a good look at you. It feels as if you've been gone for months," she exclaimed. "How was it?"

"Beah, there was one little boy. His mother had to tie him to a stick that was hammered into the ground. She has five other children. Her husband and one of her sons were killed. Mohammed, the boy, runs away when he's not tied. I'd sit next to him singing him songs from my childhood. I swear to you, Beah, that I felt his spirit. It was wounded but still so full of life."

She scrutinized me, as if searching for a hidden message. Maybe she thought I had said something unbelievable.

"I know it sounds — " She hushed me by patting my cheeks.

"You look great, but you're sunburned."

"I wore sunscreen."

"We better go before I get towed."

"What? Beah, this isn't the 1970s. You can't leave your car parked curbside."

"Sweetie, I'm not that out of it. I parked in a Hertz parking spot." She grabbed my duffel bag and took off like the day when I first moved into Fallow Springs. That day played out in my head as a lifetime ago. "The arrows point you one place and you end up somewhere else," she offered as an explanation.

On our drive from the airport I was sure I would sleep. But I couldn't. Stories began to spill out of me.

"Thad put me to work in the medical clinic. I wasn't just an observer. I held together wounds while he sewed them up. One thing that I found weird, Beah, was that there weren't as many tears as I would have thought. There were tears," I added. But now I wondered if tears were a luxury. It takes time and energy and bodily fluids to cry. "But in their eyes there was pain — it was all in their eyes. Who said eyes are the windows to the soul?"

"Shakespeare. You'll find there are a lot of reasons to read the classics. The more you live, the more you'll need to read."

I didn't comment. I was beginning to think that she was right.

When we were fifteen miles away from home, I couldn't keep my eyes open. I thought just for a minute, and I let my eyelids shut. They hurt. I relaxed my brow.

I woke hours later in my bed. The room was at a perfect temperature, and I was snuggled in my comforter. I wished Thad were next to me. I fell back to sleep, remembering his arms around me, the taste of his body.

When I woke again, it was three in the morning, and I found myself unable to go back to sleep. I started writing a letter to President Bush, asking him to place more pressure on Omar al Bashir to let in a United Nation Peace Keeping Force, asking him to support the African Union, and asking him to support divestment. I had so many thoughts about what I wanted to accomplish. My mind was spinning. Cheadle and Prendergast in *Not on Our Watch* talked about American's inertia and apathy, but at the moment I couldn't seem to rope in my energy. After I finished the letter to the President, I went for a walk in the garden to try and put some thoughts together.

Winter was hanging on. The leafless trees stood in stately fashion in the early morning moonlight. There was an elegance, a life in them that wasn't in the trees in Darfur. Water. I was sure that was the reason. I looked over at Zahir's place. It was dark. Seeing his home made me miss Thad again. Would they be friends? Did Zahir have friends? Did he used to have friends? I was his friend. He was mine. I needed to thank him for believing in me, for helping me to see that I, Jamie Shire, could do something so seemingly absurd as to go to Africa.

In the east there was a slit of bright fuchsia, a wonderful time of day when the world was lit by both the moon and the sun. I looked down at my fingers. I cleaned my left thumbnail and touched again the dust of Sudan. When I looked up, I saw Zahir walking over the lawn toward the stone path. He was carrying a fishing pole. I remembered the underground lake. The one that was supposed to be unknown, forgotten. The one Zahir had been to and told me wasn't any big deal.

He hadn't seen me, as I was still in shadow. I watched him. He watched his feet. A curl had fallen over his left eye, making him look mysterious. He brushed it aside.

"Zahir." I stepped toward him. He stopped.

"Jamie," he said, and then resumed walking. "It's early, or late, depending."

"Jet lag," I said, falling in beside him.

"Five hours is all I ever seem to need."

"Are you fishing for koi? In these little ponds, that doesn't quite seem fair," I laughed.

"Life's not fair. I went to see you earlier."

"I did it. I went and met the people in Darfur. Thank you for believing in me."

"By the look on your face, I can see. Well, I'm not sure what I see. Tell me."

"By the lake." He took a deep breath. I thought he might say, "What lake?"

"No one knows that I go there; that I know about it."

"Is there some kind of secret? Are we not supposed to go there?"

"No secret that I know of, and I'm sure Akasha doesn't mind. I don't know if she's ever been there. Maybe she has. I've never seen her there and she's never mentioned it."

"I thought there wasn't much to see."

"I was fishing for perch, to answer your earlier question." He set his pole against the bridge. "I'll show you."

We took off, running over the lawn, past the pool. Everything from this point on was new to me. I was reminded of the scene in the movie, *Dead Poets Society*, when the boys take off in the middle of the night to the dead poets' cave, except Zahir and I weren't wearing anything so romantic as capes with hoods. He wore his Stanford sweatshirt and I wore the one emblazoned with "Paris" that I had bought at Charles de Gaulle airport the day before.

Mist rose from the ground. The leaves that we ran across didn't crunch but were instead soft from the dew and months of rain. Then we stepped into a thicket of pine trees. I ducked often to keep from getting hit by the boughs. I heard an owl and then some songbirds. I wanted to look up to see if I could catch a glimpse of the owl. I had never seen one other than at a zoo. But I was afraid of stopping, as if I'd lose Zahir, as if he'd keep running. But then Zahir looked back to see if I was still coming.

"Do we have to run?" I panted. He stopped and waited for me to catch up.

"I missed you," he said. "I didn't want to miss anyone ever again." His breath made smoke in the cool air.

"I missed you, too. I wished you were there." I didn't tell him that I stopped missing him after I met Thad. That Thad had a way of filling all my empty spots. When I was around him, I was consumed with desire and fulfillment at the same time. "Especially in the beginning," I added and hoped I took away what could have been understood as yearning. For the first time, I questioned if Zahir wanted something more than friendship. He had always been so reserved with me, yet I knew that could mean a number of things. "The Darfuris want safety. They want their homes back and peace. They want their families together again. "

"Yes." Zahir knew tragedy as a way of life. He had been born in Afghanistan. He'd left when he was nine. He had said this to me, Ana, and Beah over dinner as a matter of fact, without emotion attached to the facts. I was ashamed that I just now realized how much his life had been defined by those early years. Like mine, like everyone's, like the children in the refugee camps. I wanted to ask him about his life: where did he go when he left Kabul? What was it like growing up as an immigrant? What had happened to his mother and uncle? He never talked about them. He never left Fallow Springs to visit relatives.

"Let's keep going," he said. I thought he must have sensed my desire to want to know more.

We came upon a rock formation. It jetted up like a steeple reaching the sky. The boulders looked out of place in this lush landscape. Nothing grew amongst them. Zahir glanced down at my shoes.

"Flip flops aren't great climbing shoes. You'd be better to take them off."

"Not everyone has feet like yours," I said.

"True. But trust me."

"How did you find this place?"

"When I was a boy, I loved to explore. I wanted a piece of that boy back." He wasn't looking at me, but at the rock. He reached toward a natural shelf and pulled himself up. "Is part of learning to be an adult learning how to be a kid again?"

"I've often wished for that girl again. At least the one I remember."

"What were you like as a child?" he asked.

"Before my mother died, I was a dreamer. I believed I could do anything, be anything. Everything was possible. Have you ever loved someone so much that you were sure you'd die? But the tragedy is the fact that you don't die, that you live, that your lungs continue to breathe, and to your own dismay, you drink the water and soon eat the food that someone has laid out for you. Nothing was the same after Mom died. Everyone went back to life as normal; even I did, but I hated myself for doing it, for going back to school, for going to birthday parties. I even started to laugh again. But the truth remained that my mother was gone. And then she started to fade. There were times at first that I wanted her smile, her laughter, the warmth of her hand on my thigh as we drove to school to go away. But other times I'd spend hours lying in bed trying to remember what dress she wore to my back-to-school night, or exactly how many cups of coffee she drank in the morning. Then I'd go back to wanting to forget her again, to hate my mother like the girls my age always said they hated theirs. I became an escapist, to escape all the pain, all the confusing feelings."

"That explains your love for movies. Let's get going."

I followed him up the steep incline. The rocks were cool, almost cold. The sun wouldn't warm these boulders for hours.

"Ouch." I jammed my big toe on a boulder.

"You okay?"

"Just stubbed my toe."

As we climbed higher, the air and boulders became even colder. Then, for some reason, I remembered the days I tried to picture what Clara would have looked like. How I tried to place flesh on that one sonogram picture. How I imagined holding her in my arms. Did I want to forget the love and dreams I had for my baby, like I wanted to forget my mother?

"Jamie." Zahir stopped and turned toward me.

"Yeah? I'm sorry, did you ask me something?"

Zahir looked at me with the kindest eyes at that moment, and I couldn't help but think he was reading my thoughts. "I just asked what's the difference between being a dreamer and an escapist."

"A dreamer is someone with hope. An escapist is one without hope." I had never thought about those words and their definitions before and was surprised how fast I rattled off the difference.

"You don't strike me as a woman without hope."

"I'm not. No, I'm not. I have been, though. Maybe I vacillate between the two."

Before we reached the top, we came upon a rock that was different from all the rest. Zahir said it was slate. The only slate rock around the place. We stepped around it and I spied a small, dark opening. Cold air came from it. Zahir began to crawl through the tunnel.

"You've done this lots of times, right?" I called after him.

"It opens up. You don't have to crawl for long."

I slid my feet down. "Too cold for snakes, right?" My blood pumped faster. But I wasn't feeling fear. Or at least the fear was transient; the excitement was steadfast.

"Right."

Breathing deeply, I inched my way through the small passageway.

"It's not too much farther," he said.

"Why does Fallow Springs have so many hidden passageways?"

"I am not sure they're meant to be hidden."

"What do you mean?"

"Why haven't you ever studied philosophy or psychology? You're always looking for something in between the lines, outside of what is readily apparent."

"I've always had a thing for shadows," I said. I pictured Caravaggio's *Death of the Virgin*, but said, "I loved how John Ford used shadows in *The Grapes of Wrath*. Can't do that with colored film. Just like you can't have a Charlie Chaplin and *Modern Times* in a sound movie. And *Citizen Kane* would not be the same movie in color. When I was in Chad, I was watching shadows on the wall from a candle flame. Something shifted inside of me. It's hard to explain. Maybe it's been wrong of me to be so intrigued by shadows. Shadows are just representations of what is real."

"Have you ever read Plato's 'Allegory of the Cave'?"

"Who's Plato?" It felt good to joke with Zahir again. "Just kidding. No. I haven't." Then the cave opened up and I could stand. Sun rays shone down from a small hole up high. He reached for my hand and helped me up. His hand wasn't cold like mine.

"The children in Darfur were so precious," I said. "They were like all kids, wanting to play, find a tree branch to swing from or a can to play soccer with. I taught some kids how to play baseball. It was my favorite sport as a kid. One minute Saud would be smiling and then, the next, the ball would be thrown to her and she'd miss it. Not from lack of skill but because her mind transported her to a place no child should go."

We walked another couple of hundred of yards in silence. It was cold in the cave. I slipped my hood onto my damp hair. Only days ago I was so hot I knew I'd never feel cold again. And, now, here I was.

The sound of water falling filled the cave.

"Just through here."

The tunnel wasn't as tight as the last one, but we still had to bend down and crawl.

"You are one brave man to have found this place on your own."

"You're brave, too."

I wasn't sure what he was referring to. I was about to ask him but my words jumbled together into a ball when I gasped, holding in my breath and my words. Beauty had the same effect on me as horror. I searched for a thought to express myself. The tunnel had come to an end, and I stepped into a large underground room. Water as still as the sky and colored in shades of aquamarine blanketed the large room. Light from small, star-like holes in the ceiling dimly lit the room.

"I thought you said this place was nothing to see." I felt paralyzed. The beauty. The mystery. It took me several moments to process the scene. "Can you swim in it?"

"I have," Zahir said. "It's cold. Clear and cold." He was looking at the lake, too. "It's beautiful, I know."

The only vegetation was moss. And when rays from the small openings struck it, the color went from pine green to a fluorescent green. We walked along the rocky edge of the lake. One-third of the lake pressed up against a wall of rock, as if a waterfall once flowed there. Zahir sat on a rounded boulder.

"Here," he patted a smooth rock less than an arm's length away from his.

Sitting, I tucked my knees under my chin.

"I'm sorry you're cold. I should have warned you."

We sat in silence. There was so much I had to share, but sitting in quiet felt right. I had so many faces and stories of suffering crammed into my mind. I wanted my mind to rest just for a few moments. I wanted to forget and not forget the image of the mother who buried her face in the sand. Again, I thought about what she must have been thinking as she dug the hole. How did she force herself to keep her mouth and nose covered? Was the desire for death so strong that her head had fallen limp and become too heavy to lift? No, I wouldn't forget.

"I talk to her," Zahir said. "This is where I feel her the most. This is why I didn't want to bring you here. I know it sounds crazy, but this place felt like mine." He laughed a sardonic laugh. "I guess. Like I thought she was mine."

"Who? Who are you talking about?"

"Sam, Samira. My wife."

"You have a wife?" He didn't look at me, but out toward the middle of the lake.

"I'll never know what happened to her. Not really, but the imagination has a way of filling in blank spaces. I do know she was the tenderest person I ever knew. She spoke softly; she touched softly. When she looked at me, my tension drained. But she was also funny. At first, I loved her wit. I'd laugh. And I thought I was the luckiest man alive. After a while, I learned that her days of humor were followed by days of depression. I always thought I needed to watch her on those days, the days she didn't eat, or sat in front of the television. It was on one of her funny days that she walked off the roof of our apartment building." He took both his hands and placed them on both sides of his head and squeezed. Dark curls latched on to his fingers. "I had gone to work. I was teaching at San Jose State. She kissed me and as I was leaving she chased me and jumped on my back and bit my neck. 'What kind of animal am I?' she asked. I could have said a rabbit, or a kitten, or a bear. She would have taken any answer. I said, 'You are jackal.' She said that was a terrible animal. I told her that I needed to leave. I'd be late for my morning class. As I left, I heard her laugh and repeat, 'jackal.' Later that morning, while I was in class, two officers walked in. I thought that maybe they came to arrest some student for selling marijuana. It had happened in a colleague's class the week prior — a crackdown, the sergeant had told the

290

school president. But instead of escorting a student out, they asked to speak to me. I grew embarrassed in front of my students. Ashamed of being called away. That was the last thing I remember about being at school."

His cheeks were wet. I moved to sit closer to him.

"Her father and sisters were at the hospital morgue. I haven't seen them since the funeral. They said I ask too many questions. Her father had said when I first met him that she was lucky to be alive. We were all lucky to be alive, I told him. He didn't appreciate the comparison. He said his daughter was spoiled, ruined property while he, he was a victim. He didn't use the words, but he thought them. I knew this and she knew it."

We listened to drips of water. Then he said, "I needed a place to think, to not interact with people. Akasha offered me that. I've come to believe this is what Akasha is offering to all of us, a refuge." He picked up a handful of pebbles and threw them one by one into the lake. Each pebble fell into the water, making the sound of a raindrop hitting an empty tin can. "I sometimes wish I had called Sam a lion. If she had felt stronger, she would have gone to the grocery store like she said she was going to do. Or, maybe if I had called her a butterfly, she would have flown off the building. I miss her. I love her. And yet, I realize I didn't know her. She only let me know a part of her. I think that is a fault with Afghans. Women don't feel they can open up. She said I'd be ashamed of her. The Talibs abuse women. They abuse men, too, but for women, their gender is reason enough. And the fact is, she was lucky to be alive. She was lucky they didn't stone her after abusing her, blaming her for their lust, their perversion."

I laid my hand on his. I didn't know what to say. I tried to read between the lines of his story and then wondered if I were being fair in doing so. Questions seemed invasive, as if he'd think I wanted to place my thoughts and opinions into his story, creating something new. Why was this so? But I knew why — because for me stories were sacred. I know the difficulty of whole, complex stories; sometimes it felt less painful to talk in fragments. I felt for Sam. It was easy to imagine what things happened to her that she felt others would blame her for and shame her for. History had been consistent and cruel to women in this way.

"You have no idea how heartless some of them can be. I never really believed in evil until the Taliban ruled." He fell silent for a moment, then said, "I wish I knew more."

"Maybe in time her family will open up," I said.

"They won't have anything to do with me. They never liked me before she died, said I had grown too Americanized. Her father has moved back to Kabul. He hated living here. Being an outsider is very difficult, I give him that. He's probably back in Pakistan again by now.

"My own father was a gardener. I learned a lot from him, but not enough. I never cared for plants and soil as a boy. He and my mother were happy. Truly. Maybe if I hadn't been so intrigued by ideas, books, maybe if I had learned how to touch, nurture … There have been times that I have wanted to talk with him, ask him …" He didn't finish his sentence.

"It wasn't your fault, Zahir."

"I have a list of should haves."

"It wasn't your fault."

"I knew she had been abused. I thought that if I treated her well, gave her a new life … if I were man enough — I should have known better."

"Tell me about your should haves and then I'll tell you mine."

He laughed. "Is this kind of like, 'if you show me yours, I'll show you mine?'"

"You have that game in Afghanistan?" I was truly surprised.

"Everywhere, kids are kids." After spending time with the children in Darfur, I knew that to be true. Zahir looked at me.

"Let's go for a swim."

"You're crazy."

"Maybe." He stood and smiled. Then turning his back to me, he pulled off his sweatshirt and t-shirt in one movement. "I won't look," he said.

As he slid off his jeans, he joked, "You're not watching, are you?"

"No," I lied and stripped down to my panties and bra. When I turned back toward the lake, Zahir was swimming out in broad strokes toward the center.

"If you go slowly, you won't do it," he warned.

I stepped in. "Oh shit, it's freezing!" Then, in one not-so-graceful movement, I dove and swam out toward Zahir.

Chapter Twenty-Three

The banner I ordered from the Save Darfur Coalition arrived. Zahir helped me hang it on the iron canopy that designated Fallow Springs, where it would catch the attention of everyone who drove by. I was playing on the town's infatuation with Akasha.

I stood back, looking at it. It was big, almost oversized at twenty by five feet: SAVE DARFUR, it said. I felt proud. This is for you, Mohammed.

"Did you ask her?" Zahir asked, on our walk back to the mansion. He carried the front of the ladder while I supported the back. The air was cooling; evening had come.

"No."

"Maybe she won't notice."

"Funny," I said. She had to be okay with it. "It's what she was paying me to do," I said, suddenly defensive.

The next afternoon, I had another meeting with the local high school principal. Maybe he'd listen to me now. Now that I had stories to tell. Now that I had credentials as he mentioned I hadn't had before. I sat across from him and told him about the refugee camps, about Mohammed, about the mother and her child.

"Amazing stories, " he said. "But we simply don't get involved in politics." He sat back in his chair, his hands together as if in prayer.

"This isn't about politics. It's a humanitarian issue." I couldn't believe he wasn't seeing it. Hadn't he heard about STAND? What was he scared of? Taking too much of the students' time? His controlled expression didn't look scared, but that was the word that came to my mind as he sat there in his wrinkled, buttoned up shirt.

"Same thing."

"No," I said. "It's not the same thing." I knew arguing would get me nowhere. "Have you heard about the student organization, STAND? It has over seven hundred chapters worldwide. Started with a bunch of college students."

"This isn't college. I have test scores to think about. Bush, according to you, said, *'Not on my watch,'* but he also said, 'No child left behind.' And if you had the time and energy, I could explain what that has done to education. We don't have time for politics or humanitarian issues."

He didn't say anything else. I was sure this was how he used his power with students. He'd just sit on the other side of his big desk and not say anything.

"Thank you for your time." I stood. With my hand on the door handle, I thought of Abdul caring for her sister and brother at the age of fifteen. I turned back to face him.

"You know, in the refugee camps there are young girls, the same age as the girls at your high school, who are feeding and caring for their siblings. Many are pregnant from being raped. These girls, these women, need their stories told. I wonder, just maybe, if your students knew about these women — yes, these African women — maybe, just maybe they would care more about geography, or English, or history. And then maybe their tests scores would be higher."

"I'm sorry, Mrs. ..." He had forgotten my name.

"Ms. Duval." And I walked out. Why I had played that card I wasn't so sure. I remembered the women at the coffeehouse, and I hoped he'd sweat, or piss his pants. Hadn't the school board written Akasha about a donation for a new gym or something?

"Same thing," I muttered to myself derisively on the way to the car. "How could politics and human lives be the same thing? No time to learn about humanitarian crises? No time to learn about other people's suffering?" Next to my car, a group of kids were hanging out, some in their car, others standing alongside, listening to the music coming from the sound system. As I got closer, I recognized the music.

"U2," I said.

They became rigid as I approached. Were they supposed to be in class? Did they think I was a truant officer?

"Yeah," one of the kids said.

"Is that their newest album?"

"Yeah. It's sweet."

"I'm sure it is." I unlocked Akasha's car with the remote. I started to open the driver's door, then paused. "Hey, have any of you ever heard of Darfur?"

"Are they new?" a tall lanky boy asked. He had beautiful, curly hair; it puffed out and fell right to the top of his shoulders.

"No. The Darfuris are from Africa. They're being killed — slaughtered. Men, women, boys, girls, all of them. Is that something you care about?" I wasn't trying to be cynical, or condescending.

"Smart," another boy teased and pushed the arm of the boy with the wonderful hair. The boy who made the mistake turned red.

"What do you mean?" he asked. His cheeks still pulsing with embarrassment.

"Genocide. Their government is killing them off."

"Like in WWII?"

"Not exactly the same, but the same in that kids, mothers, brothers are being killed for no other reason than that they are black and are living in what some like to think of as an Arab country."

"That sucks."

"That it does," I said. A bell rang.

"We gotta go," the girl sitting in the driver's seat said.

"If you have time," I said, "check out savedarfur.org."

I sat down in Akasha's beamer and began to sing, "I can't believe the news today …," as I watched the kids with the speed of walruses head toward their classes.

Later that day, I felt like a child when I went to tell each person that Ana had dinner on the table. It was good to feel like a child in this way. We were seated at the kitchen table, just beginning to eat, when Akasha came in. I scooted down the bench to make room.

"I'm not here to eat." Her eyes were on me, and I wondered why she addressed me. I hadn't ask her to eat with us. I had learned that Ana brought Akasha's dinner up to her on a silver tray before any of us sat down. Then her eyes moved to Ana. "Thank you, Ana. It was delicious."

I was about to ask Zahir to pass the salad when Akasha's attention returned to me. "Jamie, what is going on with that ugly banner? A banner? Reminds me of a car wash. Did you not think it was appropriate to ask me first?"

"That ugly banner is a call for change. That ugly banner is what you pay me for." I forgot my food and jumped up to grab the folded newspaper page that Beah had given me earlier. "Look — there's a letter to the editor. Someone wrote about that ugly banner in front of the elusive Duval Mansion. Now everyone who reads the newspaper today will think about the people of Darfur. Some may learn about Darfur for the first time. The kids I talked to at the high school thought Darfur was a rock band."

She looked at the paper and actually said, "Nice work." She left the kitchen, taking the newspaper with her, leaving her expensive perfume lingering in the room.

I sat back down to dinner. I noticed no one else had touched their food while Akasha was in the room.

"That went well," Zahir said.

For a moment, I thought he was being sarcastic, but the fact was, it did go well. Although they were small changes, I was still making change happen. I closed my eyes and took a deep breath. An image of the Sahel appeared, making me feel sad, but also energized that I could do something to help the Darfuris.

"Anyone up for a movie after dinner?"

"What's playing?" Zahir asked.

While I was waiting in line to get popcorn, one of the young men from the high school passed by me and said hi.

"I went home and looked at that website you mentioned," he said. "Wow. I had no idea. What can we do?"

"Get as many of your friends together as you can. Do you know where Fallow Springs is? I'm Jamie and you are — ?"

"Max."

Zahir kept going through the line.

"Popcorn. Anything else?" he asked over his shoulder.

Max and I made plans for him and some of his buddies to come over the following Thursday.

"We'll be there after youth group."

Hearing the term "youth group" made me cringe. I couldn't help but think about Joel, his desire to help the poor while advertising Christianity.

"Good. And bring anyone else who wants to come, too. This is for everyone." A pang shot through my gut. I missed Joel. I hadn't talked to him since we had run into each other at Mom's gravesite. I would call him, I decided, and really try to keep our conversation to what we had in common — our childhood, Mom, and Dad, and the desire to help.

When we got home, Zahir invited me to his cottage. I asked to see childhood pictures; he said he didn't have any because when they fled Kabul, they left everything behind. They didn't want anyone knowing that they were escaping the country.

"But I have these books of what the city used to look like," he told me. "Many people are shocked when they discover it snows." We sat down and paged through one of the books together. The first pictures were of modern Kabul life. Homes stacked up on mountains. Hundreds and thousands of cars lining the roads in disarray. People in market places, wearing tattered robes. Everything looked dusty and old. There was one picture of a corner building with large glass windows; it looked as if it could have been taken in Los Angeles or Chicago. There were no lakes, no gardens, no trees in bloom lining a road, no parks. I could see no beauty in the pictures and wondered if Zahir did. Maybe beauty was truly in the eyes of the beholder. Maybe it was based on some personal ideal of what we want ourselves to look like, in what city, in what job. My thoughts wandered until he turned another page, showing the snow-covered mountains that encircled the city. "Every day my father would stare into those mountains and say, 'What a beautiful place we live in.'"

"Did you find it beautiful?" I was surprised at his comment though the snow-capped mountains were stunning.

"I was a boy. Sweets and balls and kites were what were beautiful to me."

Looking at the next page, I asked, "What's that?"

"A mosque."

Its blue top reminded me of pictures I had seen of Greece. "Did you and your family go here? To— " I wasn't sure what to call it. "To service?"

"Not here. My mother preferred more intimate settings for worship. This mosque attracted everyone —

worshippers, tourists." Several of the following pages showed more mosques. Inside were bright ornate paintings covering the ceilings. I liked the architecture of the doorways. "These doorways and the ceiling looks Moorish," I said, not exactly certain what I meant by that. "Sort of like St. Mark's in Venice." I knew this from a large picture book of Italy Aunt Gazella had given me. The pages had become frayed from all the times I studied the art, architecture, and cultural sites.

"Yes. It's Islam meeting Greece. St. Mark's is far more ornate. But same idea." He turned the page. Although Zahir and I were sitting next to one another, I could tell he made sure our thighs didn't touch. The book would sway in the middle and he'd have to use his hand to steady it.

"This is the Column of Knowledge and Ignorance."

A tall stone column stood on a hill amongst rocks. It towered into a cobalt blue sky, several cumulus clouds crowning the column. The picture was powerful, even beautiful — stone against sky.

"My father sometimes would take me here when I fell behind on my studies. He'd say ignorance was costly. The edifice was erected to remind the coming generation what reactionary ignorance could do. There are beautiful symbols etched into the column: books and pens. And then there were the names of the people who died during the rebellion. "

"What a great memory. Your dad didn't come to the United States with you?"

"No. He died from cancer, a year earlier. I guess I could call that a blessing. He loved Kabul; he loved his culture. But he would have adjusted here, so it really wasn't a blessing. It just happened." He closed the book and set it on the coffee table. I was getting sleepy. I glanced around the room for a clock, a sign to justify my tiredness. There wasn't one I could see.

"Kabul is over three thousand years old," he said. Around his desk area, he began to look for another book, picking one up and then another. On the floor against the wall he found what he was searching for and brought it back. "I wanted to show you some Buddhist remains. My country was a Buddhist land long before the Muslims took it over. The Taliban have destroyed many of these sights." We looked at a large Buddha built into rock. The next page showed smoke from the Taliban blasts, and nothing but an empty shell.

"Poof! Gone. All that history gone. Because of ignorance. Without recorded history, we can't know facts, we can't know truth."

"D'you think so? I thought truth was found on an intellectual, spiritual level. I think that's how I see it, anyway." Zahir turned the page. Drawings in red, orange, and black covered the walls of caves.

"We live in a material world," he said. "We are material. This fact leads us to truths. Knowing our history, studying it, making as much sense of it as possible will help us move forward. When you look at your life, I imagine you don't look at it simply from where you are at this moment, but in relation to where you came from. That's your history."

I pondered his words. "Yeah, I see what you mean." And he was right; everything I say, do, and think comes from a thought or an action from the past. "Ironically, isn't it the Buddhists who teach living in the here and now. Whereas Muslims and Christians live for a better life after death?"

"The leader of the Taliban has said to destroy all Buddhist structures and relics because he says they are idolatrous. But what he is really doing is showing the world how much power he possesses. He wants to wipe out everything that doesn't speak to what he believes. He's smart enough to know that history and culture are needed and give people strength. By destroying our history, he takes the people's power. He demands eyes on him, on his view of Islam. In a sense, he is demanding to be worshipped. He is another example of evil materialized. Evil under the right conditions takes on a life of its own."

"I think you've lost me. What do you mean by 'evil materialized?'"

"Saddam Hussein was an awful, hateful person. But by himself, he was just a man. What made him powerful was his ability to create evil by making people suffer, his ability to get other people to do the same. Once that power is taken away, we see the man in him." Zahir said he couldn't get that picture of Saddam Hussein hiding in a dirt hole out of his mind. "He was reduced, his ability to perform evil acts taken away. The upside is, I think good works the same way. If a person decides to do good, honorable, moral acts, it creates movement. You're creating movement."

"Thank you for saying that." Zahir turned back to the page we had just looked at and stared at it, then closed the book. "I felt evil when I was in Chad. I saw it and felt it around me."

"How are you dealing with your experience with the rebels?"

"Sometimes I wake with my heart pounding. But, you know, the image of the mother and her baby is more real than being hit in the stomach. The fear of my life being taken ... yeah, sometimes I feel scared, but I can't separate that experience from the mother's dead child. And so, my experience seems less tragic. I'm still alive. No one is trying to kill me because I have freckles, or because I'm Christian, or because I'm flat-footed."

He opened the book again and thumbed through the pages. We didn't talk.

"Akasha wants me to go home. She said it would be good to let my family and friends know about the work I'm doing. It feels like a crazy assignment. I want to be through with my hometown, a done deal, poof, gone." I considered the irony of what I just said in light of the conversation we had just had about the Taliban destroying history.

"Do you have unfinished business there?"

I did, but could a person ever leave anywhere without having some kid of unfinished business? "It's not the kind of thing a two-day trip will cure. It sort of would be like if you went back to Kabul."

"That's different."

"I'm sure it is."

"You say that, but I'm not sure you believe it."

"I do believe it. I'm not comparing my life to yours. Really I'm not." I felt argumentative, grumpy, maybe just tired. I didn't want to go to Grass Valley, yet I wanted to see Lily and Brianna. I wanted to prove to my family that I had made something of myself, that people believed in me. That I had it in me to travel to Africa. If Thad were here, he'd tell me to leave Grass Valley, my father's low expectations, my brother's condemnation all behind. Zahir turned toward me.

"What are you thinking about?"

"Just how people have different ways of going through life. Thad, a friend I met in Chad, would have me leave Grass Valley behind." I felt my face grow hot.

"And you respect him."

"Yeah. You should see all he does. All the aid workers. They're amazing!"

"Did you fall for him?" Zahir closed his book and set it on the table next to him. He stood, for no other reason than to get away from me, I thought. I realized that he felt much the same way for me as I did for Thad. I cared for Zahir, too. He'd been a great friend. I didn't want to hurt him.

"You don't have to answer that. I was too personal."

"We can't be friends if we don't get personal. Yes." I laughed to myself to rid the pain of it, not the humor. "I'll probably never see him again." Zahir didn't look back at me. He wanted me to leave, but he wouldn't ask me to. "Zahir, you look tired. I'll go now."

I thought he'd say, yes, I'm tired, and graciously walk me to his door. Instead, he said, "No, I'm not tired, but goodnight, Jamie."

I stood. "Okay. I enjoyed the pictures of Kabul. Thank you." He led me to the door and said good night again.

As I walked back toward the house, I wondered what I could have said or done. I no longer felt tired; instead, I ached. Sadness fell over me, like rain. I missed Thad. I loved Thad. But Zahir was my friend. I searched for words, explanations I could give him to let him know that I cared for him.

I hadn't shared all of me, and the losses in Chad had both helped and reopened my wound. Zahir had invited me into his home to share a large part of himself and what had I shared with him? But sometimes the longer I kept Clara a secret, the harder it became to talk about her. Like not knowing a familiar person's name. Every day that goes by that you don't ask the person her name makes it harder, and the more absurd it seems to do it. Zahir had asked me in his way, a profound way, to be his friend and I was only half-heartedly doing it. I felt a fool.

I knocked on Zahir's door.

"Hi, Jamie," he said in a tone like he hadn't seen me for a while.

"There's something I want to tell you. May I come in?"

A few nights later at 11:10, there was a knock on my door. I was preparing for the Darfur Awareness evening in Grass Valley. I had been working on what I was going to say about my trip to the refugee camps. I wanted the audience to relate to the refugees: how they love and suffer and laugh just like we do. After my talk, I was going to show Freedman's *Sand and Sorrow*. But just thinking about the evening was difficult. I was nervous about going back home.

"Come in." I was sitting crossed-legged in the center of my bed, writing an email to Joel. Akasha walked in. I was sure she was going to give me shit about inviting people into her home without permission. I supposed I should have asked. Four teenaged boys had come to learn about the genocide. We had only met for forty minutes, long enough to talk about organizing a group and drink a Coke. Akasha asked what I was doing. Which from any other person would have felt normal, but she normally never asked.

"Emailing my brother. He's going to help me advertise the event in Grass Valley."

"How is it working with your brother?" She came and sat at the foot of the bed, her back erect, her hair pinned with a common drug store barrette.

"It's fine. I'm not sure what to expect from him. Maybe nothing. He's trying to be helpful. About the kids.

We didn't have anywhere else to meet. I guess we could have met in a coffeehouse, but — "

"I heard you guys. Sounds like a great idea, getting high school kids involved." I had been sure that was what she came in for, to reprimand me, but then she handed me a book.

"I saw this and I thought of you." It was a book about the history of film. Like the night of my birthday, I was touched. I flipped through the book, looking at nothing in particular. "I thought you'd enjoy it. Knowledge is powerful. And you know so much about movies already. Anyway, well, I'm tired." She started to leave.

"Akasha — "

"Yes?" I wanted to ask her to sit, have a cup of tea or a glass of wine. She looked sad. I'd spent all this time wanting her to be my friend, but maybe she needed a friend, maybe I needed to reach out more.

"Are you okay? Would you like something to drink?"

"I'm leaving early for a couple of days. I'd better get some sleep." She turned to go. "Hey, good luck. Or, break a leg, as they say."

"Yeah, okay. I just thought. "

"I need my rest. Good night."

After I sent the email to Joel, I spent hours reading about women directors. In the early days of film, until men began ruling the film industry in the 1920s, there were several successful women directors. Names I had never come across before, even when I'd taken that film class at the college. Cleo Madison, Alice Guy-Blache, Ruth Ann Baldwin, and Lois Weber. In the 1930s and 1940s, Dorothy Arzner was the only woman who directed movies. Lina Wertmuller was the first woman director to be nominated for an Academy Award. It was in 1976 for her film, *Seven Beauties*. I had never seen it. And then, of course, there was mention of Jane Campion who directed one of my favorites, *The Piano*; Sofia Coppola who directed *Lost in Translation*; and Julie Taymor who directed *Frida*.

I was stunned and saddened to read that only seven percent of American films had been directed by women in 2005, a drop from eleven percent in 2000.

What would it be like to see a shot and have the cinematographer, the actors, the crew make that image appear as I imagined it? What would it be like to have a story I wanted the world to see and have the means to create that story on film?

I thought of the ways I might direct the scene when we'd been stopped by the SLA. How would I communicate Thad's, Ibrahim's, and my fear? How would I show the way the young boy's fear had turned to hate? Would the viewers see the irony of the use of a cell phone in that situation? Like a bad Verizon commercial. I read through the journal I'd kept while in Chad. I remembered how Inaya and I brought back to life our childhood dreams, back when we thought anything we wanted could and would happen.

Later, curiosity led me to research how and where directors got their start and their education. I had done this several times in my past. When I used to volunteer at the film festivals, I'd spend time reading the directors' bios. Professor Irving at Sac State would start name- and school-dropping during class. I'd later spend time looking at schools I felt I'd never go to. California College of the Arts, Columbia University School of the Arts, UCLA School of Theater, Film and Television, USC School of Cinematic Arts were among the many film schools. Names like Pollack, Lucas, Scorsese, Howard, and Spielberg were listed as alumni. While I was doing this research, I ended up on the page for USC's Production Program, as I had many times before. In the past, the online registration form intimidated me.

Maybe because I was tired and feeling spunky, maybe because I was beginning to believe in myself, I filled it out. The questionnaire asked questions about applicant's parents, not to mention spouse's name, titles, company names, business addresses, saying that the information was used to send newsletters to them upon acceptance. Did they really expect me to believe that? Did they not realize that I knew if I wrote that my father's name was Dustin Hoffman, that my application would receive a second glance even though my GPA was 2.2? I wrote John Doe under "father," and under "mother," Deceased. I hit the apply button.

I was aware that not all successful directors had gone to school. Quentin Tarantino had once stated that students were better using their college money to make a full-length film.

I also knew that many student and novice directors had mentors and even had the luck to be an intern. These situations were based on who you knew, or how well you were doing at your prestigious film school. I Googled director internships. There were many internships available at companies I had never heard of before. Then I saw names like Lucas Films, Miramax. But the one name that caught my attention was James Mangold. He was offering an internship this summer while making *3:10 to Yuma*. Yes. That would be great. All I had to do was send a short two-minute film or storyboard, an essay and my résumé, and I could soon be standing next to Russell Crowe in the Arizona desert.

"I'll get right on that," I said, and then shut my computer. Done for the night.

Kimberly Carlson

I fell asleep and dreamed of sand and sun and wind and horses. In the dream, I felt I was really doing something, really growing into my skin. When I awoke, I was sure I was remembering my trip to Chad and the refugee camp, but as I climbed out of my bed, I remembered that in my dream I'd been sitting at an outdoor café drinking Sierra Nevada and not Chari beer, and I wasn't sitting next to Thad and Doc, but James and Russell. I smiled and fell back onto my bed, closed my eyes, and tried to relive each scene, every word Mangold had uttered.

I sat up and began an essay for the application. I had no thoughts of getting the position, but I could at least apply. The application asked for an essay on film. Essay Topic: Film. Although I hadn't written an essay in years, I had more than enough thoughts about film. I had a great storyboard, though I suspected most applicants would send a film. All I'd have to do was open up my journal. I knew exactly which experience I'd use. I'd need to rework it to capture the feelings of grief, of horror, of evil, of the beautiful red cloth blowing in the wind.

310

Chapter Twenty-Four

"*Y*ou're different." Lily stood by her sliding back door, which was open a few inches. Her hand held a burning cigarette through the crack. She brought the cigarette to her lips and then blew the smoke out the slit.

I waved the remaining smoke away from my face. "Different how?" I took her comment as a criticism; maybe it was the way she said it. But the fact was, I knew I was different. I felt different. Yet being in her apartment was a sad reminder of what had happened to me, to my baby.

Lily studied my face. In a softer voice she said, "You look good, Jamie. You do. I was worried. For a long time I was worried. I know I'm not much to use the telephone. And I still believe texting is for people who can't keep their thumbs from going up their asses." She shrugged. "And, while I was dating that prick, I let

everything go. I'm hands on. You know that about me."
She picked at paint that seemed to always be on her
fingers. By the table stood her easel. On the canvas a
woman stared at the viewer. She was beautiful except for
the blue paint splattering her face.

I did know that about her. Lily was the kind of
woman who adored the one she was with. She lived in the
moment. This was what I loved about her, but this was also
why I had a hard time relying on her. Lily threw her lit
cigarette in the wet grass.

"Trying to quit," she said. She closed the slider and
asked, "Would you like a drink? Margarita? Cosmo?"

"It's only 12:30."

"Never stopped you before."

"Margarita," I said, to ease the tension of time spent
apart.

She had the mix, ice and tequila in the blender
faster than most people make coffee. While the blender
ground the ice, I watched the burning tip of her cigarette
through the sliding door until I was sure it was out. The
door was covered with handprints. She handed me the
drink and we went and sat on the couch. I thought it odd
she never poured herself a drink.

"When do you pick up Brianna?"

"Three-thirty. She's missed you."

"I've missed her." All those empty days after I lost
Clara and during the trial, her kisses and little arms
wrapped around my neck fed my empty, broken heart.
Sitting on the couch, I ached to hold her, kiss her soft,
wind-chapped cheek. "I'll go with you to pick her up," I
offered. I felt bad for not sending her cards and letters. I
could have done that much. I took a drink and picked up a
Victoria's Secret catalog that lay open on her coffee table.

"Let's go shopping. I'll buy you an outfit. To pay you back for all those weeks I slept on your couch."

"I don't do paybacks." She threw her feet up on the table as an exclamation point.

"No payback. I just have the money."

As we walked around American Eagle looking at the racks, I insisted, "No sales." Other than a few items I had ordered on the Internet, it had been months since I had gone shopping.

"What?"

"Remember how we used to say it would be nice not to have to shop sales? This is our day." Lily shook her head and turned to look at a table piled high with underwear. "Unless what you want is on sale," I added. I hoped I wasn't making her feel uncomfortable. This was supposed to be fun. I wondered if this were the reason why most people hung out with people of the same socioeconomic level. It had just as much to do with the person with less as the person with more. Lily and I used to brag about our great finds at TJ Maxx and tell each other exactly how much we'd paid.

"No sales," Lily agreed, and took off toward the front of the store where they place all the new season favorites.

We each took an armful of clothes into one large dressing room, jeans, skirts, tops, and dresses. As she slid her jeans off to try on a short denim skirt, Lily said, "Your brother and I got it on. I thought you should hear it from me."

I stood looking at my shirtless self in the mirror. I stared at my boring beige bra and felt I needed to cover myself after hearing this news. My brother? As in Joel? As in purity? As in the youth leader? Who else would I hear it from, him? She folded her jeans and set them on the bench.

Lily never folded anything. I'd always known that Lily had a crush on Joel. She'd flirt and he'd put up with her. It was painful to watch. I sat on her folded jeans.

She looked at herself in the mirror. "Who am I kidding? I can never wear mini-skirts. I hate my thighs." She paused. "Well, say something!"

"I'm not sure what to say. Was it a one night stand? Are you two dating?"

Lily handed me the skirt and her t-shirt. "Not funny."

"No. And I'm not laughing. It's just that he's really not your type."

"It's no secret to you that I always liked your brother."

"No. No secret. It's just that it's Joel."

Joel was always so condemning about people who engaged in premarital sex. He even had a hard time watching sitcoms and movies with sex scenes. Now, violence and men killing one another was a different story, nothing unchristian about that. Nothing unchristian about seeing war movies like *The Thin Red Line, Saving Private Ryan, Midway, The Bridge on the River Kwai,* and *Black Hawk Down.* "Democracy. Those movies fight for democracy," he'd say to me.

"I didn't know Christ was political," I'd reply.

"Are you listening to me?" Lily demanded. "I guess you haven't changed after all. Still leaving the real world and living in your head world." She bopped me on top of the head with the backside of her hand and smiled. "Good. Glad to have you back. You were making me nervous there for a while."

But it wasn't just that. Lily wasn't the one for Joel, either. I pictured him with a sweet, kind girl. Maybe someone I'd grow to love and want to have over on Christmas.

Lily told me that he'd come into Chili's on a night when she happened to be tending bar and not serving. He ate fish tacos and had a Coors Light. On the house, Lily had offered, but he said he couldn't do that. "I asked, 'Do what?' He said, 'Let you steal from the corporation.' So I called him a prick."

"So far the story is very romantic," I said, handing her an A-line skirt. "Try this."

She looked at it, holding it out. "Too pretty."

"Just try it."

"So, I gave him his bill with only the tacos on it," she told me, while she wiggled into the skirt. "I screwed the Cor-Por-A-Shun and later him," she laughed. "It does look good." She stood to the side looking at herself in the mirror. She slid her palms down her thighs. "I like it after all. Sexy, eh?"

I slid my shirt back on. "I'll go find you a top." I left the dressing room, partly to find something to go with the skirt, partly to get away. Lily and Joel together. The thought hurt and pissed me off. I loved both of them, but they each held a different part in my life. Mixing them didn't make sense. Joel was simply getting off. I was sure it was all about the sex. Good sex. Best sex of his life, most likely. But Lily had always cared for Joel. As ill-matched as two people could be, she liked him. And what if they did get together? Lily was my friend, not Joel's. A bit of jealousy flared, but I quickly sent it on its way, knowing that this affair was simply that, an affair. My stomach churned in knots and I hurt for Lily.

I went back into the dressing room with three shirts, a sweater, and a dress.

"Here you go, madame."

"Aren't you going to try your stuff on?"

"Sure." I slipped out of the jeans I was wearing and tried on a pair of khakis. She tried on the sweater I gave her, chocolate brown with pink flowers.

"Perfecto." She hung the other shirts outside the door on a hook. She wouldn't try them on.

"So, your brother left Chili's without saying goodbye, which was fine. But I was bothered that he didn't even mention you — ask if I had heard from you or anything like that. I started washing glasses. Ten minutes later he was back, asking if I had jumper cables. I gave him my keys. But his battery wouldn't charge. He said he'd leave his car until morning and that his roommate would pick him up. I told him that I'd be off in fifteen and that I could take him home since he was your brother and all." Lily sat down on the bench, wearing nothing but her thong and bra.

"Don't you think you should put some pants on?"

"I'm hot."

"It's just that your ass is on a public bench."

"Little-miss-grandma-underwear, I'll be okay. Well, he stayed, your brother, and had another beer. I made him buy. Upfront, I told him."

I had tried on three pairs of pants. Nothing looked right. I had gained back some of the weight I'd lost after losing Clara, but it had all landed on my stomach. I handed the pants for Lily to fold. She held them in her lap, unwavering in her need to tell me her and Joel's story.

"On our way to his house, I asked if it was okay if I stopped at my house to get Brianna's jammies. She was staying at my mom's. I told him it would be just a minute and hopped out, leaving the car running.

"While I was in Brianna's room, my mom called and said that the little pumpkin had already fallen asleep. There was no reason to drive all the way out just to give her pajamas. I had to be at work at 8:00 a.m. for a fucking mandatory meeting. Employers never give a lick for their employees. I started crying after I hung up the phone. I hadn't seen Brianna all day and I wouldn't see her until 8:00 p.m. the following night."

I handed Lily a pair of jeans that were too big for me.

"Face it, girl, you need another size." She looked at the size of the pants I gave her. "Shit. Must be nice."

"I'm done," I said.

"Don't be stupid. Try the dress. Anyway, as I started back down the stairs, Joel was coming up. I wiped my tears and said, 'Let's go.' He asked me where the PJs were. And I said she was already asleep. Then he asked to use my bathroom. I told him, 'Yeah, beer has that effect.'" Lily's cell phone rang, interrupting her tale. She looked at the number. "Hmm. I think this must be for you." She handed me the phone. It was Beah asking if I had made it safely.

"I gave her your numbers," I said, after I hung up.

"How sweet. Interesting place you work."

"Yeah, it is." I sensed that Lily wanted to ask me more about my life but also wanted to continue with her story. "I'll tell you about it later. Go on."

"He asked about you then. I told him how much I missed you and what an awful friend I was for not keeping in touch."

"I haven't been that great, either. I've missed you, believe me. But I had to get away. I had to."

"I know you did." Lily, for all her tough exterior, had had a difficult life. A foster kid. Young mother. She knew pain and how to cry. "I asked Joel if he wanted another beer. To my surprise, he did. A couple of years ago

I would have been going nuts having him in my home drinking a beer while I drank a gin and tonic."

I remembered asking Joel to just be nice to Lily when she'd come over to my birthday party.

"I had recently sworn off men, after dickhead cheated on me," Lily said.

"Hurt you pretty bad, huh?" The dress was yellow with spaghetti straps. It had bright blue embroidered birds flying across it. I liked how it made my skin glow. I liked how feminine I felt. I missed Thad. I wanted him to see me in this dress. I wanted to take this dress off in front of him. I was surprised by the ache I felt in missing him. I had told him I'd write, but hadn't. He never told me he'd write, or email, or call. When I told him I'd write, he said, you might, for a while.

"Mostly the cheating." She twisted a hemp bracelet around her wrist. "He bought me this."

"I like the bead."

Lily took it off and threw it against the dressing room wall, and then she picked it up and tossed it into her purse. "It's a fucking piece of string with a cheap bead."

True. I noticed then that she wasn't wearing any eyeliner. She normally wore thick black liner, never taking it off before bed, always painting it back on after showering. "Your eyes look even bluer without makeup."

"Sometimes you just need a change."

Those words sounded like mine.

"You know, your brother seems to really care for those kids in his youth group." She looked at me, as if trying to convince me.

"I believe he does," I said. "I know he tries to do good, like all of us. His ways are just different than what we're used to."

318

"He told me about one kid who was thinking about suicide and how he'd helped him. I was still drinking my tonic when he told me this. When I finished, he kept looking at the empty glass. I told him give me a half and I'd be ready to drive him home.

"He sat back on the couch, looking straight ahead. I figured he was done talking. 'Sorry,' I said, for making him wait, and picked up a *Victoria's Secret* catalog.

"I offered him another beer, but he was still sucking on the one he had. So then I said, 'Beautiful, isn't she?' holding open the catalog. I told him she was my favorite model, the one with the exotic eyes and cat lips."

"'Cat lips?'" he said.

"'They're always puckered,' I said. He moved closer to get a better look. He asked me if I ordered from Victoria's Secret. I told him sometimes, but that it's all very expensive. We looked through the catalog, page by page. He loved the photos with the girls' butts pushed out and their chests jetted forward. Like this." Lily stood and posed and then cracked up.

"You missed your calling, Lily." She hadn't commented on the dress, but I had already made up my mind.

"I know it. He was amazed that there were pictures of butts. You know, wearing thongs. It was fun. It was as if he'd never seen a woman before, never masturbated to *Playboy*. And, wouldn't you know it. Your brother got a hard-on. I've heard that *Victoria's Secret* catalogs turned men on, but this was the first time I actually witnessed it." Lily laughed.

"Uh, he is my brother and I'm getting kind of grossed out here."

"Understood." I took Lily's skirt and sweater to the register.

319

"Aren't you getting that dress? You looked hot."

"No." She looked at her watch.

"It's about that time."

Teenagers now out of school were walking around the mall, eyeing each other suspiciously. Lily swung her bag and walked quickly through the crowd.

"Thanks," she said. "I'll think of you every time I wear it. Your brother is ... I don't even know what to say. We did it twice that night. He then had the audacity to ask me to take him home, right after he finished. I mean, within seconds. I didn't speak to him all the way to his house."

"Sorry about that. That really sucks. But I think I am done hearing about this."

"Not your fault. He came back the next day after my morning meeting before I had to work to apologize. And to, well…. All that was three weeks ago." I gave Lily a hug before we got into the car.

"He'd drive you crazy, Lily."

"I know it. He's fanatical."

I met with Joel at Java by the Trees. After we got our coffee and sat at a small, nondescript table, I searched for some visible change in him, something that would make him more compassionate, less hypercritical of the so-called secular world. Then, I remembered him at Mom's gravesite holding an umbrella over me and I softened. He was my brother and he loved me.

"It must have been crazy weird running into Inaya after all these years. What happened to her — wow, how awful."

"I know. I can't imagine," I said, but then I remembered the women and girls I met in the camps with similar stories.

"You two hit it off. I remember feeling a bit like an outsider with her in the house. Is she the reason you've taken up this issue, helping the people in Africa?"

"Yeah. At first I was at a loss about what Akasha wanted me to do. Then, at a rally … it seems a bit fated." I told him about my struggles getting people to listen to me and take this issue seriously. "All this is new to me."

"I'm glad you're helping others," he said. A familiar feeling washed over me, like Joel was the older sibling, needing to guide me, be a role model for me.

"Remember that boy from Ethiopia, that one I adopted with Mom? After Inaya left, and you and she were sending letters once a week?" he asked.

I hadn't remembered until just that moment, but now I recalled Mom wanting Joel to have a pen pal, too. I took a drink of my too-sweet latté and wished I had ordered plain coffee.

"I used to color pictures for him." Joel unfolded his napkin and pressed out the wrinkles. I thought he might draw a picture, maybe reimagine one he'd drawn years earlier. "Mom and I'd sit down and she'd help me address the envelope and place the check and my art inside. Makes me miss her all over again." He took a deep breath. "He sent me pictures he drew of animals. There was one of a rainbow. What happened to him I guess I'll never know." Joel looked into his coffee and swirled it. Frothy cream stuck to the sides of the cup like a soapy film. "After Mom died, I asked Dad if I could keep sending the money. I believed that if I stopped he'd starve. Remember the commercials we used to watch? Little kids with swollen bellies and flies coming out of their noses? We used to say 'yuck' while eating our Cap'n Crunch. The commercial said for just 47 cents a day we could feed a child. To me, it seemed so little."

"I remember. We'd laugh, but I had a hard time finishing my breakfast after those commercials. I hated them. But I think it was great what you did for that boy. Mom would've been proud. I was so wrapped up in my own pain at that time."

"Don't be too impressed." He took his folded napkin and quickly balled it up. "Dad said that he'd give me the money but that it would be my responsibility to send it." Joel turned red. I knew then that he was confessing.

"I sent the money one time. That was it. Just one time. Then I started making excuses. I would lie to myself, saying that, after I bought this or that, I'd send in double. It never ever happened. I hate the guilt, hated it then but, I don't know, I didn't know how to get it to go away." He tapped his fingertips on the table.

"You were a kid. Your mother had just died." I took his restless hands in mine. "Don't be so hard on yourself. I stopped writing Inaya after Mom passed, too."

"I pray that he's okay. I pray that he found Christ."

I felt conflicted. I felt sorry for my brother harboring that guilt all these years, but I also hated it when he'd then say something like "found Christ." What about finding food and medical care? What about finding a job and a safe home in which to raise his children?

"Do you really believe that everyone who hasn't accepted Jesus Christ as their personal savior will go to hell and won't be allowed into heaven?" I let go of his hand. I took a drink, and he combed his fingers through his hair.

"I do. The scripture says, 'Only through me.' I have to believe the word of God." I wanted us to get back to where we had been a few minutes ago on common ground.

"I think we both want to help people who can't help themselves. So let's talk about the genocide in Darfur." Joel attended the largest church in town and this was where I assumed I would be advertising the event. The church was popular with both young people and families. Its casual image, where the pastor wore jeans, attracted blue-collar workers and young kids.

"I think what you're doing is great, Jamie."

"What time should I show up? I have the trailer ready. I just need about five minutes to give some statistics and say a little about my trip to the refugee camps."

"Actually, I talked to the pastor and he said because you aren't a regular member ... " Joel shredded his napkin. I looked at him.

"I don't understand." And I didn't, just like I didn't understand the school principal, just like Doc didn't understand the international community.

"You know. It's nothing personal. He said it's policy."

"What the fuck does 'policy' mean?" I remembered one of the first rules laid out by John Prendergast: don't become emotional. Yet I felt that Joel was embarrassed by the pastor's response.

"I can't talk to you if you resort to profanity."

"You're right. I'm sorry. So explain to me this policy. There is genocide going on. Hundreds of thousands of people are being killed. It's the biggest humanitarian crisis of our time. So talk to me about policy."

"You have to know that churches get asked to support lots of events."

My blood was boiling but I needed to stay level-headed. I needed to think about what my ultimate goal was — it was to get people to come to the movie, to educate people, to inspire people to write letters to the President, to their senators and representatives.

"Okay. Yes, Joel. I understand policy. Why don't you get up and tell your congregation that hundreds of thousands of women are getting raped. That children are being chained up and burned alive. That boys are being killed in front of their fathers. You. You do it. You're a member."

"I just don't know enough."

"I'll tell you what to say." I felt tears coming to my eyes. I looked up at the ceiling and blinked them back.

"Let me ask."

I finished my cold coffee. Neither one of us spoke. I was afraid of my anger. I hated that Akasha made me do this. I thought of getting up and leaving, going for a walk, something.

"You've changed," he said.

"So I've been told."

"You're harder."

"I prefer to think of myself as stronger."

"That, too, I guess."

"You are the youth pastor, Joel. That should count for something. If you choose for it to."

"You'd be surprised how things work."

"I'm sure I would." He looked back down, and I could see that he felt powerless, like the back wheels on a wagon, having no say in the matter, no control.

In the parking lot, I gave him flyers and the DVD.

"See you at Dad's. I'll order pizza," Joel said.

I glanced at my watch. I had six hours before we were supposed to meet up with our dad for his birthday.

"I'll pick up a cake. What are you getting him? I hate to get him yet another shirt."

"Don't knock yourself out. A shirt is fine."

Chapter Twenty-Five

I had six hours to try to understand this angst inside of me. Instead of heading to the mall, I walked across the street to Target, thinking they had fine shirts. I wished I had bought a cell phone for this trip alone. There was no need to have one at Fallow Springs and I often thought how nice it was that no one used them there. None of that looking at a little screen during dinner or a conversation. No not-so-although-trying-to-be-original ring tones going off. Yet I wanted to call Beah to tell her that Joel and I were giving a birthday party for Dad and that the thought was giving me a stomachache. Was I afraid he was going to reject me? Was I becoming too different for him to be able to relate to me? It wasn't as if I'd dyed my hair purple, like I had done as a preteen, and all he could do was shake his head and say that he had heard there were people in the world like me, but he didn't know one would ever live in his house. I still sought his approval. I wanted him to take me in his arms and tell me how proud he was of me. I guess that's what I really wanted. Not too much to ask.

And Joel's pastor. Really, what was I to think of that? I was upset at the church, but I also felt pain and humiliation for Joel. He gave so much of himself, so much of his time. But he also let it define him, become him.

I bought a couple of t-shirts, and a DVD collection of the history of American sports.

The three of us sat around the table that seated eight, eating Round Table pizza. I was the one who had set the table, so at least we had cloth napkins. Dad and Joel talked about football players arrested for fighting.

"It doesn't seem fair that they could be accused of assault with a deadly weapon if they have no weapon," Dad said.

"It's because of their strength, their size. Their bodies are considered deadly," Joel said.

"It makes no sense to me. No man is equal in size and strength. They could lose their careers over it."

I picked mushrooms off my pizza, eating them one by one. Dad hadn't asked about my trip to Africa or what was going on in Sudan. I guessed he had a limit for how shocked he wanted to be.

"Maybe they should," said Joel. "If you weigh three hundred pounds and have the luxury to work out every day, you have a responsibility not to go around punching people in the face because you don't like men who work on computers."

Joel defended what he felt was right. There were so many times I felt it was Dad and Joel on one side and me on another because they enjoyed a lot of the same things.

Although I loved them both, I liked seeing them as separate. Joel was different from Dad in many ways.

"What ever happened to Manning, Jr., anyway?" Dad asked.

I figured he was the player who had hit the innocent man.

"Don't know. Probably did a pay-off."

"I wish some NFL player would hit me in the face," Dad said. I thought he might laugh after that comment, but he didn't.

"I hear you're driving a BMW." He directed his gaze at me, although his head was still turned toward Joel.

"I am. My boss, Akasha Duval, lets me use it. My car — well, you know all about the condition of my car." It came to me suddenly that I could now afford my own car. For a second I thought about the kind I might buy.

"What does this Akasha Duval do?"

I had wanted him to ask about me, but not like this, not these kinds of questions that were not really about me.

"I don't know exactly."

"Where does she work?"

"Out of her home. I think."

My pizza now was only bread and sauce. I let it slide from my greasy fingers back onto the plate. I was shrinking as he asked questions I couldn't answer. My inability to answer his seemingly simple questions gave him a new energy. And no longer did his body language communicate that he was put off by the fact that I was driving a BMW, by the fact that I made more money than he did. He was the father and I his child.

"You don't know how she makes her money. And you're living with her?"

"That's right, Dad." Like all the times past, I felt myself wanting to separate myself from him. How else could I live with his lack of kindness, lack of love toward his own daughter? "And if you also knew that I was living with a woman who harbored Jews, and a man from Afghanistan, you'd really feel superior. And you know, I love them. Beah, Akasha, Ana, and Zahir have taken me in and made me feel more at home, more valued than I ever did with you." I pushed my plate away. I hated pizza. I hated mass-produced food. I was eating it to be nice, eating it to make Joel and Dad feel I was one of them, that I, too, was part of the Shire clan. Dad sat back in his chair and pushed himself away from the table.

"Jamie, I should have told you this a long time ago. You're obviously ready for it now."

"Dad, no!" Joel stood and took my nearly full glass of water. His eyes were wide, trying to communicate what his words couldn't. "You told me you wouldn't."

Dad didn't acknowledge Joel, his favorite child. The one who didn't remind him of Mom, the one who wasn't artistic and dreamy. The one who caused no problems in school. The one he didn't have to buy tampons or hairspray for. The one who could fix his own tires. I was the one who loved foreign movies and wanted out of this place, not Joel. And yet Dad kept his eyes on me. Joel turned to me.

"He's just making conversation, Jamie."

"I won't sugarcoat this." Dad finally turned his body and faced me. "I'm not your father."

The clock ticked, one second, two, three, four. I looked at it and wondered why I had never noticed before how loud it was. It was forest green plastic. The face was white with large black numbers. Both Joel and Dad stared at me. Were they waiting for an outburst? Anger? Tears? But I continued to look at the clock, wondering why I had never noticed its ticking before. And I called myself observant? Sensitive and artistic? If I were all these things, how could I have missed this loud, insistent, revolting noise that was now making me feel crazy, keeping me from concentrating on what really mattered? Memories came to me as if I had just opened a book I had forgotten about. Searching audiences for a familiar face. Seeing my unread English essays left untouched on the table. Never hearing questions about my day, my dreams. All the disappointments, all the pain of never feeling good enough, worthy enough for just a little bit of his love. But he had called me princess, he had kissed me goodnight for years, he had rescued me on the side of the road more times than I cared to remember. Those things were signs of love, weren't they?

I felt myself deflating. Not only was I small, tiny, like Alice in her Wonderland, but I was now only two-dimensional. I had a front and a back, but no sides, no depth, like the paper dolls I used to play with, the kind that you try to make stand up but never do. What self-esteem I had walked in with felt taken, and I was left with a life full of lies.

"Jamie," Joel said.

"Yeah," I answered, but kept listening to the tick of the clock, looking at it, questioning whether it were new. Then I heard my dad speak.

"It was time."

I felt the sting of tears, but I didn't want to cry, not now, not in front of him, the man who called me weak, so I asked him, "Why did you lie to me?"

"Your mother asked me to. She asked me to raise you like my own."

"And did you? Did he, Joel?" Joel took his seat again, but I stood. My anger held the tears back.

"I tried." His hand came up and covered his mouth; his elbow rested on the table. His eyes blinked.

Yes, there were times he did try, like when he stayed home with me when I had chicken pox and the flu at the same time. I was twelve and so, so sick. All I wanted was to sleep, and he stayed home from work for two whole days before he called Gazella.

"So who in this man's world is my father?"

"I don't know. She'd never tell me."

"How can I believe you?"

"She didn't want me to know. She didn't want you to know."

Joel had tears on his cheeks. I registered this but felt none of his pain.

"Why? Why wouldn't she want me to know?" He didn't answer. I thought of the reasons: he's a politician, married with other children; he's a druggie, a loser. Maybe she was raped. None of the reasons she wouldn't want me to know seemed honorable, something to be proud of. Maybe I would have been better off if he really was my dad.

Joel and the man I had called Dad all my life looked down at their cold pizza. Joel was tearing his into little mouse-sized bites. Again the clocked ticked, one second, two, three, four, five.

"I guess it's goodbye, then?" I took my purse off the back of the chair.

"I didn't tell you because I didn't want to hurt you."

"Nice work."

Neither of them came after me. Once outside, I turned to look at the home I'd grown up in. I'd never call it home again. I'd probably never see it again. There was a newly planted tree next to the porch. I had always wanted to plant fruit trees, thought it could be cool, even romantic to be able to pick a peach from my own backyard. My eyes were filling with heavy tears. I blinked, and when I opened them again, I saw Mom sitting on the steps. She had on her blue housedress with the apples and pears all over it. Her hair was pulled back in a loose ponytail. She, too, had tears in her eyes but she was also smiling. She waved.

"I love you. And I'm sorry. Be what you are meant to be," she said. "I am so proud of you."

I stood in the lobby of the theater willing more people to walk through the door. Lily was manning the table that I had set with pamphlets, hats, and bumper stickers. It was only yesterday that she had learned of the genocide in Darfur. She was great, though. "Hey, excuse me, do you have a bumper sticker?" she asked an innocent-looking girl with long straight hair and soft features.

The theater was old and run-down, smelling of popcorn butter turned toxic. The red carpet was soiled, darker in spots from spilled sodas. The theater didn't get box office new releases, but movies that were a week away from being available on DVD. The price was the draw, a buck-fifty to watch a movie on the silver screen. It was great. I had loved the old theater, always wished they'd renovate it. The manager, whom I had known for years and who had great taste in movies, gave me the venue at no cost.

"I love to see a good film," he had said.

The theater held three hundred. About fifty of the seats were filled. I had hoped for at least a hundred. Joel waved to me from where he sat with his group of church friends. He had brought three young men from his youth group. He was trying to be supportive. But seven people from a church with five hundred members seemed feeble to

me. I had to remind myself that a year ago I wouldn't
gone to this if Joel had asked me. And I still didn't kno
about most of the horrors that were taking place in all parts
of the world at this very moment. Our own lives really do
take center stage. And possibly for a good reason.

I looked at my watch. It was three minutes until
seven. At the exact same moment that Joel walked by and
mumbled, "bathroom," Beah and Zahir walked through the
glass doors. Beah wore an old felt hat. She took it off and
shook it. "Ugh, it's raining."

I ran over and hugged her. She was wet. Joel
stopped heading to the restroom and stood watching me.
He was checking out who the strangers were. I felt closer
to Joel now, but I was also feeling something I was having
a hard time naming, like shame — but, no, not that,
exactly. But somehow as if I had done something wrong,
had been the one playing the wrong role all these years.

"We would have been here sooner, but we ran into
road construction."

"Thank you for coming," I said, fervently. Beah had
called that morning to get directions. I was open-mouthed
in my shock that they'd travel so far for one event, for me. I
wanted to introduce Lily and Joel to Beah and Zahir, and
then, again, I didn't. It came to me that I liked keeping my
two worlds separate. I worried that Lily and Joel would
think my new friends were weird and foreign. I looked at
my watch again. It was two minutes past.

"It was his idea," Beah said, cocking her head at
Zahir. I could feel Lily's stare.

"This is Beah and Zahir," I said to Lily and Joel.

Joel shook hands with both of them and said,
"Excuse me, nature calls."

ou like a hat?" Lily held out a Save
ap toward Zahir. Zahir took the hat but

"Zahir. Where is that name from?" Lily stayed
behind the table and leaned back in her chair.

"My mother named me after King Zahir. He was
the ruler— " I knew what Lily was getting at.

"Not the name. You. Where are you from?"

"Afghanistan."

"As in Osama."

"As in Kabul. Rumi. Khaled. As in Opium. Heroin.
Not Osama." He didn't sound angry. If anything, he
sounded hurt.

It was now seven after. I felt the need to protect
Zahir while also letting him know how important Lily was
to me, but I had to go.

Joel rejoined us, and we all walked into the theater.
Walking down the aisle toward the podium to talk about
the people who had died in Darfur, the Janjaweed, the
rebels, the refugees and the camps, I felt weightless, like
the slightest breeze would lift me and I'd be floating above
the heads of the fifty people who sat talking, looking at
their watches. I stopped twenty feet from the front; I
breathed to gain mass, to keep my feet on the ground.

"You'll be great," Lily said. "I don't know shit about
Darfur and Sudan, but I know you'll be great."

Beah, who was on the other side of me, took my
hand. "You're in your hometown. Show them who you
really are, darling."

Once behind the podium, I began: "Good evening.
In 2003 ..." The words came; the images came; their stories
came. When I finished, I motioned for the man in the
control booth to start *Sand and Sorrow*. Everyone was quiet.
Were they bored? Asleep? Or being respectful? I sat

down. Lily leaned over. On the screen, a boy shot in the back lay on a sandy ground.

"Jamie," she said. Sitting never felt so good, so deserved; I felt I had accomplished something.

"Yeah?" I thought she'd say something, like "Nice work," or "I can't believe this shit."

"Jamie. Well, I'm pregnant. We're officially related."

I turned to her, and for a second, felt anger. "This isn't the right time! This wasn't the right time."

"Face it, no time is the right time. It wasn't the right time for me and I peed on the stick on a sunny Sunday when I had nothing else to do. Even then wasn't the right time."

She was right.

"And when in the fuck do you think will be the right time to tell your shithead brother?"

"Half-brother," I said, defensive of her, and of me, but then I felt guilty. He wasn't treating me like a half-sister. If anything, he was being more supportive, more involved in my life.

"He's just as much your brother today as he was last month."

I took Lily's hand. It was cold. I grabbed her other hand as well and warmed them. "Thanks for saying that. And thanks for telling me. I can't wait to hold your baby," I whispered in her ear. And we watched the rest of the documentary without a word.

Silence punctuated with sniffling filled the theater after the show. I stood and thanked everyone for coming and then answered questions, or at least the ones I knew the anwers to. The others I countered by directing the audience to savedarfur.org or ajws.org, the American Jewish World Service.

As people left, Lily exhausted her supply of hats and bumper stickers. She urged people to stay informed and get involved. Joel left quickly, saying he needed to get some of the boys home.

Lily invited Beah and Zahir to crash at her place. This made me happy, though I knew they'd decline.

"I've got plenty of room," she said, meaning it.

"I'm a sucker for my own bed," Beah said. "I used to travel a lot. Now, I just want my own bed." It dawned on me then that although I had always felt I knew Beah better than Akasha, Ana, or Zahir, I now thought I knew her the least, at least about her past. And our pasts did shape us, maybe even defined what we were in the present moment.

While Lily graciously packed up the leftover information sheets, I walked Beah and Zahir to their car.

"Where have you traveled to?" I asked Beah as we stepped out into the night, my old passion taking flame.

"The usual places."

"Like Sudan? Chad? Afghanistan?" I teased, but wanting her to answer.

"France, Germany, Italy, Switzerland, Ireland, Russia." The air was damp. It wasn't rain, but you could see tiny drops of water suspended in the night air. Beah began to walk ahead of me and Zahir.

"Got to get out of the rain."

"It's not really raining," I pointed out, but she was already plowing through the mist to the car. "I want to hear more about your travels at some time," I called after her.

Zahir hadn't said a word, since — I tried to remember — since Lily had asked about his name. I wanted to explain.

"Lily sometimes comes across wrong. She really is a 'love the world' sort of person. Her art shows her desire to connect with others. It's images of herself that she shatters with paint."

"She sees me as different," Zahir responded. "I am different and I don't find fault in people who see me as what I am. This isn't Kabul. It isn't even Santa Rosa." I remembered him telling me once that there was a large population of Afghans in the Bay Area, in Santa Rosa, where he and his family had settled. "I respect people like Lily. What you see is what you get. I didn't feel judged." I smiled. He got Lily!

"She probably gets her facts about the world from blips on the news, like most Americans do. And those are so wrong, simply because they're sensational and because they're fragments."

"She's not much of a news-watching woman." For a moment I felt deflated, maybe because I could sense that Zahir was hurt, not by Lily necessarily but maybe by Americans, people like me, who did get their facts from news blips.

"I want to say I'm proud of you, but that sounds so fatherly."

That word stung. I told Zahir about my dad. We walked slowly. I could see Beah in the car. It looked like she was rummaging through her purse.

"Do you want us to stay? I can talk to Beah." We stopped several feet from the car.

"No. Really. I'll be fine. I'm hurting, but he was such a prick to me." A wave of guilt flooded me. "No, that's not fair. Not always. Not always. He was good sometimes, too." I looked at him. "I'm coming back in another day. I'll tell you more later." He started toward the car again. "Thanks for saying you were proud. I was scared."

"No one knew. You speak so beautifully."

"You can tell her about my dad." I gestured toward Beah. "Thanks again. " I started to walk away, but then paused to watch them drive out. I had thought about giving Zahir a hug, but I was unsure what it would mean. How would his arms feel around me? It hadn't even been a month since I had been with Thad. I missed Thad. I didn't want to lead Zahir on.

"I'll see you in a couple of days," I called out.

I couldn't remember when someone had done something so inconvenient for me. Then I remembered Lily. Yes, Lily had.

The clouds were breaking. In the night sky, the moon lightly colored them gray. It was the first time I saw how beautiful the color gray was, something between the color of a wet rock or a violet wild flower. Maybe it was the mixture of the two. Lily carried the box labeled "Darfur" toward me.

"Let's go," she said. "I need to take this bra off. My tits are killing me."

"I remember what that's like, nothing like being premenstrual. " I took the box out of her arms.

"Hey, I'm sorry."

"Don't be sorry. I want to hear all about your pregnancy. I can't wait to be an aunt." I could say that now without the familiar ache. "Woo hoo! I did it!"

"You did it! Now can I drive? I've always wanted to own a BMW.

"Yeah. You drive."

As I was pumping gas two days later on my way out of town, Joel surprised me by coming up and grabbing the hose out of my hand.

"Let me do that," he said.

We hadn't planned to see each other again, but here we were. Seeing a familiar face at this station wasn't unusual. It always had the cheapest gas in town.

"Lily called me, said she needed to talk," Joel said.

"Yeah, I know."

"She's just not my type. I'm sure she has some good qualities, but ..." His voice trailed off.

"Great qualities."

"I just don't feel anything for her. Do you know what she wants to talk to me about? Sure you do."

I thought about telling him, to make it easier on Lily, to soften the blow for him. But I decided it was an issue they needed to work out together.

"She wanted to meet at her apartment. I told her I thought Starbucks would work better for me."

"She's not going to try to seduce you, if that's what you're thinking." Joel topped off my gas. A few drops dripped down the side of the car. He got a wet rag and cleaned the gas off.

"There you go. When will you be back up?" When I didn't answer right away, he answered his own question. "Probably never." He turned and started toward his truck.

"I'll want to come up. To see Lily, Brianna. I'll want to see you, too," I said.

Joel unscrewed the gas cap on his car. As he fitted the nozzle into the tank, I watched him. He had Mom's nose. I had Mom's nose. Although we had different fathers, it was obvious we were siblings.

"Did you know, Joel?"

"He told me during the trial. I was angry that he wasn't being more supportive. He told me he just didn't feel it, that he couldn't fake it any longer. He assured me it would be different if it was me." Joel laughed, as if he wasn't sure he believed his own father's devotion. "But, before that, I knew he treated me differently. It made me feel uncomfortable. I knew I was his favorite. You may not believe this, but I never liked being the favorite. It made me like him less. Parents shouldn't have favorites."

A couple of cars were lined up behind ours, and I could feel the eyes of one impatient woman watching us. I wanted to tell her to use the other side. There was a pump open.

"You'll make a great father, some day." I took a breath between "father" and "some day." Did he notice?

"Thanks. That's my ultimate goal."

The woman gave us a "friendly" toot. Joel and I both looked at her. I pointed to the open pump. I hugged Joel. "See you soon."

Getting in the BMW still felt both awkward and luxurious. I wondered how long would it take to feel like I wasn't wearing someone else's underwear. That this was who I was meant to be, someone who could accomplish things that were important to her, like a Darfur awareness evening. Someone who drove a reliable car. As I pulled away, I heard no loud clinks, clanks or rattles. Not long, I promised myself. It wouldn't take long.

It wouldn't take long to get used to the painful fact that I didn't have a dad, either. And I suspected it wouldn't take long for Joel to come to accept that fatherhood might be different than he first dreamed it would be.

Chapter Twenty-Six

As I pulled into Fallow Springs, I felt the grip of my childhood loosen. The facts were still painful. I couldn't yet make sense of the memories. I had gone from having a father I'd had a difficult relationship with to having no father. Or, at least, a father I would never know about. I wondered what my mother was hiding. Who was she protecting? After I parked Akasha's car, I walked past mine. It seemed such an eyesore. Dad, or Jake, as I should now call him, sometimes would try to listen to my dreams, my ideas for scripts I'd spent days writing. I felt both angry and sad. I wasn't sure if I was more upset that he tried to listen and couldn't, that he wanted to love and was unable to, or that I was such an inconvenience to him.

Beah would have told Akasha about my father. She would have told her about the Darfur awareness evening. I was glad for both.

I wanted to thank Akasha for the book she'd given me. I had almost forgotten how much I missed thinking about the makings of a movie, how I loved to think about shots, lighting, pacing. I wanted to thank Beah and Zahir again for coming all the way to Grass Valley. I loved them for it. But, mostly, I wanted to sit next to Ana and eat a few of her homemade spice butter cookies.

Leaving my suitcase by the front door, I started toward the kitchen. As I walked through the room with the piano, Akasha walked out of the kitchen yelling, "… no matter what you give me!" Her hair was not held by the customary barrette or band, making her look more beautiful and untamed. Tears dripped down her face as if the world had cracked open and all that was good and beautiful had fallen through.

Beah followed her. Dressed in white linen pants and a caramel-colored sweater, at first glance, she looked younger. But her face looked strained, her jaw set. She was wearing her hair down and styled, so unlike the tightly pinned bun that she normally wore. I turned, hoping that I hadn't been seen, and started backing out of the room.

"Jamie, welcome home," Akasha called.

I froze. "Thanks," I said. "I need to unpack."

"Don't go. Please." Akasha sat at the beautiful Steinway that I had never heard her or anyone play. Beah slid into a chair on the other side of the piano. I leaned against the wall. It was the first time I'd noticed the small box sitting by itself on a large, ornate, wooden side table. The painting on top was of a royal Russian girl. She had beautiful cobalt eyes and a perfect complexion, pearls draped snugly around her neck.

Akasha rubbed her hands down her legs and stretched her fingers. I breathed deeply. Then Akasha placed her fingers on the keys and played "Chopsticks." She stood.

"That's it." She held her arms out, in Christ-like fashion, but her face and body held no serenity. Then she bowed toward Beah and then toward me. No one clapped. I wasn't sure what to do, what to say. I could play "Chopsticks." Everyone could. Every white, middle class, uneducated, piece of shit girl could play "Chopsticks." Akasha should be playing sonatas and concertos by all those brilliant composers that I could only barely begin to name.

"Okay, your turn," she said. At first I thought she meant me, that she wanted me to play "Chopsticks," too. But she pointed at Beah. "Little baroness, blue-blooded American," she taunted.

"Stop this, Akasha." Beah stood up.

"Play," she demanded. She hit the keys with her fist.

I thought Beah was going to decline. She stood straight, her shoulders back, her breasts jutted forward, announcing I'm not ashamed or weak. She looked at Akasha as if she were going to scold her. But then her shoulders fell. Beah sat down and she played music, sounding nothing like I expected to come from a housekeeper. Now tears rolled down her cheeks. Some door inside her had been pushed open. I thought it must be the music. But music represents our innermost selves — the feelings, the experience must come first. Beah was in pain and her choice of song told of that heartache. At first the music was sharp and loud with lots of quick movement, but then it changed and it became heartbreaking.

Leaning harder against the wood-paneled wall that I loved so well, I wished there were some lever to push, some dial to spin around and rid me from this fight. This fight was too personal for a stranger like me, and too confusing, telling me truths I didn't want to know. I slid to the floor.

Akasha started to cry again, and without realizing it, I had tears dripping down my face. They were warm at first, but as I brushed them away, they turned cold. Akasha came and sat on the floor next to me. This had something to do with Akasha losing her leg, I felt sure. Maybe Beah was somehow responsible. Maybe Akasha had been picking Beah up at the airport. Or Beah was driving. And she'd been drunk.

While Beah played, Akasha asked me, "What would you do if someone took your life away, your soul?" I would be devastated by losing a leg. I almost said it would be hard. I wondered then, for the first time, if Akasha had been a famous ballet dancer. She looked liked one, moved like one, held her head like one. But then she asked, "What would you do if someone took your child?"

Didn't I want Santos back in Cuba being jailed or even tortured after he hit me and Clara? Didn't I still? I thought of the mother who suffocated herself, breathing sand into her lungs. Did she want the Janjaweed killed? President al Bashir prosecuted?

Though there were two doors open in this large room, it seemed we were all trapped, locked in, unable to leave. The space in front of me, on top of me, on each side of me, filled as my body grew — my life, my love, my pain, my spirit filled more than my physical body. Then I felt Akasha's body grow to fill all the space around her. And Beah's body expanded, taking the piano with her. Our bodies touched, our lives. Then I felt another person's body pushing against my space. It wasn't Akasha or Beah.

Akasha murmured, "Dvorak, he's my favorite. I have always loved his music. Even though I was raised in a town where everyone listened to good ol' three-chord country music."

I couldn't ignore this other energy, this other person next to me and Akasha. The air in the room felt thick. My brain even felt expanded, as if my skull was confining the soft tissue.

I murmured Akasha's name. I wanted to ask her if she felt this other presence, too, but I didn't know how. I watched as she pulled out a large, square locket that she wore concealed beneath her blouse. She opened it gingerly and held it out to me.

"Penelope. Her name is Penelope. She's eight, in the second grade. She loves soccer; she's great at passing. She gets all A's in math and likes to read. See her eyes?" Akasha moved in even closer to me. "This picture is really small. But in the corner of her green eye there's a brown mark shaped like a leaf."

This little girl was the same as the one in the photo that I had seen in Akasha's room when I had sneaked in to look for the letter.

"Look." She pointed to her own right eye.

"She's yours?" She had the same mark — definitive, original. I had never noticed it before.

Akasha smiled while her tears continued to fall. "That's the thing ... she is, but she isn't. I gave my child up. Just like she did." Akasha directed her gaze at Beah, who still sat playing the most heartbreaking music I had ever heard.

"She didn't have to give me up. She could have found the means to keep me." She snapped her head, as if ridding herself of a pesky gnat, but I knew it was a painful thought she was trying to rid. "And, yes, I guess I could have kept Penelope, too."

I felt light-headed. All this information, all this information had been in front of me for months.

"Beah's your mother?"

"She is. She found me over four years ago. Four years too late." She looked again at Penelope's picture.

I put my arms around her and held her, as I had wanted Akasha to hold me with her powerful strength in the past. In my mind's eye, I saw my mother resting by the lake's edge with her arms wrapped around herself, crying. I thought about her loss of life, her loss of motherhood, of me and Joel. I started shushing in Akasha's ear as I have seen mothers do to their babies. More tears filled my eyes and spilled. What would happen if the room filled with salty tears? Would we be able to use the piano as our life raft? Then the lullaby came back to me and I sang, underneath Beah's impassioned playing, "Hush, little baby, don't say a word, Momma's going to buy you a mockingbird …."

I held Akasha. Long shadows, as the sun moved around the world, fell into the room. My mother's presence was now gone. The final chord of Beah's piece faded.

"You've suffered loss, too," Akasha whispered. "I knew that."

Some time later, Ana came into the room and took in the scene.

"Oh, my," she said. "It's time we moved forward."

"I'm trying to," Akasha said. She stood, took a step toward Beah. I thought they might touch. Beah didn't move toward her. She didn't stand, or hold her hand out. Instead, she closed the lid of the piano. Akasha took a step back.

"Thanks for playing," Akasha said and walked out without looking back. I listened to her footsteps as she mounted the marble steps.

Chapter Twenty-Seven

The next day I received my first guest at Fallow Springs. I had just gone for a run and was cooling down, drinking water by the pond. I hadn't seen anyone. I assumed Akasha was sleeping and Beah was keeping busy.

I heard Beah call my name. I thought she might want to give me her side of the story. Not that I had all of Akasha's. All I knew was that Beah was her mother, that Beah had given her up for adoption, and that Akasha had a daughter. That was it. I hadn't even had time to process all the feelings from yesterday, and I was still working through the new information about my own life. But I couldn't avoid Beah. I loved her, too. She had been good to me, believing in me, loving me. I didn't share Akasha's feelings, nor should I.

"Coming," I yelled. As I tied my shoes, it occurred to me that Akasha and I had both lost our mothers and we had both lost our daughters. The situations were completely different, but we shared similar losses, similar angers, and similar feelings of being victimized. Yet I couldn't think of a victim the same way I did before going to Darfur, where everything was stripped away from a person, leaving nothing but body and spirit. I wasn't a victim in this profound way. I wasn't a victim but for one awful moment in time.

I headed in the direction of Beah's call. I heard Beah talking to someone. They were walking toward me. It was a man. The UPS man? Zahir? And then he laughed. I stopped on the stone path next to the statue of a woman with a bow and arrow on her back, feeling faint. They came toward me. I couldn't move.

"Jamie," Thad said.

"Good morning, Jamie. May I bring coffee, or tea?" Beah asked. She was already back to the Beah I had known.

I didn't answer. Thad didn't answer.

"Smelling salts?" she asked. "Whiskey?"

Thad looked at his watch. "Not yet. Maybe in about six hours."

"Will you be here that long?" Beah asked.

"Thad, hi," I finally said.

"Depends. I'd like to be."

I was glad that he and Beah were talking. I didn't know if my tongue could form words. I loved Thad. I knew that. But he certainly didn't seem like the kind of man to pursue a woman to another town, let alone halfway across the world. Birds chirped in the tree above me. I could have sworn I heard an owl hooting. A gentle breeze chilled the sweat from my run.

349

"Seeing that Jamie has forgotten her manners," Beah said, "and seeing that she has turned to stone like these other goddamn goddesses in this garden, I will introduce myself. Beah Duval." It was the first time I heard her use Akasha's name. I wondered how Akasha ended up with her mother's name. Maybe it was in the adoption papers?

"Duval? 'Duval' as in the Duval Steel industry?" Thad asked.

"Yes. It has been sold. It's now owned by corporate conglomerates. Currently, I am housekeeper, butler, keeper of affairs."

"Smart transition."

My mouth flew open. When I had Googled "Akasha Duval," the Duval Steel Company did come up, but never was the name Akasha associated with it. Of course, I dismissed it. It was in Missouri, Minnesota, Minneapolis — somewhere in the Midwest. It just didn't fit. Thad, on the other hand, took the information as I had seen him take all information, simply as it was. Everything was believable, nothing extraordinary.

Thad held out his hand. "Thad. Thad Davenport. My dad was in the steel industry until he decided he liked drinking and whoring better."

"Can't say I blame him. Glad you're with us and I will leave you to breathe life into this one. I have my own mending to do. But I'll tell you, I'm running out of breath."

I wanted to walk up to him and place my arms around him and kiss him. But I feared my heart would break. I feared that I wouldn't be able to let go and I'd smother him and he'd leave, and I'd be left shamed and lonely and broken.

"I'm off to Sierra Leone."

"Isn't California out of the way?" Thad took a step toward me. My feet still felt heavy.

"I wanted to see you." He lifted my chin. As he leaned in to kiss me, I kept my eyes open, needing to see this moment that I knew I would play out over and over in my head.

"What about the Darfuri refugees?"

"Every day I learned something new from them, something about resilience, love, and the need for home and family. But I work for an organization whose needs change. It's my job to move when they say move. It's okay. I'm used to it. I don't think I'll ever want to stay in one place too long." He took a deep breath. "Show me around. This is Zahir's garden?"

"Yeah. He lives over there." I pointed toward the cottage. "Actually, I'm surprised I haven't seen him. He's an early riser."

We walked slowly over the stone path that I had spent so much time on during these last months. Thad reached down, picked a flower, then placed the petals against his lips. "I missed these," he said. "Land must have the ability to make flowers."

I thought of asking if flowers bloomed in Darfur, but my mind was full. I couldn't believe that he was here. I had missed him. In my heart Thad was another loss, someone to think and dream about.

"I've missed you."

"I want you to come with me. That's why I'm here." He stopped and took me by the shoulders, turning me toward him. Nothing happened in shadows for Thad. He faced life straight on. "We're starting a women's clinic. There'll be lots of work."

I wasn't sure if he was going to pick me up and carry me out toward the mountains, or if an orchestra would start playing in full crescendo, or I'd look up and start to see movie credits scroll down from the sky, but his words evoked a vision of a life filled with passion and purpose and love, the final scene in a good love story.

I led Thad through the back door and up the spiral staircase to my room. On my bed lay the film book Akasha had given me; a novel about the Congo, *The Poisonwood Bible*; my laptop; and my journal. Carefully, Thad removed each and set it on my dresser. "I always thought they should have made a movie from this book," he said as he held up Kingsolver's novel. "Maybe someday. Maybe you," he said, holding the film book out to me.

I accepted the book and for a moment I thought that, yes, maybe I would. Maybe I could become a director. If this could happen, anything was possible.

I brought him down to dinner, though a little sheepishly. I worried about Zahir's feelings. I wanted to talk to him about Thad, to somehow explain that his visit wasn't meant to hurt him. Then I thought that Zahir would already know this. He would know that sometimes people got hurt despite the best of intentions.

"Ana, is it okay if Thad eats with us?" I whispered in her ear as she added salt to a soup that was simmering over the stove. The salt looked more like sand than table salt. The label read Hallstatt Salt Mine, Hallstatt, Austria. She kissed my flushed cheeks. Then she dipped her finger in the jar and placed it on my tongue.

"Good?" she asked.

"Salty."

"Like tears. Like lovemaking. Like the earth."

Ana carried a silver tray out of the kitchen. "That must be for— " Thad began.

"Yes. It's for Akasha. She doesn't eat with her hired help," Beah said.

"Some things are consistent no matter what part of the world you're in," Thad said.

The weirdness of this situation hit me. Beah was asking for forgiveness by giving her all that she had, her money, her time, her position. But it wasn't working.

The meal was soup and bread, but as with all of Ana's cooking, perfect. I liked how she made no apologies for not having a roast, Hawaiian chicken, or one of her fancy pasta dishes.

I assumed Zahir would eat and leave respectfully, but instead he stayed with all of us for over two hours, talking. I looked for signs of pain in Zahir. He seemed more intrigued with Thad than jealous of him.

Thad underplayed his experiences. He lived a colorful life full of instability, travel, hard work, passion, but devoid of the romance most seek from going to Florence to study art, or Venice to study music, to Chile to learn Spanish, or Paris to learn French, or to India to stay in an ashram. He worked under very difficult circumstances. Yet Ana and Zahir had lived just as interesting lives. Thad knew this. He knew he was new in their company but not any more special than they were.

After dinner, as I was gathering everyone's bowls, Zahir invited him to go fishing.

"Jamie, you should come, too," Zahir said, as our eyes caught.

I thought about it for a moment. I had never really fished before, but I loved being at that the lake and I loved being with Thad and Zahir. But together? I wasn't so sure. "I have an early conference call. It's with Gabriel and the I-Act team. They're currently in Chad."

"Do you think you'll learn anything new?" Thad asked. His voice was tinged with bitterness. I felt that he must tire from working so hard and seeing such little change.

"Maybe not. But my job is to stay current."

"The current situation is worse off than it was yesterday. And leaders of countries like the U.S. and Germany, call it genocide. Bashir calls it tribal war. I hate the pricks who run nations."

"Port, anyone?" Beah asked, standing up and reclaiming the congenial energy. Without waiting for an answer, she walked down the stairs to the wine cellar.

"Where will we be going?" Thad asked Zahir.

"There's a lake behind the mansion. Not many know about it. Not so easy to get to it, but there are fish. Good-tasting ones. Right, Ana?" She smiled and nodded.

Beah returned, carrying small wine glasses and a bottle of Port. She poured everyone a glass. I had drunk Port once and gotten awfully sick from it. I sipped with caution.

"I've heard both a Fur sheikh and a Masalit sheikh claim there was an ancient lake in Darfur," Thad said. "They both believe it's hidden under the sand. Makes sense to me. Why else would so many people have settled in that region? There had to be a reason. In the '80s, a lake was detected by satellite in East Uweinat, Egypt. They drilled and now there are over 500 wells in that basin."

"You mean, there may be enough water to fill the needs of every village in Darfur?" I asked, hardly believing that no one had spent time looking into this.

"Isn't water one of the main issues that caused the nomads to begin killing the farmers?" Zahir asked.

"Yeah. But Bashir wants the blacks off that land, out of his country. There may not be water. There may be.

But there is oil," Thad said and then drank his Port in one swallow. "Now, if humans valued the grape as much as we do oil, I might understand all the fuss."

The next morning, Thad rolled out of bed and I listened to him dressing in the dark. I moved over to his side of the bed and nestled in his warmth and smell. Life could really be like this, I thought. I could wake with Thad next to me every morning. Before he left, he leaned down to kiss my head, thinking I was still asleep. I wrapped my arms around him, pulling him towards me, and kissed him.

"Careful," he said. "I hate to keep men waiting, but I will."

I kissed him again, feeling his weight give into me. "No, go. Zahir will be waiting."

After I heard the door click closed, I rose and made coffee in my room. I turned on my computer to read *The New York Times*, a new habit of mine. And then I opened my emails. The one that caught my attention was from USC. It was a form letter asking for transcripts and SAT scores, due to the online application I had filled out in a moment of insanity. "Okay," I said sarcastically. "I'll get right on that."

Out of curiosity, out of desire, I researched how to study and take an SAT. I didn't even know what SAT stood for. Lily used to say, "Silly Ass Test for Dumb Fucks."

At the stated time, I called the conference call number and listened to the struggles of the refugees. Gabriel spoke of the suffering but also of hope, that we were their hope. When goodbyes were said, I pressed the "off" button. Looking out the window, I wished for Thad to return soon. I thought about what to eat for breakfast — a muffin? Cold cereal? I dreamed of studying film. Then I remembered the suffering in Darfur and prayed, "God teach me how to care for people so far away and not become complacent."

During the ensuing days, Thad and I barely spoke of Sierra Leone. He had made his offer, an offer I was sure he hadn't ever given to any other woman. He had brought travel books on the country. He didn't leave them on top of his bag as if to entice me. He simply handed them to me and said, "These are for you to look through. It's beautiful there, unlike Darfur."

He told me about the issues in Sierra Leone, the political climate, the people, but very little about the job. Any time I asked anything about what I'd be doing or how'd we live, he'd say, "I don't want to romanticize the place, or even me. Come or don't come. You know what I want."

When I had asked Akasha if Thad could stay, she'd said, "Sure. It's a big house." So our days were filled. He'd fish with Zahir or spend hours out by the chilly pool or in the library reading medical journals.

One evening before dinner, Thad and I were sitting in the library when Akasha came in to retrieve a book. She must have just returned from her fencing lesson; she was still wearing her fencing clothes and holding her saber.

Thad looked up and smiled. " I haven't seen one of those for awhile."

"What exactly?" Akasha asked. I sensed Akasha wanted to leave the room when she saw we were in it. She was private and wouldn't want to be caught exposing this part of herself.

"I meant the saber, but I guess the whole getup."

"Oh."

Wanting to take Thad's attention from Akasha to help her feel more comfortable, I said, "Yes, she fences. Out in the woods there's a small arena."

Akasha picked up the book she must have left on a table.

"Let's duel," Thad said.

"You fence?" she asked.

"It's been a long time. A long, long time." He stood and gently took the saber from her hand. I thought he might try some move right there in the library, but he didn't, which I felt glad about.

"I don't duel."

Thad laughed. "Of course you do. You don't fence if you don't duel."

Akasha met his gaze. They both played by the same rules when it came to words — no bothering with niceties, saying what one doesn't mean.

"Okay, then, tomorrow morning at seven." She turned to me. "I don't want any of you there. I'm not a performer. I don't want any cheering on." She left the library with her book and saber under the same arm.

"Why does she do that?" I mused.

"Fence? Or keep herself fenced in?" Thad asked, sitting back down. I shrugged. I wasn't sure exactly what I was asking. "Doesn't matter," he said. "Both answers are the same. Seems to me she's taking her power back."

"Good. Good for her," I said.

All I heard from Thad after the duel was that she fenced well. But in uncharacteristic fashion, when Thad, Zahir, and I went wine tasting the next day, she came along. Although Thad never said so, I figured she'd lost, and this was her payment. A day out with people.

We rode in a limo. Zahir mapped out our course. By the third winery, I was laughing, dreaming of Africa, and loving the people I was with. The past held depth for me, not pain. The future was going to be mine and wonderful, and I was living in the present.

Thad and Zahir began to talk about the war in Afghanistan. Akasha swirled her wine and drank her taste.

"May I see her picture again?" I asked. Akasha pulled out the locket, slipped it over her head and opened it. She glanced at the picture and then handed it to me.

"She's lovely," I said.

"I sometimes think the pain would be less if she were dead. And then I hate myself for being so selfish. Maybe that's how Beatrice thought about me. Maybe she simply envisioned me dead."

I was about to tell her about Clara, when Zahir said, "Let's go," and grabbed my arm. It was unlike him not to be sensitive to conversations around him. His continual movement was out of character, too. I would go visit him alone to see how he is doing.

On our way to the limo, Akasha excused herself to use the restroom. We sat in the limo, conversations halted. Ten minutes later, Thad said, "Maybe you should go and check on her."

As I stepped out of the limo, she and a tall, well-dressed man walked toward us. As she said goodbye, he handed her his card.

"Don't ask," she said, as she climbed into the back. She threw the card out the window as we drove away.

The principal of the school who had blown me off ended up contacting Akasha, apologizing and asking if I'd come to the high school during its assembly as a special guest.

He had changed his mind and thought a little current events information would be good for the kids. It was important to me to get the information out, so I agreed. At the assembly, he introduced me as Jamie Duval, I guess because he believed I was a relative. I introduced Thad. I liked listing off all the places he'd been. I had a reason to be speaking for the people of Darfur before Thad came but, with him, I dared anyone to question what right we had. The kids I had met with from the high school got up and spoke about the chapter of STAND they were starting.

Max said, "I know how our lives sometimes feel powerless and meaningless, but come on, life doesn't have to be that way. We have the power to add meaning to our lives." As I watched the two young boys, I felt proud, proud of them for doing something good with their time, and proud of myself for helping to make it happen. After they sat, I showed a slide show presentation full of maps, statistics, and pictures.

"Why Darfur?" a student asked. "Aren't people dying and being killed all over the world? Where would we stop? Shouldn't we take care of Americans first?"

Thad said, "Being that I'm African, I can't answer that question. Jamie, do you have anything to say to such an impressive question?"

I watched as Thad sat down. "It can be overwhelming," I said, then stopped. "Let me see. Let's go over some of the issues here in America. What are they? Call some out."

"Gang violence."

"Yes," I said. "More — ?"

"Homeless people."

"Drugs."

"Child abuse."

"Hurricane Katrina."

"Domestic violence."

"Abortion." I raised an eyebrow.

"Well, okay, I understand that is a big issue for many people," I said. "Any more?"

"Mexicans."

"Hey," I demanded. "Who said that?" I heard a faint "Fuck you." A few teachers who sat on the lowest bench turned and looked up the bleachers. One teacher even stood, but no one answered. I hated the tension that now exploded in the gym. I heard Thad move in his chair behind me. I cast my mind about quickly to think of something to say to ease the tension.

"Maybe what that person meant was, how do we help immigrants?"

"Yeah, I'm sure that's what he meant," a sarcastic voice said.

"What about unemployment?" a boy asked in the second row.

"Yes. Unemployment can be devastating."

"Cancer research."

"Yep. Cancer pretty much affects everyone in America and everywhere else." I thought of my mom. Then I said, "Okay, that's enough. Do a quick search in your heart. Do any of those issues fire you up? Or any other issue that wasn't named? If so, name it to yourself, and keep it in your pocket."

"Now let's name some international issues." I had never thought about being a teacher, but standing up before these young people, I saw how easily one could have a passion for helping others to think for themselves.

"Drug trafficking."

"Yes," I said.

"Fathers selling off their daughters to prostitution."

"The war in the Congo."

"Good, keep going, though I'm sure we don't a have lot of time left."

"Refugees. Like the ones in Darfur."

"The poor."

"Orphans in China."

"Nuclear weapons and terrorism."

"The war in Iraq."

"That's an American issue as well, even though it isn't taking place on our soil," I said. "Our troops and the people of Iraq need our attention. And again, if any of those issues touched you, pick it and take it. What if some of you gave time, energy, and resources to the American issues and some gave to the international issues. Or what if you gave an hour a month to an American issue and an hour to an international issue? This could simply mean reading websites, going to a meeting of some kind, writing a letter to your leaders. Maybe spending a few dollars here and sending a few dollars out there. If we all pitched in just a little, policies could change, children could be vaccinated and fed, and girls might not be sold off for prostitution. I'm not saying these issues will ever go away. Who was it who said the poor will always be with us?" I asked, knowing the answer.

"Jesus," someone yelled out.

"But I don't think that gives us any reason to be cynical or self-absorbed. Anyway, I'm not sure I answered your questions," I glanced at my watch, "but Thad and I have only five minutes left."

A tall kid stood. He sat in the middle of a swarm of girls. "Tell us what's it like to have to work as a doctor without all the proper instruments and medications. My dad is a doctor and his biggest complaints have to do with insurance companies."

"I have never worked with insurance companies," Thad replied, "so I have no idea what that is like. But yes, it can be extremely frustrating to know that if I were in another situation, I could save this person's life. I do what I can do, and I try not to think about the what-ifs …."

Chapter Twenty-Eight

*T*he days were getting longer. And in the fashion of California spring, two warm days were all it took for flowers to pop open, leaves to unravel, birds to break free from their eggs, and bees to appear, hovering over blossoms. The gardens at Fallow Springs glowed like freshly painted scenes. The mansion's windows were opened and cleared of any dust or cobwebs that might have settled. Ana was setting the table out in the garden.

"Our first outside meal of the year," she announced. Thad and I offered to help. "With the dishes," she said. So Thad and I lay in a hammock and waited.

It wasn't often that I really looked at the sky and watched the clouds move and birds fly with purpose to a destination they couldn't name. I was happy. Many times in my past, thoughts of being happy came after a party, event, or vacation, as if the realization of happiness took time to settle in and, then, while I looked at photos or discussed the day or trip with a friend, I'd say, "Yeah, it was a good time." I'm not sure I'd felt happy at the time, though. But today, with the breeze bringing the smell of wisteria blossoms, Thad lying next to me, and the gargoyles peering down from the side of the mansion looking goofy and playful, not ugly and forbidding, my body resonated with joy.

Ana walked over the stone path. She stopped in front of a white rosebush and cut a few stems, and then she reached behind it to get a few from the yellow bush. She wore a white cotton dress with large pockets at the side and a lace collar. Her hair was newly braided, still wet, pinned tightly, crisscrossing on top of her head. She wore an expression of peace — there wasn't a taut muscle on her face. She cut the thorns from each stem and then held them all together as if she were a bride walking into a life full of promises sure to be fulfilled. How did she do it? One day, I'd ask her to take me to Belgium. I wanted to know more about who she was, what made her so strong and gracious.

Thad and I swayed in the hammock. The tall maple trees supporting the hammock created our shade. How did shade and shadows differ? How did shade and shadows differ on film?

I turned toward Thad and closed my eyes. Not to block out anything, but to remember it: the fragrance of wisteria and pine, the rustle of the breeze blowing the branches above our heads, dishes clinking and Ana humming, the clouds that floated in the sky, the flowers around us, the trees that held us, the hammock, the man on the hammock. I wanted to file this time away to be remembered again and again. My hand lay on his chest. It was a man's chest, thick and solid and capable. Small black hairs poked out of his white linen shirt. He breathed slowly and rhythmically. I tried to breathe in rhythm with him, wanting to feel our lungs become one, our breaths dissolve into each other, like waves reaching shore. But the more I tried, the more out of breath I became. And for a brief moment, I felt I was drowning. Until I returned to my own rhythm and fell asleep.

Thad and I woke to the sound of a bell. Beah stood several feet away from us ringing a brass bell. I had never heard or seen it, but nonetheless she stood staring at us with it, ringing away. The sun was shining behind her. I squinted as I'm sure Thad did. She must have mistaken our looks as grimaces.

"How else was I to wake you love birds?"

"How about saying, 'Dinner is ready?'" Thad said.

As if mocking him, she said, "Dinner is ready," and walked toward the table that sat under the large, red-leafed Japanese maple. As we came to the most beautifully appointed table I have ever seen, Akasha walked over.

She had just returned from being gone for several days, and like the times before, she looked sad and withdrawn. I guessed it was from coming home and realizing that nothing had changed. She was still angry with Beah. Penelope was still not hers. I still hadn't asked her why she had to give Penelope up. Didn't hundreds of thousands, even millions of women raise their children alone?

We sat on the long wooden bench. I unfolded my yellow napkin. I imagined using it to wipe off butter or avocado and staining it.

"Just sit and have a Chardonnay and then I'll take your tray up," Ana said to Akasha. Akasha sat.

"I'll eat here. Thanks, Ana."

"Good trip?" Thad asked Akasha. She sat opposite Thad, between Beah and Zahir. Thad's hand rested between my thighs. I wore a blue cotton skirt. I liked his warmth on my bare skin.

Ana, who sat on the other side of me, patted my leg. I was sure she must have felt Thad's hand when she did so. I reddened.

"Yes, it was."

"If Beah sold Duval Steel and you are living off the interests, as I presume, do you leave to check on investments? Meet with lawyers? Or do you have a clandestine lover?" Thad smiled, enjoying himself. "Do you go down to Mexico to smoke some weed? What is it? Jamie said you leave often."

My heart sank. The sound of serving spoons clinking against china plates continued as everyone passed green beans, salad, and salmon. I watched Akasha. Ana said something to Beah. The question didn't affect her like it did me, as if she knew the answer and had known it for years. Zahir poured more wine in Akasha's glass. All this happened within seconds. It felt to me as if everything had been pulled away from where it was supposed to be — the plates from the table, the forks from the plates, the roses from the vase — and now were slowly making their way back.

"I leave to see my daughter, Penelope. I assume Jamie told you I have a daughter. A closed adoption daughter."

"I didn't know," Thad said.

"I'm sorry. I had no idea." Zahir turned and looked at Akasha.

"I try to keep it to myself." She looked at her plate. "Sounds kind of weird. Maybe I could get into trouble for stalking. I don't know. Her parents don't want me in her life. I've tried to reason with them. They believe I'm a bad influence."

"People usually don't see money as a bad influence," Thad said.

"They have their own."

A bee landed on the butter. Thad, with his thick index finger, lifted it off so it could fly away.

"So how do you see her? Are you stalking her?" Thad asked. He ate his last bite of bread, then reached for another piece and spread it with the butter where the bee had landed.

Zahir had stopped eating, as I had. This story was shocking to him.

"She lives in Montecito, near Santa Barbara. I'm a teacher's aide substitute at her school. When Mrs. McCarthy can't make it, the school calls me and I head down. Works great. I get to see her. Her nanny picks her up. I never see the family. I know the situation is tenuous. I know I may get caught. I know I may have to come up with another idea later, but for now I get to see my daughter, touch her hair, or pat her hand. I get to hear her tell me stories, watch her play at recess, see what she eats for lunch." She smiled but it was a sad smile. "I picked them because they were wealthy. She'd have what I didn't. They live around the corner from Oprah. Sean Penn runs in the neighborhood. Today, I could afford a place next to them. I could afford to send her to Saints of Our Daughters Academy. If only they'd let me see her." She took a sip of her wine. "Rich people can be such power-hungry bastards."

"A lot of women losing their daughters in this home," Thad observed. As he said that, I realized I had never mentioned Clara to Akasha, Ana, or Beah.

"Jamie," Akasha said. "Tell us about your baby."

Her knowledge wasn't shocking. Had she sensed it the very first day we met? Had someone told her? Zahir's and my eyes met, and he shook his head as if to say he hadn't told her.

"Not everything is communicated through language," Akasha said.

"You have a child?" Beah asked.

"Well ..." As I reached inside to pull those memories off the shelf, I realized some things had changed. I used to curse Santos for the fact that I had never gotten to hold Clara, to smell her. I could long for that again. But really what I was longing for wasn't a chance to hold her and see her, but for her to have had a chance to live. For I knew now that there was a difference, having lost Clara while she was still in my womb. I assumed that every moment spent with a child was a blessing that caused the heart to grow larger and more connected.

I began my story, starting with the day I sat in front of Akasha while she wore her beautiful nightgown, and then I jumped back to the day Santos and I had had sex. I was attracted to his foreignness, I said, his body that was large and strong, his dark eyes. While I was explaining why I became engaged to Santos, the FedEx truck stopped in front of the house. Zahir, having heard much of my story before, got up and met the man. He returned with a large envelope

With Thad and the others in Chad, and with Zahir, I had glossed over the evening Santos hit me. How I had feared him. The anguish I felt from needing to protect Clara and not being able to. How the walls of that kitchen had been closing in on me. How he was getting bigger and stronger and more powerful, and I was shrinking, although not small enough to pass by Santos unnoticed.

When he punched me, all breath left my lungs. They stung when I gasped to refill them. It was as if I had been struck by lightning, feeling energy and pain as life struggled within me. In my womb, in the darkened place that was me, but not me, the place of creation, of life, of a soul, a spirit not of my own — in that place, she moved. She kicked, fought back. She struggled, wounded. She turned, tried to escape. But couldn't. It was my job to protect her, to escape for her, so that she could have life. I escaped, but it was too late.

Before I noticed my own tears, I saw Akasha's and Beah's.

Zahir's leg collided with mine under the table. "Sorry."

"Me, too," I said.

"I'm sorry about saying that I sometimes wished Penelope were dead," Akasha said.

"I'm sorry for yelling at you for touching my roses," Ana told me. "You can touch all the petals. You've earned the right to feel the beauty of life." Ana stood and embraced me. "And now you get to have the biggest piece of coconut cream pie." She turned toward the kitchen door. I watched Ana head toward the kitchen. I wished someone would say something. I welcomed the sound of the bees over our head, landing on blossoms, sucking nectar.

"Zahir, who's the letter for?" Beah's question helped people to breathe again. I was glad the attention was off me. Akasha, however, lifted her eyebrows and placed her hand over her face. She seemed annoyed at Beah's trivial question, but didn't say anything. Zahir reached down and picked it up.

"Jamie. It's Jamie's." He held it out to me.

I thought about all the people who might send me a FedEx letter. Santos asking me to visit him again. Maybe it was from Lily. She'd do something like that, saying it was only five dollars more. As Ana passed out pieces of pie, I opened the cardboard envelope and took out one piece of heavy white paper. Before reading the letter, I looked at the bottom of the page to see the signature. I couldn't make it out, but right below the signature was typed the name James Mangold.

I began to sweat. Even if it was a rejection, seeing his signature, his real signature, not some stamp, sent adrenaline reeling through me.

Dear Jamie Shire:

Thanks for applying for the summer intern position. Your thoughts on art and film were thoughtful, smart, and fresh. Your storyboard was powerful and the tension well thought out. Although I assume you lack some basic knowledge of production and film, all that is easily learned. What you have is an eye, and intelligence, and strength of will. You're fresh. I am giving you the intern position. Call me ASAP if you accept.

"Jamie, are you okay?" Zahir asked.

I looked up and reached for my wine glass. It was empty, so I drank my water.

"Yeah. Yeah, I'm fine."

"Tell us, who's it from?" Beah asked.

"Mangold. It's from James Mangold." I couldn't believe what I had read.

"And he is— ?" Beah pressed.

"He's a director. *Girl, Interrupted*. *Walk the Line*. And this summer he's directing a movie with Russell Crowe. Yes, Russell Crowe, a man who needs to do nothing but sit and twiddle his thumbs and a camera will find him."

"And he wrote you because— ?" Beah said. I turned to Thad. He sat comfortably, confidently back in his chair. He held a full glass of wine. He wouldn't have asked or waited for someone to fill his glass. He'd have reached across the table and filled it himself. He smiled, happy for me, maybe even proud of me, but he couldn't have guessed what the letter said. And would that smile still be on his face if he knew?

"He— " I stopped, and began again. "A few weeks ago, I applied for an internship. I did it that night you brought me that book, Akasha. I was simply dreaming. I never really thought ... or I guess I kind of thought ... I mean, I like thinking about film. I liked that someone would read what I had to say, that someone would see the images, the scenes, the stories that I have in my mind."

Thad now leaned forward toward the table. His body was rigid.

I looked at Akasha. Her eyes took me in and I concentrated on the leaf, floating in a depth of green. Now every time I looked at Akasha, I saw the leaf in her eye. I didn't know why I hadn't noticed it before, why she had to point it out to me. Her lips weren't ready for speech. She wouldn't smile either. She knew I was struggling. She wouldn't try to lift me up and protect me, choose for me, answer for me.

"He says in his letter that I'm fresh and intelligent."

"Did you need someone to tell you those things?" Thad asked.

I wanted to say, no, of course not. But that would be a lie. I did. Feeling worthy and capable was new to me. They were feelings I had only recently discovered. "I didn't say I was going."

"Congratulations," Zahir said. "What a compliment. Whether you go or not, it's wonderful that you were invited."

Ana came and kissed the top of my head. She reached for my hand that still held tightly to the water goblet. She squeezed it and then placed it on my lap.

371

"I like Johnny Cash," Beah said. "Always did. Even when he wasn't so damn popular."

Akasha reached for a tangerine from the bowl of fruit in the center of the table and peeled it. The small molecules of scent burst into the air. For a minute I could have sworn it had been an onion because for no reason my eyes grew hot and burned with tears.

Ana began to clear the table.

I hadn't touched my pie. I wanted to eat it, the largest piece, but I had lost my appetite.

"Let me help," Zahir said. He gathered serving dishes and left on his bare feet after Ana.

"Excuse me," Thad said. He walked around the house toward the hills.

I was in bed when he returned. The lights were off, but he must have known I was awake. "I'll stay another day, and then I'll go. Don't ask me what I think you should do."

He slipped out of his clothes and crawled in next to me. He smelled of whiskey. His back was toward me. And because I didn't know what I was going to choose, I didn't pull him toward me, nor did I wrap my arms around him.

Chapter Twenty-Nine

*H*ours later, I was lying on my side, facing Thad. We weren't touching. He was on his back, breathing heavily. I turned onto my stomach, folded my arms underneath me. Then I turned to my right side and pulled my knees up in a fetal position. I willed my mind to relax, saying sleep, sleep, sleep, but this exercise only made me more anxious. Then I turned over onto my back and watched the overhead fan. Moonbeams lit the room, but soon they moved across the sky and the room became darker. I dozed. I must have because I couldn't recall if I had reached over to him or he had come to me. The air in the room was cool now, and if it weren't for Thad's warm body I would have been cold.

While we made love, I couldn't believe that I had even considered not going with him, not following this man, this love. Tears fell, but I turned my face to the side. I didn't want to have to explain them, as if I could. It was as if they were my last bit of sadness. And then I began to see this scene on film, the way I have been doing for years, taking moments lived or imagined and placing them on the screen.

Before dawn, I slipped out of bed and out of the room. Ana was in the kitchen. Flour and dough lay on the large wooden table. The tangy scent of yeast filled the air. It was still dark out, and I was still unsure of the time. Before Ana said a word, she took out a mug and poured me my coffee.

"Thanks, Ana." I sat down at the table. With my index finger I began to trace squiggly lines in the flour.

Ana got out four bread tins and divided the swollen dough among them. She took three to the oven and then sat one in the open log-burning fireplace.

"That's a lot of bread," I said.

"I'm taking a couple of loaves to my niece."

"I've never met them. I want to. How come they don't come here?"

"It's not that they don't. They have, just not often. They have their own lives. And not everyone feels comfort at Fallow Springs," she said, sitting down across the table from me. "I've been working on a poem."

"Oh, yeah? What's it about? Can I see it?" I flicked the flour off my fingers.

"When it's done. The poem is about The Now."

"As in this moment?"

"Yes."

I took a sip of my coffee and sat the mug in a pile of flour I had made minutes before.

"Why is this a hard decision for you?" Ana asked. I looked up. I thought the answer to that question was obvious.

"Because I love him. And because I have always wanted to create. I have dreamed of film my whole life."

"I see."

"What should I do, Ana? What would you do?"

"Those answers don't meet. What I would do and what you should do. People confuse those. I have grown to love you. Wisdom will come to rest with you. And I do believe that either choice could be the right choice."

Ana had the outside door open as she often did. She liked the fresh air. I filled my mug and stepped outside. I thought if Ana were young, she'd follow love. That was what she would do. She didn't want to tell me this. But maybe she didn't think Thad was right for me. Or maybe she had a secret wish to be a poet but the dream wasn't fulfilled, and now she had regrets. Maybe she doesn't know what I should do.

When I returned, Beah was in the kitchen, speaking what I assumed to be French to Ana. She was stirring her black coffee as she always did. For months, I had assumed Beah took cream and sugar with her coffee from the way she stirred and stirred.

"Morning," I said.

Light slowly began to filter its way into the room. Ana turned the overhead lights off, preferring the natural light.

"Jamie, you're up early."

"I didn't know you spoke French," I said to Ana.

"Don't. Not really. Not sure why she thinks I do."

Beah picked up her purse and sweater. "I guess it's *au revoir*."

"Where are you going?" I asked, panicked. I held on to the sleeve of her sweater. It was cashmere. I didn't want anyone to leave me to make this decision alone. I wanted everyone's input. Beah let her purse slide off her shoulder. Her stance became less rigid.

"I'm taking Zahir to the city. We'll go to the Museum of Modern Art and then to a nice lunch, and if he's game, to some art galleries. Or better yet, maybe we'll go to Alcatraz. I've never been."

Of course. Zahir. Of course he wouldn't want to be here. He wouldn't want to influence me one way or the other. "That's a great idea, Beah. I'm glad."

"If it were only my idea, I'd take credit for it."

"Was it his idea? Say hey to Zahir for me."

"No. It was Akasha's. I will. And Jamie — "

"Yeah?"

"Regret is an awful feeling."

"Don't you think I know that?" Her words irritated me.

"I was told that keeping Akasha would ruin my life. That's what people told me. I was nineteen, in college, and a child would ruin my life, my chance of marrying well. I did what I thought was best, or what the adults in my life thought was best. You are the one who knows what is best."

Beah left without saying goodbye. I heard her steps on the stone path heading toward Zahir's.

Ana placed Akasha's teapot on the silver tray. Steam floated up from the spout.

"May I take that up?"

Ana simply stepped away and began to clean flour off the large wooden table. I thought she must already be tired of talking.

Walking up the marble steps, I wondered how they had become worn, indented. Although this place was old, it was barely lived in, and could marble be that soft? Part of me wanted to forgo going to Akasha's room and climb back in bed with Thad. A warm body had never felt as good as his did, ever. A life with him would be fulfilling.

I wasn't paying attention to the tray and, when I went to knock on her door, I hit the tray and hot water dripped down my leg. "Shit," I blurted. Akasha opened the door.

"Jamie," she said. "Do you need some help?"

"Thanks. How did you know it was me?"

"Ana never says 'shit' outside my door." I held out the tray for her to take.

"You can set it on the veranda."

"Right, of course." Akasha hadn't put on her prosthetic leg. And with the elegance of a child hopscotching, she made it to her chair outside. Her hair was down and unbrushed, her face puffy from sleep. Why didn't she have a boyfriend or a lover? Why hadn't Zahir fallen for her? I watched her tip the pot, holding the lid as she did. Light amber tea cascaded into her cup. She poured cream and stirred. Before she lifted the cup, she sat back and breathed. For a moment I tried to breathe like she did, deeply, but my heart was beating too rapidly.

"Please, sit. You're making me nervous. Either way, you're going, and I'll miss you."

I hadn't really thought of leaving Fallow Springs. I loved it here. In my confusion, I had almost forgotten I had another choice. I could just stay, stay here with Akasha, Beah, Ana, and Zahir. This was where I felt safe, strong, cared for, and valued. Could I take those feelings with me? Was I strong enough to do that?

"What are you thinking about?"

"Staying. Leaving."

"And going?"

"I don't know. One minute I can't imagine leaving Thad and then the next, when I think about being on a real movie set, getting to learn and be a part of a major movie, I can barely control my excitement."

"Could you have both? Could you do the summer internship and then meet up later with Thad?"

"Maybe. I guess. But that doesn't feel like a possibility. If I do the internship, Thad will have moved on."

"Are you more worried that Thad will have moved on or that you might? I doubt he will that quickly."

I pictured myself working on a film set. I saw myself moving to L.A. Maybe even going to film school. "I'd have to let movies die, if I ever left with Thad."

"Or they could become what they are to the rest of us."

"No." The thought of sitting in a theater without knowing who the director and the actors were before buying the ticket, not thinking about the cinematography, the shots, and lighting pierced me. "Maybe. The thought of it feels painful. The thought of losing Thad feels awful, too."

"Love is hard to come by."

"Did you love Penelope's father?"

"I can safely say no."

"Who is he?"

"I don't know."

"You don't know?"

"I could guess. But I won't. I wouldn't mind telling you about my life, though I know you think I keep a vault full of secrets. It's not like you're going to tell anyone." And then she laughed. "Well, maybe you will. Maybe my life would make a good B movie."

"I'm not a screenwriter, and biographies aren't so popular. And I think someday you will get to see Penelope more often. Things change."

I stood.

"What about *A Beautiful Mind*?"

"What about it?"

"It's a biography."

"It's Russell Crowe."

"Where are you going?"

"To see Thad. I miss him."

"Already?"

"Already."

"You've done well," she said to me but looking out toward the curvaceous hills. I followed her gaze and saw that the sun had begun to give them color and life.

On my way out of her room, I thought about asking her, "What have I done well?" But I didn't need to. I finally knew what she meant. What I asked her was, "How did you know I'd call you and ask for the job back, way back in the beginning?"

"I sometimes get these feelings. I thought you needed a place to heal. I wanted to give you that."

I reached for her hand. It was warm from holding her tea. I kissed it.

"You've saved me," I said.

After gently closing her bedroom door, I ran down the marble stairs and up the spiral staircase that led to my room. I pictured Thad still lying in bed. I would slide into the covers and cuddle up next to him. I opened the door slowly to not disturb him. He wasn't on the bed. My heart fell. I looked in the corner where he had his duffel bag. It wasn't there. He couldn't have already left. He wouldn't have. Where would I find him? I could call the Doctors without Borders 800 number. But he couldn't have left. I began to pace the room. I didn't know if he had a cell phone. I never asked him, never saw him use one. I walked into the bathroom and there, on the floor, was his stuff. He had some of his clothes folded on the counter. "Thad?" I called. The shower wasn't going.

I began to fold his shirts that were thrown in balls in his bag, but then stopped. I ran to the library, then to the kitchen, the pool, and the garden. He could have left a note, but I hadn't, either. I ran through the back fields toward the rocks. He must have taken off early to fish. Was that something he'd do? I didn't know. I ran through the wet fields. Everything was spring green, new and fresh. The air was wet and heavy. I thought about the movie *Oh Brother, Where Art Thou*. The movie was filmed in the south. The trees, the grass were crisp green. The movie wasn't released that way. The film was colorized with a brownish hue to create a worn feeling. The feeling of how Ulysses felt after punishing travels. But today, if I were filming this day, I'd keep the grass green, the sky blue.

Before sliding down the hole, I stood over the darkened space and thought about all that could be lurking. I pushed my fears of spiders and snakes aside and slid down.

"Thad," I yelled, as I got closer to the lake. "Thad!" My voice echoed through the cavernous space. I began to worry that he wasn't here, that I had made a wrong call. That I hadn't looked for him well enough in the house. Maybe he went to town.

The lake was still. There was no sign of life. No sign that life had been here, no beer bottles, fishing wire, graffiti. I sat down to catch my breath. My pajama bottoms were wet, and I shivered. I looked at my reflection in the water. There was no moonlight like the night I was with my mom. There was no breeze to ripple the water to cause me to dance. The sun shone through the opening, giving just enough light to see. On the water there appeared an exact replica of myself. I recognized her immediately, the self I always wanted to be, maybe the person my mother saw in me. I had an urge to dive right in and retain her, take her home, keep her inside me. The water had been so cold the time I'd swum with Zahir. Even now, sitting on the lake's edge, I had goose bumps. Before I could talk myself out of anything, I dove in, reaching for her, for me. And she enveloped me.

When I walked back into my room, Thad was packing his bag. He folded a grey t-shirt. His stacks of folded clothing resembled the work of a two-year-old. Before he said a word, he went into the bathroom and threw me a towel. As I dried off, he zipped up his bag.

"Goodbye," he said, standing in front of me with his bag over his shoulder.

"I'm not coming," I said.

"I know."

"How? How did you know? I didn't know."

"Because I love you. If you came, well, that would be too much like an American ending."

"I'm American," I said, in my defense, in my desire to be with him.

"I'm not." He kissed one of my cheeks and then the other. "I'm African." He walked out, closing the door behind him.

I listened as his steps went down the stairs. I took the pillow that he had been using, breathed in his smell, then crumpled to the floor. In my mind, I watched him getting in the taxi, arriving at the airport, boarding the plane … but then I lost sight of him and fell asleep. In my dreams, I pictured myself being sucked under the bed, through the wine cellar tunnel, under the foundation, through the center of the earth, and popping out in Sierra Leone, where I'd see him, watch him work, and wait until night fell when I could hold him and make love with him.

When I woke, I stuck in the DVD of the 1957 production of *3:10 to Yuma* that I had ordered the day I sent in the application.

The next morning, I found a box outside my door. When I came back from Chad, I had ordered a ship in a bottle from a master craftsman in Spain named Javier Zafón. I opened the box. It was wrapped and taped in hard Styrofoam. And still the bottle was broken. Cracked in two as if someone had struck it on a table.

I set it on my dresser and went and changed my clothes. Then I turned on the radio. Looking in the mirror that hung over the dresser, I pulled my hair back to see if it could fit into a ponytail yet. Half of it, and just barely. If I kept busy, perhaps the pain would lessen.

I picked up the ship again. The sails were made of canvas. I could smell varnish, or maybe it was paint. I placed my nose on the bow and breathed in, as if I could tell, as if it would make any fucking difference. The radio DJ gave the time and temperature, but I didn't register either. Did he say it was 9:15 a.m. or 11:00? Was it going to be 85 degrees or did we have a drop in the weather? But then Dave Matthews began, and I registered everything.

I slid to the floor. Wind blew in through the window. Hairs on my arms brushed across my skin. Salt water dripped from my eyes.

A ship in a bottle won't sail

All we can do is dream that the wind will blow us across the water

A ship in a bottle set sail ...

Chapter Thirty

I saw Mangold and Crowe standing against the bar at the Four Seasons in Phoenix, Arizona. Russell Crowe held a glass of whiskey. I smelled Thad from where I stood. People watched Crowe. He was like a shark in water. His presence dictated the movement around him. One lady with a purse larger than half her body snapped a picture. Others got up to use the restroom, just so they could walk past him. The manager of the hotel stopped by and checked on them. Part of me wanted to just watch, take in the scene.

Instead, I breathed. I breathed in my mother's love, my love and devotion for Clara. I breathed out the pain caused by Santos. My dad. I breathed out my low self-worth and breathed in Akasha's, Beah's, Ana's, and Zahir's belief in me, my belief in myself. I breathed in the power of friendship, Lily's, Zahir's. I breathed in my strength and all the good I did for the people of Darfur. I breathed out the belief that mediocrity was all that I was capable of. I breathed in Thad's warm breath.

I walked over to the men.

"Excuse me, Mr. Mangold. I'm Jamie Shire."

"Jamie, glad you made it. This is Russell."

"It's a pleasure," we both said.

"Tell us what you have seen lately. We've been talking about all the trash out there."

"I've been watching *3:10 to Yuma*. And other westerns. All of John Ford's. And *Tombstone*. I love Doc Holliday, that ill man."

"Ah, doing your homework," Mangold said.

"Yes."

"Where is the weak point in *3:10*? What would you change?" He leaned against the bar.

"What makes *3:10* a great western are the characters, Ben Wade and Dan Evans," I said. "The 1957 version doesn't develop these men and their relationship. The movie goes from Ben Wade being captured to Ben Wade and Dan Evans stuck in a room for several hours. If the relationship were developed with action instead of dialogue, two things could happen. First, the scene in the hotel room could be shorter and more poignant. Second, Dan Evans's actions could be made more believable."

"I'll give you the script to read. You'll like it," Mangold said.

"Plus, I hate the sappy love scene with Dan and his wife. This is a movie about men and what motivates them to behave as men do. They don't do sappy. That was for the women in the theater. Dan's vision of love is to bring home money to save his home."

Both Crowe and Mangold looked at each other. Russell drank down his whiskey. I felt like I had taken a drink, too.

"What would you like?" Crowe asked me, as he held up his glass to the bartender. I looked to see what was on tap.

"I'll take the Downtown Brown. Someone recently said I had bad taste in beer and that I needed to expand."

"Someone you respect?" Crowe said.

"Yes." I thought back to all the people at Fallow Springs. "Yes. His name is Zahir Abdalla. He's my good friend. From Afghanistan."

"Jamie recently got back from the refugee camps in Sudan." Mangold sat down on one of the bar stools.

"Chad, actually."

"Did you see George?" Russell Crowe asked.

"No. I didn't. I've never seen Clooney, Cheadle, Farrow, or Jolie. But I can tell you about the people I did meet. Fantastic people."

"That storyboard you sent me. Did you witness that?" Mangold said.

The image of the mother lying face down drowning in sand with her baby tightly swaddled next to her came to me. Her love and her heartbreak. I thought of Thad's devotion to finding her and her baby. I thought of Mohammed and the day he had smiled.

"I did."

I kept my shoulders squared, my ears open, and my feet ready to move when Mangold asked. I learned more in a day with him than I did from any book, class, or film festival. I was grateful for his time, his talent, and I hoped he didn't see me as a drooling fan. I did what I could to make myself helpful even if it was simply moving his chair. Film was more physical than I had ever imagined.

After the last cut was shouted, after bags were packed, I went away to school. I did get into the School of Theater, Film, and Television at UCLA. Do I want to know how? A call from Mangold? Crowe? Akasha? Maybe all of them.

When I finish my studies for the evening, quiet in my little studio room, I turn off the lights and close the curtains. The lights from the city play magical games on my walls and ceiling.

When I was in Darfur, a woman gave me an amulet. She slipped it from her neck and told me to wear it as protection. I asked her from what, protect me from what, but she simply repeated the word "protect." The amulet is a leather pouch. Inside, I was told a sheikh had written a message and sealed the pouch. I sometimes think about opening it up to see what was written, as if I could read Arabic or whatever language he used, but I don't, of course I don't.

The truth is I haven't felt so protected since my mother passed. Not only does it seem harm is being kept away, but my life is rich, sensual, comforting, and full. I laugh often and love my friends and family with little fear.

Every month I drive up to Fallow Springs to stay a couple of nights. There I eat and sleep well. I spend time with Ana in her kitchen; sometimes Beah plays piano for me. Zahir now teaches a class at Sonoma State while still attending to the gardens at Fallow Springs. He and I pal around drinking wine, watching movies. Akasha continues to stay to herself. Penelope's adoptive parents are divorcing. Akasha hurts for her daughter but has hope that somehow this change will open a crack that she can slip through, maybe even on the adoption papers.

Last month, my nephew Zachary took his first breath. Later, he slept on my belly, giving me no desire to move, his breaths warming my face. Joel moved into a vacant apartment two doors down from Lily. When not at work, he is at Lily's caring for his son, playing with Brianna.

There are nights I awake sweating or cold, knowing I dreamed of Thad. His memory and my love feels deep, fossilized. I fantasize him with me. Sometimes my eyes play tricks, and I see him in the market or the pub I frequent. I ask myself, if he loved me, why couldn't he have made the sacrifice of following me, instead of expecting it of me?

Next week, Inaya will be coming to stay with me for ten days. She will be speaking at UCLA with other activists, telling her story so that it might touch others, so that maybe one or two more people will be inspired to call the White House or join the Save Darfur Coalition. Maybe a handful of people will begin to ask questions of themselves, of our leaders.

"A good film will ask questions," Mangold told me one day as we walked toward the set in the blazing Arizona sun. "Wade uses Bible verses to justify his actions." I think about the questions Inaya's story poses.

I always thought that if a film were to be made about Darfur, it should come from the eyes of a person from the Fur, Masalit, or Zaghawa tribe. But now I wonder if Americans would be more engaged if the story came from an American. I'm going to keep thinking about it.

I sit on my couch and close my eyes. Scenes I have never seen before play. I know they are waiting for life. I will give them the life they need. It is what I am here to do.

Acknowledgments

I envisioned writing this page while my kids played with their dad at Turtle Bay Exploration Park. I'd glance out my window to see that large snowflakes just started to fall. I'd sip on a Sierra Nevada Celebration Ale. Next to me a fire would crackle and warm. As reality has it, I am zipping high on coffee; my children are watching *Curious George* on television (I feel little guilt about this), and I am stressed about getting this done in time. And, yet the sun shines through my window sending rainbows around my desk as it prisms off my crystal lamp. A light breeze blows pink and white blossoms around our yard, and I am wearing a Sierra Nevada Pale Ale t-shirt.

Here is a short list of books while writing *Out of the Shadows* that were essential to me: *Tears of the Desert*, by Halima Bashir; *The Translator*, by Daoud Hari; *Not on Our Watch*, by Don Cheadle and John Prendergast; *The Devil Came on Horseback*, by Brian Steidle; and *Fighting for Darfur*, by Rebecca Hamilton. Thanks to Stop Genocide Now (stopgenocidenow.org) and the American World Jewish Service (AJWS.org). Both organizations offered invaluable information. Thanks to Paul Freedman, writer and director of *Sand and Sorrow*, for offering crucial facts about Darfur.

As a fiction writer, fiction nourishes and inspires me. Books that influenced me while writing the novel include *The Shadow of the Wind*, by Carlos Ruiz Zafón; *East of Eden*, by John Steinbeck; *West of the Night*, by Beryl Markham; *Uncle Tom's Cabin*, by Harriet Beecher Stowe; *All the King's Men*, by Robert Penn Warren; and *Paint it Black*, by Janet Fitch.

Thanks to all women writers, present, past, and future, women who risk and sacrifice so much for believing in the power of story.

Thanks to Robert Sofian for teaching me a bit about the history of film.

Joan Pechanec, thank you for showing me my strength and worth.

Thanks to Dr. John Powell who let me sit in on his philosophy courses. Thanks to my English professors, Dr. Michel Small, Dr. James Brock, Dr. Tom Gage, Dr. John Schafer, Dr. Kathleen Doty, Dr. Mary Ann Creadon, and my graduate advisor, Dr. Susan Bennett. Thanks to my writing retreat instructors, Karen Joy Fowler, Sharon Oard Warner, and Jane Hamilton.

Connecting with others through literature is intimate and powerful. I am forever grateful for my book club friends who share the love and power of the written story. These women call me a writer, have read my loose-paged manuscripts, offering to pay for the pages and ink. I thank you and love you, Elizabeth Jorde, Alexandra Stephens, Dorothy Tello, and Sue Waits.

AHWOOO to my wolf pack: Lisa Kielich, Cindy Martinusen Coloma, Alexandra Stephens, and Rebecca Calkins. Our time together where we share feelings, dreams, fears, and wine feels deep, real, and full of old wisdoms. Your acceptance of the whole Kimberly, the maiden, the queen, the beast, the crone, and the wild woman, gives me soil to blossom.

Thanks to Omer Ismail, a Darfuri, an advisor for the Enough Project. Your friendship and encouragement is deeply felt.

I started attending Genocide No More—Save Darfur over five years ago. Through the years, the group has raised money for Darfuris and awareness about the genocide in Darfur. I have never worked with more devoted, caring, awesome people: Mary Burns, Nola Wade, Lynn Wonacott, Art Tilles, Janet Wall, Vicki Ono, Greg Lawson, Debbie Livingston, Ann & Damon Cropsey, Sharon Brisolara, Donna Holscher, Andrew Deckert, Peggy Rebol, and Judy Champagne. Thank you Marv Steinberg, the founder of Genocide No More. Your devotion to the Darfuris is unparalleled; you give your time, your passion, and your heart. Your belief in peace and justice is admirable. Your belief in me is moving; thanks.

I met Sandra Schofield over twelve years ago at the Ashland Writers Conference. She has mentored me as a writer. She is one of the few people who have read through all three of my manuscripts, and still she keeps cheering me along. I have been a guest in her home; I have been her guest in this life. And I always think on her with warmth and kindness, strength, and love. Thank you, Sandra.

Thanks to Sharon Brisolara for reading an early draft and offering needed advice. Thanks to my proofreader, who lives in a small cottage in France, Siobhán Gallagher. Thanks to Kimberly Glyder for the fabulous cover design. Thanks to Judy Champagne, my sophomore English teacher, who taught me to care for all Jews during the Holocaust by reading one Jewish girl's story. Thank you for reading and editing my almost final draft, thanks for encouragement during the final days. Thanks to my friend and sister wolf, Alexandra Stephens, for being my final reader—your words of affirmation were needed.

To my editor, my mentor, and my friend, Celeste White, your wisdom first showed me and then pushed me to make the manuscript fuller, more complete. You were forever available to answer any question I had...but more than that, I felt your intense faith in my work, in me. If courage can be handed to a person, you gave me a cupful or two when it was needed most. Thanks.

To my dear friend, Cindy Martinusen Coloma, thank you for all the times you have been there for me as I suffered the hardship of being a writer. When I hear you tell others that I will someday be on *The New York Times* Best Sellers list, I know you believe this, and though I smile, and I hope, your belief in me is more fully felt than any affirmation of my work.

To my nephew, Bret, and nieces, Ashley and Hannah Namihas, you are amazing people.

Thanks to my uncle, Chuck Jones, for all you do. You are probably my greatest fan.

My siblings married fabulous people. Tim Calkins —thanks for helping to raise me; you are my family. Thanks to Jeff Johnston, who reads more than anyone I know, a man who loves passionately; thanks to Mandee Carlson Spear, who loves and works for peace among us all; thanks to Destiny Carlson, who gives and shares her time and talents and love with abundance.

Blessings to my nieces and nephews: Brooke, who is full of devotion and intelligence; Cade, your passion and love and zest is amazing—thanks for placing me on your list of favorite authors, second only to Dr. Seuss; Denver, how my heart aches to hold you; your humor and love stabilizes; and Kolae, who is so articulate, full of smiles, kisses and hugs. I am blessed.

Thanks to my sisters and brothers. I feel Rebecca, Tommy, Kenny, and Elizabeth as if their arms are part of mine; their laughter mingled with mine; their aches as if my own. When I was seven years old, my mother drove us home from Glendora to Fullerton in her blue VW Bug. I nestled in the way back. Mom said, "Life is tough. You kids need to learn to stick together." Stick, we did. I feel love in my deepest darkest times; I feel love at my most joyous times. To Rebecca, whose arms hold me, and whose friendship nourishes me. To Tommy, whose loyalty is felt like earth under my feet, your actions work toward justice, giving people's spirits room to fly. To Kenny, my first buddy, whose levity lifts and tenacity encourages. To Elizabeth, who shows love through her hugs and kisses, who reminds me to love daily by actually saying, "I love you." My life is full.

To my father, Robert Carlson, you gave me heart. You gave me the strength to cry and hold on. Someday, peace will lie with you.

To my mother, Marcella, only after I had Elias and Anika did I understand your love for me, how complete, unparallelled, and deep. You did the drudge work: the cleaning of the diapers, the making of the dinners, the wiping of all the tears. Your love and devotion is written on my bones. I can't imagine a more tender, hardworking, self-sacrificing gift from God. Your touch is felt, and I am regiving your motherly love to Elias and Anika.

I wonder if when my husband, Steve Namihas, married a writer, he felt he married the one who writes when he is at work, sells loads of books, cheers and says witty things at parties, and sleeps soundly. The reality is I am sometimes grumpy when I don't get time to write, or when I wake at 4 a.m. in order to write, or after watching videos about girls being raped and stories from the Holocaust. I require loads of time to myself. And as of today, I have only sold one book. Thanks for sticking it out with me. Thanks for freely supporting my *Room of One's Own*. This novel wouldn't be without you. Thank you and I love you.

My son, Elias, reconnected me to Love; and my daughter, Anika, to Joy. Thank you Elias and Anika for helping me to stop and play and cry and nap and look at the color of leaves and collect acorns and revere princesses and pick flowers and eat lots of sugar and read loads of books in one sitting and find elephants in the clouds and forgive easily and kiss all day long. In thanking them and accepting them as a gift, I am thanking Yahweh, the giver of all gifts.

Now that I have written arguably the longest acknowledgment pages in printing history, one last thanks—to you, my readers.

Blessings: love and joy; peace and justice.

Kimberly Carlson
kimberly-carlson.com